The
Devil in
Jerusalem

Also by Naomi Ragen

FICTION

Sotah

Jephte's Daughter

The Sacrifice of Tamar

The Ghost of Hannah Mendes

Chains Around the Grass

The Covenant

The Saturday Wife

The Tenth Song

The Sisters Weiss

PLAY

Women's Minyan, A Play

The Devil in Jerusalem

Naomi Ragen

ST. MARTIN'S PRESS ❊ NEW YORK

THE DEVIL IN JERUSALEM. Copyright © 2015 by Naomi Ragen. All rights reserved. Printed in the United States of America. For information, address St. Martin's Press, 175 Fifth Avenue, New York, N.Y. 10010.

www.stmartins.com

Designed by Steven Seighman

Library of Congress Cataloging-in-Publication Data

Ragen, Naomi.
    The Devil in Jerusalem : a novel / Naomi Ragen.—First U.S. edition.
        pages ; cm
    ISBN 978-1-250-04313-9 (hardcover)
    ISBN 978-1-4668-4123-9 (e-book)
    1. Women detectives—Israel—Jerusalem—Fiction.   2. Jewish fiction.   I. Title.
    PS3568.A4118D48 2015
    813'.54—dc23

                                                    2015027338

Our books may be purchased in bulk for promotional, educational, or business use. Please contact your local bookseller or the Macmillan Corporate and Premium Sales Department at (800) 221-7945, extension 5442, or by e-mail at MacmillanSpecialMarkets@macmillan.com.

First Edition: October 2015

10   9   8   7   6   5   4   3   2   1

For Yehudit Rotem, one of Israel's finest novelists,
and a precious, generous, giving friend

Until when, O Lord? Will You forget me forever? How long will You hide Your face from me? How long must I seek counsel within myself and find only sorrow in my heart . . . ?

—Psalm XIII

If there appears before you a prophet or a dream-diviner . . . do not heed his words.

—Deuteronomy 13:1

PROLOGUE

There is an ancient rabbinic saying that you may enter hell either through the wilderness or the sea, or through Jerusalem.

Few of those who have actually walked the cobblestone streets behind the ancient, discolored stone walls of the Holy City, their souls stirred and their eyes focused on a higher plane of existence, have ever felt that other, darker current that has always been part of Jerusalem's legacy as well. But there, just to the south of the Western Wall, Al-Aqsa, and the Church of the Holy Sepulchre, the earth dips down into the Valley of Kidron, forming a deep ravine of dark, green shadows.

Named after its owner, Gei-Hinnom, the ravine became "Gehenna," a place known for depravities so horrifying their potency has not been diluted by the centuries and which continue to terrify even in our unshockable age.

The prophet Jeremiah railed against it, saying, "And they have built the high places of Topheth, which is in the valley of the son of Hinnom, to burn their sons and their daughters in the fire, which I commanded not, neither came it into my mind. Therefore, behold, the day will come when it will no longer be called . . . the valley of the son of Hinnom, but the valley of slaughter, for they shall bury [there] for lack of room. And the carcasses of this people shall be food for the fowls of the air and the beasts of the earth; and none shall frighten them away."

There once the idol Moloch stood, his face like a calf and his body human, his hands outstretched to receive his offerings, while inside his vast and empty belly his priests lit a roaring fire. Seven fences with seven gates were erected around him. Those bringing sacrificial birds were allowed to pass only through the first gate; those with goats, the second; with sheep, the third; with calves, the fourth; with cows, the fifth; and with oxen, the sixth. Only those who brought their babies were allowed through the seventh gate, close enough to feel the heat.

And the parents would kiss their child and lay it in the red-hot arms of Moloch, while the people beat their drums, the noise drowning out the screaming of the child, to keep the parents from feeling pity. Hinnom, the sages said, was not the name of a person, but rather from the Hebrew word *nohem*—"to groan in agony." Some said it was the child or its parents who groaned. But others, perhaps wiser, said it was those who watched and could do nothing.

Unlike the barren white hills of the Dead Sea just beyond, destroyed for eternity by fire and brimstone for the wickedness of its inhabitants, Gehenna is still verdant, quiet, lovely, a picnic ground for the ignorant and obtuse of soul, or those willing and able to bury and forget the past, drinking their Cokes and eating their cheese sandwiches where once innocent children were sacrificed to their parents' perverse conception of holiness.

Part One

1

The siren pierced the early morning serenity of Jerusalem's silent streets, deserted except for an occasional man returning from morning prayers. The ambulance sped down the almost empty road, bordered on both sides by old trees leaning against the aging white stone buildings of 1949 immigrant housing, which gradually gave way to expensive, modern villas with red-tiled roofs. On the right side loomed the Monster, a hill-sized black-and-white head with three bloodred slides spilling from its mouth that delighted Jerusalem's children.

Seeing it, the driver thought of his own small children, shaking his head sadly as he glanced into the rearview mirror at the little boy stretched out and motionless, surrounded by paramedics.

"Hurry!" one of the paramedics called out.

The driver turned quickly into the long, winding road to Hadassah Hospital, barely allowing himself a glance at the spectacular gold spires of the Gorney Convent rising up from the valley of Ein Karem as he concentrated on the road, speeding forward through barren hillsides peppered with dark bushes that flourished between the ancient white stones, barely slowing down even when he reached the hospital's security gates. Instead, he motioned urgently to the guards, who quickly raised the barriers, waving him through.

He pulled to a stop in front of the emergency room, jumping down and scrambling to fling open the back doors. As one paramedic pumped air into the child's lungs and the other held an intravenous drip high above his head, the driver navigated the gurney urgently through the beige and apricot corridors crowded with donor plaques straight into the Pediatric Trauma Center.

"Unconscious child. Heartbeat barely stabilized," the paramedics shouted. A flurry of nurses, almost all of them mothers, pulled around the gurney like metal shavings to a magnet. Slowly, and with a heavy heart, the driver backed away.

A senior nurse split the crowd in half, making her way to the patient.

He couldn't have been more than two or three, she thought. His wide eyes were closed and his round, cherubic face was bloated with scars in various stages of healing, the most prominent a black-and-blue mark on his right temple. The nurse placed a stethoscope under his little pajama top: "Get Dr. Freund!" she shouted.

An intern pushed his way through. "What's the history? Where's the mother?"

No one responded.

When the senior doctor arrived, the nurses drifted reluctantly back to their stations, shaking their heads slowly as they glanced briefly over their shoulders, their troubled eyes catching each other's glances.

The child was wearing soft, fuzzy Carter pajamas—an American brand not found in Israel—in a pale shade of blue with tiny yellow bunnies, Dr. Freund noted with the practiced eye of an experienced grandfather sent on numerous solo shopping trips before and after medical conferences in San Diego and New York. Gently, he lifted the top over the child's chest, then drew down the bottoms. What he saw made him catch his breath. After so many years of intimacy with the human body in every condition, he had assumed himself to be impervious to shock.

But this . . .

He cleared his throat, taking off his glasses and pinching both sides of his nose to discreetly remove the moisture that had gathered there.

"Well, what are you waiting for?" he said, gathering himself together. He held out one hand for the paperwork and scans, while with the other he pinched the child's finger and felt his chest, testing him for some response. There was none.

"How old is he? How much does he weigh?"

"Almost three. Weight approximated . . . there was no time . . . ," a paramedic answered.

Dr. Freund looked up. "Where is the mother?" he asked, repeating the intern's unanswered question. Again, there was silence.

"Well, then, who brought him in here?"

The paramedic holding the intravenous bag leaned forward. "We got a call about four in the morning. Took us ten minutes to get there. He was on the floor. His heart had stopped and he wasn't breathing. There was no mother or father, just some older siblings and a Hassid, no relation, who said he was a friend of the family. He told us he was baby-sitting when the child started crying and suddenly collapsed. We got him stabilized, then took him to Shaare Zedek for a CT scan."

"So why is he here?" Dr. Freund asked. But he already knew. Shaare Zedek wasn't equipped to handle extensive brain injury. His eyes narrowed and his breath quickened as he studied the CT scan. "Call the pediatric anesthesiologist. Tell him it's urgent. The child must be intubated immediately."

"Yes, Doctor."

"Someone will need to sign. . . . Isn't anybody here from the family?"

The paramedics shrugged.

"Well, do you at least have a name?"

"An older brother said the baby's name was Menachem— Menchie—Goodman."

A passing nurse stopped. "Goodman? Are you sure?"

Dr. Freund looked up at her.

"It's just that . . . There's a Daniella Goodman who came in a few hours ago with another child. A four-year-old. He had extensive third-degree burns on his legs. We sent him to the burn unit. I think they said he's going to need skin grafts."

"Get on the phone," he told her, "and call the police."

2

Dr. Freund found her sitting silently by the bedside, a slim, petite young woman with blond brows and gentle hands, wordlessly mouthing psalms from a small book she held in one hand, while with the other she clutched the space over her heart. For some reason, he felt surprised by her youth, guessing her to be in her early twenties. He would have been startled to learn he was off by more than a decade.

She didn't seem altogether present, swaying slightly, her eyes barely open, her head swathed in a white headscarf. The rest of her clothing—a skirt that touched the tops of her shoes, a clavicle-covering, wrist-length blouse—was also white, the kind of outfit devout women wore to the synagogue on Yom Kippur eve as a plea to a compassionate God to bleach their sins "though they be as scarlet." What dark sins did she hope to whiten? he wondered.

She seemed oblivious to his entrance, neither lifting her head to turn in his direction nor allowing her moving lips to rest. In general, she presented a picture of a pious mother pouring out her heart to God to heal her injured child. He would not have guessed that the only thought going through Daniella Goodman's head at that moment was, *Don't tell, don't tell, don't tell.*

"Mrs. Goodman?" Dr. Freund ventured, peering at her warily.

"Rebbetzin," she corrected him, still not looking up.

"Rebbetzin," he repeated, holding back his contempt at this vain and wildly inappropriate demand for respect as he reached for the chart on the bedside of yet another horrendously injured child.

The boy was four, little more than a year or so older than his brother, a painfully thin, dark-haired child with silky long side curls. He lay quietly in bed, his eyes open vacantly, his calves covered in bandages, not uttering a single moan or cry. He seemed almost unconcerned, apathetic, Dr. Freund thought in surprise, which slowly turned to astonishment bordering on fear as he studied the child's chart.

"My God!" suddenly burst from his lips.

Only then did she raise her head and look at him.

"You are?"

"I'm Dr. Freund."

"You're not the doctor I saw before. I asked him when we can go, but he didn't tell me. Do you know?"

She spoke Hebrew fluently but with a pronounced American accent, he noted, which would explain the baby's clothing. "Go? You want to go?" he answered incredulously, his eyes never moving from the chart:

> *. . . burn wounds on scalp, neck, chest, and right and left arms. A long scar on the upper abdomen, judged to be the result of a heated object held against it because of the clear perimeters of the scarring and the various changes in skin color. . . .*

The list of injuries went on and on and on. But the worst were:

> *. . . two deep, wide third-degree burns the entire length of the backs of calves fitting the profile of burns caused by either a hot liquid poured on them or they were placed into the liquid, or a burning*

object strongly and forcibly held against them. The burns are mirror images, probably caused by an identical process. As for the age of the wounds, it is difficult to assess given the influence of numerous factors: infection, scratching, various attempts at healing. The damaged skin requires surgical intervention and extensive skin grafts.

Dr. Freund lifted the blanket off the child, examining his battered body and extensively bandaged legs. The chart indicated both legs were infected, yet the child wasn't displaying even mild discomfort. Morphine would explain that. He guessed a relatively high dosage. One really didn't like to drug such small children, but in a case like this . . . But morphine wasn't listed. In fact, aside from ibuprofen, he couldn't find any pain medication at all on the chart.

"I . . . I'll . . . return in a moment," he murmured, more out of habit than a desire to communicate with this strange, stony presence at the child's bedside. He hurried out the door looking for a nurse. Outside, he found two waiting men, one in police uniform.

"Dr. Freund? I'm Detective Morris Klein, and this is Officer Cohen. We're responding to your call."

Dr. Freund held up his hand, gesturing to them to hold on a minute. Hurriedly, he cornered a nurse. "I can't find the pain medication on the Goodman child's chart. What is he taking and in what dosage?"

She looked down, shaking her head. "He's not taking anything, Doctor, except ibuprofen. And that only when we insist."

He couldn't move. "*What?*"

She shrugged. "He isn't showing signs of distress, so we . . ."

The hairs on the back of his neck stood up. "It's impossible."

"I know," she said. "No one can believe it. Even when we change the bandages over his raw skin, he doesn't cry or even complain. He seems . . . indifferent."

For a moment, a cold current of fear raced up his spine. He had once seen a veteran combat soldier reduced to a howling animal clawing the walls during bandage changes on similar burns. And this was just a little boy, a baby, really.

It was unimaginable. It was unnatural. It was, he realized—even to a veteran practitioner of the medical profession who specialized in treating children with traumatic injuries—inexplicable. He had never come across anything remotely similar.

"Did you talk to the mother? Has she said what happened?"

"She hasn't said anything. Not since they were brought in."

"Brought in? You mean she didn't call the ambulance herself?"

"No. Apparently social services did. They brought him in against her wishes."

"About what time was this?"

"I think the ER sent him up here yesterday, about five p.m."

And only a few hours later, his brother was brought in! Dr. Freund was glad, then, he'd involved the police, any residual guilt disappearing.

He returned to the officers. "Please, follow me."

Daniella looked up at them, closing her book of psalms and setting it aside.

"Ima!" the child suddenly sobbed at the sudden crowding of strangers, his small hands clutching her desperately.

"Who did this to you, Eli?" the detective suddenly demanded. "Who burnt you?"

"Don't talk!" she warned the child, even as he buried his head in her bosom. "Don't talk, don't talk, don't talk. . . ."

The contrast between the child's obvious attachment and love and the mother's pitiless words left all three men reeling.

"Would you mind coming with us for a few moments, Mrs. Goodman?" Detective Klein asked politely.

"Rebbetzin," she replied, pulling the child's hands off her and standing up.

To their surprise, the child made no move to protest, obediently crawling back beneath the covers. She was walked down the corridor flanked by the detective and the police officer, trailing the doctor, who led them into an empty conference room.

"Would you sit down, please? I'm Detective Klein and I need to ask you a few questions."

"Open the door!" she demanded.

All three men glanced at each other in confusion.

"Why?" Dr. Freund asked.

"A married woman is not allowed to be in a closed room with men who are not her husband, father, or brother. Even with a son, it is questionable. . . . It's a religious prohibition, *yichud*," she said piously.

"Look, lady, cut the crap!" Detective Klein ordered with sudden harshness. "Tell us what happened to your children! Who did this to them?"

At first, she didn't hear the word "children." Perhaps because she was so focused on what she would say—what the Messiah wanted her to say. She had practiced it, rehearsed it like a child about to go onstage in a school production, still unsure of her lines. She put her hand into the pocket of her skirt, searching for the paper on which it had all been written out for her in case she forgot. But she wouldn't forget. She would rather die.

"There was a fire in our apartment in the Old City. A blanket too close to an electric heater. The child was hurt. We took him to a private doctor. His wounds are healing—anyone can see that."

"How long ago was this?" Dr. Freund asked.

"Two weeks ago."

He jumped up. "You mean to say he has been walking around with those burns for weeks!"

"I took him to a burn expert! Someone we all go to in our community."

"An 'expert' or a doctor?" Detective Klein asked pointedly.

"I didn't ask to see the degree."

Detective Klein looked down at his papers. "And who is Rabbanit Chana Toledano?"

She lifted her head sharply. "A friend, a healer, who agreed to look after him."

"Why did you take your four-year-old to a friend instead of look-ing after him yourself?"

"I told you. There was a fire. We needed to move out temporarily. He needed rest. She took him in as a *chesed*, a kindness."

"She is the one who called social services. She says she asked you for your medical insurance card so she could have his wounds treated at a hospital and that you refused. She says you came and picked him up that same day and took him away. Is that true?"

"I thought I knew better how to take care of my own son than she did, a stranger."

"I thought you said she was a friend. Why would you leave your injured son with a stranger?"

She looked down, her grip tightening around her book of psalms.

"What's your answer?" Detective Klein pressed.

"I don't know what you want from me."

"Why not try the truth for a change?" the policeman cut in.

"I take care of my children! I'm a good mother! I took care of my son!"

"How?"

"I'm sitting here in the hospital with him, aren't I?"

"Only because social services sent the police to your house after Rabbanit Toledano called them to report her suspicions," the detective said dryly. "But we'll get to your son and his burns later. Tell us, Rebbetzin Goodman, why is your other son, your three-year-old, lying in the emergency room unconscious?"

She looked up, stunned, her distress real and overwhelming. "Menchie? My Menchie?"

For the first time, the doctor and the police saw something human and recognizable in her face.

"I must go to him!" She jumped up, starting for the door. The policeman barred her way.

"Where's your husband?" the detective asked.

"Which one?" she said softly, looking down.

The men raised their eyebrows. "Maybe you didn't hear us. We asked about your husband," the detective probed.

"I'm divorced."

"Have you remarried?"

She hesitated for a surprisingly long time before finally shaking her head no, a fact that did not go unnoticed by Detective Klein.

"Your ex, then. Could he have done this?"

"I told you. It was an accident. Besides, I haven't seen Shlomie . . . in . . ." She suddenly stopped, as if changing her mind about what she wanted to tell them. "Can I go now to see my baby?"

"No." The doctor shook his head. "Not until we get some answers. Sit down!"

"Please! What answers can I give you? I've been here all night!"

Detective Klein and the police officer exchanged a glance, raising their shoulders in a slight shrug. That at least was verifiably true.

"Let her go," Detective Klein told the doctor.

"If you say so," Dr. Freund agreed reluctantly, feeling disgusted and angry, like a moviegoer who finds himself confronted by scenes of sickening violence to which he had no idea he'd bought a ticket.

3

Daniella Whartman and Steven (Shlomie) Goodman met in an Orthodox Jewish summer camp in upstate New York in July 1994. She was seventeen years old, a precocious high school graduate of a religious Jewish day school in Pittsburgh, and he was twenty, a born-again Jew from a thoroughly assimilated family who had surprisingly found joy and a new life beckoning to him ever since his Bar Mitzvah introduced him to God.

Certain smells still triggered Daniella's memories of that time: wet bathing suits, Sun-In oil, and the sugary scent of raspberry juice served in large, plastic pitchers that the campers called "bug juice." It was her sixth year at camp, her first as counselor. Before that, she had been a *chanicha*. All the campers were *chanichim*, the Hebrew word for student. They were all encouraged to speak Hebrew—the language they would need when they all presumably immigrated to Israel to build their homeland. At least, that was the ideal of the camp.

But for most campers' parents, the real incentive to part with the hefty camp fees each summer was something else entirely: the hope that their children would be inoculated with enough Jewish identity to give them immunity from the lure of a *shagetz* or a *shiksa*.

When the camp offered Daniella the job, her mother—who felt it only fair Daniella earn back a tiny bit of what had been spent on her over the years—insisted she take it. Even though it was her last summer before college, Daniella, whose hopes of traveling to Israel and Europe with friends had been dashed by her family's sudden financial straits, whether real or imagined, reluctantly agreed. "College tuition is bad enough, now especially with your father out of work . . . ," her mother moaned dramatically.

But it was just her mother trying to make a point, Daniella knew. As owners of a chain of jewelry stores founded by her great-grandfather, Daniella came from a wealthy family. "That's Grandma's money, not ours," her mother would shout whenever the topic came up. But her mother ran the main store and was well paid. Besides, Daniella couldn't see that her mother had economized on her own spending, trading in a practically new car for an even newer one.

Still, she didn't complain. Being a counselor was certainly a much better option than being stuck in the house in the unbearable, wet heat of a Pittsburgh summer.

There was basketball, canoeing, archery, and swimming interspersed with prayer and study sessions as well as arts and crafts—*omanut*—where they labored over wire mezuzah holders and clay menorahs. It was strictly Orthodox, but not crazy like some of the Hassidic camps where boys and girls were sent to different parts of the country. While there were no formal dances, or other organized coed activities, the two groups were often left alone to mingle naturally.

The first sign of a coupling occurred during the traditional Friday-night walk by the dimly lit lake. It was all so innocent, the religious prohibition against *negiah*, physical contact, having been firmly pounded into their heads on numerous occasions so that even the most daring didn't go beyond gentle hand holding or a chaste kiss. And while there possibly might have been an occasional rebel who got to first base, no one ever got to second. As for home runs . . . well, you might as well have dreamt of being a blond goy in Norway.

Saturdays were Sabbath days, reserved for communal prayers and lively dinners with Sabbath songs and Grace After Meals sung out loud, each table competing with the other to show how much *ruach* they had. Given the materialism in which most of the overindulged chanichim were drowning in 1990s America, *ruach*, spirit, spirituality, was at the root of all the camp wished to instill.

Their success was mixed.

The boys spoke Hebrew and joined prayer quorums but wore Izod shirts with collars turned up, their hair stiff with gel, while the girls willingly made challah bread and crocheted skullcaps but also spritzed on Sun-In to lighten their hair and were slavishly addicted to Birkenstock sandals, Dr. Martens, and skorts.

Although Daniella didn't know it, she was very beautiful that summer, her lithe young body as graceful as a dancer's as her strong, rhythmic strokes lifted her blond head and white shoulders out of the water.

The boys noticed. All of them. To this, she was not oblivious. Still, while she thought constantly and surreptitiously about the opposite sex, her upbringing and schooling had reinforced her shyness, making it impossible for her even to daydream about a boy outside the context of marriage.

Unlike most of her girlfriends, she didn't want to "catch" an Orthodox doctor, lawyer, or engineer. Born into a wealthy family, money had never really been important to Daniella. All she wanted was sincerity, someone deeply committed to a different life than the one she'd grown up in: a confection of erstwhile spiritual values and religious rituals iced in materialism—a religious life that was more social convention than anything else, barely touching the hearts and minds of those who prayed by rote, their eyes all the while wandering in search of the opposite sex, or what people were wearing. She couldn't imagine living the life she wanted in America. And so, unlike almost all her friends, she often considered moving to the Jewish homeland, her inspiration less the choppy, 1950s black-and-white Zionist movies showing kibbutz girls in frightfully immodest short shorts and silly hats wielding hoes in very dusty-looking places, but rather the words of the Bible itself. It was Genesis, chapter 12, verses 1 through 3: *Leave your father's house and your birthplace and go to the land that I will show you.* She had no doubt that as Abraham's descendant, God was also talking to her.

Both her parents strenuously objected. Fulfilling that dream had seemed a long way off until a sudden tsunami swept through her family, disrupting everything in its path and leaving her bobbing in uncharted waters.

It began slowly in the middle of her junior year when her father suddenly lost his job as personnel manager at a midsized insurance company gobbled up by a huge conglomerate. According to his version, he had found it impossible to find another. Months went by. There had been door-rattling arguments, her father furious, her mother adamant, loudly objecting to paying the bills with her family money. From there it turned pitiable, her father reduced to begging as he fought tooth and nail to keep the family together. But as a poor boy who had married into a rich family and had never really succeeded much at anything, he was in a weak position, and he knew it.

While Daniella could understand her mother's disappointment and anger, she found her alacrity to pursue a legal separation and a divorce unfair to the point of being unforgivable. He *was* her father, after all, and she loved him. Besides, being strong and successful wasn't the most important quality in a man, she thought; being kind and good was. And he had always been a good-hearted, if inattentive, father and a decent person. She hoped her mother would appreciate that at some point and back down. They apparently were in counseling.

She lay on the warm, summer grass, the back of her slim young arm shielding her pretty brown eyes against the afternoon sun.

"Ready for the little monsters?"

It was Mark, the boys' swim counselor. He leaned over her, grinning, his large, muscular body putting her small one into shadow.

"I guess," she answered, as she pulled her towel more tightly around her modest swimsuit, sitting up. Quickly, she tucked all her long blond hair inside her Speedo cap.

He was six feet tall and two years older than her, with a smooth, manly chest and slim, powerful thighs. His dark hair swept into laughing blue eyes that crinkled adorably at the edges as he brushed it away, squinting into the sun. While he wore a knitted skullcap—all the males in the camp did—she could tell he wasn't the type that pored over the Talmud in his spare time. All the girls, she knew, were gaga over him. She just wasn't one of them.

She jumped up, lowering her head and staring at her toes as she walked away toward the little girls lining up for their swim lesson.

"Well, see you later, Daniella," he called out hopefully, his ego deflated but not crushed. She had a reputation for being shy and serious, and very religious.

A week into camp, a new counselor showed up. He was introduced right before Friday-night prayers.

"This is Shlomie, and he's our song master and ruach booster," announced the head counselor, a paunchy Israeli married to the camp nurse. Daniella wondered at the job title. Their usual song material consisted of old Hebrew rock tunes that had long ago represented Israel at the Eurovision song contest: songs like *"Abanibi Aboebe"* and "Hallelujah." But this year, it was a more recent Israeli hit, *"Kan Noladeti"* (*Here was I born and here were born my children / Here I built my home with my own hands / and here is the end of my two thousand years of wandering. . . .*). She loved that song, wondering what he could do to improve on it.

He was dark and thin, and just slightly taller than her, with beautiful blue eyes, a long nose, and high forehead. His thick, black hair was cut short while his sideburns dipped past his earlobes. She wondered if this was deliberate—a religious statement—or simply carelessness, in tune with his wrinkled, uncool corduroy pants and the worn sweatshirt on which the words "Coca-Cola" were written in Hebrew letters.

Then, he began to sing.

He had a strong, melodious tenor that lifted the notes out of cliché no matter what the song. He sang, she thought, the way he smiled: with joy and innocence and sincerity and an overflowing sweetness that was as clean and pure and wholesome as a glass of milk. It came out of his eyes, blue, happy pools, like waters in the Bahamas, with nothing dark underneath, which made you feel you could see right down to the bottom of his uncomplicated soul.

"My parents wanted me to go to college, but I decided to go to Israel instead," he told a group of them around a Saturday-night bonfire. She uncharacteristically joined in, sitting across from him, just watching and listening.

"But you came back," someone pointed out.

"Only temporarily." He shrugged, smiling.

"How was it there?"

"I got off the plane and right away, I felt like I was really, really home. Can't even explain it to you. Just that feeling, you know, in your gut, your stomach. Your soul."

He didn't have to explain it to her. She felt she understood completely.

He picked up a guitar and started to strum. "This is a *havdalah nigun* from Reb Shlomo Carlebach," he told them, strumming softly, accompanying a tune without words. And the more he sang in his rich, clear voice, the more the wordless tune took on meaning, filling her heart, creating an intense longing for something undefinable but real, something permanent and good. It was as if he was sharing some secret. He sang on and on until everyone had joined in. Suddenly, without warning, he picked up the tempo, the tune getting faster and more frenzied, everyone clapping in wild rhythm.

The flames of the bonfire crackled and snapped, sending lively sparks into the night sky that illuminated their joyous faces. He put down his guitar and stood up, his body swaying, his arms moving from side to side. He closed his eyes, his young face clenched with intensity as his head swung to and fro. And then everyone was up and dancing, clapping their hands off, singing their lungs out, part of something larger, something magical that lifted Daniella off her feet as well, pulling her out of her shy self-consciousness, allowing her body to stamp out its own rhythm, to sway and move.

She never wanted it to end. And when it did, she saw him staring at her, smiling that beautiful, pure smile. She smiled back, dazzled, a small thrill flying through her stomach.

All that summer, they were both too shy to take a private walk together, meeting only as part of a group. But when they said their good-byes at camp's end, she felt an irresistible urge to walk over to him.

"I really enjoyed your singing," she said.

"Oh, thanks. I really, really enjoyed your dancing," he answered shyly.

There was a short pause.

"I'm so happy . . . that is . . . I'm glad . . . you know . . . we met," he said quietly.

She caught her breath. "So . . . am I," she whispered, her voice trembling, feeling awkward and unprepared, as if she'd been twelve and one of his *chanichim*. "What's happening with you next year?"

"Oh, I think I'll look for a job in education, or maybe work for a youth organization. "

"Like Bnei Akiva?"

"Yeah, or maybe Ezra."

Bnei Akiva was coed. Ezra—its more religiously stringent counterpart—was not. She wondered if that had significance and what it said about him.

"Where will you be living?"

"I guess that'll depend on where I get a job." He shrugged cheerfully, unconcerned.

"You don't seem too worried." She laughed.

"I'm not. This is all just temporary. I'm going to move back to Israel, as soon as I can talk my parents into agreeing."

"Oh, that's . . . great. I was thinking of going there next summer, during college break."

"College? Already?"

She nodded. "Early admissions. The University of Pennsylvania."

He mouthed a "wow." "You must have really good grades!"

She gave a modest shrug. "I like to read."

"What will you be studying?"

"I was thinking pre-med."

Again, a silent "wow" made his mouth open wide. "That's wonderful. The good that doctors do in the world! They're so close to God."

She smiled shyly. "I want to do good."

"I'm sure you will, Daniella."

And then, there was suddenly nothing, and everything, left to say. But it was up to him, she realized, hoping he would boldly ask for her number. He didn't. Disappointed and a bit hurt, she picked up her bag.

"Well, bye. And good luck with everything."

"Oh, you, too, Daniella. Hope we'll meet again!"

She put down her bag. "Do you?"

"Of course." He smiled but didn't continue.

She picked up her bag once more and boarded her bus. All the way back to Pittsburgh, she leaned her forehead against the window, chilled now with a sudden rainfall, and felt her eyes moisten with regret. With half an ear, she listened to a fellow counselor chatter on about her plans for buying clothes for the upcoming Rosh Hashanah holiday. She felt heartsick.

Standing in front of the door to the beautiful old Victorian house she had always lived in and taken for granted, she rang the bell. She was disappointed when no one answered. She took out her key.

"Mom?" she called through the open door.

"She not home," answered the maid, coming up from the basement.

"Oh, hi, Emelda. Is my dad around?"

The woman's sad brown eyes looked even sadder. "Oh, Missy Daniella. Your dad, he move out. Las' Sunday."

"Oh, yeah. Well, thanks for telling me." She hurried up the steps, throwing her suitcase and bags onto the thick rose carpeting of her room and then slamming the door behind her. She lay facedown, moaning, wetting her lovely satin bedspread with tears.

Her mother, who finally arrived three hours later, was unapologetic. "It had to happen sometime, Daniella. You are old enough to understand the situation. It couldn't go on. It wasn't good for anyone."

She studied her mother's mouth as it formed the words, not hearing anything, thinking it looked like some yawning, spongy whirlpool of quicksand that swallowed people whole. The more you struggled against it, the deeper you'd sink. She'd never been able to win an argument with her mother.

The next day, her dad called, asking her out to dinner. Sitting across the table from him in a dark restaurant, she realized that in his own way, he was no easier to talk to than her mother. He seemed to have lost his grip on reality, talking about a "little break" and how "things would soon be getting back to normal." Any attempt to talk realistically about how he would manage, where he was going to live, what he was going to do, floundered into silence.

She wished so much that her older brother, Joel, was home. She needed his confident, flippant practicality, his sense of humor, his big-brotherly advice. But he was off in Boston doing a summer internship at a prestigious law firm. While in their long-distance phone conversations, he tried his best to be helpful, what she really needed was a hug and for them to take a long bike ride together.

The only other person she could open her heart to was her granny, who told her wisely, "Your relationship with your father has nothing to do with your mother's. Remember that."

"But, Granny, why does she have to be so cruel to him?"

She sighed. "Honey, your mother is a very tough businesswoman. She believes in cutting her losses. She's always felt she got the wrong end of the bargain when she married your father. Don't count on her developing a soft heart all of a sudden. There is nothing to be done."

Nevertheless, Daniella ached for him, for his summary dismissal, never doubting that the same fate awaited her, too, should her mother ever discover she was not the clever, accomplished daughter she felt she had coming to her after so determined an investment of time and money.

She was glad when the horrible awkwardness of High Holy Days dinners, split between her parents, was finally over and her first semester began. Her father offered to drop her off at campus. He looked weary and gray as he struggled with her suitcases.

"Try to have a good time, not just study all the time," he told her as they walked side by side through the campus.

"Oh, Dad!"

"Yeah, glad your mother can't hear me, right? She doesn't know everything, Daniella. Remember that."

She sighed.

"Look, this is just temporary between your mother and me. You'll see. Sometimes separation makes the heart grow fonder."

She looked into his dark, distracted eyes, hooded by newly sagging eyelids, then looked away, walking with him in silence toward her dorm. What could she say? Try to convince him there was no hope? Better unrealistic dreams than no dreams at all, she told herself.

"Well, this looks nice," he said, putting down the suitcases, his eyes briefly and hurriedly flitting around the dorm room. He patted her shoulder absently, then turned to go.

"Dad?"

He turned around. "Hmm?"

"The rest of my stuff? It's still in the trunk."

"Oh, is there more stuff? Well, sure, let's go back and get it."

They worked silently, like two strangers going up in an elevator, each waiting to get off at his or her own stop. His clothes looked unironed, she thought, and there was a distinct stain on his sweater that looked like baby spit-up but was probably yogurt. Where would he find a baby?

She kissed him lightly. "You take care of yourself, Dad. Even if Mom . . . even if it doesn't . . . she doesn't . . . Don't . . . don't depend on Mom."

"You know your mother. She can be harsh. But she doesn't mean it. She'll come around, she'll come around," he murmured, as if to himself, his head nodding as he walked out the door.

She was alone, her one acquaintance—a large, rather morose girl who'd been in her Bnei Akiva group—having chosen to study art history and live off campus. Her roommate was a polite girl from Idaho named McAllister. Daniella considered switching—there was no shortage of Orthodox Jewish girls like her on campus—but decided there was no point in going to college if you were not going to open yourself up to new experiences. Besides, McAllister was also pre-med.

Despite her best efforts and intentions, she found it hard. The campus was a Gentile outpost saturated with unfamiliar symbols and loyalties. Even the library, with its opulent windows looking out at the verdant campus, seemed grandly foreign, somehow, a place for the descendants of the *Mayflower* or the offspring of foreign oligarchs to study about the Pilgrims or the French Revolution. What had it to do with a Jewish girl from Pittsburgh? Brought up to see the world through the binoculars of faith, heritage, and peoplehood, for Daniella Benjamin Franklin and the Founding Fathers seemed distant and small, while Maimonides, Rashi, and Herzl loomed large and demanding.

She tried joining the vibrant and multifaceted programs for religious Jews on campus. They were a smorgasbord: Shabbat, holidays, Israel, social justice. And for a time, she felt hopeful she might yet find a place for herself there. After all, these people were not so different from those she had befriended in school and camp. But while she had grown to know her school friends over a dozen years, this new crowd felt unwelcoming, her attempts at friendliness strained and unreal. She never considered the truth: that she had become estranged from herself, weaving a bandaging cocoon around the raw wounds caused by her family's implosion, shutting down protectively, afraid to open up to new activities, new friends, new ideas,

She might as well be an orphan, she thought with a self-pity that was often debilitating. She was furious at her mother, pitying and a bit contemptuous of her father, neither of whom had time for her anymore. Even her brother, Joel, seemed to have abandoned her, apologetically cutting their conversations short, explaining he was just trying to keep his head above water during his demanding senior year at Harvard.

Besides, she thought, beneath his flippant attitude toward the family woes, he was no doubt nursing his own wounds.

She felt lost and alone.

It didn't help that pre-med was as difficult as they said it would be. There was absolutely no time for anything else but study. Calculus with analytic geometry, basic concepts in biology and biodiversity, chemical principles, honors English, and her one elective, Hebrew. That first semester was like walking uphill in a snowstorm, dragging a heavy sled behind her.

She'd always been so good at science and math and had breezed through her high school courses. But now she wondered: Was that simply because she'd been in yeshiva, among yeshiva girls, a big fish in a small pond? Here, her classmates—most of them top of their class, valedictorians of large, competitive high schools—were all so smart, so quick to catch on. She just forced herself to work harder, and the harder she worked, the more isolated she felt.

At the end of the first semester, her grades were passing but not brilliant. She was heartbroken, vowing to do better. But the second semester was mostly a continuation of courses she'd stumbled through in her first semester, only more difficult. She found it almost impossible to fall asleep at night, and when she awoke in the morning, her heart began to pound even before she got out of bed.

Her hair grew out of its cut, but there was no time to go to the hairdresser, so she tied it back messily. Her meals consisted of pizza and a Coke, or pasta and cheese, anything filling and easy. She ate alone, quickly, never looking down at her food, her eyes fastened on the pages of a textbook. All the information began to merge: periodic tables and math formulas and biological terminology. It swam around in her head, like little silver fishes, flashing information at random intervals, then merging into an inseparable goo, like the combination of all colors that produces, simply, black. She was tired, irritable, lonely, overwhelmed with stress.

On holidays, she avoided going home, telling her parents she had to study. Only Joel didn't buy it. "You're driving yourself nuts, Daniella. Nothing is worth that."

But she couldn't fail. She couldn't go home and face her mother's disdain, admit she was another loser, like her father—that she'd wasted a year's tuition.

Besides, ever since she was small, she'd been taught to finish what she started. Piano lessons, for example. She'd started at ten and despite knowing early on she had no talent for it, she had taken seven years of lessons, practicing diligently but without pleasure, producing correct but uninspired music she—and everyone else—never really enjoyed. By age twelve, she declared her desire to become a doctor, repressing her horror of blood, her squeamish dislike of hospitals, delighted at the gleam in her parents' eyes. It proved she was smart, capable, a winner. She, like them, was entranced by the title, the status.

But now, second-semester finals over and her grades only marginally better than before, she felt like those little kids in her tadpole swimmers group who paddled and flailed with all their might but still only managed to keep their heads slightly above water. She decided not to take the summer off but to volunteer at a hospital.

"Yes, that's exactly what you should do!" her mother agreed. "Exactly what you *need* to do. You know the competition out there for medical school, internships, residencies. . . . You need to be up on your game, Daniella."

"Take the summer off," her father advised her.

"Go to Israel and cover yourself with black mud from the Dead Sea," Joel agreed. "Really, Dani, what you need is rest. You're killing yourself," he warned.

"So says the man who interned at law offices during every college break," she mocked.

"Yeah, but I enjoyed it," he answered pointedly. He knew her better than anyone.

She joined the pre-med volunteer program at Bellington Hospital, spending her first week bringing doctors and nurses coffee, emptying bedpans, and sterilizing beds while the orderlies whose jobs these were sat and watched her. But then she was assigned to the ICU.

A young man with leukemia arrived, unable to breathe, accompanied by his panicked girlfriend and frantic family. The young intern wanted to intubate him, but the young man resisted. "No, no!" he kept saying. "All I want is painkillers. Give me painkillers!" All the while his parents and girlfriend hovered over him, shouting, trying to convince him, making it impossible for the young doctor to even get close to him. And then suddenly, in the middle of resisting, the young man collapsed, setting off all kinds of bells and whistles and doomsday buzzers, which felt like stone pellets raining down on Daniella's head.

The blond girlfriend, who looked fifteen, backed up against the wall and stared, while the family screamed and moaned until they were herded into the corridor to make room for nurses wheeling in machines, followed by senior doctors. Daniella listened to the noises coming from the closed and curtained room, the doctors' low, frantic tones punctuated by the hiss and pump of machines that seemed to go on forever. And then the door opened and the young intern, no older than the patient, emerged, the bad news written all over his face. A scream went up, a roar of disbelief and raw grief.

This, she thought, nauseated, was the sound in Egypt during the final plague. The family pushed open the doors, invading the room, circling the dead man's bed protectively as they hugged each other and wept. The keening went on for hours.

Daniella was stunned. Just moments before, he'd been alive, a handsome young man. And now he was dead and absolutely nothing could be done about it. No one had been able to save him. Or, perhaps, there had been some mistake, some lapse, that had cost him the remaining fifty years of his life? And if so, who had made that error? Was it the family for not trying hard enough? Or the patient himself, battle-scarred and weary, who had decided he'd had enough of doctors and hospitals and lifesaving techniques? Or in the final tally, had it been the young intern, who hadn't intubated him fast enough, who hadn't been wise, persuasive, or simply commanding enough to convince him and his family to do the right thing in time? It was one thing to get a mediocre grade on an exam, but quite another to fail in the actual practice of medicine, she thought, suddenly terrified.

Slowly, imperceptibly, it began to dawn on her that she couldn't, mustn't, do this, take lives into her own hands. She didn't want that responsibility. She didn't want to play God. She told no one, because there was no one in her life to tell, no one who would understand and not condemn.

So when the summer was over, she decided to do what she'd done with her piano lessons: keep plunking away, ignoring her feelings, which she had never been taught to trust. Instead, she went back for her third semester as pre-med. She took seventeen credits, including organic chemistry, well known as the Scylla and Charybdis of all pre-med students, and had been since 1910. She wasn't overly concerned. Plenty of people still passed it. Why shouldn't she be one of them?

But nothing prepared her for the reality of studying how molecules containing carbon interact. For the first time, all her tried-and-true methods of intensive study and memorization simply didn't work. It wasn't the same as math or physics, where there were equations you could master. There were too many exceptions to the rule, the same molecule dancing to a different tune in base or acid, dark or sunlight, heat or cold. You needed to use intuition, to extrapolate the answer from specific examples. Someone once likened it to the skill of diagnosis. And as with music, she knew she had no aptitude for it, however hard she tried and however long she studied.

For the first time in her life, she knew she was headed for certain failure. There was going to be an *F* in organic chemistry on her record: an indelible black mark that nothing could erase. So deep was her depression and foreboding that she actually decided to spend less time studying.

For some reason, she found herself wandering into the Sabbath service at Chabad House. It was not really a place in which she felt comfortable; most of the students congregating there were either Hassidic wannabees from secular homes or rebels from her own background exploring the idea of giving the finger to their parents' boring, comfortable, middle-of-the-road Orthodoxy. There, on the other side of the women's partition, was Shlomie.

He looked taller, somehow, and certainly better dressed, his hair longer, the hint of *payot* gone, a newly grown mustache and goatee giving gravitas to the boyish young face she remembered. He was the cantor, leading the Morning Prayer service, his spirited voice awakening the room, setting it clapping and swaying in joyous rhythm. She smiled, singing along, feeling suddenly lighter.

When the prayers concluded, she saw him wave to her across the room. She waved back, approaching him shyly over the wine and cookies set up for kiddush.

"Wow, Daniella!"

"You remember my name." She smiled, flattered.

"What? Of course! I've thought about you a lot."

"Really?"

"Why are you so surprised?"

She touched her face, which was suddenly hot. Was she that obvious? "Well, you just didn't seem all that interested."

"I was. I just didn't think you'd be interested . . . in someone like me, that is."

"Someone like you? What does that even mean?"

"You know, no college degree, low-paying job, very religious, headed for Israel."

"And I thought you couldn't be interested in me: nerdy, all work and no play, who wore sandals and no stockings. . . ." She paused. "You never even asked for my number."

He smacked his forehead with the palm of his hand. "I know. I only thought of it when your bus had already pulled out. I'm an idiot!" He grinned.

She blushed once more. "So, what are you doing here?"

"The Chabad rabbi hired me as his assistant."

"You're Chabad!"

"No. Not exactly. At least, I don't think I am. I'm exploring it. Reading the *Tanya*."

She looked mystified.

"You know, the *Tanya*, written by Rabbi Schneur Zalman of Liadi two hundred years ago? He was the one who founded Chabad. His Hassidim are really the only ones who study it. It's their most important book."

"More important than the Bible?" she said archly with a sideways glance.

He didn't answer. He seemed confused.

"Sorry. I didn't mean to be sarcastic. What's in it, anyway?"

"Would you really like to know?"

"Sure, why not?"

"I'd be happy to teach you, at least the little I know, if you've got time," he said happily.

She certainly had that, given that studying wasn't going to save her, not this time. They met that very evening. Finding a quiet corner in the campus Chabad House wasn't easy. Something musical was going on, along with lots of eating and socializing.

"We'll just start with the first chapter," he said. "Here's a copy of the *Tanya* in English." They sat close, poring over the text together, conscious of their nearly touching shoulders, the warmth of their thighs just beneath the table.

"'An oath is administered to him,'" he read.

"To whom?"

He looked up, as if surprised she had to ask. "To your unborn soul. You are made to swear an oath before you descend to earth."

"And what do we swear?" she asked, bemused.

"That you will be righteous, not evil. But along with that, you must also swear to think of yourself as wicked."

She shook her head. "That makes no sense. Besides, isn't it written in *Ethics of the Fathers*, 'Never be wicked in your own eyes'?"

His face lit up, impressed. "Exactly! That's written here, too. Look." He pointed excitedly to the words she had just said. "And it gets even more complicated. As the *Mishnah* says, if a person considers himself wicked, he'll be depressed and not be able to serve God with joy. And if he tells himself to serve with joy anyway, then this might lead him to flippantly ignore his sins."

"So what's the answer?"

"Answer?"

"Should you think of yourself as wicked or shouldn't you?"

"I . . ." He turned the pages, studying. "They don't really say."

"But what do *you* think?" She smiled.

"I think," he pressed his lips together in concentration, "that no one should ever think of himself as wicked. You should be sorry for the wicked deeds you do, but realize that it didn't come from a wicked heart, but from mistaken ideas or a momentary weakness. If you take your mistakes too hard, then you really might become wicked. You'll think it's in your blood and you have no choice."

She leaned back, exhaling. "That's what I think, too."

"Should we keep going?"

Why not, she thought, nodding.

" 'The completely righteous man prospers materially and spiritually. He knows only good,' " he read.

She wrinkled her nose. "Plenty of righteous people suffer."

"Because they still have some evil inside them that hasn't yet been purified."

"Or because they have bad luck, or no money for a good lawyer. Anyhow, does suffering ever really purify?"

"The text seems to be saying that a truly righteous person doesn't need to suffer because he has no impurities. So, if you do suffer, it's God's way of making you a better person while you are still clothed in your earthly body, so you need not suffer in the Next World. Prospering and suffering are all part of the divine plan. The complete tzaddik, who knows only success, has succeeded in serving and loving God completely."

"I never heard of anyone who knows only success, no matter how righteous. Even the Lubavitcher Rebbe, the one his followers are now claiming is the Messiah, never had children. That must have caused him tremendous suffering."

There was a thoughtful silence. At last he said, "I guess you could say the same about Abraham. He was also childless for a long time. So . . . maybe the text isn't saying that a great tzaddik will have a perfect life, but just that his perfect faith will prevent him from suffering the way a lesser person would."

She scanned the text. "Where is that written?"

"Oh, it isn't. It's my own interpretation."

She looked up, impressed. "That makes sense to me."

"I've also heard another interpretation, not my own, which says the word *masbiyim* means 'sated' rather than 'swear'. In other words, before you are born, your soul will be sated with everything you'll need to fulfill your destiny on earth."

"I like that better than the pre-fetal soul swearing." She grinned.

"So do I," he admitted.

"It's getting late," she murmured, looking at her watch, but not really wanting to go back to the loneliness of her dorm room, the stacks of books and study notes that lay in untouched mounds on her desk, like an abandoned archaeological site that has turned up nothing of value. She hoped he'd try to talk her into staying longer.

He didn't, instead getting up and walking her back to her dorm room, his hands in his pockets. The first snows had come early; the streets were already icy.

"I hate this cold," he said, zipping up his coat. "In Israel, it never really gets cold at all. Most of the houses don't even have central heating."

"In Jerusalem and the Galilee, especially Safed, it snows," she told him. "I was there once. It can get freezing cold, especially since the houses are made of stone. But unlike here, everyone is so happy when it snows. First, because it happens only once in a blue moon, and second, because before it can get dirty and become a nuisance, the special Israeli snow-removal equipment is put to work."

He looked at her blankly. "What's that?"

"The sun." She grinned.

He laughed.

She looked at him seriously. "Do you think you'd be happy there? Away from your family, friends, American hamburgers?"

"I don't want to be like the spies Moses sent out to scout the land, who came back and complained, 'We can't possibly live in Israel! There are no Entenmann's brownies!'"

"Oh, is that what they said to Moses?" She laughed. Suddenly, she felt her feet losing their grip on hidden ice. She began to slide precariously forward. He reached out to steady her, his hand around her waist. It felt so right there, she thought, looking up at him. He was just the right height, just slightly taller than herself, with those amazing blue eyes.

He crooked his arm. "You'd better hold on."

She slid her arm through his. "Is this even allowed?" she joked.

"There is no skin-to-skin contact, and besides, all prohibitions are canceled when it comes to saving a life," he told her with the utmost seriousness.

Was he being cleverly deadpan? she wondered, looking into his face for a hint of humor. There wasn't any.

He went on, oblivious. "How many stories do you hear about people falling down during some stupid ski vacation—nothing major, just a little bump on the head—and wham, internal bleeding, rush to the hospital, the families all weeping and wailing. . . ."

She dropped his arm. "That's not funny."

He stared at her. "It wasn't meant to be! A little caution could prevent so much needless suffering."

She suddenly felt foolish. "Right, I'm sorry. It's just that . . . this summer, I was a medical volunteer in the ICU. The families . . . I saw and heard so much."

"I'm sorry. I didn't know." He sighed. "I suppose you'll just have to get used to it."

"I don't think that's possible. I can't imagine being in those situations every single day, being the one to break the horrible news to someone's mother or boyfriend. . . ."

"Well, you know, you don't have to."

"What's that supposed to mean?"

"It means that your soul has been gifted with every ability you'll need to do anything you decide to do during your time on earth. No one is restricted to just one path."

"My mother would disagree with you. She believes firmly in choosing a career path and sticking with it."

"Your mother is your role model? You want her life?"

The question left her dumbfounded. She'd never thought of it in those terms. They walked on in silence under the dark night sky until she reached her dorm. "Well, good night, and thanks for the *Tanya* lesson. And for keeping me from falling and breaking my head."

"I'll take thanks for the latter but not the former. I probably scared you off for life. I really don't know enough *Tanya* to be teaching."

"I don't scare easily. Besides, honestly? Your own insights were the things I found most interesting."

He brightened. "I'd be happy to give you another lesson."

"I'll think about it." She smiled, turning to go. Then suddenly, she turned back. "Hey," she called out.

He turned, looking at her.

"Okay. Let's do it again sometime."

"What about tomorrow?" he asked her.

From the notebooks of Menachem Shem Tov . . .

Question: Greetings to the heavens.

Answer: Greetings.

Question: Should I marry Daniella?

Answer: There is truth in this.

Question: In the next three weeks, will her husband, Shlomo, die?

Answer: Indeed, there is truth in this.

Question: Will Daniella agree to marry me?

Answer: There is truth in this (yes).

4

Daniella zipped open the long white bag holding her wedding dress. Using both hands, she delicately lifted the beaded silk free of the plastic. It was so lovely, so shiny! Like the future she held in her mind.

The wedding would take place only a week after her nineteenth birthday. Her parents had not been easy to convince, especially since it coincided with her dropping out of college.

"So you failed one course! Take it again!" her mother railed.

"I failed organic chemistry. I will never get into any decent medical school."

"There must be something you can do! Don't just give up and get married!"

"You don't understand, Mother. I don't want to be a doctor."

There was a shocked silence as her mother absorbed this new information. To her credit, her response was measured. "So, don't be a doctor," she said reasonably. "Take a different major. But why get married so young? Get your BA, at least. Without it, what will become of you?"

Her father was also less than enthusiastic. "Where's the fire? What's the big rush? You don't want to go to college? So get a job. Work in the store. Live with your mother for a while."

"Right, I'd be so much better off with Mom and her boyfriend," she'd answered, which made him look down then turn away. End of discussion.

Her mother was more difficult to put off. "The fact that I made a mistake doesn't mean you have to," she nagged.

"Why can't you just accept I'm not going to be a rich, Jewish doctor or marry one?"

"As far as I can see, your Shlomie has no education at all!"

"He's a Talmud scholar. He wants to continue learning!"

"Yes." Her mother nodded in mock respect. "Very noble. He trusts that God will support him. Unfortunately, he thinks I'm God."

"No! You're wrong! We don't care about money! We're not like you and Dad! We want to live in Israel, work the land, study, plant roots, give you grandchildren who are devout—"

"Have you thought about birth control?" she interrupted.

Daniella found the question almost brutal in its intrusiveness, especially since it had been the first major bone of contention between her and Shlomie.

"It is forbidden! A person must never prevent God from blessing them with children," he'd said almost harshly. "We must accept every soul God sends us with joy, whenever it happens."

Her response had been equally vehement: "Yeah, right, Shlomie. Sure. Easy for you to say, since I'll be the one who's pregnant and suffering through labor, and taking care of them!"

He'd taken her hand and kissed it. "Daniella, my beloved. We will do this together. You will never be alone. I will love every one of our children and care for them, the way I will love and care for you, my dearest, sweet friend."

"We've discussed it," she told her mother. To her shock, she found herself parroting the very words that Shlomie had used, and against which she had objected so fiercely. Anything was better than siding with her mother on any issue. "You know religious people don't believe in birth control. They believe that God will only send them children when they are ready, and that each child is a blessing. Don't you find your children a blessing, Mom?"

That finally shut her up. "Well, I suppose nothing I say will influence you, so I guess this discussion is at an end."

She watched her mother flounce out of the room, clearly relieved to be leaving Daniella and her brooding, judgmental stares behind. For comfort, Daniella went to see her granny.

The family's elegant, gray-haired matriarch was a cheerful, half-cup-full kind of person in whose eyes Daniella knew she could do no wrong. Heiress to a flourishing family-run business, Elizabeth Auerbach lived in a stunning mansion in the most expensive area in the city. All her life she had been coddled and pampered by a doting husband and handsome, clever children. The blessings of her charmed life had made her warm and loving and generous, and there was no one in the world she loved more than her only granddaughter, Daniella. Ever since Daniella was a baby, there had been this special bond between them. Perhaps because the girl was the opposite of her mother, Claire, whose own reaction to her good fortune was to guard it jealously, becoming shrewd, demanding, and greedy.

"Don't let your parents discourage you, Daniella. Not all marriages turn out badly."

"I won't, Granny," she said, hugging her, buoyed by her warmth and optimism.

"Daniella, my baby. A bride! I can't believe it. And she's going to make me a great-grandmother, of sabras, no less, dear little brown babies born in Israel! Are they going to wear those side curls and the long dresses? Are you going to wear a wig?"

"I don't know, Granny. Maybe."

"Just don't get too fanatic. Promise me?"

"Never!"

The truth was, she wasn't sure of anything. All she had was the broad outlines of a life imagined in uncomplicated, youthful passion, a life of total, uncompromising commitment to ideals. Some of her ideals were religious—a love for spiritual purity, for sanctity, for truth and goodness—and some were half-formed visions drawn from books, movies, Zionist youth groups, and summer camp. But it was all so abstract. She had no idea what that kind of life would actually look like, or where it would take her, when put into practice.

Only one thing filled her with absolute certainty: she wanted to be a mother. Her youthful passion to help others, to save lives, she now poured into her desire physically to create and nurture life. That was now her highest ideal, the purest way she could imagine to fulfill both her destiny as well as her womanliness: to be the person whom God had intended her to be. Her entire education at the hands of kind, learned rabbis and rebbetzins had reinforced that longing, and her relationship with Shlomie cemented it as the cornerstone of their lives together. Motherhood was the ideal of Jewish womanhood, Shlomie often said. After having failed at her studies, she allowed herself to agree.

Although in her younger years she had felt just the opposite, now when she looked at photos of haredi women and their numerous children—all beautifully dressed for the Sabbath and the holidays, the mother herself in her finely coiffed wig wearing designer dresses, calm and smiling—she saw the face of God.

She would be nothing like her own mother, she convinced herself. Her kids would have fun. There would always be time to read stories, and comb dolls' hair, and play catch. She didn't want to be admired for her medical degree, beautiful house, jewels, clothes, accomplished husband, she told herself. She wanted to be called a great mom.

That's why it didn't matter about college and birth control, she told herself. She would have no profession other than mothering, no outside interests that would interfere with taking care of her children, every one a precious, multifaceted gem that she would fashion and polish, bringing out their full potential for godliness.

She fingered the material of her wedding gown. It was fancier than she'd wanted. She would have been happy getting married the way they did on a kibbutz: in a white cotton dress with a garland of fresh flowers around her head, followed by a ride on a hay wagon and a picnic. Instead, it was going to be black tie in some ostentatious hotel with obscenely expensive kosher catering. Her mother and even her understanding granny had insisted. And everyone would have to be dressed *just so.* Her mother was even calling up distant cousins to interrogate them on what they were planning to wear!

Her grandmother had connections with a bead salesman who got Daniella into one of the few bridal gown factories still on American soil (although the seamstresses were illegal aliens paid wages little higher than those of their overseas counterparts). They'd custom-fitted her dress, lining the sheer sleeves completely so that no flesh at all peeked through.

While she'd wanted to do her own hair and makeup, she'd compromised, allowing her mother to engage a religious woman who would come to the house on the day of the wedding. She had nothing against makeup per se; she just didn't want to look like Jezebel when she walked down the aisle, like so many other, usually sensible girls who mistakenly relinquished their faces to the ministrations of "experts" on their crucial day. And even though no one ever said anything bad about a bride on her wedding day, it was obvious to her that this was the case.

She'd already had a consultation the week before. A little lipstick and mascara, that was it, she'd insisted. "Shlomie, my fiancé, doesn't like thick makeup and, after all, it's for him I want to look nice, right?" she'd explained to the affable, bewigged young woman, who nodded approvingly. "My hair—can you just put it up with tendrils floating gently down on either side of my cheeks? With all that dancing, it's bound to come undone anyway, so I might as well start out that way!"

The only extravagance she'd permitted herself was the loan of her grandmother's diamond coming-out tiara, to which she planned to attach her veil. Ever since she'd been a little girl, she'd admired the photos of her granny in her white debutante dress at the Cinderella Ball. She'd been one of the only Jewish girls in Pittsburgh to be invited, thanks to Daniella's great-grandfather's wealth and well-known philanthropic works. No one could say no to his face, no matter what they surely must have said behind his back in those anti-Semitic days.

Daniella's mother, Claire, had also participated in the ball, even though by that time the family had become more religiously observant. She simply wore a dress with less cleavage, danced with her brother, and avoided the non-kosher champagne.

The Cinderella Ball was still going strong. Daniella, too, had been invited but refused. What would have been the point? Was there ever anyone less eligible to be presented to Pittsburgh society in hopes of finding a suitable husband than herself? She had found the only man she could envision being married to: a kind, gentle, scholarly, devoutly pious boy who shared her dreams and ideals and who had never owned a pair of black, lace-up dress shoes, much less learned how to waltz.

They were very much in love, very much in sync, she told herself. She understood that her family couldn't begin to fathom this, but that was not her problem. She was going to live a better life than the one they'd chosen, a life in which every act and emotion was genuine and pure, unpolluted by hypocritical social demands or money and materialism. No one in the yeshiva world had lots of money, but they all managed somehow. With God's help, she and Shlomie would, too.

Across town, at the very same time, Shlomie Goodman was trying on a brand-new black suit. As was usual with religious Jews, he had not seen or spoken to Daniella for more than a week. Their next meeting would be in front of hundreds of people as he walked toward her, accompanied by his parents, and a twenty-piece orchestra, smiling into her face just before veiling it, as had been the custom ever since Jacob got stuck with Leah.

"What about a tie, Dad?" he asked his father, who wasn't really an expert.

A machinist in a tool and die factory, Arthur Goodman had exactly two suits and two ties hanging in his closet: the ones in which he had gotten married and which no longer fit him, and the ones his wife had picked out for him for his son's upcoming wedding.

"Well, son, you know, you should really ask your mom about such things." He cleared his throat. "How you doin', Steven?"

"*Shlomie*, Dad. I'm called Shlomie now."

"Right. Shlomie," his father said, pronouncing it "Slo-me."

"Oh, I'm great, great! She's . . . Daniella's . . . I just . . . well . . ."

His father patted him on the back. "Yeah, she's a doll, your Daniella. A real sweetheart. I want you to know that. Your mom and I, we're real happy for you. Just—and don't take this the wrong way, son—how are you going to support yourselves?"

"Always so practical!" Shlomie grinned. "You don't understand, Dad, the world I'm in . . . it's not the same as yours. People aren't practical. They want to study, to bring themselves closer to God. There are thousands and thousands of such people sitting in yeshivas all day long, just studying."

His father scratched his head. "Who pays for their lunch?"

"They don't starve, Dad!"

"Yeah, but how does it work, exactly?"

"I don't know. Government subsidies for yeshiva students, charities . . ."

"What, like welfare?"

"No, no, Dad, nothing like that!" He sighed. "It's, like, to learn is the highest purpose in life. To learn Torah, that is. And people who can't do that, they get part of the merit of those who do by helping them. It's mutual. You take, but you also give."

"I can't get my head around that—I'm sorry, son. I wanted you to . . . We wanted a better life for you than ours, me and your mother. We wanted you to go to college, make something of yourself. But ever since your Bar Mitzvah, you've gone places I've never been in my life. I respect that. It's why I never dragged you into the tool and die makers union. But now, I'm not so sure I did you a favor."

"Oh, Dad! Can you see me with my math skills learning computer drafting? Or juggling weights and gauges?"

His father chuckled. "Dropping them on your own or someone

else's foot, more likely!" Then he turned serious. "I was never much of a philosopher myself, and I'm not a great reader. But I remember this one book they made us read in high school, *David Copperfield*. There was this character, Mr. Micawber, who was a great guy, really kind, nice to his family, but always in debt. I remember this line that went something like this: 'Annual income twenty pounds, annual expenditure nineteen, result happiness. Annual income twenty pounds, annual expenditure twenty-one pounds, result misery.'"

"Oh, Dad!"

"Remember it, son!"

Shlomie looked at his father. He was a tall man, taller than he'd ever be, his body large and solid, two feet planted firmly on the ground. His hands were also big, work roughened, full of scars from abrasions and scratches, the leathery ridges between his fingers permanently stained with paints and oils that could never be entirely removed.

He'd long ago given up on the idea of competing with his father. He'd taken another path entirely, one his father had never trodden. He patted his father's shoulder. "I'll be fine, Dad. Don't worry. Eventually I'll get a job. I'll support my family."

"What are you both doing up there?" his mother's voice drifted up the steps.

"Hi, Mom! Dad's giving me his philosophy of life."

His father looked at him oddly, then looked away.

"Oh, didn't know he had any! Leastways, he never shared it with me." She laughed, entering the room. She patted her son's shoulders, almost giddy with happiness.

He was her child, small-framed and almost delicate for a boy, with what people like to call an intelligent forehead and big, gentle blue eyes like her own, which still had a shine of innocence about them, like when he was a newborn; a boy who didn't like rough sports and enjoyed reading.

While they couldn't say it to each other, both she and her husband had breathed an enormous sigh of relief when he'd brought home Daniella. A woman, after all, no confusion about that, thank God! Of course they—she—would have loved him all the same. But this was so much less complicated both for Steven and for them all, wasn't it?

And such a lovely, lovely girl! From such a fine family. Everyone in Pittsburgh had heard of the Auerbachs and the Whartmans. Old money. That lovely Victorian mansion in Highland Park. But a sweet, modest girl, without her nose stuck up in the air like you'd expect, wouldn't you? Though you couldn't say the same for the mother. A new boyfriend. At her age. Imagine! She laughed to herself, nodding. Money didn't buy class, that was for sure.

"What's so funny, Mom?"

"No, nothing. I'm happy, Steven. Really, really happy. Never had a grandmother of my own. And now, I might actually be one!"

"Hey, what's the rush! Let them get married first, Marsha!"

She chuckled, dimpling like a girl as she hugged her son.

Shlomie put a smile on his face but he couldn't help wondering: *Was* he rushing into this? Or was he simply taking advantage of something wonderful that had been granted to him like an unexpected gift, this pretty, smart, spirited girl who was so attentive and admiring?

He had never experienced anything remotely like it. How could he not want it all settled, before the clouds vanished before her eyes and she realized who he really was? He had no doubt that it would happen one day but hoped there would be a good life and a few children tying them together before it all unraveled.

Other times, he was more optimistic. Was it not written: forty days before conception, a heavenly voice calls out, This man for this woman? She had been chosen for him, a heavenly gift, a reward. It was humbling. He would spend the rest of his life trying to be worthy of her, trying to bring them both closer to God and to holiness.

He didn't feel any guilt for her dropping out of school. It had never been his idea. He would have waited patiently for her if she'd wanted to be a doctor. But she didn't want to. She'd opened her heart to him about that. She'd never wanted to.

So there it was. Who knew the future? As the Baal Shem Tov wrote, "A leaf cannot fall from a tree, unless it be God's will." He would trust in Providence.

5

Hearing the screeching of jets, Detective Bina Tzedek looked up, squinting at the blue, Mediterranean skies, wondering if it was just practice or if they were actually going somewhere. As an Israeli, her ear had become attuned to the sounds that ushered in momentous, life-changing events in her small country. From personal experience, she knew that you could just be going along, your day completely ordinary when—*whoop*—out of nowhere, a siren would sound, signaling the end of normalcy and the beginning of anything from a civilian drill to a rocket attack to even the beginnings of a war.

It was the same with her job. Every morning, she just never knew what was going to land on her desk. She took a deep, calming breath, taking in the blooming rows of colored violets that bordered Yemin Moshe. She loved this daily morning walk from her home in Talbiya to the bus stop. No one could understand why she didn't drive to work, a detective, a modern, powerful professional in control of her own life and those of many others. What was it about steering wheels and horns and the screech of tires that she found so distasteful that she avoided them whenever possible?

What she usually told people who asked was that other drivers were crazy and parking spaces such a problem. If they looked at her oddly, she'd add that she lived a short bus ride away from everywhere she needed to go and hiring taxis was cheaper than owning a second car.

All this was true, but not really the truth.

The real reason she didn't want to drive was because she loved the extra time it took to walk down the street, to wait for a bus, to sit back and look out the window in peace before she got to work—time leached out of her crowded day to think about her life. It was in such short supply these days, with two-year-old Lilach and five-year-old Ronnie and a briefcase bulging with reports studied late into the night that hung heavily, physically and metaphorically, on her slim shoulders. She always got the worst ones: wife beaters, pedophiles, rapists.

Lately, though, she and her husband, Noah, had been talking about having another child. They missed having a baby: that delicious smell of a warm bath and baby powder, the soft little kissable face and bottom. But the last birth had been a horror: a detached umbilical cord, an emergency cesarean, hemorrhaging. But she knew she couldn't wait too long. Statistically the chances of birth defects went zooming up with every passing year once you hit your thirties. She was thirty-four. She'd already seen the first wrinkles around her eyes and between her brows, little lines that used to disappear immediately after a frown but now lingered.

She drew her fingers through her hair, recently cut and a full-blown disaster, the hairdresser misinterpreting her "give me something cute and youthful" into a license to chop up her curly, shoulder-length auburn hair into a ridiculous pixie that had no chance in hell of looking good on anyone over six. For the millionth time, she tugged on her bangs, trying to stretch them to cover her forehead. It was useless.

She walked into the modern police headquarters, surrounded by shopping malls and car dealerships, taking the elevator up to her floor.

"Hi, Bina. Just the girl I want to see," Morris said as soon as she stepped out into the corridor. He frowned. "New haircut?"

She grimaced, nodding.

"Want me to bring in the guy who did it?" He grinned.

She shook her head. "It's useless. There is no death penalty in Israel."

He put a sympathetic arm around her shoulder.

Morris Klein was a senior detective with forty years' experience. A former paratrooper who had been through three major wars and uncountable skirmishes, he had lost two fingers of his left hand and wore a prosthetic leg. Everyone in the department looked up to him. She was flattered he had sought her out.

"What's up?"

"It's on your desk."

He hovered by the door as she hung up her purse, settling herself in her chair. He seemed impatient, begrudging every extra second. She looked down at the pile of material and began to read, her face slowly draining of color. She looked up at him. "Tell me, Morris, is it because I'm inexperienced? Or is this the most sickening case ever? I feel nauseous."

She was shocked to see his face change color as well. He shook his head. "It's the worst one anyone in the department has ever come across. It goes way beyond crime. There's something truly satanic about it. It's like a true-crime novel, or one of those tabloid stories that happen in far-off places. These kinds of things just don't happen in Israel, among Jews, especially religious Jews. Certainly, it doesn't happen in Jerusalem, the Holy City."

Two young children, he told her, victims of horrific child abuse that had left one in a coma and the second with horrifying burns. Five other children who were so traumatized they refused to say anything. And a mother and father in custody, the former reading psalms all day and the latter proclaiming his innocence and ignorance.

"Unless we come up with something, we're going to have to let the father go."

She was shocked. "Why?"

"He's separated from the mother, divorced, something, living outside Jerusalem. He hasn't seen the children in months and he has an iron-clad alibi for the days the kids were injured."

"What's he like?"

"Weird, American, dressed in prophet-wannabe flowing white robes. But not evil. Incredibly naïve, though, a born-again Jew, brainwashed by all that Breslov stuff, the red strings, amulets, and whatnot. My gut tells me he wasn't involved. Maybe he's a fool, but he isn't a monster."

"Did you get anything from him?"

"Hard to tell at this point. He rambled. But he did say something curious we need to follow up on. He said the divorce itself wasn't supposed to be permanent. It was simply a temporary *tikkun.*"

"He used that word? From the kabbalah?" *Tikkun,* a correction, a way of returning the divine sparks of holiness that had been lost—she remembered from her days in the religious public school system.

He nodded slowly. "He said he divorced his wife in order to, get this, *improve* their relationship! Go figure that one out. While he was gone, his fellow yeshiva students had apparently started living in the house to help his ex, who was finding it hard to manage alone with all seven kids."

"What?"

"You're religious, Bina. Tell me, is that normal, for three yeshiva guys to move in with a religious woman who's just gotten divorced?"

"Absolutely not! Especially if you're telling me we are dealing with haredim." She shook her head. "What else did the ex say?"

"Nothing, really. He just looked stunned by the whole thing, saying that there had to be some mistake, that his lovely, gentle wife was a wonderful mother and would never, ever hurt their children."

"Did he ask about his children?"

"Many times. He really seemed distraught and anxious to take care of them. Of course, we told him he wasn't allowed to go anywhere near them until we had more information."

"Good. Even if he isn't directly responsible for child abuse, they *were* his kids, after all. He can't just think he is going to walk away from all this."

Morris shrugged. "Okay, right. But he's not the problem, Bina. Think about it. If the mother wouldn't hurt a fly, and the father isn't responsible, then who is?"

She looked down at the papers in front of her. "Have you spoken to the mother?"

He nodded, pulling up a chair and looking into her eyes. "If he was eccentric, then she is certifiable. Dressed like the prophetess Deborah, too busy muttering prayers nonstop to worry about her damaged kids. You grew up in a religious home. What do you make of the 'holy' act?"

She shrugged. "Haven't you and I seen the worst serial rapists and child abusers suddenly put on a skullcap when they have to face a judge? It's easy enough to wear long sleeves and cover your hair."

"It never impresses the court, but that doesn't seem to stop them trying." He grimaced. "And afterwards, they whine their way into the 'religious' wing of any prison, where they spend their days as pious Talmud scholars instead of working. But a woman trying that tack? I haven't seen it before. Also, she doesn't appear to be evil or insane, the Andrea Yates, Susan Smith kind of psychopath. And the kids? They are dying to see her and keep asking about her. Even the one in the hospital with the burns hugged her and clung to her. I've never seen children treat an abusive parent that way."

"Actually, it's not that uncommon, believe it or not. Give me some time to study the material and I'll let you know what I think."

"Don't take too long. This is urgent. But I'm stumped. I figure you're our best shot, being a woman, religious, a mother—"

"Please, don't compare me to her," she said, already dreading diving headfirst into this polluted cesspool. But like someone who has already paid for tickets to a particularly wild and dangerous amusement park ride, she felt she had no choice but to get on.

She read over the preliminary information and the transcripts of the early interviews. From what she could see, Daniella Goodman wasn't faking. She really was in another world, but no place Bina had ever visited on planet Earth.

What kind of mother watches a child with an irreversible brain injury without crying out for revenge? What kind of mother turns around and blames a husband she hasn't let near her kids in months? What kind of mother hides the truth, protects the abuser? There had to be someone else involved. After all, the mother had been in the hospital when her youngest child had been brought in. Who had put a three-year-old into a coma? And—not that it really mattered—why? Who had done this? And why did Daniella Goodman refuse to cooperate in bringing that person to justice?

And how could they make her?

6

They were excited young newlyweds, getting ready for their new life. Almost immediately, they began gathering together those wedding presents that could not make the trip to Israel with them: all the electrical appliances that ran on the wrong voltage, the fragile crystal, the frivolous tchotchkes that would be expensive to ship and were unsuited to the serious life they planned, a life of family, study, and prayer. A life of simple pleasures.

And just as suddenly, all their plans were suspended.

She was pregnant. Honeymoon pregnancy, the doctor called it cheerfully. Shlomie was thrilled. She was devastated. It meant postponing their Aliyah indefinitely. And she had so wanted to get away, to leave behind her mother's disappointment, her father's irritated compassion.

Her grandmother found them an apartment and paid for it. Shlomie got his old job back. And she waited, growing heavier and heavier and more despondent each day as the lethargy of idleness made her sleepy and indifferent.

"Why don't you come to the store and help me out?" her mother suggested, emphasizing the "me," making it judgmental and personal rather than an innocent question.

"I don't know the first thing about jewelry. You know that."

"You could learn, though, couldn't you?"

It was better than nothing, Daniella supposed. At least it would get her out of the house and away from the refrigerator. Her weight gain was alarming.

The store, founded in 1911, was immense, with lush, turn-of-the-century fittings that made it a landmark, historic building. Daniella sat behind sparkling glass counters lit by clever overhead lighting, her eyes mesmerized by the flash of well-cut diamonds, emeralds, and rubies. But aside from using Windex on the cases, there was little else she was really qualified to do, she thought listlessly. There was no way her mother would trust her to serve a serious customer shopping for a $20,000 diamond engagement ring. And not without good reason, she admitted to herself.

"Look, over there," her mother said one morning, nodding toward a young couple with tattoos. "They're yours." She snickered snobbishly.

"Can I help you?" Daniella asked, smiling, feeling an immediate kinship with others her mother had found unworthy of her precious time and attention.

"No," the young man answered, a half smile, ironic and dismissive, on his face.

"Sure," the young woman said, glaring at him. "We'd like to see an engagement ring. But with a black diamond."

Daniella swallowed. Was there such a thing? A black diamond? Wasn't the whole beauty of a diamond in its whiteness, its dazzling purity?

"Just a moment; I'll check what's available."

"Of course there are black diamonds! Right over there, see? The black and white diamond cocktail ring," her mother hissed, moving her head slowly from side to side at her daughter's hopelessness. "They are extremely fashionable and very expensive."

"Like how expensive?"

"For a real, unenhanced one of a decent size? Thousands."

"And 'enhanced'? What does that mean, by the way?"

"It means heated and filled with a substance that will change the color to whatever color you want."

"A fake?"

"No," her mother said patiently, holding back a sigh. "Real diamond, fake color."

"Do we carry those?"

"Sure. Everyone does. They're over there, by the fissure-filled rubies."

"Fissure-filled?"

"Natural rubies are pretty ugly. Mostly they fill the holes inside with glass to make it prettier."

"So, this is all a big fake?"

She bristled. "There is nothing wrong with improving on nature. Why should millionaires be the only ones to wear a black diamond or a pretty ruby? Your customers are waiting."

They were talking softly but with growing vehemence to each other. When she drew near, they stopped, falling into a sullen silence.

"We have black diamonds. Enhanced black diamonds."

"Are they real?"

"Yes, they are real, but they get a little help in the lab with their color."

"Oh, I don't know." The young woman shook her head. "I wanted a real one."

"Can I ask why? White diamonds are so much more—"

The girl cocked her head, staring belligerently.

Daniella swallowed. "Traditional."

The young man spoke up. "Black diamonds come from a supernova explosion that took place even before our solar system was formed. They dropped to the earth like meteorites."

"They absorb light," the girl said. "They don't give it back. They trap it, hold it, like a secret inside. That's what I want."

Something about what she said startled Daniella. The idea of total

blackness secretly holding light. It reminded her of a lecture on kabbalah she'd heard at a National Council of Synagogue Youth conference during tenth grade. Kabbalah had been a big fad at the time, a
few girls in her class wearing red strings on their wrists, something she
found silly. But something of the kabbalistic idea of ten holy vessels
containing God's primordial light had remained with her as a magical
image, like a fairy tale myth.

She showed them the black diamonds, little one- or two-carat soli-
taires costing a thousand dollars or less. The girl tried one on. It was
way too big for her.

"We can make it any size you need," her mother chimed in with
her eager merchant's smile.

"Sure," Daniella agreed, embarrassed she hadn't thought to say it
herself.

"Can we pay out for it?"

"My mom is the expert on that," Daniella said, smiling, and taking
a step back.

Her mother stepped up to the counter with a practiced smile,
giving them prices, offering special discounts that expired within the
hour. The couple seemed convinced, promising to decide quickly and
return.

Once the couple had left, her mother nodded approvingly.

"That was good. You're learning."

"But they didn't buy in the end."

"They'll be back."

"Why do you say that?"

"Because she won't sleep with him until he buys it for her," she said,
yawning.

Slowly, Daniella learned the business, the value of the gems according to their size, color, and clarity, the cost of each gram of precious
metal, each decorative, colored gemstone. Most important, she learned
to evaluate the men and women who were buzzed in wanting to buy
them, becoming as cynical and accurate a judge as her mother, and with
it, learning a healthy dose of self-contempt. What a shallow way to judge

people, by the material and fit of their clothing, the kind of shoes they wore, the type of handbag they carried! Even worse, though, was how accurate these things were as indicators of their value as customers.

She hated that people could be labeled and dismissed so easily. Every day, she hoped for a surprise, for some bearded stranger wearing purple Crocs and a Metallica T-shirt to ask for a delicate pink morganite. But it never happened. Except for the young couple who wanted the black diamond, there were no surprises at all, until the day she was standing behind the counter and suddenly found herself in a puddle of her own making.

"Call Shlomie!" she begged her mother, as they hurried out to the car for the ride to the hospital.

Impossibly, Shlomie was waiting for her at the entrance. She was so happy to see him! Her loyal, sweet husband! Here to rescue her from her mother!

"I can't be with you during delivery—it's not allowed," he whispered to her. "And I can't touch you. The moment you started labor, you're a *niddah*. But I will help all I can," he assured her. She felt devastated he wasn't going to be by her side but had no time to dwell on it, the contractions coming fast and furious.

"It won't be long now," the midwife said.

She was wrong. The labor took hours and hours. The pain was excruciating.

"Please, can't you give her something?" her mother begged the doctor.

"She signed up for natural childbirth, and it's too late for an epidural. I'm sorry."

In the end, the baby's heartbeat started to show distress.

"I want my husband!" Daniella shouted. But he was nowhere to be found. Then she forgot about Shlomie completely, engrossed in the expression on the faces of her doctor and the midwife as they exchanged somber glances of terrifying seriousness, nodding in wordless agreement.

The next thing she knew, they were cutting her and inserting a vacuum extractor as the midwife pressed down hard on her stomach. It was like a Holocaust movie, she thought with horror. But seconds later, there was the cry of the baby.

"A beautiful, healthy girl!" the midwife said as she wrapped the baby in a blanket and showed her to Daniella.

"A girl," she whispered, shocked as she stared at the tiny, bluish, wrinkled bundle. She was accustomed to magazine photos of plump three-month-olds masquerading as newborns; this was her first encounter with the reality of a human being newly emerged from the womb.

"What's wrong with her? Why does she look so old, so damaged?"

The midwife and doctor laughed. "She looks exactly the way every newborn baby looks, maybe a little bluer because she had a bit of a stressful entry. But by tomorrow, she'll be pink and shiny and new—trust me," the doctor assured her.

He would say that, Daniella told herself, not in the least reassured. Doctors always worried about their malpractice insurance going up. So she wavered between hopefulness and the fear that something had gone terribly wrong because of something she'd done. Maybe it was her resistance to the idea of being pregnant, her despair at having her plans disrupted? Perhaps all that stress had somehow been communicated to the child in her womb? If there was anything wrong, she would never forgive herself. She prayed, "Please, God. Don't punish her for my sins. Let her be perfect."

The prayer was still on her lips when they wheeled Daniella to her room. Physically and emotionally exhausted, she closed her eyes and slept. When she awoke, Shlomie was standing beside her bed, a huge smile on his face. He was flabbergasted when he saw the silent tears roll down her cheeks. "Was it very hard?" he asked kindly.

"Oh, Shlomie, it's not that! There's something horribly wrong with her! I just know it! And it's all my fault."

"No, no. The doctor said she was perfect. Eight pounds six ounces. A beautiful little girl. You did a great job."

She shook her head in despair. "She's wrinkled and ugly! We're never going to marry her off!"

He threw back his head and laughed. "You just need rest, Daniella. You'll feel better tomorrow. The doctors want me to go now."

"No, Shlomie, don't go!" She reached out for him, holding his arm.

Gently, he pried himself loose. Religious law forbade physical contact between a husband and wife after childbirth until the bleeding stopped and the woman could immerse herself in the ritual bath for spiritual purification. It was a stricture that no one could really explain.

"I don't understand that. Why should bringing forth a new life make a woman impure? It's the holiest thing a woman can do, isn't it?" she asked him.

He shrugged. He knew no more than she did. "Some say it's because of all the curses a wife lobs at her husband during labor." He smiled, showing her he wasn't serious.

She found herself weeping softly, the whole experience overwhelming in its unfamiliarity, its shocking immodesty and pain. It was like nothing she could have imagined. Raw, animalistic, the opposite of the lofty spiritual experience she'd led herself to expect. She hurt all over.

She spent a fitful night trying to find a comfortable position, taking forever to turn slowly from one side to the next, afraid each small shift would evoke the knife-like, stabbing pain where they'd stitched her up. In the morning, she was exhausted.

Shlomie came at eight, bringing a small bunch of flowers.

"Did you see her?" she demanded.

He smiled. "I went to the nursery and I looked into the window at all the babies. And I focused on this one baby. It was so healthy looking, with such a full head of black hair, and it was laying there, kicking its little feet and waving its arms but not crying. Just looking around at the world. And I thought: What a perfect baby! Then the nurse came over and asked me my name. When I told her, she went over and picked it up—the very baby I was looking at!—and said, 'This is yours.' God be blessed!"

She saw his smile, so genuine and heartfelt, as the tears streamed down his cheeks. And she thought: I can do this. Be married to this man. Have his children. It was all right then, the baby, her husband, her marriage. God had not punished her. He had blessed her. Because He was kind. He was compassionate.

"Don't cry," she told him softly. "Don't cry."

They named her Amalya, because it sounded so Israeli, and they wanted an Israeli child. Soon after Amalya's first birthday, Daniella found herself pregnant again. Busy raising her little daughter, the pregnancy went amazingly quickly. But three months before her child was born, Shlomie lost his job.

"Chabad is sending someone down from New York." He shrugged. "They say they'll give me a good reference."

But with the economy, no one was hiring. She had no choice but to turn to her mother.

"Do I look like an ATM?" Claire shouted. "But I'll tell you what I will do. I will offer that husband of yours a job in the business. He can earn a salary."

"You want him to sell jewelry?" Daniella asked, aghast.

"No. He'd be useless at that. But he can do deliveries."

Shlomie agreed, but after a month, the number of parking tickets he accumulated was more than his salary.

"He's useless," her mother reported.

The birth was the opposite of Daniella's first, taking less than two hours. Wiser, this time she got an epidural and the delivery was almost painless. Unlike Amalya, her newborn son was remarkably beautiful, with a pink complexion, light blond hair, and brown eyes like her own. They named him David, after the Jewish king of Israel, but everyone called him Duvie.

Soon after his bris, she confronted her husband. "We need to make Aliyah, Shlomie. Like we planned. We can't wait anymore. I'll just get pregnant again." Concerned for his dignity, she didn't mention that her mother was about to fire him.

He was thrilled, the impracticality of moving across the world with two babies and no job not entering his mind at all. He lived with faith. He was sitting in God's palm, and God would take care of him.

They arranged to send their things, a dining room set and china closet that Daniella adored and refused to part with—notwithstanding her purported desire for a modest lifestyle—as well as their dishes and pots and pans (all four sets: milk, meat, and Passover milk and meat). They arranged to live in a Jewish Agency Absorption Center for new immigrants in Kfar Shoshan until Shlomie found work and they could afford to rent an apartment.

They left on a dark, gray winter's day, a month before the turn of the century. It was a new millennium, and a new life, Daniella exulted. Two-year-old Amalya and two-month-old Duvie were wrapped up warmly, their small faces barely visible inside their hats and scarves and snowsuits.

They emerged from the jumbo jet in Tel Aviv to a shining sun and the vast blue skies of the Mediterranean. Happily, they unwrapped themselves and their children, basking in the spring-like warmth. It felt like a new world, a new beginning, all the old failures and doubts sloughing off with their heavy winter clothing.

Someone from the Jewish Agency was there waiting to meet them, holding a placard bearing their names. He accompanied them through customs, then helped to wheel their heavily laden luggage carts filled with suitcases, baby carriages, and infant car seats through to a waiting van. They set up the car seats, strapping in their children and then themselves. Exhausted, they leaned back, surrendering to the forward momentum of the vehicle as it carried them toward their unknown destination. Their eyes feasted on the scenery, enchanted by the blossoming plants, the verdant green fields, the dazzling glare of uninterrupted sunlight, and the endlessly deep blue sky. It seemed not only like a different country but a different planet, a parallel world to the cold, grayish Pittsburgh winter they'd left behind.

Somewhere near Tel Aviv, the van took a left turn and the tangy scent of oranges suddenly filled the vehicle. They drove down a narrow, winding road through orange orchards heavy with ripe fruit as far as their astonished and delighted eyes could see.

Shlomie reached out, gently squeezing Daniella's hand. "We did it!" he rejoiced. "We're really here!" She squeezed him back, his joy infectious, putting to rest for the moment all the unanswered questions that flitted through her mind like dangerous insects she wished she could swat away.

The driver parked the van in front of the Absorption Center, a modest, low building with porches that looked pleasantly like a motel. Ushered inside, they were met with a flurry of greetings and paperwork, all in Hebrew. Finally, they were given the keys to their apartment.

It was almost brand new, smelling of fresh paint and turpentine and unopened new kitchen cabinets. It had two tiny bedrooms, an even tinier kitchen, and a small open space with a couch and chair. Daniella looked around, shocked. The whole thing was barely larger than her teenage bedroom.

"It's only for a little while," Shlomie comforted her, bustling around to find a place for their luggage and numerous bags, an impossible task he soon abandoned. Duvie began to wail, and then Amalya chimed in, whining with exhaustion and hunger.

"Do you want me to change the baby?" Shlomie asked. He was being generous. He never touched diapers.

"No, I'll do it. Why don't you find a grocery store and get us something to eat?"

"What should I buy?"

"Well, that depends on what they have, doesn't it?" she answered, exasperated. "Buy what you can."

"Right," he said, going out the door.

She sat down and unbuttoned her dress, taking out a breast. She felt the immediate determined latch of Duvie's eager lips around her nipple. Amalya pulled at her dress, whimpering.

"Hungry!" she complained.

She caressed her daughter's plump, red, unhappy face gently with her spare hand.

"I know. Mommy knows." She got up, balancing the baby carefully in the crook of her arm so as not to disturb his nursing, then walked through the rooms searching for the diaper bag they'd taken on the plane. Hopefully, there still might be some fruit or perhaps an uneaten sandwich. As she searched, Duvie left off nursing, his wails becoming louder and more insistent in a way that was becoming unfortunately familiar to her. Her heart clenched. Once allowed to start down this road, if not immediately distracted, he became impossible to pacify. Like a ticking time bomb, he would simply explode. It was dreadful.

Where the hell was that bag! she thought desperately. But Shlomie had just piled everything on top of each other. She needed both hands to unravel the mess. Reluctantly, she put a pacifier into Duvie's mouth, laying him down on the bed. At this, his cries ceased as he held his breath, almost turning blue, before releasing a wail like a crack of thunder.

Finally she spotted the bag. Wrenching it free from a pile of suitcases, she rummaged through it desperately. But all she found was one small box of raisins and a few broken cookies.

"Here, here, take this, Amalya sweetie," she said, handing it to her. "Soon Daddy will be home with real food."

Amalya took it gratefully.

Duvie, in full-blown meltdown, was by now choking with rage, the silences between his cries lengthening disturbingly as his legs flailed and his tiny hands tattooed his stomach.

"Stop, you'll hurt yourself!" she cried out to him, attempting to pry his tiny fists off his body, gathering them in her hands and holding them still as she took him back into her arms. In what seemed like hours, his sobs slowly subsided. Patiently, she guided his mouth back to her nipple. She sat there afraid to budge lest she disturb him, feeling her own stomach ache with hunger pangs. She was starving, beyond tired, feeling the full weight of the life she had chosen in all its intensity as she waited helplessly for Shlomie to return with food.

Finally, she heard the door open and Shlomie's unhurried footsteps. She rubbed her eyes, realizing that she and the children had all fallen asleep. She looked at her watch. He had been gone two hours.

"Where were you! What took you so long?" she hissed.

He seemed shocked at her anger. She never got angry.

"I went to the grocery, like you asked. It's about a twenty-minute walk uphill. But they have nothing on open shelves. Everything is behind the counter and you have to ask for it. Until I remembered the Hebrew words for milk and bread and coffee . . ." He chuckled. "The grocer was this Hassid, so friendly. We had a little talk—"

"I was here alone with two hungry, screaming babies and you . . . you were *schmoozing* with the grocery man?" she whispered incredulously, with cold fury.

He looked down, ashamed. "You're right. Sometimes I forget myself. To be friendly is a good thing. But to everything there is a season, as it is written: a time to talk and a time to hurry. Please forgive me?"

She sighed. "What did you buy?"

"They didn't have any brands I recognized. So I got bread, milk, butter, some yogurts, and a box of cereal. You can go yourself tomorrow and stock up."

"We need a car."

"But, Daniella, a car is so expensive! And I still don't have a job."

"You expect me to walk for forty minutes carrying groceries?"

"It won't be so bad. We'll put the baby in the carriage. It's lovely weather outside!"

But the next day, it rained.

"I'll go back," he offered, but she didn't trust him to shop. She couldn't stand having no food in the house to make normal meals.

"No, no. You just watch the children. I'll go." Then she turned to him and looked at him as if she'd never seen him before, searching his face. "You can do that, can't you?"

He nodded, hurt.

She walked along dirt roads rutted with car tracks and soft with mud. When she finally reached the center of the village, she rubbed her eyes. It looked like a stage set for *Fiddler on the Roof*: run-down wooden buildings housing tiny shops. She began to feel a little more sympathy for Shlomie. He was right: if you didn't know how to ask for it in Hebrew, you couldn't buy it. She didn't fare much better than he. But at least she found out which of the little shops sold meat and vegetables and fruit. She bought what she could, piling it into the empty carriage and making a mental note to buy a shopping cart. With each purchase, she tried to convert the shekel price into dollars. That way, things seemed much cheaper, except for meat, which was prohibitively expensive no matter how you calculated it.

They managed to live on bread and butter and spaghetti with sauce for a while, getting simple take-out food for Shabbat—roast chickens, potato kugels, vegetable salads—which was thankfully delivered to the center. But the longing to once again visit a supermarket was intense, especially since Tel Aviv and its modern urban conveniences were just a short bus ride away. Unfortunately, the bus to Tel Aviv didn't come into the village. One needed to walk down the dirt road through the orange groves until one reached the highway. The sun beat down on their heads, and the rough, rock-strewn road stubbed their sandal-shod feet, making their toes bleed, and blocking the baby carriage wheels.

But it was all worth it when the bus let them off in Tel Aviv. A modern supermarket! A place where you could browse goods laid out on shelves! They had Hellmann's mayonnaise, and Heinz ketchup, and Nestlé cereals. It was like crossing a border into another country. They filled their cart, only to realize that they would have to lug it all back by bus then carry it down the road. They considered taking a taxi but rejected the idea as extravagant, which it certainly was, considering the alarming speed at which their supply of ready cash was dwindling as Shlomie unsuccessfully scanned the job ads, his weak command of Hebrew disqualifying him for almost everything.

Reluctantly, they put back half of the things in their cart, things that were too heavy or that wouldn't last the long trip home: the ripe, juicy half of a watermelon, cans of tuna fish, a pint of ice cream, frozen dinners. The bags were still too heavy, and by the time they reached home, they were both falling off their feet.

They unpacked in silence. Without a word, she fed and bathed a cranky Duvie, putting him to bed, then read Amalya a story. In the middle, she suddenly felt unwell. She hurried to the toilet, throwing up.

No, she thought, shaking her head as the bile rose in her throat. No, no, no. It can't be!

But it was. Another pregnancy.

"But you can't be sure. I mean, not until you have a test. If you are, it's a great blessing. We will manage, my dear wife. . . ."

She had lost interest in anything he had to say. She wanted to go home, she realized. To Pittsburgh. Where she would have help. Where her grandmother would make sure she lacked for nothing, and her mother would come over to baby-sit, and her father would bring her packages of food from the supermarket. Where she had a car.

She hated her new life.

She came back into the living room, where Shlomie was sitting by the dining room table. Books were piled beside him, and one was open. He studied it intently, humming to himself as he swayed to and fro, repeating words softly under his breath.

She found this suddenly intolerable. "Do you need to make so much noise?" she exploded. "Why can't you study quietly? You'll wake the children after I've finally gotten them both to sleep!"

He looked up, shocked. "I'm . . . sorry," he stuttered. "It helps me to concentrate. It's not so easy for me to study. I have to keep myself motivated. Feeling happy helps my motivation and gives me the incentive to keep going. Singing makes me happy. But if you want me to stop, I'll stop."

Guilt washed over her. Contritely, she placed an arm on his. A wife shared in the merit of her husband's good deeds, his Torah learning. So why couldn't she be more supportive when he was trying so hard to be a good person, a spiritual person? Because of him, you are living your dream, she reminded herself. She sighed. But why does it seem like a nightmare? Why does it have to be so hard? Where was the merit in that? She pressed her lips together, tightening her jaw.

"Shlomie, we have to buy a car. We just can't manage without one, not with the children."

He put down his book. "But, Dani dearest, how many times have we discussed this? We just don't have the money for a car."

"My grandmother does. She'd be happy to help us."

He shook his head, sincerely bewildered. "I thought we decided to do this on our own. To live simply, modestly—"

"*I'm pregnant! What do you want me to do, lug three babies up the road and eat bread and butter for the rest of my life!*"

He felt a stirring of anger. Had they not discussed all these things beforehand? Had he forced any of this on her? But then he saw the tears run down her cheeks. A saying from the Talmud echoed through his head: *God does not forgive a single tear a wife sheds.* He stood up, putting his arms around her. "I'm so sorry, so sorry! It's so hard for you, and I don't help enough. You are right. We need a car. And if your grandmother will lend us the money, we'll take it gratefully and pay her back as soon as we can."

A week later there was a bank transfer. They rode home from Tel Aviv in a brand-new Fiat, a modest little sardine of a car that made American cars seem like whales. It was bright red. And as they filled the trunk with food from the supermarket and drove back to the Absorption Center, they sang all the Zionist songs they remembered from campfires, as Amalya clapped and attempted to sing along and even baby Duvie made noises to keep up.

The baby was born in October. They named him Joseph but everyone immediately called him Yossi. Daniella's grandmother, her parents and their new partners, her brother, Joel, and his new fiancée—a pretty blond legal secretary named Esther—all flew in for the circumcision ceremony. Only Shlomie's parents weren't there. They apologized, explaining that they just couldn't afford the airfare, sending a nice check and some baby clothes instead. Shlomie was deeply disappointed. Daniella's mother arranged for a lavish party in a Tel Aviv catering hall for the celebration.

"Now it's your turn, Joel and Esther," Claire teased them.

"Give us a chance, Mom!" Joel complained, his arm around his blushing fiancée. Their wedding was set for February. Granny had already ordered and paid for round-trip tickets for Daniella and her family.

"Any luck in finding a job, Shlomie?" Claire asked pointedly.

"With God's help, it will be all right, Mrs. Whartman."

"Yes, well, you know that joke, right?"

He cocked his head innocently.

"Martin is in deep trouble. His business is bankrupt and his bank account almost empty. So he prays to God: 'Please, help me. I've lost my business and if I don't get some money soon, the bank is going to foreclose my mortgage and I'll be out on the street. Please, God, help me. Let me win the lottery.' Lottery night comes and goes. Another person wins. So Martin prays again, 'God, I've already lost my business and my house and I'm about to lose my car. My wife and children are starving. Please, please, let me win the lottery this one time so I can get my life back in order!' Suddenly there is a roar of thunder and a blinding streak of light, and the voice of God Himself rings out: 'First you've got to buy a ticket!'"

His mother-in-law cackled, and her new husband howled. Daniella, fortunately, had been out of hearing range in the bathroom changing the baby's diaper.

"Did I miss something?" she said with a smile, coming back to a table groaning under the weight of expensive pastries and other mouth-watering desserts, enough for twice the small gathering who had come to celebrate.

"No, you didn't," muttered Joel, squeezing his sister's hand. "I'm sure Shlomie is doing his best, Mom. Let it be," he whispered.

Claire Whartman looked around innocently. "It was just a joke."

Responding to his wife's questioning gaze, Shlomie's pale face stretched into a tight smile. "Nothing serious. Just talking," he assured her.

Granny took the newborn into her arms, cradling him. "God has blessed you once again. Such a handsome child!" Before she left for the airport, she put a well-stuffed envelope into Daniella's hand. "Buy yourself something."

"Oh, Granny. You've already been so generous."

"What do you care? There's lots more where that came from. You just take care of yourself and the children."

"I will, Granny. Thank you." Daniella put her arms around the elderly woman, embracing her, shocked by the sudden thinness of her shrinking frame, the delicate frailty of her almost meatless bones. When had this happened? But saying good-bye to Joel was the hardest. "I'll miss you so much, brother. Who's going to yell at me when I say something stupid?"

"I know, it's a sacrifice for me, too." He grinned, then turned serious. "How is it going, really? Tell me the truth."

She swallowed. "It's hard, Joel. Very, very hard. Harder than I thought it would be."

Joel, of course, wanted details, but her loyalty to her husband made that impossible. "God will help us. It will be all right."

"Daniella, is this really what you want? This life?"

She hesitated, but as much as she wanted to pour her heart out, she found she couldn't. It was too embarrassing. She didn't want to lose the last shred of respect Joel might still have for her. "It is the deepest desire of my life, Joel," she told him, swallowing her doubts.

He shrugged, almost convinced. "But you're coming to the wedding, right?"

"How can you even ask that? Would I miss your wedding?"

He smiled, pointing a finger. "You know that I'd track you down and find you. Okay then. Take care of yourself and the munchkins. But you could call me more often. Write."

"You know, I heard this rumor that the phone cables carry calls in both directions. Same thing about the post office. But okay, I'll try. If I ever have a minute to myself."

"Well then, you are leaving me no choice. You're forcing me to add 'call sister' to the weekly schedule on my PalmPilot."

"Damn right."

"Oh, I love it when my pious sister uses curse words." He put his big arms around her, hugging her close.

She never wanted him to let go.

———

Soon after everyone left, their Jewish Agency caseworker asked Shlomie the same question his mother-in-law had asked, except with greater urgency: "Any luck in finding a job, Shlomie?"

He shrugged.

"Well, you know you arrived in December and now it's October. New immigrants usually only get six months here. You really have to move."

"But we have no place to go!" Shlomie pleaded.

"Well, in that case, I have an idea for you. The government is trying to add people to communities in the Western Negev. They'll give you land and a mortgage to build a house, along with a mobile home to live in while it's being built. They'll lend you money to buy equipment to set up hothouses for growing tomatoes and peppers and flowers—"

"You want me to be a farmer!" Shlomie scoffed, shaking his head, amused. "What do I know about growing things?"

"None of the other families knew anything either, when they began. They were teachers, computer programmers, editors. You just need to be willing to learn. We'll teach you everything you need to know."

"Where is that exactly, the Western Negev?"

The Jewish Agency employee cleared his throat. "It's a lovely place, not far from the sea."

"Right near the Gaza Strip . . . ," Daniella broke in.

"Yes, yes, that's true, but our soldiers will be stationed all around you. You needn't have any concerns about your security. After all, the entire state of Israel borders enemies everywhere you look. You'll be pioneers, and you'll be making a very profitable living. Some of our older farmers are exporting a hundred thousand dollars' worth of produce a year."

"Are there any religious people there?" Daniella asked.

"Oh, is that important to you?"

Daniella and Shlomie eyed each other. True, Daniella's hair covering was an expensive wig, but surely even this secular Israeli could see that Shlomie was wearing a kippah.

"Ah, yes. Very important," she answered.

The caseworker seemed crestfallen. But then his face lit up. "I have just the place for you. Yahalom, in the Jordan Valley, not far from Jericho . . . and," he added hurriedly as he saw their expressions sour, "only an hour's drive from Jerusalem! Fifty young, religious families just like you! They grow figs, passion fruit, grapes. They have a wonderful day care center for young children. Why, they even have a *kollel*! I even heard all the families join together every Sabbath for communal meals."

Shlomie's eyes shone. "A kollel. Where I could learn full-time?"

Daniella glanced swiftly at her husband, mortified.

"Oh, you couldn't do that. The kollel students are all single men. You'd have to work to support your family."

He looked crestfallen.

Fortunately, tiny baby Yossi began to whimper and squirm. "We'd better go," Daniella said, thankful to escape further humiliation.

"Think about it, okay? We'll talk next week."

But Shlomie wouldn't budge. "It's ridiculous, Daniella. Me, a farmer?"

"Then what will you do, Shlomie?"

"I'll find a job. You'll see. My Hebrew is getting better every day."

Three months later, the showdown finally came. After nursing the baby, feeding and bathing the children and putting them to bed, Daniella sat down opposite her husband at the small kitchen table.

His eyes were glued to a book about Hassidic wonder workers, a subject that of late fascinated him.

"Shlomie, we need to talk."

"Sure." He nodded affably, not lifting his eyes from the page.

"Can you please put down the book?"

"Right now?" he asked, aggrieved.

She nodded, trying to keep her emotions in check. Something inside her was coming together, building up, like the first indication of a lava flow about to blow the head off a volcano.

Unhappily, he set his book aside.

She closed her eyes, taking a deep breath. Then she took out a letter, unfolding it slowly and laying it down on the table between them. "It's an eviction notice. If we don't vacate the apartment in thirty days, 'legal proceedings will be initiated' against us."

"They can't do that!"

"Why not? These apartments are meant for six months. How many times did they tell us that? We've been here nearly double that."

He tapped the white paper nervously with his forefinger.

"And there's something else."

A strange urgency in her tone made him face her at last.

"I'm pregnant."

For the first time, his face showed uncertainty. "God be blessed!" he said by rote. "But is it possible? Yossi is only three months old and you're still nursing."

"You can get pregnant while you're nursing."

"Really?"

She nodded, growing more furious by the second. "Didn't you notice I was still nursing Duvie when I got pregnant with Yossi?"

"No," he said honestly, his face full of wonder. "I didn't."

"It seems to be a pattern with me. Thank God Israel has socialized medicine and the hospital stays are covered, but we need to find a way to support ourselves! If you haven't noticed, our wedding gifts are running out."

He blinked, taking the rebuke without comment.

"Even if we could stay here, it's a chicken coop. We need a real apartment for a normal-sized family. What are we going to do?"

"You know, I've been looking into different kollels. A few in Jerusalem and Petah Tikva have offered me a place. They'll pay me a monthly stipend."

"A stipend? Shlomie, I know what they pay yeshiva students to study. It won't even cover our gas and insurance for the car."

"You were the one who wanted a car!" he accused sullenly, feeling suddenly aggrieved.

"Yes, I know. But how else could we have managed?"

He thought for a moment. "Well, maybe your grandmother—"

"*No.* Absolutely not. Never again."

"Well, your mother, then . . ."

"As if . . . After all the money she wasted on my tuition? Forget it! I can't ask her for the time of day."

"I don't know why not," he said, peeved. "It's a mitzvah to support Torah learning."

"Damn it to hell, you've got to get a *job!*" she shouted, out of control for the first time in their relationship. She felt enraged, all the accumulated tiredness and work and disappointments falling on her with a crushing blow. She felt as if she were being squeezed through a very narrow tunnel with hardly room to breathe and no certainty of making it out the other end.

He must have sensed it because he suddenly stood up and leaned over, gently touching her shoulder. "You're tired. Let me do the dishes."

"It's not about the goddamn dishes!" she shouted.

He was devastated, looking at her as if he'd never seen her before. He was paralyzed, unsure of how to react. "Tomorrow, you take the day off," he said hurriedly. "I'll do everything—feed the kids, do the laundry, the shopping. We'll go to Tel Aviv for dinner."

She felt her knees buckle in fury and pressed her lips together, suddenly cognizant of the thin walls and her nosy neighbors, who would be listening to their every word. "Is that what we've been talking about?" she said in a heated whisper. "Dinner in Burger Ranch! That's not the point, Shlomie."

He collapsed heavily into a chair, frightened by this sudden transformation of his kind, gentle, adoring Dani. . . . He was at a loss. He covered his eyes with his hands. "What is it you want?"

"I want us to have a life. Is that so hard to understand? Free money is the least free thing in the world. It comes with all kinds of strings attached. You have no idea what my family can be like. I don't want them to rule our lives."

"So, you want to move to that place in the desert and grow figs?" he mocked.

Her face sagged, the anger draining, leaving a pale, exhausted fury in its wake. "I don't want to be dependent on anyone ever again, whatever it takes. I want to teach our children—the children *we* are bringing into the world—the value of hard work and achievement."

"But a farmer . . ." He gestured helplessly.

"It's not like it used to be, Shlomie. It's all computerized now, the watering, the fertilizer. Very high tech. It's a real opportunity for us to learn a profitable business." She paused, taking a deep breath. "We need to work hard, to learn new skills, to contribute, especially now that we have debts to repay. What do you say, Shlomie?"

He smiled and took her hand in his, almost convinced. Besides, it felt so much easier just to give in. "Please God, He will bless us and we'll succeed."

And so yet another chapter in their marriage began, but not the last, which was as yet still inconceivable.

7

Bina Tzedek stood outside the door of the interrogation room with Morris and another senior detective, who between them had more than sixty years of experience in interviewing suspects.

"I'm surprised you think you need me along," she said.

"You're a woman, a mother," Morris explained.

"That person is not a mother. No mother—animal or human— behaves the way she has. She's a monster."

"No, she's not," Morris answered, shaking his head slowly. "She's young. She has no record of any kind. There is a secret buried here. Something we need to dig out."

"How many times has she been interrogated? She's worse than the most hardened crime lord. She won't budge. I'm not a miracle worker."

"Just try," the other detective encouraged her.

Daniella sat in front of the desk, looking small and incredibly child-like, dressed in the same outfit she had worn in the hospital, but wrinkled now and stained with perspiration and spots the color of tea.

"Let's stop the nonsense, shall we, Daniella?" Morris began.

"Rebbetzin Goodman," she interrupted him wearily, her hubris gone, clinging to some shred of dignity.

"Why don't you tell us the truth? We are going to get it out of you, one way or the other, Daniella," Morris continued briskly, ignoring her request. He was done playing games.

"I've told you everything about my ex-husband!" she insisted, tears in her eyes.

"We know, we know, you told us. How he beat you and abused you. How he abused the children . . . ," the other detective chimed in, his tone skeptical, almost mocking.

"So what do you want from me?"

Bina put a restraining hand on Morris, slipping forward and pulling up a chair. She smiled, reaching out her hand across the desk.

"Hi, Rebbetzin Goodman. My name is Bina. I want you to know that I talked to your ex-husband, Shlomie. He denies all you say, and I believe him. He really doesn't seem like the type at all."

Daniella ignored the proffered hand but looked up, suddenly wary, her eyes darting to and fro like those of a trapped animal searching for a place to hide.

"Rebbetzin, even if what you say is true about your ex, you divorced him and threw him out of the house three months ago. He has many reliable witnesses who have testified he was many kilometers away in Pardes Chana when the children were injured."

"They're lying!"

Bina went on mildly, ignoring all interruptions. "One of them is a very well-known rabbi who said Shlomie was in his kollel the night Eli and then Menchie were brought in. There were thirty other students in the kollel who saw him there." She paused. "So, Rebbetzin Goodman, my question to you is this: If your ex-husband didn't do it, and you didn't do it, who did?"

Daniella wiped her eyes, looking at her questioner alertly. "Nobody. It was an accident."

The other detective stepped forward, about to say something. Bina quickly caught his eye, nodding curtly. He stepped back. "Look, Rebbetzin, we are here to help you, to help your children. You have a baby lying unconscious—"

Daniella flinched.

"—another child with third-degree burns. Don't you want those who did this to your children punished? Why don't you simply help us, so we can help you—and them?" Bina said gently.

Daniella put her hands into her pockets, kneading something. "My ex-husband did it."

Suddenly, Bina slammed her hand on the desk. The pencils jumped. "I have a child, almost the same age as your baby. She walks, she talks, she has chubby little arms and legs. I'd kill anyone who tried to harm a single hair on her head! What kind of monster are you to cover for someone who did these things to your babies!"

Daniella suddenly covered her face with her hands.

Morris and the other detective nodded to each other approvingly. Bina pressed her advantage. "Tell us what happened! Be strong, purify yourself, get rid of your guilt, spit it out of you. Those tears aren't helping anyone."

Daniella pressed her lips together.

"Look, let's say there are three kids in the kitchen and you hear a glass breaking. You go inside but no one is talking. So you ask, 'Which one of you did it?' No one answers you. But you see that one of them is standing on the countertop opening a closet, and you know it was him. So you'd get even angrier with him, wouldn't you? But if he admitted it and said, 'Sorry, Mom, it fell by accident,' you'd say to him, 'Not so terrible, sweetie. It happens. Next time be careful.' That's the position you're in, Daniella. You're holding the broken glass in your hand, and you have the chance now to cleanse your conscience by telling the truth."

The silence lengthened.

Bina slammed both fists on the table.

Daniella twitched uncontrollably, visibly shaken.

"Tell me what happened with the heater!"

"I already told you!" She wept.

"What, that the child put himself up against the heater and you right away grabbed him away?"

"Yes."

"*Liar*! Those kind of burns don't come from brushing against a heater! He was forcibly held against it for a long time, the doctors said. Tell the truth already!"

"The child . . . the child who was burnt . . ."

"Yes, yes. Your son. Your four-year-old son. Your Eli . . ."

"Yes, Eli. It was his own fault. He stood there; he didn't move!"

"A normal child who touches fire runs away immediately!"

"That's true. It's amazing that he didn't . . ."

"What? That he didn't want to move away? Wow, you're trying to sell us that?"

Morris broke in: "Who are you protecting? The court will decide your punishment, but the person who did this must also be punished. You can't save them. We'll catch them. And in the meantime, your behavior is disgusting. And you pretend to be religious, God-fearing—"

"I'm not pretending!" Daniella shouted, standing up.

"Sit down! You know, a highly respected rabbi who saw you in your white clothes with the psalmbook in your hand said it was sickening," Bina told her, something she'd read in the newspaper.

"Which rabbi?"

"Never mind. A well-respected Hassidic rabbi from Meah Shearim."

Daniella sat down, her strength draining.

"She's not religious. No religious, God-fearing person hurts an innocent child or let's someone else do it while she watches. I feel like we're talking to a brick wall," Bina said, thinking of the little boy with the horrible burns. She felt the bile rising in her throat. "Where are the handcuffs? Come, let's go back to your cell, Your Holiness. You're not going to see us for another eight days. Such a hypocrite!"

"We rolled out the red carpet for you to tell the truth. We couldn't have been kinder or more understanding. We don't want to see your act anymore," Morris added.

"Your poor kids! You should burn in hell—you have it coming! I'm going to make sure you get yours: that you don't live to see the light of day again, let alone your children!" Bina suddenly shouted, standing up and leaning across the desk.

"Whoa!" Morris glanced at the other detective, who put a restraining arm around Bina's shoulder, steering her out the door.

Outside, she leaned against the wall, shaking. She felt defeated.

"Don't take it personally, Bina," Morris comforted her. "Sometimes, it's like this. But usually, they are hard-boiled criminals, Mafia types, murderers. But a young mother? I've never seen anything like it."

"So now what?" she asked him.

"Now we offer her a carrot. We let her meet her children. She's been demanding it all week."

"You can't be serious. She could influence them, threaten them to keep quiet."

"If she does, we'll know about it. We'll be watching and recording the whole thing. If she tries to shut them up, the judge will know about it."

"Go back in and tell her," Morris said to Bina.

"No, I've burnt my bridges."

"Don't be naïve. She respects you now. She realizes she can't fool you. Go back in and offer her time with her children if she talks."

Bina took a deep breath, opening the door.

Daniella looked up fearfully.

"I'm sorry I got carried away. It's just . . . the idea of anyone hurting children the way yours have been hurt. It makes me crazy."

"When can I see them?"

"We'll arrange something. They are missing you terribly."

Daniella's shoulders slumped, her back losing its defiance.

"My poor children . . . ," she said softly.

The sudden contradiction of this statement compared to this woman's heartless behavior was absolutely dumbfounding. Bina tried to decipher this creature in front of her. It was like working on a jigsaw puzzle with tiny pieces when you had no picture to compare them to, no way of knowing how many pieces were missing or how the ones you had fit together. What she had so far showed her nothing comprehensible.

Two days later they brought Daniella back. Her children were waiting for her: fourteen-year-old Amalya, thirteen-year-old Duvie, twelve-year-old Yossi, eleven-year-old Gabriel, and seven-year-old Shoshana. They were in a bad way, divided up among several foster families, missing their parents and each other. But with both their parents under investigation, social services didn't have a better solution at the moment.

On the other side of a two-way mirror, Bina watched the drama unfold. An interrogation room's gray walls, and five children who cried when they saw each other, the older ones hugging the little ones. The door opened, and Daniella Goodman walked in, dressed in her now filthy white clothes. The children's sobs immediately rose into hysterics. They wailed, a white-hot sound that physically hurt Bina Tzedek's heart. She stared at the mother, who was facing away from her, appalled once more at her youth, her slenderness. Her body was erect, stiff, like a stone sculpture or some robot in a sci-fi thriller. She didn't try to hug her children or comfort them. She didn't ask them who was taking care of them, and if they were all right. When Daniella Goodman finally did begin to speak, Bina couldn't believe her ears.

"Am I hearing her right?" she asked, turning to Morris, who was standing beside her.

He nodded. "She's saying the same thing, over and over and over: 'Don't talk, don't talk, don't talk. . . .'"

Bina felt her face grow hot with fury. Not one hug. Not one word of comfort to those heartbroken children! She had to stay objective, she must, she told herself, trying to reason with some unreasoning impulse that wanted to smash Daniella Goodman's face in, to shake her until her pious white hair covering went flying across the room and her long-sleeved dress was stained with blood. She closed her eyes, wiping her forehead and trying to settle the turmoil that ripped through her bowels. This had touched some primitive, animalistic part of her, she realized. Something all creatures capable of having offspring must feel in the most primal way. I want revenge, she admitted to herself. I want to hurt her. And then that suddenly gave way to another primal emotion: fear. Who could stand up against such pain from her own children without trying to help them? It was inhuman.

The longer she watched Daniella Goodman standing stoically, allowing herself to be hugged, the greater her disgust for this woman grew. "Remember everything you were taught, children," she told her screaming children without emotion.

"We miss you so much, Ima," Amalya sobbed helplessly. "What's going to happen to us now?"

"The most important thing is to pray all the time," Daniella told her. "Ask God to get me out of here. They're yelling at me, and cursing me, and saying terrible things to your mother. But I won't answer. I'll be strong. You also have to be strong."

"Listen to her!" Bina fumed, feeling her face grow hot once more. "The only thing she is worried about is her own neck! She's telling them to keep their mouths shut! We need to end this!"

"Wait," Morris said quietly.

The children's sobs increased. It came from a place so filled with agony and loss and pain, it made Bina feel as if she had never heard anyone cry before. What could these children have experienced in their short lives that had opened wounds that deep and full of suffering? she wondered, goose bumps covering her arms and the skin across her back. And how could their mother witness it now without collapsing in tears herself, spilling her guts, wanting to kill somebody?

Perhaps, after all, she truly was a monster. Or someone who had sold her soul to the devil.

"So, what do you think?" Bina asked Morris.

"I think we need to call in a child interrogator, the best one we have. We need to call in Johnny Mann."

8

Three days after they returned from Joel and Esther's wedding, Daniella and Shlomie packed their things into a small moving van, piled into the little Fiat, and bid farewell to the Absorption Center. Weighted down with three children, pots and pans and paper diapers, the little Fiat moved heavily down the road toward the Dead Sea, past ancient Jericho, their ears popping as they reached almost a thousand feet below sea level.

Three-year-old Amalya was strapped into her car seat happily playing with her expensive new American Girl doll from Granny, while eighteen-month-old Duvie clasped the plastic steering wheel attached to his car seat, liberally pounding on the squeaky toy horn no matter how many times Daniella begged him to stop. Despite the racket, baby Yossi slept soundly in his expensive, super-safe baby car seat, also brought back from America, lulled by the engine's steady hum.

The air was dry, but the area around the old town of Jericho was bright with wildflowers and palm trees, their magnificent fronds swaying in the desert wind.

"An oasis in the desert!" Shlomie exclaimed. He had developed a sudden enthusiasm for the move, for their new life together. He was anxious to be more active in the world, to support his growing family, he told her, not for practical reasons but for spiritual ones. He'd decided that manual labor was a holy thing.

"Doesn't the prophet Isaiah tell us that it is God who teaches the farmers how to farm? Don't we read in the Psalms, 'Happy are all who fear the Lord. . . . You shall enjoy the fruit of your labors'? The Torah condemns idleness: 'Through slothfulness the ceiling sags, through lazy hands the house caves in,' King Solomon wrote. And Rabbi Yehuda and Rabbi Shimon said, 'Great is labor for it honors those who engage in it.' As it is written, 'A pious person should never say: I will eat and drink and enjoy the good life and not exert myself and Heaven shall take pity on me.' A person must toil and work with his hands and then God sends His blessing!"

Daniella, who didn't know what to make of this recent conversion, said nothing. She was relieved but skeptical. Shlomie was always developing new philosophies and enthusiasms. They seldom lasted very long, replaced by others that he advocated with equal conviction.

As for herself, she was just trying to keep her head above water. The nausea from her fourth pregnancy was making her feel tired and wretched. Taking care of three children, two of them essentially babies, was exhausting. She worried how she would manage with yet another one. Shlomie would just have to pitch in more. I have to talk to him, to make him, she thought. But every time she was determined to have it out, something stopped her. She didn't want to be negative, not now when he'd agreed to cooperate, to move out to this new community, to start a new job. She didn't want to be the nagging, complaining wife. She wanted to be a woman of valor, the kind Jewish lore praised as the ideal of womanhood, a woman who both knitted woolen clothes to keep her family warm while also trading goods to support and feed them. She wanted to be worthy of her new, exalted pioneer status in the Holy Land. Most of all, after what she saw as all her failures, she wanted to succeed at something. She couldn't stand the idea of yet another downfall.

They pulled to a full stop in front of a massive iron security gate. "Now what?"

She squinted at the gate. "They've posted a number to call," she said patiently, lifting the crying baby out of his car seat and pulling out a breast heavy with milk. Gently, she pressed the infant to her breast, inhaling sharply as his eager mouth latched on to the nipple, tender from the new pregnancy. With her other hand, she took out her cell phone and dialed. "Here, Shlomie, it's ringing." She handed it to him.

"Hello? Hello? We're the Goodmans, your new neighbors," Shlomie said brightly, smiling and nodding as he listened.

The gate slowly pulled back.

"Such nice, friendly people! He said to follow the signs that point to the office. Someone is waiting there for us."

They inched along like sightseers, charmed by the small, private homes surrounded by blooming gardens. There were playgrounds filled with small children, and large grassy communal areas. A sudden hope blossomed in her heart.

Perhaps, after all, this would work out.

A young couple who introduced themselves as Yochanon and Essie Meyers were waiting for them outside a small caravan with a hand-printed sign in Hebrew that said, OFFICE. The woman was dressed religious pioneer-style: a long, blue cotton skirt and a long-sleeved white shirt, her hair covered with an elaborate headdress of bright turquoise. No one else in the country dressed exactly like that. No one else in the world, Daniella thought with a touch of pride that she would soon be joining this unique fellowship. The young man had a warm smile beneath a bushy beard. He wore jeans and a work shirt and the colorful knitted skullcap favored by modern Orthodox Jews. His hands looked brown and work roughened, nothing like the hands of Orthodox Jews with whom she was familiar back in Pittsburgh.

"*Baruchim Haba'im*! Welcome! How was your trip down?"

"Very nice, very nice," Shlomie said, extending his hand through the window and shaking the other man's warmly, preparing for a long chat. From the back of the car, Duvie's whining and Amalya's demands rose.

"Oh, poor things!" Essie sympathized, bending down and looking into the car, as her husband moved away. "Such a long drive from Jerusalem. Here, let me get them something." Ignoring Daniella's polite protestations, she disappeared back inside the office, soon returning with ice pops.

"It'll turn their tongues and lips blue, but they'll be happy, I guarantee," she said, handing one to Amalya and one to Duvie, both of whom eagerly grasped the icy treat.

The women smiled at each other with instant connection.

"When are you due?" Daniella asked Essie.

"In two months," she answered, smiling.

"I've got another seven."

"That means you'll be pregnant through the summer," Essie commiserated. "It's really hot here, but we all get used to it, and the houses are air-conditioned. The upside is that it never really gets cold down here. I wouldn't want to give birth in December in New York!" She laughed. "*B'sha'ah tovah.*"

"Thank you. The same to you," Daniella blessed her. In a good hour.

"Well, I guess you'd like to get settled? Please follow us in your car," Essie said briskly to Daniella's relief, walking away and taking her husband with her, leaving Shlomie no one with whom to shmooze. Daniella watched them as they climbed into an old pickup that had seen better days.

Shlomie started the car, the little Fiat following behind over ever more primitive roads, until finally the paving disappeared altogether, turning into rutted layers of mud and gravel. They bumped brutally along for ten minutes until thankfully coming to a stop.

"You've got to be kidding," Daniella murmured under her breath as she peered through the windshield.

"What?" Shlomie asked.

"Nothing." That's all her husband needed, discouragement.

It looked like a trailer park, she thought, aghast, places no respectable, middle-class American would ever set foot in. She counted about fifteen caravans, spread out over the rocky, dusty earth where nothing seemed to grow.

She got out of the car, baby Yossi still at her breast, her back aching.

"It's not as bad as it looks." Yochanon grinned, noting Daniella's dismay. "I remember the first time Essie saw a caravan! But inside, they've got everything you need—a kitchen, a bathroom, beds, water, electricity. It's sometimes cold in winter and very hot in summer. But there's a heater–slash–air conditioner. Electricity is expensive, but we've got no choice, especially if you've got little kids."

"What you have to try to remember," Essie added, "is that it's only temporary, until you can build your house. Have you seen our members' houses?"

"Yes, when we came in. They were lovely," Daniella said, smiling.

"Thank you. Nothing luxurious, but it's a good life."

"How long . . . that is . . . when can we start . . . ?"

"Building?" Essie smiled.

"That's always the first thing all the women want to know." Yochanon laughed.

Daniella's face reddened, embarrassed that she'd been outed as a typical, materialistic American.

"In a few months, when you're sure this is the right place for you, you can apply to the building committee for a piece of land," Yochanon assured them.

"Come inside?" Essie invited, opening the caravan door.

Daniella followed her inside. A hot, dry blast of air and the sharp, chemical smell of desert dust and metal baking in the sun assaulted her immediately. And this was February! She didn't even want to imagine June. She took a few cautious steps farther inside. It was surprisingly roomy, at least compared to the Absorption Center. There was a fully equipped kitchen, a small couch, and three bedrooms, already fitted with beds and cribs.

You know what? This is not so bad, she told herself, setting the baby down in the new crib, which had been thoughtfully made up with clean sheets and a baby blanket.

"Why don't you get settled, Daniella? Essie will stay behind with you, while I take Shlomie to see the orchards and hothouses."

She was just about to protest being left behind and to assert her intention of being a full partner to her husband in the agricultural work, when Duvie began to cry. She laid him down to change his diaper. That done, she took him and Amalya into the bathroom to wash the blue off their faces and hands. "You look like little Smurfs," she said, holding them up to the bathroom mirror. They giggled riotously. She heard the door open and close. Yochanon and Shlomie had gone.

She sighed, taking out the sandwiches she'd prepared for the children and for herself and offering one to Essie.

"No thanks—they look delicious, though. I'm trying to keep a lid on my weight gain."

Daniella suddenly stumbled, assailed by a momentary dizziness. She sat down by the small kitchen table, holding Duvie in her lap.

"Are you all right?"

"I'm exhausted."

"Why don't I put up some water for tea and coffee?" Essie offered kindly.

"I don't know if we have any. I haven't gone shopping yet. . . ."

"If you look in your cupboards and the refrigerator, you'll see it's stocked for the next few days."

After her experience in the government-run Absorption Center, Daniella was shocked to see that this was true. "That's really so thoughtful of you. Thank you," she said with sincere gratitude.

Essie made a dismissive gesture. "Oh, don't thank me. We have a welcome committee who does this for every new family. We've all been there, where you are now, Daniella: a new country, a fairly new husband, lots of little, needy 'blessings.' And on top of that, to be pregnant with another 'blessing' . . ." She rolled her eyes heavenward and laughed. "You'll do the same for the next family who moves in, believe me."

Yes, she thought. I will. She exhaled, the tightness in her chest suddenly dissipating. It was such a relief to feel wanted and needed, to feel she had found a home.

Shlomie returned, bubbling with excitement. He set his alarm clock for five thirty in the morning.

"Why so early?"

"I want to have time to pray with a minyan and get in a little learning before I start working."

She was astounded by his newfound energy, amazed that he didn't complain even though farming turned out to be way more complicated than either one of them had imagined. Luckily, he had a helper, an Arab from Jericho named Marwan, who was very experienced. She felt a sudden surge of pride and affection for her husband as she packed his lunch each day, slicing the still-warm rye bread delivered fresh each morning to the local grocery.

Her life took on its own rhythm. Waking with the children, tidying the small living space, cooking Shlomie a hearty, mostly organic dinner. Often, neighbors would knock on her door, bringing cakes or fruits, flowers, and vegetables from their hothouses. Or they'd casually stop by just wanting to be friendly. Everyone always kept their front doors open, she learned, and you didn't need a formal invitation to stop by and sit down for a cup of coffee while all the kids, including your own, were outside playing with dozens of other kids. It was a very sheltered place, all outsiders carefully screened before being permitted to enter. Besides, invariably there was some adult outside supervising not only their own but everyone else's children. If you found a hungry child, you didn't care if it was yours, you'd feed him. If a child fell, motherly hands were never far away to pick him up and wash his wound, sending him home with a Band-Aid.

She found the atmosphere kibbutz-like in the best way. People were sincerely friendly with no guile or ulterior motives, honestly wanting to be helpful. Here, love your brother as yourself wasn't a tired old saying; it was a way of life. The women arranged play groups so that Daniella had time to go shopping and to do the laundry. They exchanged recipes, translating local ingredients to those she was familiar with from America. They offered cleaning tips on how to rout the invasive desert dust and hard-water stains.

Most important, they kept her abreast of the weekly lectures and other cultural activities being offered for both men and women, encouraging her to get out of the house. The talks were always on some interesting or practical subject, the lecturer usually a member of the community. There was no coercion to join in. If you wanted to come, you came; if not, not. No one thought any less of you if you simply said you were too tired. Everyone in the community worked hard.

Daniella loved the interaction with the other mothers. It was wonderful to finally be part of a community in which most members were exactly on her wavelength when it came to the kind of life they were seeking. Religiously, there were many like her: Americans brought up in the liberal Orthodox day-school tradition that assumed college was your goal, and Israel your destination.

Most of the women covered their hair with cotton scarves, but a few wore wigs, and some wore nothing at all. Their clothing was eclectic. too: everything from jeans and sweatshirts to shirts with buttoned-up collars and calf- or ankle-length skirts. No one made a big deal out of it, which suited Daniella perfectly. She gladly parted with her expensive wardrobe and skull-pinching, handmade wig, happily wearing long jean skirts, light inexpensive T-shirts, and a simple headscarf she hardly felt was there.

Some native Israelis on the *yishuv* seemed a bit more stringent religiously, dressing in black outfits, their women in wigs and long-sleeved, dark dresses down to their ankles. But they, too, were not pushy or judgmental about their beliefs, and everyone—except for the two dozen or so kollel boys—worked in the agricultural industry whether as farmers, pickers, distributors, or exporters.

She was happy, loving the fresh morning air, the abundant blue skies, and her rugged-looking husband, whose body had become handsomely muscular and tan. They grew hothouse strawberries and lettuce and cherry tomatoes, which he brought home in abundance. And because the vegetables were grown indoors, they used no pesticides. She had never tasted anything so delicious! At the end of the year, their crop was large and top grade. They made a good profit, enough to begin paying off some of their loans for equipment and seeds and the use of the caravan.

She wrote long, detailed letters to her mother and father and Joel that were humorous and expressive, her happiness evident in every line. She was so glad she could honestly say her life was working out, and that her husband was busy providing for them.

When Gabriel was born in September, Daniella found herself surrounded by caring friends who took turns baby-sitting her children when she was in the hospital, bringing over casseroles and doing the laundry so that Shlomie didn't have to take too much time off from work. She came home with her newborn to an ordered house and happy children, who continued to be watched over by various friends and neighbors for a few hours every day in order to give her time to recuperate.

While her mother and father came for the *brit,* Joel and Esther, expecting their first child, begged off. It had been a difficult pregnancy, Joel explained, and Esther's doctor urged her to skip long plane rides. Daniella understood, but Joel's absence marred the joy of the celebration. She missed him terribly. She was anxious to show him her new life. She trusted his judgment and would have loved his seal of approval. She also wanted him to be proud of her, the way she was of him.

The following year began with an unusually cold winter. In the evenings the caravan shook from strong winds as it was battered by icy rain. It didn't take them long to realize that despite their air-conditioning and heating system, the caravan was just too flimsy to keep out the elements. Amalya developed bronchitis, and Yossi had ear and lung infections from the dampness. Most worrying, baby Gabriel seemed to be developing asthma.

The winter was followed by a brutally hot summer in which all the children suffered from the sweltering temperatures inside the caravan, which was often hotter than it was outside, not to mention insect stings and sunburn.

For the first time, she felt real despair. "Shlomie, how much longer can we live this way?"

"It will be all right, Daniella. God will provide. The crop was good this year. It will be even better next year. We are saving money. It won't be long now."

"Another year!" She shook her head adamantly. "We can't put off building for another year, Shlomie! I can't live in this tin box three more years with four children!"

"But, darling, what do you want me to do? We can't take out a big mortgage while we are still paying off our other loans."

He was right. But so was she.

Without discussing it with him, she wrote to her grandmother.

When the money was transferred to her account, she joyously told Shlomie what she had done, and that they could now begin to plan their comfortable new home.

His reaction left her dumbfounded.

"You wrote to her, behind my back?" he accused. She had never seen him so angry.

"What can we do? We are a young couple. We need help. Everybody here has gotten help from their parents or family to build their first home."

"It's never good enough for you, is it, Daniella?" he said coldly. "I planned to learn Torah my whole life, but I put that all aside because you wanted me to. I am working every day, all day. But you'll always want more than I can give you."

"Shlomie, it's not like that!" she pleaded.

He ignored her. "You know how you make me feel? Like I'm not a man. Our sages tell us not to ask for handouts. To earn our bread through the sweat of our brows."

"That wasn't always the tune you sang," she said levelly, looking him in the eye.

He blanched. "I turned over a new leaf. I did it for you. You were the one who insisted we do this on our own, remember?"

"I know I did! But that was before we had to house four kids in a crumbling sardine can that bakes in the summer and freezes in the winter. You know Yossi was on antibiotics all winter, and the baby is on the verge of developing asthma. It's not right! We are their parents. We have to take care of them."

"So, now I'm not a good father either, right?"

For some reason, it hurt her to hear him say that. For everything he was, he loved the children. "I never said that! I . . . I'm so proud of you!"

"But it's not enough . . . never enough."

He opened the door and went out, slamming it behind him.

Daniella sat down heavily. What can I do? she thought, looking around her. It would take two years to build. If they put off starting another year, that would make it three. Three more years! Maybe even four if they put off starting, which was more than likely. Even if she was willing to wait, she couldn't do that to her children. She was a mother first. Shlomie would just have to get over himself.

Shlomie showed minimal interest in the architectural plans she had drawn up. Whatever you want, he said dully. He spent more and more time away from the house, learning with the boys in the yeshiva. He went to sleep late at night, and often it was difficult for him to get up in the morning, his tread slower and heavier as he left for work.

Daniella, busy with four small children, overseeing the building of her home, didn't have time to notice. She was supervising the contractors, keeping track of the cost of materials, and making sure the workers didn't steal them blind when floor and ceramic tiles were delivered. Building a house by herself wasn't what she'd had in mind, but in the end she found she rather enjoyed it. Everything was to her taste, unrestrained by compromises to please her husband.

"You're lucky," a friend told her. "My husband had his nose in everything. Whenever we disagreed, there was a fight, which I usually won. Still, you're lucky to have a free hand."

Lucky, yes, but somehow it didn't feel that way. It felt downright lonely, especially when the children were in bed at night and she had a few moments to herself and Shlomie was off somewhere at the yeshiva.

"Can we talk?" She cornered him one Friday night after dinner, when the children had all been put to bed.

"Whatever you want." He nodded warily.

"What is that supposed to mean?"

"Nothing. What do you want to talk about, Daniella?"

"You are never home. I need your help, and you are never home."

"My help?" He seemed truly surprised. "I never get the feeling you need me at all."

She bit her lip, her eyes filling with tears. "I need you, Shlomie. So much."

He looked into her face, wiping tears from the corners of her eyes with his thumbs. "I don't know why you married me. I'm not very smart. I didn't get into an ivy league college like you did. I come from a working-class family. You could have had anyone, some rich lawyer, a doctor, and you'd have a big house, a full-time maid, an au pair. . . ."

"I married you because I love you," she said, trying to feel sincere about the words, wanting them to be true. But honestly, she wasn't sure, not anymore, not the way she'd once been.

He didn't pick up on her hesitation. Instead, he swallowed her words whole, the way a starving man eats bread, without even chewing. "I feel so blessed with you and the children, this beautiful family we're building. I know I don't do enough to help you. I'll try harder to be around more."

And for a while, he did. He came home directly after work, helping to feed and bathe the children, washing the supper dishes, allowing her to get out of the house and join her friends at some evening lecture or folk dancing class. For a while the situation between them improved, both of them doing their best to be loving and accepting, encouraged by regular visits to the yishuv's rabbi, who also acted as a marriage counselor.

He was an older man with twinkling blue eyes and eleven children of his own. His wife, the rebbetzin, always had a lovely smile on her face that seemed to rise up from her soul. She was a woman that took care of herself, wearing well-made, fashionable clothes on her still-slim body, her expensive wig always coiffed just so. All of the women envied and admired her and the relationship she had with her husband.

"Remember this," the rabbi told Shlomie and Daniella, "it takes two to make a marriage and it takes two to destroy one. Both of you are equally responsible. When was the last time you went out on a date? To the movies, a play, a concert? When was the last time you went to a hotel together without the children?"

They looked at each other, blushing. Such things had never occurred to either of them.

He shook his head. "Just what I thought. Now, don't give me excuses. There are plenty of baby-sitters in this yishuv. Go out to dinner in Jerusalem. And you are not allowed to talk about the children, building your house, money, or anything else. Just focus on each other, like you were on a first date. That's number one. But in between dates, make time to connect during every single day."

"It's hard; I work all day in the hothouses."

"So go home for lunch, Shlomie, instead of taking it with you! Sit down, talk to your wife, find out what's going on in her life. And you," he turned to Daniella, "make him something good to eat, something he likes, that will keep him healthy and happy. Not just a sandwich. I know you don't have time, but it doesn't take more time if while you're cooking anyway, for Shabbat, for example, you cook double and freeze it. This I learned from my dear wife. You know, when I was a young kollel husband, I'd be away from the house all day. So you know what I used to do? I'd write love notes on the eggs so that every time my wife cooked, she'd find a good word from me."

Daniella and Shlomie looked at each other shyly. They laughed.

The rabbi's blue eyes danced. "And if you can't get home for lunch, then make it a habit to call her, or you call him. Talk at least once during the day when you're apart. And when you get a chance to be together, don't just chatter. Look into each other's eyes, feel each other's soul. Make each other feel loved and appreciated." He took Shlomie aside: "Make her laugh. Tell her she's beautiful, that you like her eyes, her dress, her smile. Buy her presents, perfume, jewelry—pretty, thoughtful things. It doesn't have to be expensive. Let her know that you love and *appreciate* her."

Shlomie nodded gratefully, hugging the rabbi.

Later, when they looked back at this time, it all seemed like a happy dream, even the problems, which in hindsight shrank into insignificance, like a small child's worries over ice cream or a toy he craves and cannot have. They were good problems, human problems. Like people lost in one of those medieval mazes, they could not remember how they had veered so far off course, and how everything had gone so horribly, horribly wrong.

9

"It's time," Bina said to Daniella Goodman, more coldly than she felt. Even though she knew what this prisoner was guilty of, still, to remove a mother forcibly from her crying children was something she'd only seen in films about the Nazis. It was upsetting.

The children shrieked as hysterically as Bina had expected when their mother was led away, her arms clutched on either side by policewomen. Out of consideration for the children, they waited until they got her outside to handcuff her. The policewomen were also mothers.

"Are you ready to talk now?" Bina asked her without much hope.

"I want a lawyer!"

Bina shrugged. "Take her back to her cell."

"No!" Daniella lifted her head and peered at her. "Let's . . . let me . . . it's not my . . ."

"Look, we have nothing to talk about until you come out of your shell. Go get your lawyer. But it won't help you or your children. I have no sympathy for you. It's your poor kids I feel sorry for. You've left them orphans, with no one to take care of them."

"You won't let me!"

Bina turned her back and walked away, not trusting herself to maintain her outward show of indifference. Behind her, she could hear Daniella pleading, then shouting, a tussle, a commotion. She stiffened her shoulders and continued walking. Let the bitch suffer the way her children were suffering. Let her open her stupid mouth already, the monster.

It was a short ride in a paddy wagon back to her holding cell. Daniella covered her face and turned from the window, terrified of seeing someone in the streets of Jerusalem who might recognize her.

She had to get a lawyer, but how? She was confused, unable to think of anyone to call when they allowed her to make a phone call. Joel? But then she'd have to tell him why. . . . She shuddered. She hadn't spoken to him in years, ever since the Messiah had revealed the truth to her about her brother, about what terrible things he'd done to her, things she'd repressed and had refused to recognize until the Messiah, in his great wisdom, had revealed them to her.

As the cell door clanged behind her, Daniella pressed her forehead against the iron bars. She couldn't bear to turn around and take in the ugliness of the colorless, gray room with its steel bunk beds and stained, exposed toilet. There was no privacy.

"Well, look who's back—the Saint," her cellmate, a heroin-thin woman with straw-like blond hair, mocked. She wore a short, tight tank top that shamelessly displayed the track marks that climbed up both her arms.

"Please, leave me alone!"

To Daniella's shock, the woman lunged for her neck, wrapping both hands around it. "Didja hear that, girls? The 'Holy One' wants to be left alone!" She increased the pressure. Daniella half-turned, frightened, struggling, trying to enlist the help of the others. "Please, help me!" she begged them, choking.

"She wants to be left alone, she wants your help, you hear that?" the blonde sneered, shaking her like a rag doll, calling out to the other two women who lay in their bunks. At this, they lifted themselves up, resting on their elbows, lazily watching the action. Anything was better than the boredom.

"Vhy you dress up in outfit? Who you zink you fool?" said the heavy Russian in the top bunk. "Take hands off throat, whore; let her talk."

The blonde dropped her hands. Daniella rubbed her throat, coughing, terrified. "What do you want from me, all of you? I'm here, the same as you. Why do you want to hurt me?"

"She wants to know. Why don't you tell her, Russkie?"

"Tell yourself, whore."

"Okay. Because in prison there are people who steal. Most of them are poor, and they don't steal much, but they get caught. And then there are people who steal because they need money for drugs. That's me. Then there are people who murder, because they are afraid of getting murdered; that's Russkie over there, with her fat vodka-boy who tried to throw her out the window and by accident fell on his own knife—that's her story and, you know, I believe her. Then there are the ones like the little flower over there with the blue streak in her hair, who sell their bodies because they are too stupid to do anything else. They are only hurting themselves. But some people here, they deserve it. Bad people, people who make other people suffer for no reason, just because they enjoy it, you know? Murderers, rapists, wife beaters. But the worst people in prison who deserve to rot here are the ones who hurt children.

"We heard all about you, Your Holiness, you in your dirty white clothes, so modest and pure, head to toe! Heard about how your baby was so badly beaten he's a vegetable, and how your four-year-old got his skin burnt clear off! Who does fucking things like that? Devils. You're a devil, so take off the white costume, you bitch!"

"Yes, enough already with ze act," the Russian agreed, dropping slowly down to the floor out of her bed, her eyes wet with tears, reaching out and tearing off Daniella's headscarf. She had two small children of her own. "From father, you sometimes expect—a man, you know? But from woman, from mama, mamochka?" She spit on the floor, hitting Daniella's shoes.

"You're a sick piece of trash! If I could kill you right now, I would and do your kids a favor!" the blonde said, taking hold of Daniella's blouse and watching it slowly rip as Daniella struggled to pull away.

"Guards! Guards!" Daniella screamed.

But if they heard her at all, they were in no hurry.

The third girl, who couldn't have been more than seventeen, suddenly joined in, slapping Daniella across the face, her nails digging in. "I know you!" she screamed. "I know exactly who you are!" She pulled back, punching Daniella hard in the stomach, then kicking her, until the Russian finally pulled her off. "You're like that woman who married Elior Chen, the one they call 'M.' You're like those religious women who dress like Muslims, fucking their own kids. Like my stepfather. You're the same, the same, as all those monsters!" It was only when the shouting grew into a riot of noise that the guards finally showed up.

They took Daniella to the infirmary, where an indifferent nurse washed off her wounds, applying a butterfly bandage to her face where a nail had scraped a small hole. Afterward, to her shock, they took her back to her old cell. "I need to be protected from them. They're animals!" she demanded. But the guards, expressionless, opened the cell door and shoved her back in.

"I'm going to report you in the morning," Daniella said coldly. "I'm going to kill myself!"

The guard blinked, opening the door and hauling her out. He walked her down the corridor toward an empty cell. Daniella hurried inside.

"No more trouble tonight, okay?" he told her. "But tomorrow, you're going home to those three, so don't get used to this. Learn how to behave."

Daniella, shocked, her body scraped and sore and aching, nodded. She sat down on the floor, her back against the bars, which felt frigid through the thin fabric of her torn blouse, pressing like icicles down her aching spine. Beneath her the stone tiles chilled her thighs and buttocks. It was like sitting in the middle of a frozen lake, she thought, hugging herself and shivering.

It was long after lights out. The dark was deep and penetrating, almost palpable, as was the silence. In the other prison cells, there was snoring and an occasional nightmare shout. But now, for the first time in months, maybe years, she found herself cocooned from all outside distractions, alone with her thoughts.

At first, her mind was like a kaleidoscope, filled with a swiftly changing array of images: the beautiful little house in Yahalom with its window boxes, backyard apple and fig trees, and wooden swing set; the luxurious home in Jerusalem with its large picture windows of the Old City walls; and then the house in Beit Shemesh, with its tiny bedrooms and sinister locked doors, the place where it had all happened. Then came the faces of her children, especially her baby, Menchie, his expression of shock and horror after that first slap that had sent him flying across the room. She held her ears, trying to block out the remembered screams of her children. But more powerful than any image was *his* face: her rabbi, her mentor, her lover, her husband. The Messiah.

Where was he? Where? Where was his wisdom and his purity, his mystical connection to God? She needed all of those things now, because without them, how could she begin to explain to anyone what had happened? How could she explain it to herself?

She looked down the corridor at her cellmates. A murderess, a prostitute, and a drug dealer. All of them looked down on her. How could that be?

They compared her lover to Elior Chen. She remembered the story, the horror of it, how he had convinced a mother to allow him to abuse her children. And they compared her to that mother. But her Messiah was nothing like Elior Chen, and she was nothing like that mother. The man she loved was truly holy, saintly, the holiest person on the face of the earth, a person who was gentle, kind, and to whom God Himself spoke every single day. And he had chosen her to be his partner, and through him she, too, had become holy, pure. She had sacrificed everything for him, to share in his vision of heaven—to be as close to God as he was, to do God's will, as he did. She closed her eyes again, trying to figure it all out, to see again his vision of the shining diamond of the World to Come, the sapphire-blue dazzle of the ladder leading up to the highest rung of purity, which he had helped her to climb, step after step, helping her to pull her children up behind her, wanting only for them, too, to experience the pure joy of goodness, of holiness, of serving a higher being. She had wanted so much for their lives to be blessed, as hers had been blessed.

She had not taken the coward's way but had bravely followed the more difficult path, a journey others would have lacked the courage to take, preferring instead to see their children consumed by the terrible evil that had taken hold of them. She had sacrificed herself, done all she had been instructed to do, to save them, no matter the consequences for herself. They were the most important thing in her life. Even if she had to endure the hell of prison for the rest of her days, she would never, ever be sorry.

But now, in the darkness, in the silence, somehow the words of these criminals, this murderess, this prostitute, this addict, sank like a stone through her heart. They had mocked her for what she had done, called her names. For the first time in a long time, she suddenly felt confused.

If she could only explain the truth to them, to the police, that she had undertaken a sacred mission out of purest love for her children! But it was impossible. However she tried to phrase it, they would only see her as evil, an abusive, monstrous mother. She would not be able to explain it to them the way it had been explained so clearly to her at the time. She could never make them understand how hard it was to watch what was being done to her children, but that to have stopped it would have endangered their very souls. It was like watching a surgeon cut open a body to cut out a cancer. The pain! The blood! The agony! But what could one do? Run into the operating theater and punch the surgeon in the face, tie his hands behind his back? What would happen then to the patient, lying there helplessly, without hope of ever becoming whole and healed again?

If only he would come, if only he would explain it to them! For whenever she tried to remember his words, it all became so jumbled in her head, whereas before, with him at her side, it had all been so very, very clear. Crystal clear.

Where was he?

All night she sat and thought and thought and thought, trying to make some sense of what she knew and what she thought she knew. And in the morning, she understood.

"Guard," she called out.

"What happened to you?" the morning-shift guard said, peering into her bruised face, concerned.

"It doesn't matter," she shook her head. "I want to speak to Detective Tzedek. There is something I need to tell her."

10

"She wants to talk."

Bina turned around in her chair and looked at Morris. "The White Witch?"

He smiled, nodding. It had become a sad joke around the office. Every day they invented nicknames for her: "the White Witch," the "Haredi Lady," or, Bina's favorite, "Mommy Dearest."

"About what?" She tapped a pencil impatiently on her desk. Although she had been taught and absolutely agreed with the importance of maintaining distance and objectivity toward the subjects of her investigations, somehow, with this woman, she had failed. Daniella had gotten under her skin. She dreaded being in the same room with her again. On the other hand, if this was a game of poker, the White Witch must be less sure of her hand if she was volunteering to talk.

In answer, he shrugged.

"So maybe we should just let her stew in her cell for a few weeks."

He shook his head. "You know the judge won't allow that. We've got to charge her or let her go."

"We've certainly got enough for that, haven't we?"

"Without the children's testimony against her, it will be hard to get a conviction."

"Child neglect, surely?"

"Yeah, that. But it won't guarantee her any major time. We need to put her there at the time the kid got burnt."

"So, you think we should bring her in again? Will you be there?"

"Actually, Bina, I think you should do it alone."

She swallowed. "Why?"

"Well, it was you she asked to see. You seem to be getting to her. But you have to promise you'll keep from flying off the handle again. Can I trust you?"

She was ashamed he needed to ask. She looked down, nodding.

"Okay then, it's in your hands. But I'll be watching from the other side of the glass."

The White Witch looked different in her prison uniform, Bina thought: smaller, more vulnerable, less full of herself somehow. She was also visibly bruised, no doubt a catfight with jailhouse moms. Who could blame them? Bina felt almost glad. Maybe it knocked a little sense into her.

"Please, can you take them off?" Daniella asked in a small voice, thrusting her handcuffed wrists forward.

Bina took out her keys and unlocked the cuffs, laying them down conspicuously within easy reach between them on the desk. Let her look at them while we're talking, Bina thought. Let her remember what's waiting for her.

They sat in silence as Daniella massaged the red circles on her wrists.

"Well?" Bina finally said, raising an eyebrow.

"Well what?"

"You're joking, right? You're here because you asked to come. Why is that?"

Daniella sighed deeply. "I want to talk. I want to . . ."

"So talk!" Bina exclaimed brutally, ready to be fed up, actually looking forward to putting those cuffs back on and sending her away.

"My husband and I, we went through a hard time. Our marriage . . . it started to break down. Oh!" She suddenly stopped, wiping her eyes on her sleeves. "I'm so afraid, so confused. I don't understand anything anymore. And I thought I did, you see? I thought it was all clear, what happened, what I have to do now. But it's not. Not at all!" She broke down and wept.

Coldly, Bina reached for a box of tissues, handing her one, her mind still filled with images of the woman's crying children.

"Thank you." Daniella blew her nose and wiped her eyes.

"Take a few minutes to compose yourself," Bina told her, shocked to see this monster show some human qualities at last. Involuntarily, she glanced at the window, wishing she could see Morris's expression. Was it just her inexperience, her soft heart, at work here? Or was the woman actually undergoing some transformation for the better?

Daniella took a deep breath. "It's so hard for me to be without my children! All my life, I did nothing else but take care of them with all my love. I was dedicated to them, body and soul."

"Was that what you wanted to confess? I'm not a psychiatrist. Or a rabbi."

"No, no. I wanted to tell you that my husband and I . . . our marriage . . . it started to break down."

"You already said that."

"Yes, you're right. But I didn't tell you this: I asked him to leave the house and to let the *tzaddikim* come stay to help me. I thought it would help the tension between us."

"Tzaddikim?" *Saints.* Bina's eyebrows shot up as she looked at the window. "Who are you talking about?"

"Yeshiva boys. Students. There were three of them. I called them my dear brothers. I couldn't manage with seven children alone. So they were sent to me to help educate my children."

Bina straightened in her chair, her back hard as a rock. "Who sent them?"

"They were yeshiva students who learned Torah together with my husband. We knew them well. They were always at the house. After my husband left, the children were very upset. They began behaving like wild animals, destroying the house. Nothing I said had any effect on them."

Bina tapped her pencil, studying the jagged, uneven lines it made on the white paper in front of her. The beginning of a story, she thought. But only that, nothing more. "And did they help you?"

"Of course! They helped me to educate my children, to feed and bathe them, to watch over them. I felt . . . I don't know if I can explain this to you. . . ."

"Try."

"I . . . I felt that there was some evil inside them that was making them act this way. Something that was hurting them. I thought they needed much more than a harsh word or a slap on the wrist to fight those demons."

Bina let the words sink into her. "Evil," "demons." *That's what we're talking about now. Like something out of a medieval village, some sick version of the dybbuk.*

"It wasn't my idea, the things the tzaddikim did to help. I thought they knew better. All I wanted was the good of the children. I wasn't always there when they were disciplining the children, but they would describe it to me afterwards—what had happened and what they had done. About the burns on Eli's legs . . . I wasn't there. . . . that is, I was in the house but not in the same room. The tzaddikim never, ever lied to me. I believed them. From what they said, I understood that they were sitting around and talking, and Eli stood too close to the heater and got burnt before they could stop him."

"And you believe this?" Bina asked incredulously.

Daniella nodded. "Why shouldn't I? They were there to help me. It was very kind of them. They were there to do tikkunim. . . ."

Bina looked into Daniella's face. That word again.

According to kabbalists, God created the universe as a vessel to hold His holiness. But it wasn't strong enough. It broke, sending sparks of holiness all over the place. A tikkun was any human activity that succeeded in returning a lost spark.

"Whoa. Take a step back. What does that mean, that word, in relation to bringing up your children?"

Daniella seemed surprised. "You've never heard that word?"

"Yes, I know what it means. It's a way of improving someone's character. When you're flawed, you try to correct it—that's the tikkun, right?"

"Well, almost. If we want to be close to God we have to be worthy. And imperfect people with spiritual flaws must try to change. A tikkun is a corrective, a way of making you change for the better."

"And you're saying that these men, these tzaddikim from your husband's yeshiva, were involved in administering tikkunim to your babies?" She saw Daniella stiffen. Bina bit her lip. She shouldn't have said "babies." She was showing her hand. She must remain neutral.

"They weren't babies!" Daniella cried.

Bina waited.

"The youngest were toddlers, two and a half and three and a half. But even so young, they were out of control. There was something inside them that was harming them, making them misbehave. The tzaddikim were helping to expel the evil from them. I thought I was doing the right thing for my children. I couldn't let them suffer, to grow up possessed by demons. You do understand that, don't you?" She looked at Bina meaningfully, as if everything must be perfectly clear now.

Bina felt her head spin vertiginously. So much made sense now. And it was terrifying. What had happened here was beyond a crime. With a crime, you have a perpetrator with some selfish end in mind: money, sex, revenge . . . But these people . . . What had anyone gotten out of torturing small children? It was just pure evil.

"I'll be right back." Bina got up and walked out, closing the door behind her and leaning against it. She wiped the sweat off her forehead with the back of her hand.

Morris looked at her, disturbed.

"What's your take?" she asked him.

"There's a key here that will unlock everything. But you didn't follow up on it. It was the most important thing she said."

Bina stared at him, trying to recall the conversation, but she was at a loss.

"Think, Bina. What did you ask her, and what did she answer?"

"I asked her who the tzaddikim were. And . . ." Then it suddenly dawned on her, like a bright light at the end of a dark road. "I asked her who had sent them."

Morris nodded. "And what did she answer you?"

Bina closed her eyes, breathing deeply. "She didn't."

She went back in and sat down. "Tell me more about the tzaddikim."

"I've told you everything! What more do you want to know?"

"Let's start with their names."

To Bina's surprise, she didn't hesitate: "Kuni Batlan, Shmaya Hod, and Yissaschar Goldschmidt. Kuni and Shmaya would shake the children if they didn't listen. Once, I saw them tie Menchie's hands so he wouldn't scratch himself in the face. I thought it was for his own good! I never heard them beating the children or doing anything harsh to them. There wasn't anything deliberate to hurt them or wound them. It was, you know, just the way things sometimes go with naughty children. I and the tzaddikim kept hoping at every moment that the situation would change for the better so that more tikkunim wouldn't be necessary. Sometimes, though, mistakes were made. . . ." She went silent.

"Mistakes?"

Daniella hesitated. "They hit them a little too hard, and I trusted them completely! They said it was an accident. But I never heard that they hit the children in the head with a hammer or handcuffed them. And I know for sure they never starved them."

Bina looked at her, wide-eyed.

Daniella stopped. "At least, that's what the children told me happened to them."

"Your children told you those things?" Again, she felt herself losing control, the nausea rising up inside her.

She nodded. "The older ones. But they were angry . . . about their father leaving. I didn't believe them. It wasn't possible. They, the tzaddikim, were . . . are . . . good, gentle boys." She suddenly stopped, jumping up.

"I love my children! I'm a good mother! I would never, ever hurt them! Neither would the yeshiva boys, whose whole lives are goodness and kindness and purity! Why would we suddenly go crazy and decide to abuse innocent children? God forbid! God forbid!"

"Sit down!" Bina commanded her.

She sat.

Bina gripped the sides of her chair, steadying herself. "I asked you a question before but you didn't answer me."

Daniella looked surprised. "I answered all your questions."

Bina shook her head. "I asked you before who was it that sent them, the tzaddikim, to help you. What's his name?

"It was our rebbe. A God-fearing, gentle man, a sensitive man whose educational methods don't include violence. Despite his greatness, he has always been very modest and unassuming. He never wanted to gather hundreds of people around him, but because he was so wise and beloved everyone wanted to be with him. But he only allowed a chosen few. We—my husband and I—were among them. We were so fortunate! Everything he told us to do was so wise. We were blessed because we listened to him. So when he told my husband to leave the house and not to bother me . . . when he said the children were in need of tikkunim, of course I understood it was for the best. When he saw how hard it was for me to manage the children alone, he sent Kuni, Shmaya, and Yissaschar to help me."

Bina stood up. "What's his name?"

"Oh," she said. "I can't tell you that. I'll never tell you that."

11

A few months before their house was ready, Daniella gave birth to their fifth child, a little girl they called Shoshana, meaning "rose." She was strikingly beautiful, with peachy-warm skin tone, blue eyes, and blond, almost platinum hair. Among themselves, the baby nurses called her Marilyn Monroe. It had been a difficult time, the late summer heat baking the caravan, the odor of soiled diapers almost suffocating. For Daniella, who was home all day caring for her children, it was often more than she could bear.

"It's like the old story about the house and the goat," Shlomie said, trying in his way to be comforting when Daniella seemed ready to explode.

"What story is that?" she asked, exasperated.

"The man comes to the rebbe and complains: 'Rebbe, we can't stand it! So many children in such a small house. We're suffocating!' So the rebbe says: 'You have a goat?' The man nods. 'So bring the goat into the house.'"

She rolled her eyes.

"What, you've heard it before?"

"No, I'm sorry. Go on," she murmured. Of course she'd heard it before. Everybody had heard it before. But she didn't want to hurt his feelings, not when he was trying to be helpful.

"He comes back to the rebbe the next week. 'We can't stand it, Rebbe! If before it was terrible, now it's a nightmare! The noise, the smells, the crowding! It's impossible!' So the rebbe asks him, 'You have a donkey?' The man nods. 'So now bring the donkey inside. . . .'"

Daniella couldn't stand it. "And he does it, right?"

"Right. And the next week he runs back to the rebbe and says, 'You have to help me! I'm losing my mind! The filth . . . and all night the donkey braying, and in the morning bumping into the goat. We have no room even to turn around!' So the rebbe says—"

"I know, I know. He says, 'You have a cow?'" she murmured through clenched teeth.

He stopped. "So you have heard it before?"

Could he really be that stupid? She shrugged.

"The week after that he goes back to the rebbe and says, 'My life is not worth living. I know it's a sin, but I'm going to kill myself.' So the rebbe says, 'Now take all the animals out of the house—'"

"—and the next week," she cut him short, "he comes back and says, 'A *mechayeh*, so wonderful! I can't believe how much room we have, how quiet it is, how clean! Thank you so much, Rebbe!'" She lifted her blouse wearily, exposing her nipple to the crying newborn. "Too bad we don't have a goat."

"I could borrow one," Shlomie answered.

Her head shot up, studying his face. She saw his eyes twinkle and they both laughed.

He put his arms around her and kissed her. "I know it's hard right now. But just try to remember how blessed we are. In a little while, we'll move into our new house and it will feel like a palace! Just be patient."

He turned out to be right. And even though they moved in before it was completely finished (everyone in Israel moves into their homes before they are completely finished because otherwise it drags out forever, they were told), amid dust, workmen, painters, unfinished bathrooms, and a yard full of building debris, even then it was a marvel.

By American standards it was a modest four-bedroom ranch house, with the children's three bedrooms on the small side, and a master suite with an en suite bathroom too small to fit anything larger than a stall shower. Still, it was considered by their friends—especially those still stuck in caravans—to be the height of luxury. And Daniella and Shlomie had been in Israel just long enough to agree. Just having a separate room in which to put the new baby was going to be amazing, holding out the tantalizing promise of a few precious hours of undisturbed sleep.

Their lives fell into place. Each morning about 5 a.m., Shlomie would get up and bring her the newly diapered Shoshana to nurse. Afterward, he'd place a freshly brewed cup of coffee along with a sweet biscuit on a tray on her bedside table. After he'd left for work and the baby was settled, she'd slip back into bed for an hour, looking out of the windows that faced the golden, rising sun and their newly planted fruit trees and grapevines. She'd drowse deliciously, almost stupefied with happiness simply to be alive, as the glorious pink-red light washed slowly through their rooms.

"Such a blessing from God!" Shlomie often declared, surveying their new domain.

"And from my grandmother," she'd add pointedly.

"Of course! I will write her. We must invite her to come and stay with us."

Daniella thought that was a wonderful idea. While her grandmother had not felt well enough to come for Gabriel's bris, she'd promised to visit when Shoshana was born. But in the end she'd backed out, saying she still wasn't feeling up to it. She hadn't given any details. Her mother came, though, combining the trip with a visit to diamond cutters in Tel Aviv and leaving her new husband home, explaining that his business needed his full attention right now. Daniella searched her mother's face, wondering if things had already gone south with the relationship. Her mother was stoic, revealing no clues.

Her father came also, accompanied by his new wife, a shrewish blond widow who, her mother whispered, had more money than brains. "After all, she married your father."

Joel and Esther, who had one small child and were expecting another, sadly gave their regrets but promised to visit as soon as they could. Daniella and Shlomie's heavy disappointment was mitigated by the arrival of Shlomie's parents, who had carefully saved up for the trip. While they expressed limitless joy in their grandchildren, they hardly recognized their son.

"A farmer!" his father said with a hearty laugh, slapping his Shlomie on the back, impressed with his new muscles and work-roughened hands. He toured the hothouses and orchards with pride, the opposite of Daniella's parents.

"How can you live this way, Daniella?" Her mother shook her head, utterly shocked. Menial manual labor was something that had been absent from her family for many generations. Daniella's father and his wife, who felt the same, were more polite, careful to be encouraging and kind, even if they were unable to hide their misgivings completely.

If only Joel had come! Daniella mourned. He would have understood her pioneer life and spirit, what she and her husband had achieved! But most of all, she missed her grandmother. There is nothing lonelier than making a family celebration without your family, Daniella thought.

"Is it anything serious with Granny?" she asked her mother, who moved her head from side to side in vigorous denial.

"Your grandmother just doesn't like that long plane ride. When baby Shoshana is a little older, you'll take the whole family back to Pittsburgh to see everyone. That is, if you don't have another baby in the meantime."

Daniella made a face.

"Well, you can't blame me. That seems to be your pattern, no?"

"What's the problem, Mom? Too many grandchildren for you? An overload of *nachas*? I'm sure you brag about them all the time to your friends."

That was absolutely true. "No mother likes to see her daughter turned into a baby machine, especially when her daughter has so much else going for her. Is it Shlomie? Is he forcing you?"

"What? How can you even say such a thing! We are partners. And no one was ever sorry they had another baby."

That stopped her mother. But the conversation gnawed at Daniella.

She took a few long walks and had a private talk with God. They *were* blessings, she told Him, and He shouldn't think her ungrateful. But why so *many* blessings in such a short time? she asked Him.

Eventually, she made her peace with it. After all, this was the life she'd chosen, and she wasn't sorry. Her aspirations to be someone, to have a degree, a job, had all fallen by the wayside. This was her life now: A wife. A mother. All her thwarted ambition, her competitive striving for excellence, she poured into this new avocation. She would be the best wife, but especially the best mother.

She knew she had a way with children. Unlike other mothers she met, who treated children like another species, she always treated them like equals whose opinions mattered and should be respected as far as humanly possible. They were people, she'd tell skeptical friends, if you bothered to get to know them. From the moment they were born, each one had their own personality, interests, loves, and hates.

Amalya, her firstborn, had been a delicious baby. Beautiful, with her father's dark hair and her grandmother's sapphire blue eyes, she was placid and good-natured, the kind of child who only woke when she was hungry and then almost immediately went back to sleep. She grew up to be a sweet, docile, kind little girl, who looked after her younger siblings and was quietly helpful without even being asked. Naturally devout, she memorized all the Bible stories she learned in school each week and was stringent about ritually washing her hands and reciting her blessings at mealtimes. She loved crayons and blank paper, drawing charming, imaginary little animals that she kept in a folder. A shelf in her pink and lavender bedroom overflowed with Steiff teddy bears and expensive dolls her great-grandmother, grandmother, and grand-father had sent her for birthdays and Chanukah: American Girl dolls with fancy wardrobes, Barbies, and Bratzs. Soon, they'd need a room of their own, Daniella smiled to herself. But no matter how much Amalya was given, she took care of her things, and in her own childish way, cherished them and could always tell you exactly who had given her what and for what occasion. Sometimes, with her quiet ways, she got lost among her more vocal siblings.

"We should have called her Blessing," Shlomie always said, strok-ing her long, straight, almost black hair. And on those rare occasions that she needed to be disciplined, Daniella felt almost guilty at raising her voice. "It's like yelling at an angel," she told her husband.

David, or Duvie, her firstborn son, was just the opposite. A hell-raiser, he ran almost as soon as he could walk. He loved anything with wheels, graduating from a tricycle to a bicycle in record time. He was a cut-up with a lot of energy, playing soccer, flying down the road on a skateboard, or helping his father in the hothouses. He was a master of practical jokes but never did anything remotely mean or hurtful. He watched over his younger siblings, who idolized him.

Daniella's biggest problem with Duvie was his teachers. Ever since nursery school, they were always complaining that he wasn't focused, that he daydreamed and didn't listen. But as they got to know him, they realized that his quick mind usually grasped the material so speedily that it wandered off as they catered to slower wits. He learned to read by himself in record time. He had just turned five when they moved into the new house. He looked nothing like his father. Blond and brown-eyed, he'd inherited her brother Joel's angelic, round face and large, oval eyes with almost girlish lashes, which contrasted sharply with his strong, lean, little boy's body.

Yossi, four, born during their time at the Absorption Center, had been the largest of all her babies, almost double Duvie's weight. She put it up to all that fresh bread and butter she'd eaten during her preg-nancy when her Hebrew wasn't good enough to ask for anything else in the grocery store. He was still a chunky toddler with a sweet smile who loved nothing better than to eat. He was downstairs finishing his first breakfast when his siblings came down in the morning and was always pleased to join them for a second helping. While Duvie had been trying to teach him how to play soccer, his chubby little legs didn't see the point, and he gave up in frustration, taking out his Legos along with a plateful of snacks.

Compared to his siblings, he was very slow in everything: the way he walked, the way he talked, the speed at which he did what you asked him to do. But more than any of the others, he was her cuddly bear, a little mama's boy who was never far from her side. Everyone was instinctively gentle with Yossi because he cried so easily and was so good-natured and giving. His favorite objects were not toys but picture books. He could sit for hours quietly turning pages, smiling and laughing to himself. Daniella sometimes worried about him being off in a world all his own and tried hard to get him to put down his books and run around outside with the other kids. Sometimes it worked and sometimes it didn't. But as a mother, she respected his differences and didn't try too hard to make him into another Duvie. In nursery school, he tended to sit quietly in corners, seldom raising his voice. But his teacher had no complaints. "I wish more of them were like him," she told Daniella, who nodded, her concern lightening.

Gabriel followed Duvie around worshipfully, begging to try out his skateboard and to be given a ride on his bicycle. He was covered with cuts and scrapes, but there was nothing to be done other than locking him in the house.

Shoshana, four months, was an easy baby, waking at five and going back to sleep until almost noon, so that Daniella had time to get the others ready and out the door. When she looked back at this time in her life, she could almost feel the soft flesh of tiny, demanding arms, legs, and bottoms all over her, her flesh and theirs mingling, becoming one. She loved them so much.

But it was a constant struggle to keep her head above water. The mountains of laundry that seemed as high and insurmountable as Everest each day. The larger and larger cooking pots that needed to be refilled constantly with nourishing, tasty food. The constant running low on milk and diapers and toilet paper and having to shop, again and again and again. And the house, as much as she loved and appreciated it, was hard to keep clean without household help of any kind, which they simply couldn't afford. Yes, it was all that. But a joy, too.

She managed, but just. And then she was pregnant again. When she reached month four, she suddenly started spotting. Her doctor put her on complete bed rest.

"It's impossible! I have five little kids."

"Well, if you want to have six you'll have to find a way to manage."

Shlomie wrote her grandmother, who immediately sent a check for full-time, live-in household help. She was furious he'd gone behind her back.

"To save a life, all is permissible," he'd answered with equanimity, refusing to apologize. After all, he was only following her lead, no? The children came first, before their parents' silly pride and even self-respect. Whatever harsh thing she said (oh, she could be very harsh!) he let roll off him like oil on a Teflon pan. While domestic harmony was important, saving a life was paramount per all the laws of the Torah.

Holed up in the bedroom with Shoshana, there was little Daniella could do but accept the situation. They found a very efficient woman who cooked, cleaned, and took care of the children. In addition, the entire community chipped in, making a rotation schedule in which every day another volunteer picked up the children from school, while someone else took the baby for an hour or two, and someone else dropped off a lovely dinner.

Daniella, used to endless activity, felt she was in prison. But soon she got used to it, secretly reveling in her newfound idleness, making up for years of overwork. She relished the undivided time with baby Shoshana, something she'd never had with the others. Even with Duvie she'd been working in the jewelry store. If you had nothing else to do, having a little baby by your side all the time was the most marvelous thing in the world.

But then, despite all their efforts, she awoke one morning to find the bed soaked with blood. Rushed to the hospital, there was nothing anyone could do to save the fetus.

"You're young, you're healthy. There is no reason you shouldn't have more if you want them," her doctor assured her.

At home, she took to her bed. She felt useless, guilty, cursed. Why would God do this to her? What was she being punished for? she wondered, completely convinced that the baby's loss was preventable. Perhaps she hadn't prayed hard enough? Or perhaps God could see inside the dark shadows of her heart where she kept hidden the shameful secret of her ingratitude, her unhappiness, and her fatigue? God had known that she didn't want this baby, even if she hadn't been able to admit it to herself.

She wrote her grandmother, asking her to come. "I don't know when I'll be up to bringing all the kids on a plane. I miss you so much! I want you to see your great-grandchildren."

To her surprise, she got a phone call from her mother. "Your grandmother has cancer. She doesn't have long. There's no question of her, or any of us, traveling just now. If you want to see her, you'd better get here fast."

Daniella was numb with shock.

Only two weeks after the miscarriage, she found herself on board a flight to America with all five children, Shlomie staying behind, unable to leave the hothouses. The trip was a nightmare: eleven hours with four kids running up and down the aisles, spilling cups of juice and soda, vomiting, the two youngest screaming with ear pain and fatigue.

Gabriel, and especially baby Shoshana, really should not have been on an airplane filled with dangerous germs. But sometimes, she thought, you have to make difficult decisions for your children. Would it be better for them never to have met their great-grandmother? Or for her grandmother to die without ever having seen them? She couldn't bear the thought of such a loss.

They stayed three weeks in her mother's spacious home. Almost immediately Duvie, Yossi, and Gabriel came down with the flu, keeping her up all night. But thankfully, Amalya and the baby were fine. The problem was, she couldn't take the sick ones into her grandmother's hospital room, which broke her heart. But at least she took her oldest and her youngest.

Her grandmother was propped up on a pillow, her hair carefully coiffed by Phillipa, the woman who had been looking after her all these years. A swipe of pink lipstick gave color to her pale face, and matching nail polish highlighted her still beautifully manicured fingernails. Still, her face was haggard, and there was no question—as much as she desperately wanted and tried to hide it—that she was in terrible pain.

"Don't keep her too long. She needs her rest," Daniella's mother warned.

"Oh, don't be a yenta, Claire! This is the best medicine in the whole world. My granddaughter and her babies," her grandmother scolded, holding out her arms. "Come, my darlings." Carefully, Daniella placed Shoshana in them.

"I wish I had a camera," Phillipa said.

Her mother took out her cell phone and snapped a picture. "Now, you get in with Amalya," she instructed Daniella, who crouched down beside her grandmother's bed, her arm around her daughters, her face resting next to her grandmother's on the pillow.

Later, she would never be able to look at that picture, look at the expression of terror on her own face.

Her mother and Phillipa took Amalya and Shoshana down to the cafeteria to get themselves coffee and something sweet to share with Amalya, leaving her alone. Daniella pulled a chair close to the bed. Her grandmother's elegant hands with their long fingers and magnificent rings reached out to her. She clasped them.

"So tell me, Dani, are you happy?"

She nodded. "You can't imagine. Thanks to you, we built a lovely house. Shlomie is getting really good at being a farmer. You wouldn't believe all the tomatoes and strawberries . . . imagine!"

They both laughed at the irony.

"You shouldn't have come here so soon after losing the baby." Her grandmother shook her head.

"I had to. Next time, I won't wait so long to come."

"Oh, darling, there isn't going to be a next time," she said softly, stroking Daniella's hand.

Daniella put her hand over her grandmother's. Tears stung her eyes. "What am I going to do without you, Granny?"

"You'll do fine. I want you to know, you and your family are never going to have to worry about money."

"Please . . . don't!"

"Oh, don't act silly. Don't pretend. You and I don't have that kind of fakery between us. We never did."

Daniella nodded, dabbing her eyes.

"They are beautiful, beautiful children, Daniella. Such a blessing! I could only have the two, your mother and your uncle Arthur, God rest his soul. In such a dangerous world, you need a lot of children. Take care of them well."

"It's my life, Granny," she said with simple sincerity.

"I know, I know. But take care of yourself, too. Children need a strong, healthy, happy mother with her feet on the ground. Especially if their father is a *luftmensch.*"

Daniella knew what that meant. It meant a person floating in the air, with no real profession or connection to the realities of life. I should be insulted, she thought. If only it wasn't such a perfect description of the man she'd married.

Truthfully, she worried all the time about the work Shlomie was doing. Often, he'd forget to turn off the taps, which flooded the plants' roots, rotting them; or he'd put in too much fertilizer, risking burning them. So far, Marwan had always been able to save him in the nick of time. But she wondered if the day wasn't far off when he'd succeed in achieving a disaster so complete it would ruin them.

"Don't worry, Granny. I'll take care of him, too."

"Ha, right—that's the spirit, girl!" Her face suddenly went from palest white to deep red. She groaned and closed her eyes. "Go, Dani! Take care of your babies. I don't want you to see me like this." She pressed a button. The room filled with nurses. Daniella felt herself crowded out toward the exit. She couldn't even manage to say good-bye.

12

The police rounded up Yissaschar Goldschmidt and Shmaya Hod, but they couldn't find Kuni Batlan.

"All these guys look the same, with the beards and black hats and suits," the sergeant said.

Bina winced. "I know. Like all the Chinese look the same, right? You know, Sergeant, the Chinese think all us Westerners look the same."

He looked at her sideways, wondering if she was trying to be funny.

"All I'm trying to say is, these three are vital to our investigation. We must talk to all of them. Can't you put out an alert in the haredi community? Talk to some of the more influential rabbis? After all, these guys are dangerous child abusers. I'm sure they don't want them running around loose in their communities either."

"Thing is, Detective," the sergeant drawled, "at the moment, we are on the outs with the haredi community, big-time."

There was no need for him to elaborate. Not a day went by when there wasn't some other headline-producing battle between police and an increasingly vocal and belligerent minority among haredim. First, haredim had a campaign to put women at the back of public buses, abusing and insulting any female who resisted. When they tried this on gun-toting girl soldiers, though, the police had to be called in, and the men were arrested, causing riots and the burning of tires and garbage cans in haredi neighborhoods. This was followed by the beating of women at the Western Wall who wanted to form their own prayer quorums and read from the Torah, some of them choosing to wear the hitherto male religious accoutrements of prayer shawls and skullcaps like their Conservative and Reform American sisters. They were cursed, physically accosted, threatened, and even had chairs thrown at them. But when the police were called, they oddly decided to haul the women off for creating a "disturbance of the peace." Soon, the indignant women returned with court orders, and the police had to spend time hauling off the belligerent men.

And then there was the haredi campaign to keep public parking lots in Jerusalem closed on Saturdays in order to encourage people not to drive and thus, in their minds at least, prevent the desecration of the Sabbath. To that end, every Saturday, haredi hotheads blocked roads with noisy demonstrations, which police had no choice but to break up, thus ruining their own Sabbath rest. Resenting overtime on the weekend, the cops broke up the demonstrations a bit more roughly than was strictly necessary, at least according to the demonstrators.

Adding fuel to the fire was a challenging social upheaval in which the average Israeli was finally fed up with yeshiva students who not only had draft exemptions but were also being supported by monthly stipends from the public till, even though their families paid virtually no taxes. Police, who had all served in the army and sent their sons, and who paid a considerable amount in income taxes, were only human.

For all these reasons, police contacts with haredim were fraught. The result was a simmering public volcano ready to explode in which the police were given the impossible task of keeping order and preventing incidents that would trigger widespread tensions overflowing into violence. Yes, you could say the police loved going into haredi neighborhoods about as much as the haredim loved having them there.

"Look, Sergeant, I appreciate the difficulties. But just get it done, okay?"

He nodded. "What about the two we found?"

"We're talking to them. We'll talk to them some more," she said evenly.

"No luck, huh?" He shrugged. "Now you know what I'm up against."

Unfortunately, she did. She thought about her first session with Shmaya Hod.

He came in looking like a typical yeshiva student, but on steroids: side curls down to his shoulders, white socks pulled up over his pants, a long satin black waistcoat straight out of the closet of an overweight, medieval Polish landowner. The first thing he did was demand that Bina leave the room, because it "wasn't modest" for them to be alone together.

"Don't worry, we're not alone. You see that window? It's two-way glass. Two male detectives are out there watching every move you make—just in case you're suddenly overcome by irresistible lust."

He sat down, his face reddening. He refused to look at her. "What do you want from me?"

"Tell me about Daniella Goodman and her children."

"I was asked to help her, as a *chesed*, a good deed."

"I know what the word 'chesed' means," she cut in. "Not only that, but I know what the word 'tikkunim' means as well," she said evenly.

He suddenly stared directly into her face. "What did she say? Did she lie about me?"

"Who?"

"The mother. Because whatever she said, she was responsible. She was the mother."

"So why don't you tell me what happened?"

"I am a God-fearing man who was doing a mitzvah! I had nothing to gain from it. And now she accuses me of all kinds of evil! Such a lack of *hakarat tova*!"

"Oh, so you think she should be *grateful* for what you did to her children?"

She saw the color drain from his face. He reached into his pocket for a cigarette.

"No smoking."

Reluctantly, he put it back. He closed his mouth, pinching his lips together, his fat arms enfolded over his heavy chest, his thumb and forefinger picking nervously at the mustache hairs around his twitching lips.

"Whose idea was it for you to move in with her and 'help' her? And, by the way, if you are too *frum* to be in the same room with a woman, how is it you had no problem moving in with Daniella Goodman after her husband left?"

"It wasn't like that at all!" he sputtered in rage. "I am a God-fearing man!"

"Yeah, so you already said. So, I'll ask you again: How did it happen you moved in with her?"

"She asked us to come! I was never alone with her."

"That's funny. She says you and the others were sent to her."

"Did she say a name? Did she say who sent us?"

The rise in his anxiety level did not go unnoticed by any of the detectives.

"That's for me to know," she answered. "But why don't you tell us your side. Otherwise," her voice rose dramatically, "you are going to jail for a long, long time, you *Scumbag*! Hitting children in the head with hammers, starving them, holding them up against burning heaters until their skin peels off . . . Not to mention," here she took a deep breath, almost unable to go on, "what happened to the baby, to Menchie. If he dies, that's murder. You know how long a murderer spends behind bars? Especially someone who murders a child?"

He jumped up. "I had nothing to do with that! Menchie wasn't assigned to me. That was Kuni Batlan."

"Oh, so you each had assignments? Who made up these assignments?"

He sat down. "I want to talk to a lawyer."

She leaned back in her chair. "Do you have a lawyer?"

"No. But I know you have to get me one."

"That's true. But a lawyer isn't going to be able to save you. Not with all the evidence we have against you."

He tapped his foot nervously.

"So why don't you try to cooperate? If you tell what happened first, if you help us, then we can cut you a deal. Believe me, the other two are going to sing when they understand we know everything. One of them will get the deal, because then we won't need you. We are talking about life behind bars."

She could see the information register. He sat up stiffly.

"I . . . First I want to speak to a lawyer."

"Who was behind all this!" she screamed, pounding the desk. *"Whose idea was it to torture these children"*

He looked up, a sudden, secret gleam in his eye. *"Ve Tahar libanu, be Torah techa,"* he suddenly sang loudly, banging his fist on the table, his eyes closed.

And purify our hearts in your Torah, and dedicate our lives to your commandments.

"Get him out of here!" she said to the window.

Handcuffed, his feet in chains, they dragged Shmaya back to his cell, but not before he looked back at her and smiled.

She put her head down on the desk and covered it with her hands. She could feel a migraine coming on.

"I think I'm going home early," she told Morris. "I don't feel well."

"Look, kid, you can't let this get to you," he said mildly, not wanting to risk discouraging her. He needed her. "If you do, you're not going to last long in this profession."

"I feel tainted just being in the same room with these people."

He nodded, patting her shoulder understandingly.

"I used to think we were all more or less the same, you know? But that sometimes the worst in people took over. They get stupid or greedy or both. But this . . ."

"Just remember, it's not your job to figure out the universe. All you need to do is put two and two together until you get four."

She stared at him. "You're telling me this is not getting to you?"

He exhaled, running his fingers through his thin, graying hair. "You see this mown lawn? Every case, I lose a few more hairs. It was the only thing Kojak got right."

"Who?"

"Ah, was that before your time, little one? A television show with a detective who was completely bald."

"So what now?"

"We find Batlan. We come down twice as hard on Goldschmidt. Put him into solitary for a week so he'll be well marinated and softened enough to spill his guts. But in the meantime, there is someone else you should talk to."

"Okay, send them over."

He shook his head. "She hasn't been arrested. The opposite. She's the one who blew the whistle on this whole horror. A haredi woman who lives out in Ashdod. The White Witch brought Eli to her after he got burnt. This woman was the one who eventually alerted social services and got us involved. I think she could be helpful."

"You want me to call her?"

He shook his head. "I want you to go down there and sit across the kitchen table from her and get her to tell you everything she knows not only about this case but about this world. When you are trying to catch fish who are hell-bent on avoiding the bait, sometimes you have to dive deep into the water holding a net."

13

Ten days after they returned home, Daniella got the call from her mother.

"Your grandmother passed peacefully last night."

And though it was expected, Daniella felt a tidal wave of grief batter her body, her heart, her mind. Phone still in hand, she felt her knees hit the floor, hard.

"Why didn't you call me earlier!" She rocked up and back on her haunches.

"What could you have done?"

"Gotten on a plane to be at the funeral!"

"Ima!" Yossi said, wrapping his fat little arms around her neck, while Gabriel crawled over, and Shoshana started to cry in her crib.

"Take care of your children," her mother said.

"Don't you dare hang up!" she shouted into the phone. "Do I still have time to make it? "

"It's in two hours," her mother informed her.

"What! You can't do that to me!"

"What does this have to do with you? It's Jewish tradition to bury the dead as soon as possible. You know that."

"But exceptions can be made! Did you ask a rabbi?"

"There was no need. No need at all," Claire huffed, offended. "This is what the family decided, what your grandmother would have wanted."

"What, for me not to be there?" she shouted, frightening the children, who now all began to cry. "Listen, I'll call you back." She hung up, gathering Yossi and Gabriel into her arms and picking up Shoshana from her crib. She sat down on the floor, holding them.

"Shh . . . shhh," she crooned, trying to comfort them even as tears of grief and loss fell in torrents down her own cheeks.

"Don't cry, Mommy," Yossi said, wiping away her tears with his chubby little fingers.

She buried her head in his sweet-smelling tender neck. "What would Mommy do without her cuddly bear?" she told him, kissing the soft, pudgy folds.

When Shlomie came home, he was sympathetic. "She had a long, happy life and now she is in Paradise."

Daniella stared at him, thinking, What an idiot! But she only said, "What does that matter? They are burying her, and I can't even be there." She felt empty, inconsolable. "I won't even be able to make a shiva call. I hate being so far away. I just hate it."

"Do you want to go? I'll watch the kids."

"Really? You'd do that?"

"I'm sure the neighbors will help me out."

"I'll take Shoshana with me. Are you sure you'll be able to manage?"

"Yes, of course. It's only for a week."

If it had not been during her unclean days before immersion in the *mikva,* a time when no physical contact was allowed between husband and wife, she would have hugged him. Still, while she was immensely grateful, she couldn't bury her serious doubts about Shlomie being able to manage on his own. Had her need to be with her family and visit her grandmother's grave been less compelling, she might have put off going altogether. But as it was, she felt she had no choice.

She forced herself to overcome her fears. After all, it was just for a few days and he wasn't really going to be on his own. Her wonderful friends and neighbors would be there to help. Whatever she thought of *him*, she trusted *them* completely to make sure nothing bad happened to her children. Nevertheless, it was with a heavy and foreboding heart that she kissed them all good-bye, boarding the long flight to New York for the second time in a month, this time with only baby Shoshana to care for.

Shiva was such a wise custom, she thought as she sat on her grandmother's couch. Seven days of complete abandon to mourning and loss surrounded by friends and relatives and neighbors who dropped by to pay their condolences. It felt so right to be sitting there, next to her mother and brother, the baby in her lap, as they passed around photos of her grandmother.

"Such a fantastic, elegant lady," someone murmured. Daniella opened up the picture album, studying the photo of her grandmother as a debutante: the abundant blond hair piled high like a crown, encircled by the diamond tiara, the striking blue eyes staring a bit rebelliously and with a touch of contempt at the camera, the small, perfect bouquet in her white-gloved hands. It was everyone's favorite photo.

"She was never like the other girls. She always had a mind of her own," Daniella's mother murmured, shaking her head as if such a thing needed to be excused, Daniella noticed, annoyed. Typical.

Later, when the house had emptied out a bit, Daniella fed Shoshana, put her down for a nap, then curled up on the sofa leafing through the rest of the photographs.

So, this was the whole of life, she thought, beginning with the first page: Granny sitting in an old-fashioned pram pushed by a nanny in uniform; a toddler on the beach in a big floppy hat, squinting at the sun; the third-grade class photo, her shining face framed by two long, blond braids, as she smiled into the camera. And suddenly, there she was a young teenager, sitting on a horse during a vacation in California when she was in junior high school, all loose, thin, gangly limbs, her golden hair long and straight beneath a smart riding helmet. And there was her coming-out ball, her engagement photo, her bridal gown, and then her first child . . . and so soon, it seemed, her first grandchild.

And with each page, the years seemed to spill like water from a jug, until there was not a drop left. There was the last page, filled entirely by the photo they'd taken together in the hospital with Amalya and Shoshana, just two weeks before her grandmother died.

Daniella closed the book, her heart aching, the tears spilling down her cheeks. And now there were no more pages left, no more time to create and record events. Her grandmother had vanished from the earth. And there was no one to take her place.

That will be my life, too, she thought, if I'm lucky. When I die, the people I loved will say: there is no one to take her place. She hoped at least her children would feel that way, because as far as she could see into the future, there didn't seem to be any other way she would make herself useful in this world. It saddened her in a way, that she, who had had such ambitions, such high hopes of saving lives and making the world a better place, would be reduced to caring for only a handful. But if that was the destiny she had been handed by fate, she would pour everything she had into it, caring for those few, her family, making sure her children were nurtured to become the very best people they could be in this life, she told herself.

On the last day of shiva, the mourners and their friends went to visit the grave. Without a gravestone, which had not yet been laid, it was just a naked, rough, rectangular patch of newly turned earth, rather brutal and disturbing, Daniella thought as she stood there reading psalms that had been chosen for her grandmother according to the Hebrew letters of her name. She tried to imagine her granny's soul now freed, floating with the angels. Closing her eyes, she strained to feel her grandmother's spirit, her loving arm draped around her shoulder, smiling one of those wicked, conspiratorial smiles they had so often shared behind her mother's back.

To her surprise, she felt a warm glow of happiness suddenly fill her heart.

There were spirits, she believed. There were angels. If only we could break through those barriers between the dream of life and the reality of the inexhaustible creativity of God; if there were some way we could bring ourselves closer to Him, to the wonder and holiness of a truer reality, which could overcome and banish the horrendous illusion that was death. If we could but see life and death for what they really were: part of an endless cycle of decay and rejuvenation. If we could only comprehend what holy creatures we were, with every chance of touching the God Who created us and resided within us at every passing moment of flowing time.

Back at the house, the family partook of a catered buffet, picking at slices of smoked salmon, sushi, and roast beef, which they carried around in small, square plates, talking in subdued tones. Daniella sat in a corner, holding a sleeping Shoshana in her arms. Joel sat down next to her. He put his arm around her.

"How are you doing, Dani?" His eyes were full of compassion.

She leaned her head on his shoulder wordlessly. "What am I going to do without her? I feel so empty."

"She really loved you."

"She loved you, too."

"Of course, but with you, it was always something special. Now that I have kids I sort of understand it better. You love them all the same, but not really. You love them each differently, because they aren't just a generic 'child.' They are people. You can't help getting attached to some of their qualities and being turned off by others. You and Granny just clicked. You brought her so much happiness."

She looked up at him. "Do you really think so? I was so needy."

"I don't think so. I *know* so. And helping you was her greatest joy. I know you don't feel that way, but as an objective observer, I can tell you that allowing her to help you, getting her involved in your life, gave her some of her happiest moments on earth. Believe me."

She buried her head deeper into his warm, strong shoulder. "I miss you so much, Joel! You have no idea."

"Hey, I'm always just a phone call away."

"And *I* never call, I know. . . . I just don't ever have that minute I need to sit down and spend it on a phone call. I love the kids, but five kids, all so young. It's crazy."

"I'm sorry about the miscarriage. That must have been hell."

She nodded. "I guess God figured I wouldn't be able to cope. He was probably right. My biggest fear is not bringing them up right, neglecting them. Sometimes, I think I'm a big fake. That I'm not really equipped to do any of the things I promised myself I'd succeed at."

"That's human. Everybody feels that way sometimes, Dani. We are all faking it, hoping no one finds out," he said, grinning.

She laughed, punching him playfully. "You have never in your life thought you couldn't succeed at anything. You are such a hard act to follow."

"We are not in competition, sister. And from where I'm sitting, your life looks pretty wonderful."

"Really?" She was sincerely surprised.

"Really. You're living the dream. Pioneer in the homeland after two thousand years of exile. Raising Jewish children who will never know what it is to live outside their own country. Farming organic vegetables. I mean, who can compete with you?"

"Well, if you really feel that way, there are plenty of empty caravans in Yahalom. . . ."

"Oh, wouldn't Esther love that!"

"She might. She's not a Jewish-American princess. I love Esther."

"So do I." He nodded.

"Wouldn't it be great to bring up our kids together?"

His eyes got a faraway look. He was getting tired of the rat race, working sixty-hour weeks to make partner, never seeing his kids until they were fast asleep every night. He shook his head. "I don't think I'm cut out for farming, not unless the carrots want to sue the potatoes."

They laughed. He squeezed her shoulder, and she patted his face.

"Can I hold the baby?"

She lifted Shoshana gently, placing her in his arms. "I guess you miss your kids."

"Well, I didn't think bringing them to a funeral and shiva was a good idea for anyone." He adjusted the baby so that her head rested comfortably in the crook of his arm. "She is gorgeous. Blond, blue-eyed, like an ad for babyGap."

She looked over her daughter lovingly. "I'm very lucky to have had five easy pregnancies and five perfect births. I have to get out of this depression I'm in. It's not fair to the children."

"Or your husband."

She didn't respond.

"How are things going between the two of you?"

"Great, just great," she murmured.

He was about to pursue it when his mother suddenly sat down beside them.

"We arranged for the will to be read now. Will you both come upstairs?"

"Do we have to do it right now?" Daniella asked, aghast.

"Well, since you're leaving tomorrow . . ."

She reached out for the baby.

"It's okay," Joel offered. "I'll carry her upstairs for you."

Reluctantly she climbed up the elegant winding staircase that led to the study. She sat down in her grandmother's favorite chair, a magnificent maroon leather studded with bright brass nail heads. It was a place she'd often crawled into as a child to leaf through a book she'd pulled randomly from the shelves. Sometimes it was a book with photographs of faraway places and sometimes a book with no pictures at all, just words. She'd sit there, unmoving, just wanting to be in the room with her grandmother as she worked.

She leaned back, motioning to Joel to hand her the baby. Shoshana was still sleeping soundly as he placed the child in her arms.

Mr. Weinstein, the family attorney, took out some papers and cleared his throat.

"I . . . I just want to say what an incredible and gracious lady your mother and grandmother was. It was a privilege to serve her. This will was updated two weeks ago."

"What!" Claire shot to her feet.

"Yes, she called me to the hospital and I came."

"She was under medication!"

"She was perfectly lucid. Her doctor will testify to that, as will several nurses, who are signed here as witnesses."

"Sit down, Mom," Daniella said, pulling on her arm, wondering at her outburst. What was she so afraid of?

"As I said, you'll find this completely in order," he said, coughing uncomfortably.

" 'I, Elizabeth Auerbach, a resident of Pittsburgh, Pennsylvania, make, publish, and declare this to be my Last Will and Testament—' "

"Oh, just skip the legalese and get on with it," Claire said irritably.

He stared at her, appalled.

She sighed. "Just get on with it."

He nodded. "I revoke all prior wills and codicils to wills made by me. I direct my executor to pay my funeral expenses, the expense of my last illness, and the expenses of administering my estate. I do hereby appoint my longtime attorney and trusted friend Morris Weinstein as executor of this will. My executor shall have full power and authority to sell any property of my estate at public or private sale, excluding the following personal bequests. . . ."

There was a list of fabulous jewels, which were left to Claire. That seemed to calm her down.

"In addition, I leave half ownership in Auerbach Jewelers to my daughter, Claire Auerbach Whartman, who has been a hardworking and excellent manager for many years. The remaining half I leave to my beloved grandson, Joel Whartman."

Claire shifted in her chair.

"All remaining cash, my house and furniture, property and estate of any kind and nature wherever situated, both real and personal, I give, devise, and bequeath into a trust for my beloved granddaughter, Daniella Goodman, who has always made me proud to be her grandmother and to be a Jew."

Claire was on her feet, livid. She turned to Daniella: "I can't believe it! What did you say to her in that hospital room, Daniella? What did you ask her? Well, we'll just see about all this. . . ."

"Don't answer that," Weinstein said firmly to Daniella. "Mrs. Auerbach, as executor of this estate I must tell you there is a no-contest clause."

"What is that?"

"Let me read it to you."

"Don't bother! Talk to me in English."

"It means that anyone who contests this will gets nothing. And I assure you, it will be enforced."

Claire sat down and leaned back, closing her eyes.

All eyes were on Daniella, who sat there, hardly breathing, her heart pounding so hard in her chest she was sure it would wake Shoshana.

Her grandmother *had* visited her in that graveyard. She felt her hold her hand now, leading her out and closing the door behind her on a room full of stunned relations. She winked, and Daniella, through her tears, winked back.

The door suddenly burst open. It was her mother.

"You aren't going to go along with this, are you? You know it isn't fair. It's not fair to me, or to your brother, or to his children."

"She left you and Joel the business."

"You have no idea how hard things are now in the jewelry business with this economy!" she shouted.

"But you have your own beautiful home! I'm sure you have savings!"

"It's none of your business what I have or don't have! She was *my* mother, mine! I had the bulk of her estate coming to me! That's the way these things work. If you rob me of my legacy—"

"Rob you!"

"Yes, rob me! I don't know how you sweet-talked her into this . . .

your usual Zionist sob story, what? A fortune to support you and your useless, freeloader husband pretending to be a farmer while he makes you pregnant every other day."

A strange calm came over Daniella. "Take it back," she said threateningly.

"I have no intention. I only speak the truth!"

"Then, Mother, you and I will never speak to each other again."

She turned her back, walking up to her room and slamming the door behind her. Too late she thought of Shoshana, who woke with a start, wailing. She opened her dress, nursing the baby until she calmed down. Then she put her in her crib and quickly packed her bags. There was a knock on the door. "I don't have anything to say to you, Mom," she called out.

"It's me. Joel."

She opened the door, falling into his arms. He hugged her.

"I'm so sorry, Daniella."

"I didn't say anything to Granny, Joel. You have to believe me."

"I do. This was obviously what Granny wanted. She and Mom never got along."

"So, you're not angry?"

"I got half the business; you know what that's worth?"

"But Mom says it's not doing so well . . ."

"So I'll be a millionaire, not a billionaire. Trust me, there's enough for everyone. Mom's just being greedy. And I think, deep down, she's honestly hurt. She's taking it out on you."

"I don't care, Joel. She's finally gone over every red line. I'm finished with her."

"You're packing?"

"I can't stay here another minute."

"I'll drive you to an airport hotel."

They walked out together, using the backstairs to avoid any awkward run-ins. When Joel finally pulled the car up to the hotel, Daniella got out, then lifted Shoshana from her car seat. Joel took her suitcases from the trunk. He waved to a bellboy, who quickly loaded the luggage, wheeling it into the hotel.

"Thanks, Joel. When are you going home?"

"I'm catching a plane later tonight."

"Give my love to Esther and kiss the kids for me."

"I will."

"I'm going to miss you so much, Joel. You're really the only family I have left."

"Take care of yourself, Dani. I'm always going to be there for you. Remember that."

While later she would forget those words, he would not. It made all the difference.

14

Shlomie wasn't there, Daniella realized, her eyes scanning the balloons and flowers and smiling faces of expectant welcomers crowding the arrival hall at Ben Gurion Airport. How was she supposed to get back to Yahalom in the middle of the night? She looked anxiously at Shoshana. Thankfully, she'd finally dozed off, no doubt worn out by eleven hours in the dry cabin air and all that hysterical crying as the plane's descent tortured her tiny ears.

Exasperated, Daniella took out her cell phone and dialed her husband, letting it ring until it went to voice mail. She exhaled, considering her options. Did she want to wake up her friends to find out if the house had burnt down or someone was in the hospital? Why bother? In all the worst-case scenarios her imagination could conjure, the answer was simply to get home as soon as possible.

"Taxi!"

It would cost a fortune, she knew. But that burden at least had been permanently lifted from her shoulders. How she had been looking forward to sharing that life-changing news with her husband! But now, she was too distraught to even imagine the joyous celebration she had envisioned the entire plane ride home.

It was close to dawn when the taxi pulled up to the closed gate of Yahalom. She dialed security. "Hi, it's Daniella Goodman. I'm at the entrance. Can you tell me if everything is all right with my family?"

There was a short hesitation, a throat clearing. "Sure. Your husband will tell you all about it when you get home. Welcome back."

What was that supposed to mean? she thought. A "sure" together with a "he'll tell you all about it"? What was "it"?

She paid the cab, struggling to wheel the luggage and the baby carriage across the rough gravel path to her front door, hoping the scraping and the bumps wouldn't wake Shoshana.

With a feeling of dread, she unlocked the front door of her darkened home, putting on the hall light. She looked around. The house was an astonishing mess: shoes, toys, soiled diapers, and dirty clothes littered the floor. She locked the door behind her, taking the baby out of the carriage and tiptoeing into the bedroom. Without changing Shoshana's diaper or clothes, she laid her down gently in her crib, tucking a blanket around her little body.

Quietly, she checked on her other children. They were all fast asleep, the covers half thrown off. Gabriel and Yossi were dressed only in underpants, their little legs naked to the chill air. Shlomie hadn't even put them into pajamas! She tucked warm blankets around them, furious. But no one seemed damaged in any way. She walked toward her bedroom, passing the kitchen. Dirty pots, dishes, and take-out containers littered the kitchen counter, where a long trail of ants were having a feast. She felt disgust rise up in her throat.

How could this be? Her friends, her dear friends, had promised to look in, to help out. . . . But from the look of things, Shlomie had been left totally on his own.

She walked into her bedroom, half-expecting it to be empty. But there he was, her husband, stretched out across the bed fully clothed. Had he meant to be at the airport and simply overslept? Or was there another, more sinister reason, in line with the "your husband will tell you all about it"?

"It," she thought, her anxiety somewhat quelled by the fact that the house—appallingly dirty as it was—was at least still standing, and everyone seemed alive and well. She sat down on the sofa, kicking off her shoes and stretching out, her mind slowing down. She pulled the couch blanket over her shoulders and closed her eyes. Sleep was instantaneous.

She was awakened hours later by small hands shaking her shoulder and patting her face. She heard the baby crying.

"Ima, Ima!" the children screamed in joy, climbing into her lap and hugging her.

Yossi, her big cuddly bear, and Gabriel, her sweet, baby boy. She hugged them, squeezing their little bodies close to hers. "Where are Duvie and Amalya?"

The other two, hearing their names, bounded through the house, Duvie throwing himself into the couch pillows, almost crushing Yossi, and Amalya bending in to kiss her gently on the cheek.

"Did you miss us?" Amalya asked. "We missed you so much!"

"Yeah, and Aba got into trouble and killed all the plants and now everyone is angry at us, but he says it's Hashem's decision," Duvie added breathlessly.

She looked up into his eager, childish face, inwardly groaning, catching Shlomie leaning against the wall. "You didn't come to meet us. I had to take a taxi."

He looked down. "I'm sorry. I . . . couldn't. . . . No one would . . . I had to care for the children."

"What about our friends? Yochanon, Essie?"

He rubbed his hands together. "I have something to tell you."

She got up. "Not now!" she hissed, glancing meaningfully at their children, then heading to the crib to take care of Shoshana. The baby was soaked through. Daniella took off her soiled clothes, wrapping her in a towel and hurrying into the bathroom to give her a quick, warm bath in the sink. After she'd been dried, diapered, and put into clean, warm clothes, Daniella carried her into the living room.

Exhausted, Daniella sat down on the couch to nurse the baby.

The other children crowded around.

"No one will play with us anymore!"

"They say Aba is a *mazik*!"

"Why not? Who says?" she answered in confusion, her head spinning.

"Children, please!" Shlomie said. "Ima is feeding the baby."

"I have presents for all of you!" she remembered, grateful for the distraction. "Duvie, go get Ima's green suitcase."

He ran, rolling it into the room.

"Now unzip it!"

It looked like some scene from a Christmas card, she thought, taking in her children's looks of delighted expectation. The suitcase brimmed over with wrapped packages.

"All the blue packages are for Duvie, the pink for Amalya, the green for Yossi, and the orange for Gabriel."

The children scrambled, tearing the packages out of each other's hands, gathering them in a pile, then sitting down to rip them open.

Their cries of happiness were deafening.

Shlomie stood by silently, his hands in his pockets, watching them with a pasted-on smile.

"Children, take your new toys to your rooms. Aba and Ima need some quiet, okay?"

Obediently, they took their loot and disappeared. Only Gabriel sat on the floor close to her, refusing to budge.

"Talk, Shlomie. I'm just about ready to have a heart attack."

He shuffled his feet, one hand rubbing the back of his head, the other clutching his skullcap.

"I meant to do a good deed; the neighbors have been so helpful. . . ."

"What did you do, Shlomie?" she asked levelly.

Just then Gabriel began to cry. "Amalya, come get Gabriel," she shouted, patting him on the head. Amalya dutifully picked him up, shaking a toy tiger in his face.

They were both silent, waiting for the children to leave before resuming.

"Well, I'll start at the beginning. Marwan's wife had a baby."

Her head ached. "What?"

He seemed surprised at her impatience. "His wife, she had a baby," he repeated.

"I heard you. Why are you telling me this?"

"Because he didn't come in to work for two days. And I don't know how it happened, but the plants didn't get enough water and some of them died."

She looked down at Shoshana. She had Shlomie's eyes, those beautiful blue eyes. "I'm listening."

"So, I bought some seedlings to replace them. The nursery man said they were the finest quality. . . ." He stopped. "They weren't. They were infected."

"What does this have to do with all our friends being angry at us?"

"I bought some extra, to give out. To thank our friends for all their help. I meant well."

She felt nausea rising up from the core of her being. She quickly shoved the baby into his arms and fled to the bathroom. Her stomach was empty. She heaved green bile. She washed out her mouth, cupping cool water and drenching her eyes and face. There was no clean towel, so she wiped her face with the hem of her skirt.

"How bad is it?" she asked, taking the crying Shoshana and putting her over her shoulder, patting her gently.

He stuttered. "Now everybody's greenhouse is infected. Their plants are all dying, and they all blame me."

"All of our friends?"

He nodded.

She covered her face with her hands.

"They say they will have to throw out everything and start from scratch, that they'll lose the entire growing season." He was shaking.

"Well, Mustapha will just have to pay the damages. They were his plants!"

Mustapha Quadri, a devout Muslim who lived in Jericho, had been Yahalom's sole supplier of plants for years.

"Well, it's a little more complicated than that." Shlomie shook his head sorrowfully. "You see, someone from kollel said it wasn't right that we were helping to support our enemies. He said his father had a friend who knew a devout religious Jew with a nursery in Ashkelon who would sell seedlings to me at a very reasonable price. . . ."

She looked around at the walls of her almost-brand-new home, the place they had built in the Holy Land, surrounded by friends. They had been accepted, taken care of, loved. And they had returned evil for good.

"So, did you call this 'devout Jew' where you bought the plants and tell him what he did to you and our friends? Did you demand he pay for the damages?" she asked forcefully, already knowing the answer. Inside, she felt half dead from weariness. It was the last straw.

"I tried many times, but he isn't picking up his phone. He's vanished."

"Did you call the father of the man from kollel? Did you get in touch with the friend who recommended him?"

He shook his head. "It's not their fault. I don't want to embarrass them. That would be a sin."

"And what you did to the people we know here in Yahalom, to Yochanon and Essie, that wasn't a sin? Never mind that we're ruined. . . . What are we going to do?"

"God help us!" he said fervently, his eyes brimming over with tears as he sat down on the floor next to her, patting Shoshana's small back. "I'm so sorry, Daniella. It's all my fault." He wept.

Luftmensch, she thought furiously, unmoved.

The children came bounding back into the room, their hands filled with dolls and other plastic treasures. At the sight of their father, they stopped dead and stared.

She looked at their stricken faces. He *was* their father. She reached out, patting him on the head. "It's all right, Shlomie. It's all right. God has preceded the blow with the remedy."

Slowly, and with none of the joy she'd expected to feel, she proceeded to tell him about her grandmother's last will and testament.

15

Detective Tzedek pulled up to the parking lot of one of those massive, ugly apartment complexes built back in the sixties to house dirt-poor young couples and penniless immigrants. While it had undergone subsequent renovations by the slightly more affluent people who had purchased the apartments from their original owners, the building nevertheless remained an eyesore, with cheap add-on porches of clashing styles cluttered with old appliances and children's toys. The overall aesthetic effect was appalling.

There were so many entrances labeled with numbers and letters that she finally gave up and asked someone if they knew a Rabbanit Toledano. To her surprise, she was led immediately to the woman's door by the first person she asked, who waited patiently as she knocked.

A plump, short, older woman in a dark wig covered by a kerchief opened the door. She wore a shapeless flowered dress and orthopedic shoes. She smiled at both of them.

"She was looking for you," the young man said.

"May God reward you for your kindness, Moshe," Chana Toledano blessed him.

A joyous smile spread across the young man's face, as if he'd been told he'd won the lottery.

"And God bless you, Rabbanit Chana," he thanked her, walking away beaming, satisfied.

Bina watched this display, her curiosity growing. "I'm Detective Tzedek of the Jerusalem Police. I spoke to you earlier?"

"Yes, please, come in, sit down."

The house seemed like a clinic of some kind, the tiny living room cluttered with cheap folding chairs arranged in a neat circle.

"I knew you were coming so I sent everyone away. Otherwise, this room would be overflowing."

"What is it you do, Rabbanit?"

"I have gotten the reputation of being a healer." She shrugged modestly. "The truth is, I know a few homeopathic remedies my mother taught me and which seem to help people. But I always remind them, I'm not a doctor. They need to go to a doctor."

They went into the kitchen, which was spotless. A stew boiling on the stovetop filled the small space with pungent odors of cumin and cinnamon.

"Can I offer you a drink?"

"Yes, thanks. I'd love a coffee."

She made it Middle Eastern style, thick as mud, and poured it into tiny cups. It was delicious.

"I guess you know why I'm here."

She nodded. "About the Goodman child, Eli; heaven have mercy on us! How is the child?"

"Thanks to you, he and his brother are in good medical hands. Eli is healing. But his brother . . ."

Her face went ashen. "I don't know anything about a brother."

"His younger brother, Menchie. He's in a coma."

The woman shook her head mournfully. "God watch over us. Such things among God-fearing Jews . . ."

"Apparently not," Bina said softly, taking a deep breath. "I'd like to ask you a few questions."

"Of course. Whatever I can do to help."

"Can you start from the beginning?"

"It was about a month ago. Right before Rosh Chodesh. I don't know the secular date."

"All right. Just tell me what happened."

"I got a phone call from a woman I didn't know. That isn't so strange. I get a lot of phone calls from people I don't know who have heard of me and need help. But she wanted me not only to heal her boy but to take him in and keep him."

"What did you say?"

"I told her to first bring him over. God help me, I'll never forget it. Such a sight!"

She pulled out a small amulet that hung around her neck, kissing it three times.

"Can you describe what happened?"

"She was dressed like on Yom Kippur, God save us! All white. I never saw . . . anyway, she had a small boy with her—a beautiful boy, but so skinny! He could hardly walk. He was limping, limping so badly. At first, I thought maybe he broke something, fell down, hurt his ankle. You know small boys, always running, falling, God forbid, breaking bones. I told her to take him into my examining room and to take down his pants so I could see the legs." She shifted uneasily in her chair. "God help me, I never saw such a thing! Like raw meat on the butcher's counter! No skin, no skin left at all, just covered with pus and redness and swelling. Somebody had tried to treat it but didn't know how. The wounds had been neglected for a long time, God help us. I'll tell you the truth. It made me cry just to look at them! I couldn't even think how much pain such a little child must be in from such a wound! But, God have mercy on us, he didn't cry. Not once. And the mother, she just looked at the wounds. Didn't wince, didn't say, 'oy, my poor son,' didn't say anything you'd expect a mother with such a child to say. Just stared, like she was reading a recipe for challah. I can't tell you how much this bothered me.

"I asked, 'How did this happen?' So she starts in with a story about a blanket next to a heater catching fire. . . ." The woman shook her head slowly. "Fairy tales. What she described, that kind of burn, it's like when you burn yourself on a havdalah candle, God watch over us. It's not so even. It's a red spot here, another spot there. A person moves around, tries to get away. What her boy had, it was like someone held a blow-torch to his poor little legs, the way you do to a stove when you *kasher* it for Passover.

"But I didn't press her, since I saw what I was dealing with. Instead, I asked her why she didn't take him to the hospital right away, why she waited until now. But instead of an answer, she gets up and says maybe this is not such a good idea, and she starts pulling up the child's pants, getting ready to leave.

"When I see this, I understand I can't let her leave with him—that if I don't try to help this child, no matter how he got the burns, no one will."

"So you were suspicious even then?"

She cocked her head to one side and gave Bina a shrewd look. "I've seen things in my life. But what could I do? Besides, many devout Jews avoid hospitals."

"Why is that?"

She shrugged. "They think that a God-fearing person would have more success interceding with God to heal their loved ones than a secular doctor. So in the end, I stopped asking questions. I took pity on the child and agreed to keep him and try to help him."

Bina tried and failed to understand such thinking. "You took in a stranger's injured child?"

She shrugged. "God had sent this child to me. What else could I do? But I wasn't born yesterday. First I made her sign a paper saying in what condition she brought this child to me, and that it was her wish that I keep him and try to help him heal. Here is the paper. You see the signature, the date?" She handed Bina a handwritten letter that described Eli's wounds in great detail and ended with, "I ask Rabbanit Chana Toledano to care for my child." It was signed "Daniella Goodman," and dated three days before he'd been brought to the hospital.

Bina sank back into her chair, her spine tingling. "Why . . . why would you agree, Rabbanit Toledano?"

"I didn't want to. But I couldn't let her just drag the child out of here, could I? He could hardly walk, poor baby."

"What happened?"

"She left and the child stayed. I expected him to struggle, to cry, to run after her. But he didn't do anything. He was like a toy, a doll. He didn't open his mouth." She shook her head in wonder at the memory, as if it was still undigested. "I put some healing solution on the burns and waited to see what would happen in the morning. But the next day, I could see that it wasn't what he needed. The wounds were too deep and they'd been neglected for too long. He needed a doctor, maybe even a surgeon. I called the mother and asked her to send over the child's medical insurance card so I could take him to the hospital. But she refused. She told me that under no circumstances was I to take him to a doctor. God help me, I was shocked. I screamed at her that what she was doing was *rishut*, evil, satanic! She hung up on me.

"An hour later, she was already at my door. I begged her to let me take him to the emergency room. I asked her again how he'd gotten hurt. But she just shook her head, said it was her child and it wasn't my business. God help me if she didn't pull pants over those wounded legs and drag that child, limping, out of here. That was when I called social services."

"How long was he with you?"

"Overnight and a few hours."

"Why didn't you call the police right away, Rabbanit Toledano?"

She bit her lip. "Did I do something wrong?"

Bina thought about it. If not for this woman, who knows how long this situation would have continued, how many more of the Goodman children would have been fatally injured by whoever, and whatever, had injured the two youngest? Still, in a normal society, who agrees to take in a stranger's injured child? Was it an act of incredible generosity or spine-chilling dysfunction?

"Are you going to arrest me?" the woman asked.

Bina shook her head. "No, of course not. You meant well. But the next time, Rabbanit Toledano, for your own sake, you must call the police immediately."

"If I call the police, even once, this clinic, it is closed. No one comes to me for help ever again. Are you going to close me down?"

Bina hadn't thought of that. "Are you paid for what you do?"

She shook her head, shocked at the thought. "Heaven forbid. But sometimes people bring me presents, out of gratitude. I don't want to offend them, so I take their gifts and give them my blessings."

"What kind of remedies do you use?"

"Come, I'll show you."

The "clinic" consisted of a small bedroom made up of shelves with old glass coffee jars holding all kind of herbs and liquids.

"How long have you been practicing, Rabbanit Toledano?"

She closed her eyes, thinking. "Fifty years," she said.

"And has anyone ever been injured?"

"God forbid! If it doesn't help, I send them to the doctor straight away. But sometimes, the doctors send them to me."

Bina thought about it. Maybe she should inform local police and shut her down. But people would only find another "healer," and maybe the next one wouldn't have harmless herbs, send people off to doctors, and call social services when necessary. She took a deep breath. "Rabbanit Toledano, the real reason I am here is this: While he was with you, did the child say anything about who had done this to him?"

The woman shook her head sadly. "Believe me, I asked him, again and again. But he was terrified, as if he'd been threatened, warned, not to open his mouth."

Don't talk, don't talk, don't talk, Bina suddenly thought, the words Morris had written up in his report, the words of Daniella Goodman in the hospital room.

"From your experience, Rabbanit, what do you think happened to him?"

She looked down, then suddenly she looked up, straight into Bina's eyes. "What do you know about the kabbalah?"

"What?"

"The kabbalah. You've heard of it?"

"Of course. Who hasn't?"

"Then, what do you know?"

"Nothing. Red strings and Madonna."

"Madonna?"

"Never mind. But why are you asking me? What does kabbalah have to do with this?"

"That child . . . he had fifteen amulets around his neck, with secret kabbalistic formulas, some I've seen many times and some, handwritten, that I've never in my life seen before."

Tikkun, Bina thought. "And you think . . . what?"

"The amulets were the work of someone who has delved into the forbidden. Practical kabbalah, or *kabbalah maasit*. Magic. Long ago, someone told me that sometimes, those who dabble in such magic use children in their ceremonies."

Bina felt a tremor go up her spine. "Use?"

The woman shook her head. "I don't know anything more than that. And I don't want to know! You need to go to a kabbalah master, someone who delves into these things. But I'll tell you this: that child has been touched by real evil; Satan himself polluted that child."

The words were chilling.

"Who is this Satan, Rabbanit Toledano?"

"Ask those who have met him," she answered cryptically. "Ask the children."

Bina felt suddenly weak, as if the breath had left her body.

"You look pale," the woman said, concerned.

"No, really. I'm fine." She reached into her pocket. "Here is my card; if you think of something, anything, please call me."

The woman nodded, taking it. "You do God's work. May I give you a blessing?"

"Of course!" Playing along, she lowered her head, allowing the woman to place her hands over her scalp.

"May God watch over you and see that your next birth is smooth, healthy, and without any disruption."

Bina looked up, stunned. How could she have known her last birth had been so traumatic?

Outside, she took a deep breath, placing a steadying hand against the side of the building to stop her trembling. I'm a young woman of childbearing age, she thought rationally. It was simply a good guess, completely random, nothing more. But somehow, she didn't quite believe that either, the way she could no longer believe that there was no such thing as the devil.

Her phone rang. It was Morris.

"Where are you?" His voice sounded strained.

"Interviewing Toledano."

"Get anything?"

"A few real surprises. I'll talk to you when I get back."

"Hurry. Put your siren on if you have to."

Her jaw dropped. "What's up?"

"Eli, the four-year-old with the burns? He's started talking."

16

They left like thieves in the night, Daniella thought, heartbroken. All those people who had been so kind to them—Yochanon and Essie!—all their newfound friends, their good neighbors! Instead of the hugs and kisses and exchange of phone numbers, there was a moving truck at midnight. While most of their neighbors' losses would be covered by insurance, still, she could not face them, feeling she had returned evil for good.

For even though nothing of what transpired had been her doing, she felt ultimately responsible. It had been her, after all, who flew off to America to satisfy her own selfish needs, leaving Shlomie behind to care for all the children. She beat herself up over it. How could she have done it? The accident (that's how she decided to view it, focusing solely on the watering incident, glossing over his choice to buy infected plants and distribute them) had no doubt come about from exhaustion as he tried to manage everything in her absence. If she had just been there, where she was supposed to be, where it was her responsibility to be, none of it would have happened. As his wife, she was his helpmate and partner. They were one. His failure was her failure. They were equally responsible. Humiliated and full of guilty regrets, all she wanted was to put the past behind her as quickly as possible.

They rented a large apartment in a luxurious building in central Jerusalem, then set about looking for a permanent place to live near good schools and enough yeshivoth to keep Shlomie happy. The house in Yahalom they would sell later, she thought. It should be easy enough, with new people arriving daily, and all those families still in caravans. She was heartbroken over the idea of another family moving into her dream house.

Shlomie himself went into a deep depression, hardly rising from bed except to say his morning, afternoon, and evening prayers. And then, one day, weeks later, out of the blue, he came into the kitchen, his eyes burning with excitement.

"I have the answer!" he told her ecstatically.

"What was the question?" she answered wearily.

He seemed taken aback. "What do you mean! The answer to why all these terrible things have happened to us."

She was holding Shoshana with one hand, while with the other she kneaded the dough for the Sabbath challah. "I'm listening."

"It's a punishment from God."

She looked at him, stunned.

"We came to the Holy Land to be holy, to be close to God, right? And instead, what did we do? We abandoned learning Torah for digging in the dirt! Of course God is angry with us."

Daniella listened to him halfheartedly, hearing only every other word. She was skeptical, especially since this explanation left no room for the natural consequences of stupid human choices. But she didn't tell him that. He'd been upset enough with himself. What did it matter anyway? You couldn't change the past.

"But God is merciful. That is why He has seen fit to give us this great blessing of financial security, so that we can return to doing the good we came here to do, so that I can bless our family by studying the holy texts, thereby bringing blessing upon us and our children. I promise, Daniella, this time, I won't fail."

She nodded, handing him the baby and kneading the dough with both hands. She had no time to devote to philosophy. She had five small children to care for. All she wanted was for her husband to drag himself out of bed and help her.

She wasn't disappointed. His revelation banished the dark clouds that had kept him immobilized. He baby-sat, read to the children and played with them, giving them their nightly baths and helping them into their pajamas. He even helped out with the shopping, going to the *shuk* twice a week to bring back fresh fruits and vegetables.

But his main job—and that to which he devoted the majority of his time and energy—was seeking out exactly the right framework within which he could devote himself full-time to learning Torah. There were no shortages of such places in the Holy City of Jerusalem. As part of his exploration, he went to lectures of various kinds at a diverse range of institutions and with private study groups. Some took place in modern buildings and were given by beardless, Orthodox teachers who wore knitted skullcaps—places where students came in the evening after working full-time at well-paid jobs or studying for higher degrees in the university. Others, in contrast, were informal study groups that met in run-down synagogue buildings near the shuk or in the cramped living rooms of private homes, everyone crowded around dining room tables with hardly space to move. Those attending were an eclectic group of born-again Jews in various states of Hassidic dress, people who had part-time, low-paying jobs or no jobs at all.

He quickly decided that the formal, collegiate settings in Modern Orthodox institutions were not for him. "I feel it's too dry, too rote. There is nothing there that touches my soul," he explained to Daniella. In truth, he found his educational background totally inadequate to meet the high levels of scholarship demanded at such places, and his fellow students intimidatingly clever and successful.

And so he narrowed his searches to the private study groups. Eventually, he found himself wandering the mysterious, winding alleyways of the Jewish Quarter of the Old City, whose crowded homes were always bathed in shadows. There, behind the ancient Old City walls, he found a plethora of groups that met behind closed doors to study everything from the Talmud to esoteric, sometimes forbidden books of Jewish mysticism.

At first, he studied Talmud. But before long, he was lured by his new friends and acquaintances to less intellectually rigorous and demanding pursuits. It was the kabbalah that entranced him most, with its promise of personal communion with God through mystical formulas.

"Most people live their lives like ants, pushed along by their bodily urges, their lusts. The holy kabbalah seeks to raise us up, to put us in control, so that we can be like Him. It's amazing, isn't it, that we, little ants, pieces of dust, who live on this earth for such a short time, running after food and sex and good times, who wither and die, can approach the everlasting, all-powerful God of Creation?"

The words, spoken by Reb Amos, a shaggy-haired blond guru with the large, white knitted cap of Breslov Hassidim, fascinated him. Amos was treated like a king by his followers, who stood up in awe of him when he entered and waited for his permission to sit back down. Yes, Shlomie thought, drinking in the words deeply. This is the truth I have been seeking!

Not all the students felt as Shlomie did. "What does it matter what we do then?" a student boldly challenged. "Why should we try to be like God if we are ants? Why can't we just enjoy being what God made us?"

Shlomie was shocked at the insolence. But Reb Amos was patient. "Because those who reach godliness never die. Their souls are eternal. Think of that! We have the potential for eternal life! Everyone, if they are honest, knows this is true, feels this is true."

"I've never felt it," challenged the same young man.

"Where is your will? Have you ever felt your will?" Reb Amos asked with a gentle smile.

The young man's arrogance faded. He looked confused.

"Call it God or nature, all Creation wants to give, and we want to receive. 'Kabbalah' means *to receive.* If you don't feel that inside yourself, it's because that part of you is dormant. The purpose of our existence is to *awaken* that knowledge, to begin our journey back to the light that created us. Everyone and everything is part of God. And so when you eat, if you remember to bless God for your food before and after, if you remember that the food is simply there to nourish you as a servant of God, even the food you put into your mouth becomes elevated: the wheat that is ground into flour, the truck driver who brings the bags to the grocery store, the person who puts it on the shelves—all of them are elevated."

"How do I know any of this is true?" another young man asked.

"I suspect you already know it's true—you feel it, don't you?"

The young man sat down. He said nothing.

Shlomie stared at Reb Amos. Yes, his heart was telling him: This is the truth! His mind didn't yet understand it, but his heart was one with this amazing revelation.

He became a regular, abandoning all his other studies. He'd found what he was looking for.

"Your life is a mission. If you follow your heart, you will be directed to the divine sparks that belong uniquely to your soul, and for which your soul has returned to the world again and again to gather."

Shlomie was entranced by the poetry of the words, by the intent, by the glorious purpose that was the stated ideal. He tried, clumsily, to transfer this enthusiasm to his wife.

"It's a way to reach God, face-to-face, like Moses!" he told her. "To be pure and good!"

"Yes, but what does it mean, really, Shlomie? What are you supposed to *do*? How are you supposed to live?"

"I haven't figured that part out yet," he said honestly. "I'm trying to understand. The ideas are very deep. It will take time."

More and more he attached himself to the learning group, so that he was gone almost every evening.

"You're never home," she finally complained to him. "I never see you anymore."

"Why don't you come, too, Daniella? They have classes for women. You're so smart. You'll understand it quicker than me."

"I can't get out in the evening—you know that."

"I was thinking of maybe inviting Reb Amos to give his lectures at our house."

She hesitated. At least she would see her husband more often. More than that, she could stay abreast of the kinds of things he was learning. Now she felt left out.

"It's fine with me, Shlomie. Would he really come?"

"Why not?"

It turned out that Reb Amos was not only willing but eager to come, especially when he heard the address, which was in the most expensive area of the city, Rechavia. Soon enough, he and his students began to visit regularly, eating the elaborate buffet Daniella prepared for them, which she and Amalya served.

Sitting in the kitchen folding laundry, Daniella listened, trying to unravel the meaning of the esoteric phrases that peppered Reb Amos's lectures. Almost against her will, the constant instruction began to seep inside her consciousness. She felt herself less skeptical and more accepting. She told herself that her rational, scientific mind was growing, expanding beyond its narrow confines, just as Amos said it would, the new ideas dwarfing what she had believed before. Slowly, it took over her reality. She hardly noticed.

17

"Goodman, you have a visitor."

Daniella looked up, surprised. So far, not a single person had come to see her in jail. Perhaps . . . was it? Could it be Him?

She jumped up, adjusting her head covering and smoothing down her skirt as she followed the prison guard to the visiting room.

He was sitting there at the table, his eyes cast down.

"Joel."

He looked up, their eyes a reflection of each other's, eyes awash in misery. "Daniella."

She took a step backward, turning to the guard. "Do I have to?"

"Daniella, please. I've come all the way from America. Please sit down," Joel pleaded.

She hesitated. "Was it Mom? Did she send you?"

For a moment, he considered taking the first cab back to the airport.

"Of course not! What's wrong with you?"

She looked down, ashamed. "I don't know," she whispered.

"I'm here because your children are suffering. I'm here because they're my nieces and nephews, and I love them. I'm here because you're my sister, and whatever has happened to you or whatever you've done, I love you."

The resistance holding her body stiff and upright seemed to vanish. She stumbled to the chair, sitting down heavily opposite her brother.

"I'm in terrible trouble, Joel."

"I know that. The police called me and told me everything."

"They called you in America?"

He nodded. "I can't tell you the horrible shock of this on the whole family. Dad is ill, really ill. And Mom, well, she's almost catatonic over it. Refuses to attend any social gatherings. Won't even go into the store."

Daniella twisted her lips into an ironic grin.

"You think this is funny?"

"I think Mom finally got what she deserved after all her attempts to produce the perfect daughter."

He leaned back, away from her. "I don't think you have the slightest idea what you've done. You need help, a good psychiatrist. But before that, you need a lawyer, the best one around. I have some colleagues who recommended a few here in Jerusalem. I've been to see them. Not all of them are willing to take your case—"

"A lawyer turning down a fat fee? What?"

"I'm a lawyer, Daniella. And I can tell you that no amount of money in the world would induce me to defend a child abuser."

"I didn't hurt my children! It's all lies!"

"Then why is Menchie in a coma? Why is Eli going into his fifth skin graft operation? Why are the rest of your kids hysterical?" he said in his best prosecuting-attorney voice. He could see that each question landed like a blow on her head. He paused. "Look, I'm not leaving, even if you throw me out. If you don't care anymore about your kids, I do. And Mom and Dad do. I'm coming to Israel with my family. I'm going to take in the kids and care for them. I'm going to get you a lawyer, the best one available. We are going to get through this as a family, with or without your permission, Daniella. I'm not expecting any thanks."

"Thanks? You want me to thank you for barging into my life when you're not wanted? I have all the help I need. I have God. I have angels. You'll never understand."

He shrugged. "All you have, Daniella, is a screw loose. I don't know how it happened, and frankly, at this point, I don't give a damn. While you're in la-la land, I'm going to be there for the kids, since you and your ex obviously aren't."

"You can't take my children from me without my permission."

"Where do you think your kids are now, Daniella? Who do you imagine is caring for them while you are sitting in jail with whores and drug dealers, and Shlomie has been forbidden to go near them?"

For the very first time, she thought about that, realizing she had no idea. She had somehow magically assumed Shem Tov, Ruth, or the tzaddikim would be caring for them.

"Social workers have divided them up among foster homes. Strangers are caring for them, or trying to. It isn't easy. They are all on the verge of nervous breakdowns. Your wonderful kids . . ."

She put her hands over her ears, his words unwelcome, confusing, rattling her surety and confidence, in the same way as her cellmates' abuse and name-calling.

He got up to go.

Suddenly, she leaned forward, grabbing a handful of the material of his jacket and clutching it. "Joel," she said.

He waited, staring at her the way he would a stranger.

"I'm . . . sorry."

"Tell that to your kids, Daniella. Tell that to your kids."

18

Bina Tzedek raced through the city streets of Ashdod, speeding down the highway back to Jerusalem. At the entrance to the city, her phone rang again.

"I'm almost there, Morris."

"Don't come to headquarters. Meet me in Rechavia." He gave her the address. "Don't ask any questions."

When she arrived, the door to the building was locked. She pressed the buzzer.

"Who's there?"

"Detective Tzedek."

Morris buzzed her in. He grabbed her by both shoulders. "Finally!"

She was startled. She'd never seen him like this before. "What's up?"

"The White Witch's brother, Joel, has come in from the States with his family. He's rented an apartment and taken in Eli. The child has told him things—"

"What kind of things?"

He shrugged. "Child Protective Services has sent their senior child interviewer, Johnny Mann. I've worked with him before. He's amazing."

"So what am I doing here?"

"You're a mom, right? I want your take."

"How is the child?"

"The hospital released him a few days ago. He needs to rest before undergoing another skin graft. Social services thought it would be good for him to be with the uncle."

"What's your take on him?" He was, after all, Daniella Goodman's brother. Didn't pathologies run in families?

"Honestly, from my first impression, he seems like a good guy: deeply concerned and anxious to do all he can to help his sister's children, even though they haven't been in touch for years. Yesterday, he called Johnny. Said the kid is starting to open up and talk. He wanted Johnny to record it. He wants whoever did this behind bars as much as we do."

"What has the child been saying until now?"

"Not much. Some story about a blanket catching fire and his mother and the tzaddikim saving him. You can tell he's been spoon-fed every single word."

"Will he talk if we're there?"

He shrugged. "We'll see."

Joel was sitting on the couch with Eli in his lap. Johnny Mann was sitting next to them, joking with the child, who was laughing. Joel got up and extended his hand to Bina and Morris. He wore a T-shirt with the words THE PURE AND SIMPLE TRUTH IS RARELY PURE AND NEVER SIMPLE over washed-out jeans that looked like the real thing. On his head he wore a backward Yankees baseball cap, a head covering that gave nothing away about his religious affiliation or lack of it.

"Hi, Eli. What's up?" Bina said, smiling as she crouched down so that her face was level with his.

To her surprise, he smiled back, his sweet young face alive and curious, so different from the half-dead robot she'd seen in the hospital video. "I'm good," he said, nodding, "with my uncle Joel." The man's hands tightened around him, pulling him closer. He kissed the child on the top of the head. "He's watching me now."

"Who was watching you before?"

His little face suddenly clouded over. "The tzaddikim and the Moshiach."

Bina felt a chill. *The saints and the Messiah.*

"You know, Eli, this is the first time Bina has met you. Can you tell her about yourself?" Johnny asked the child in Hebrew with a slight American accent.

The child nodded but didn't speak.

"Tell her your name."

"Eliahu Goodman, but they call me Eli. He went to heaven in a carriage with horses."

Morris and Johnny looked at him, puzzled.

"You mean Eliahu the prophet, right?" Bina asked, smiling.

The child nodded, delighted.

Johnny gave her an I-owe-you-one smile.

"And how old are you?" Johnny continued.

"Four years old and almost a half."

"I see you're wearing blue pajamas today. What would you say to someone who said you were wearing red pajamas?" Johnny continued.

The little boy giggled. "They're stupid!"

Johnny smiled, touching him lightly. "Yes, that's true. And what would you say about a boy who broke his sister's doll and said his sister did it?"

"He's making up stories!"

"Very good! You're such a smart boy. And what if I said there's an elephant sitting on my lap?"

The child laughed louder. "You're telling funny stories!"

"Right! It wouldn't be the truth, would it?"

He shook his head.

"You know the difference between the truth and a lie?"

He nodded, his face suddenly serious.

"Eli, we heard that something happened to you. Can you tell us about it?"

He snuggled closer to his uncle. "I don't know."

"You don't know or you don't want to talk about it? It's fine if you don't. No one here will be upset if you don't. Did you like it, what happened to you?"

He shook his head violently.

"Eli, how did you get those burns on your legs?"

"It was Menchie. Menchie pushed me into the heater . . . no . . . we were playing, running, I fell into it, by accident. . . ."

"And that boo-boo on your forehead? How did you get that?"

"Menchie put a nail on my head and hit it with a hammer."

"Eli, you are such a good little boy; everybody knows that."

The child looked up, as if surprised to hear this.

"But this story you are telling me, honey, it's a funny story, right?" Johnny smiled at him. "And it's okay to tell funny stories. Stories are fun to make up, I know, like the story about the elephant on my lap. But we really need to know the truth about what happened. Can you try to remember?"

The child's chin met his shoulder. "I don't know. I can't remember."

"Eli, has anyone ever asked you to keep this a secret?"

He suddenly looked up, his big, blue innocent eyes growing wider.

"You know, Eli, it's always okay to talk to doctors about anything; even secrets are okay to tell to doctors. You aren't going to get into any trouble. I'm like a doctor. I talk to lots of children about things that are bothering them. Even secrets."

Eli looked up at his uncle, who nodded encouragingly. "Just tell them what you told me, honey."

"Someone made *boom-boom* on my head."

"How?"

"With a hard hand and a big hammer."

There was a moment of silence as the adults processed this.

"Eli, who made *boom-boom* to you?"

"The tzaddikim and the Moshiach."

"Kuni Batlan, Shmaya Hod, Yissaschar Goldschmidt . . . ," Bina said.

The child looked at her, surprised. "You know the tzaddikim?"

"Yes," she nodded. "What can you tell me about the tzaddikim?"

"Yissaschar washed me in too cold water and then too hot water because I wouldn't listen"—it seemed suddenly to pour out of him—"and Kuni and the others burned my foot like a piece of toast. It was a tikkun . . . and Shmaya took a hammer and he went *boom, boom, boom* to my head. Like he was pounding a schnitzel."

She tried not to show she was reeling. She literally saw red. She stood up. Morris patted her back.

"Steady," he whispered.

She sat down heavily, trying to pull herself together.

"Eli, sweetheart, that was a good story. A real story. Can you tell us more real stories?" Johnny urged.

He shook his head. "Not about the Moshiach."

There it was again. *The Messiah.*

"Oh, please. We really want to hear about the Moshiach. It would really help us."

Eli seemed unsure. "Ima wouldn't like it."

"But I just spoke to your ima and she says now it's all right to tell. She wants you to tell."

He shook his head again. "But Duvie wouldn't like it. He says not to."

Duvie, the eldest child, his big brother. "Why do you think Duvie said that?"

"He's afraid."

"Of the Moshiach?"

He nodded. "Duvie's not a scaredy-cat. Duvie says we'll go live with him again."

"You lived with the Moshiach?"

He nodded. "In his little house with him and the tzaddikim and Ima."

"Eli, who is the Moshiach?"

She saw his whole body go into a spasm. It shook. His uncle held him tighter.

"It's okay, Eli. No one is going to hurt you anymore. You can talk now. You're safe now."

The little boy shook his head. "The Moshiach knows magic. He can fly. You can't hurt him. He took me into the kabbalah room. He made me do magic."

"And the magic hurt, right, Eli?" Bina said gently.

He nodded.

"And why do you think he hurt you?"

"Because I was bad. And he and Ima wanted me to be good. He was helping me to be good. With tikkunim."

She thought of Rabbanit Toledano's words about the amulets.

"Can you tell me about the tikkunim?"

"To stand up all night and not sleep. To drink arak. To get locked in the suitcase with a *kippah* in your mouth so you can't cry. Sometimes, though, I would cry . . . for Ima. But she didn't hear."

Bina's head began to pound. "Were you the only one the tzaddikim and the Moshiach helped with tikkunim?"

He shook his little head. "They helped all of us. Shmaya helped Menchie. Also the Moshiach helped Menchie."

Menchie. The baby in the coma . . . *My God!* "And who helped you, Eli?"

"Kuni helped me," he said, "and also the Moshiach helped me."

"And what is the name of the Moshiach?" she pressed.

The child turned around, burying his head in his uncle's chest.

"Please, Eli—"

Johnny raised his hand, then stood. "It's enough for now. Thank you, sweetheart," he said in English. Hearing his mother tongue, the child peered out at him, relieved.

Morris got up. "Thank you," he nodded toward Joel, putting his hand out to the child, "and thank you, Mr. Eli. I have something for you." He reached into his pocket and pulled out a big lollypop.

The child's eyes gleamed, but he didn't reach for it.

"It's okay. It's kosher," he assured the child, who looked to his uncle. Joel nodded approvingly. Only then did the child reach out and take it, cautiously unwrapping it from the cellophane and popping it into his mouth. He held the wrapper in his fist, afraid to release it, afraid to do anything without permission.

"You'll make a good policeman one day," Morris told the child, taking the wrapper from him and tousling his hair.

"Will I have a gun to shoot the bad people?"

"Of course."

A delighted smile spread across his somber face.

"Bye, Eli," Johnny said. "I'll come visit you again soon."

The child smiled. "Next time, bring the elephant."

"Okay. I'll try to remember."

They all laughed, even as their hearts broke for this smart, loving, articulate little boy who somehow, through all the incomprehensible pain and horror he had experienced in his short life, had managed to retain his sense of humor and his ability to trust.

He was awesome, Bina thought. That being so, she had to admit to herself, reluctantly, that someone had brought him up that way. He had certainly once known love and care.

"Mr. Whartman, please call us if you have any other news," Morris said, helping Bina to her feet.

"I will. And thank you. There's one other thing. My sister, she'd like to see the other kids. And they are desperate to see her. They hate being in foster care. They hate being separated."

"We know. We're working on it. It's complicated."

"I'm willing to take them all," he said.

"That's really good of you. I'll look into it," Johnny promised.

Bina felt wobbly on her feet. "Good-bye, Eli. You are a very, very good boy and I like you very much."

The little boy turned around, his beautiful clear eyes suddenly shiny with tears, which spilled down his pale cheeks. "I want to see my ima," he told her.

Bina walked toward the door, stumbling perilously. Morris quickly put out his hand to steady her, helping her outside.

Johnny soon joined them.

"I don't know how you do it, Mr. Mann. It's sickening. This whole case. I don't know if I can even continue, if I have the strength. . . ."

Morris stared at her. "You are on the Egyptian border and it's 1967 and they've declared war. They are coming to get you. Believe me, you don't have a choice."

"But, Morris, it's not an ordinary situation. Did you hear what the child said?"

He nodded grimly, looking at Johnny. "And I'm sure that's not the half of it."

She turned to the psychologist. "Do you think it is connected to some kind of abracadabra, black magic, sick rituals—"

"Now you're going overboard," Morris interrupted.

"No, really, Morris—"

"Why? Because the child used the word 'tikkun'?" he scoffed. "A lot of very normal people have started using that word interchangeably with 'correction'. Anyhow, kabbalah isn't black magic."

"This woman I just went to see, Rabbanit Toledano, she said when Eli was brought to her, he had fifteen amulets around his neck, some of them handwritten, a type she'd never seen before."

"Really?" Johnny said.

Morris looked suddenly less dismissive.

"What I just can't get my head around is what did they get out of it, hurting babies like that?"

"That's the real question, isn't it?" Johnny nodded, lighting up a cigarette and taking a deep drag. His hands shook.

"Tell me, Johnny, do you have kids?"

"Three, who live with their mother. The youngest is about Eli's age." His jaw flexed. "I can't even imagine what I'd do if someone, if . . ."

"Neither can I," Bina agreed, thinking of Ronnie, his agile little feet tearing up the grass on the soccer field, and Lilach, who cried from the slightest scratch.

"We need to talk to the oldest boy, to Duvie. He seems to have some control over Eli," Bina suggested.

"Over all the kids." Morris frowned. "You weren't there at that first interview, but Johnny was."

"I've never seen anything that bad." Johnny threw the half-smoked cigarette to the ground, rubbing it out forcefully with his foot. "The children were screaming; they tried to attack us. They told us we were hurting their mother. They were off-the-wall hysterical. Children who had been traumatized to a degree I've never seen before. They refused to give us any information. We're dealing with some very, very sick sons of bitches," he said bitterly.

"Eli says the Moshiach can fly," said Morris.

"And I'm sure he really believes it." Johnny nodded.

"He's a child."

"Listen, Morris, my son, Ronnie, is about his age. Kids tell stories, but they know the difference between reality and fantasy. Either he's been convinced of these things, or . . ."

"What?"

"He's seen them, or thought he did."

"I'll tell you one thing. All those kids have seen things none of us can even imagine," Johnny said grimly. "That's for sure."

"What's at the bottom of it?"

"The Moshiach," Johnny whispered just under his breath. "They are flat-out scared to death of him."

"Who or what is that?"

"That, Detective Tzedek," Morris told her, "is what we need to find out."

19

Daniella stood in the steam-filled bathroom, crouching over the tub where Shoshana was splashing and singing.

"I'm supposed to be giving you a bath, but instead you're giving me one!" she told the child with mock sternness. Shoshana crowed with happiness, her little hands flapping furiously as she churned up the bathwater.

"Okay now, Shoshana Goodman! Enough! Soon it will be Shabbos. Ima has to finish preparing."

"No, Ima. Stay!" she demanded.

Daniella shook her head. Just yesterday she was a baby, and now she was nearly two. She could argue and she had opinions. Daniella smiled, reaching down and pulling out the plug. From her experience, once the water went down the drain, so did the child's resistance to getting dried off.

She heard the front door open and close. She held up a towel. "Your aba's home. Come, quick, get dried off."

She wrapped the fluffy, thick towel around the little girl's naked, warm body, hugging her close. They were like puppies at this age, she marveled. All joy and motion. *Baruch Hashem!* Such a blessing to have healthy children. Such a gift from God! Her heart and soul whispered thanks to the power of creation that had given her so much.

On the way to Shoshana's bedroom, she noticed Shlomie sitting on a kitchen chair. He was bent over, his head in his hands as if in mourning. Her heart sank. What now?

"What happened?" she asked him, trying to contain the child, who was determined to wiggle out of her arms.

He looked up at her, his face a mask of confusion and distress. "I don't even know . . . how . . . to tell you."

A flash of fear, sharp as a piece of broken glass, cut through her contentment and peace.

"I'll . . . I've . . . wait." She hurried into Shoshana's bedroom, quickly dressing her in pajamas even as she squirmed restlessly, wanting to play. Daniella didn't stop, grimly forcing her arms through sleeves, her legs into bottoms, until finally the child burst into tears.

"I'm sorry, so sorry, Shoshana. But Ima can't play now. She has to talk to Aba." She lifted the child off the bed, taking down some dolls from the shelves and placing them on the rug. "You play for a while, okay, sweetie?"

She wiped the tears from Shoshana's face, placing a tissue over her nose. "Blow."

Then she walked back into the kitchen, sitting down opposite Shlomie at the kitchen table. In the living room, the three boys were playing Legos, while Amalya set up the Sabbath candles. She was almost ten, a lovely, sedate young girl with lustrous dark hair and sparkling blue eyes. She was like a second mother to her younger siblings and a star pupil in Beit Yaakov.

"Ima, I finished setting up the candles. What else should I do?" she said, sticking her head inside the kitchen.

Daniella saw Shlomie turn to his daughter, studying her, his face suddenly tragic. Amalya noticed it, too, her innocent, happy face suddenly somber and questioning.

Daniella quickly intervened. "It's okay. Aba's . . . just sad. He'll be fine. Help your brothers clean up the Legos and make them take their baths, okay?"

"Yes, Ima," she said, casting a worried, puzzled look at her father as she walked away. Daniella closed the kitchen door behind her.

"You're frightening the children. Just tell me already, Shlomie."

"It's Reb Amos. He says he's had a vision. He says . . . he wants to marry Amalya."

She had misheard, she thought, her mouth falling open, a frisson of horror passing through her heart. "What?"

"He says this is what the spirits have told him. Otherwise, our family will suffer a terrible tragedy. It's the only way it can be prevented."

She felt her heart squeeze in her chest, as if she were having a heart attack. She got up and stumbled to the sink, turning on the faucet and filling a glass with water. She threw back her head, draining the glass, then placed it carefully in the sink. She turned around, pressing her back against the ledge of the counter until it hurt. She looked at her husband.

"She's not even ten years old."

He lifted his palms in a gesture of helplessness. "He doesn't mean right now."

She exhaled. "Then when?"

He hesitated. "In a few years, when she's Bat Mitzvah."

"He wants to marry a twelve-year-old? Is he nuts?"

"He says at that age a girl is most divine in her purity. That God would not have given her body the ability to have children at that age if it were not the perfect time for her to marry."

"It's not even legal!"

"He says that the modern world is impure, and that she must be protected from all that impurity at the perfect moment of her own purity, so that she can have children of absolute holiness, born out of immaculate purity. Why would Reb Amos . . . why would he say such a thing if it weren't true? If he wasn't trying to help us?"

She sat down, feeling everything move around her as if she were passing through a tornado. The center of her body was hollow. Why, indeed?

Only a year ago, she would have laughed at her husband and told him to get lost and take his Reb Amos with him. She would have threatened to call the police. She would have felt her two feet on the solid ground and her mind set with steely determination.

But much had happened in a year. Every week, lecture upon lecture, explanation upon explanation describing the mystical influences in the world had soaked into her reason, making her mind as soft and spongy as oversaturated earth on the verge of collapse. More than that, the space around her, once benign and empty, was now filled with the unseen celestial beings who had become part of her reality. She felt their volatile presence watching over her and her family. Anything that happened—a glass accidentally pushed off the counter that fell and shattered, a toe that stubbed on a wall, a child's illness or recovery— revealed their presence. Everything that happened was now full of meaning, import, consequence. Reb Amos, considered a holy person and a saint by devoted followers who worshiped his every word, practically lived at their home. Everything they now knew about God, about holiness, about growing spiritually, they had learned from him. Oddly, instead of this bringing her closer to God, she had never felt more distant.

"What are we going to do?" Shlomie asked her.

"He's not going to marry our daughter. Certainly not our twelve-year-old daughter!" Daniella said emphatically, her former self breaking through the shell of enchantment, asserting itself.

"But if we refuse, we are risking a terrible tragedy befalling our family. He hinted there would be a death of a very young person."

Her face went white as her mind retreated, cowering, as she tried to assimilate this information. In saving their daughter, would they be sacrificing another of their children? Oh, the horror of such a choice! She was suddenly confused, her certainty and determination fleeing under her terrible fear.

"Before we do anything, we need to be sure," she said cautiously.

"Of what, Daniella?"

"That what Reb Amos is telling us is true. That he is truly a saint and what he says truly comes from God."

"Yes, we must be sure. But how?"

"You have to investigate. Find someone that is on the highest level possible, someone everyone you speak to agrees truly speaks to God. Let him investigate Reb Amos, to see if his words are true, if the source is from behind the curtain," she said, using the familiar euphemism for contact with the spirit of holiness. In the Holy of Holies in the Temple in Jerusalem, where God dwelled among His earthly creatures, there was such a curtain.

"Yes, yes," Shlomie said, slowly nodding in agreement, his eyes glazed over in wonder at such a remarkable solution. Before making such a decision, they must be sure.

He continued his classes with Reb Amos. And Reb Amos continued to come to the house, only now Daniella was careful that Amalya was not there at the same time.

"He has spoken to me again. He wants to know our answer," Shlomie whispered to her a month later.

"Then tell him we are still thinking," she advised him. "Tell him to wait."

"He says there is another way."

She looked up at him, but he wouldn't meet her eyes.

"He says that he could marry you instead."

"What? What are you saying?" Revulsion, mixed with fear, choked her. "You're my husband, Shlomie!"

He shrugged helplessly. "But what can I do? If it is ordained . . . ?"

She looked into her husband's frightened eyes, but they refused to meet hers. He was going to be no help at all in this, she realized, disgusted. He was going to go along with all of it, unless he became convinced his mentor was a charlatan. She felt helpless. "Shlomie, you have to investigate. You have to find someone to tell us what we must do!"

"You're right, you're right. I will." His voice trembled.

They lived in a state of suspended animation, not really living even as outwardly they made an effort for the sake of the children to seem as if they were going on with their normal lives, while all the time this horror hung over them. It was like that Edgar Allan Poe story, Daniella thought, "The Pit and the Pendulum." They were flattened against the bottom of a hole as a sharp blade swung over them, getting lower and lower as they crouched in the darkness, wondering how to stop it, how to escape.

Both of them understood it wasn't from Reb Amos they needed to run. If what he was saying was truly ordained, then there was no escape. Their fate would follow them, no matter what. The only question was whether or not he had truly gotten this information from God— if God, or the angels, had spoken to him, and if the remedy he offered was truly the only way out for them.

Shlomie spent his days feverishly discussing this with everyone he knew that was a student or master of the hidden wisdom. And one name came up again and again and again. Reb Menachem Shem Tov. People whispered it with a kind of adoration mixed with awe and fear that bordered on worship. He was young, but everyone had heard the stories about him. He was a genuine, undisputed Master of the Good Name, with particular expertise in practical kabbalah. Stories of his wondrous deeds flowed in abundance from the astonished lips of those who whispered into Shlomie Goodman's ears.

But he was hard to approach, they warned him. He chose you, not the other way around. You couldn't just walk into one of his classes. And he deliberately kept his Hassidim to a minimum. Unlike other masters, he refused to have a court of hundreds. He had perhaps ten followers at any given time, even less.

"But I'm desperate. Isn't there a way?" he pleaded with those same friends.

"He goes to pray with his Hassidim at the Tomb of Samuel the Prophet at midnight every Thursday. You must be there. See if you can talk to one of his Hassidim. They might be able to arrange a meeting." Shlomie thanked them profusely.

He didn't tell Daniella, only hinting that they might have an answer soon. The worry and tension were bringing them both close to the breaking point. They couldn't go on much longer like this, they realized, frightened. Without telling his wife anything, the following Thursday, Shlomie drove out to Ramot in northern Jerusalem, turning off the highway to where an unpaved road led to the Tomb of Samuel the Prophet. A former mosque, it was still the highest spot in the entire area, considered a landmark for nineteenth-century wayfarers, a place where they might view the Holy City of Jerusalem in its entirety.

The time was close to midnight. It was pitch-black, with only a ribbon of faint light coming from the headlights of random cars moving down the faraway Jerusalem–Tel Aviv highway and the single lightbulb illuminating the tomb itself.

Shlomie kept walking. While he saw no one, he had the strange sense that he was being followed. He kept looking over his shoulder, listening to the rustle of the branches swaying in the wind. He felt surrounded by spirits, both good and evil. Finally, a shaft of moonlight escaped from a thick cloud, revealing a group of black-garbed Hassidim in the forest. As he drew closer, he heard them howling in prayer at the moon, shaking their bodies in ecstasy. Noticing him, one of them detached himself from the group, walking toward him.

"Who are you and what do you want, brother?" he asked belligerently.

Shlomie took a step back. "I'm seeking godly advice and solace from Rebbe Shem Tov. I have heard wondrous things about him, brother."

The stranger nodded. "Come."

Shlomie blended into the group, taking out his prayer book and silently reciting psalms. But he could not concentrate. He had never in his life heard people pray this way. It was as if they were liquefying their hearts and stomachs and pouring them out in words. Their cries shattered the indifferent face of the night. He felt pure elation, as if the silent mystery of heaven had been slashed wide open, allowing him to enter. His eyes closed as he began to shout the words, letting all his fear, pain, and frustration drain like pus from his soul. He thought: They will think I'm a madman. But when finally he opened his eyes, he saw everyone smiling at him, nodding in approval.

"Reb Menachem has heard your prayer, brother. He asks you to approach."

Shlomie was thrilled.

The rebbe was a short, dark man with long payot and black glasses. "Rebbe—"

But the man motioned for him to stop speaking. "I already know your question," he said. "And the answer is yes."

"Yes?" Shlomie felt as if his heart had been pummeled with a hammer by someone intent on killing him. What did that mean? Yes to a marriage between Reb Amos and his little daughter or his wife? Yes, Reb Amos was telling the truth as he had heard it from God?

Reb Menachem seemed to understand this. "Yes, I will help you."

Relief as swift and wide as a river sent its healing solace through Shlomie's soul. He felt his breath once more move the tiny hairs in his nostrils, filling his lungs.

Menachem Shem Tov stared at him, pleased. Even in the darkness, cold moonlight gleamed from his eyes.

Part Two

20

Shlomie said nothing to Daniella about Menachem Shem Tov. First, he had to arrange a meeting between Shem Tov and Amos. Only then— or better yet, when he had Shem Tov's opinion of the matter—did he think it would be wise to reveal what he had done to his distraught wife. He did this out of kindness, the desire to spare Daniella the terrible tension and suffering he, himself, was experiencing preceding this potentially life altering encounter.

He tried not to think what would happen if Shem Tov confirmed that Reb Amos's demands were indeed the will of heaven. The mere possibility weighed on him with nightmarish intensity. If it did prove to be the will of God, he knew they could not stand against it. Like Abraham with Isaac, they would need to bind their child and bring her to the altar. Or send Daniella in her place.

Through one of Shem Tov's Hassidim, Shlomie invited the *rav* to meet Amos during his regular weekly lecture at the Goodman home. Shlomie had no idea if Shem Tov would actually show up. As usual, their living and dining rooms were packed with Reb Amos's Hassidim. There was no sign of Shem Tov. But just as Reb Amos stood up to speak, there was a knock at the door. Daniella opened it. A group of unknown Hassidim stood in her doorway, led by a short, stocky man with very black hair and extravagant payot that fell past his shoulders. He wore a large black hat and a black satin Hassidic waistcoat. There was something patchy about his beard, Daniella noticed, betraying a youth inappropriate to the stature his arrogant stance seemed to claim. His obsidian eyes met hers boldly, a look that did not befit a Torah scholar facing a strange woman, she thought. That, and something about the eerily tenebrous quality of the light in his eyes made her stumble as she bent her head. But there was no time to process her feelings as Shlomie soon appeared by her side, ushering her out of the way.

"*Kavod Harav*, welcome to our home," Shlomie said, his entire body bent obsequiously, his voice deepening with awe and respect. "Please, come in."

Shem Tov nodded briefly in acknowledgment, striding into the large, elegant living room, his calculating eyes taking in the massive china closet with its ornate silver candelabra, wine cups, and other ritual objects; the expensive custom-made drapes and matching upholstery; the fine rugs and original works of art. Behind his eyeglasses, under lowered lashes, he studied Daniella Goodman's youthful figure, her large breasts and tiny waist.

Shlomie approached Amos, whispering in his ear. Amos's head shot up, staring in the direction of Shem Tov. For a moment, the two men's eyes locked, each taking the other's measure as if they were prizefighters just about to climb into the ring. Amos stood up respectfully. "This is an honor, Reb Shem Tov," he said, nodding with a pleasant smile. "I have heard many wonderful stories about you."

"And I have never heard of you at all," replied Shem Tov brazenly.

Everyone froze.

"Please, Reb Amos," Shlomie said, almost physically shrinking before both these titans, "Reb Shem Tov asks to speak with you privately before we begin."

"With pleasure," said a now unsmiling Amos through gritted teeth.

Shlomie gestured humbly to both men to follow him, leading them into a study just off the living room and closing the door behind him.

"What is going on?" Daniella whispered hotly when he returned, confused and more than a little frightened.

"I did what you asked. I found the greatest Master of the Good Name in the Holy City. He will now tell us whether or not Reb Amos's words have come from behind the curtain."

For a split second, it occurred to her that she and Shlomie were now preparing to relinquish sovereignty over their fate and that of their children to strangers, allowing them to decide. But before she was able to comprehend fully the enormity of such a monstrous idea in all its abhorrent gravity, she found it had already slipped past her like wind, muffled by another voice, another idea that hugged her with fatherly comfort, erasing her fears. She was doing no such thing, the voice comforted. No, it was not these men deciding her fate, but God. The men had no power other than to reveal His will. She trembled, the small hairs on her arms standing on end, magnetized and electric as she waited to hear the judgment of heaven.

21

It didn't take long. The door opened and Shem Tov came out, his face blank, his dark eyes inscrutable. Amos soon followed. Without saying a word to anyone, he went straight to the front door, unlocking it and exiting. His shocked Hassidim abruptly pushed back their chairs, hurrying after him.

"I have looked behind the curtain," Shem Tov announced to a room of startled faces, including Shlomie's and Daniella's. "The person who calls himself Reb Amos is a fake! A charlatan! One who preys on the innocent and naïve. There is no holiness in him. He is not a rav or even a scholar. Nothing he has told you is true. All of it is lies."

Daniella felt her knees buckle beneath her. Shlomie caught her, carrying her to the sofa, where he laid her down, adjusting her dress modestly over her legs. Menachem Shem Tov took it all in: the guileless husband and the slim, young woman who lay prone on the expensive American sofa. He memorized every nuance, every detail, storing whatever could be of use to him.

The Goodmans' relief and gratitude to Menachem Shem Tov knew no bounds. Shlomie quickly switched allegiances and was welcomed warmly into the small inner circle of Shem Tov's Hassidim. He was enormously flattered, feeling a real sense of accomplishment, convinced that his acceptance by the great Master was a sign of his own spiritual growth.

Daniella felt the opposite, her self-worth and confidence all but destroyed. How had she allowed herself to trust such an obvious fake? How had she not been wise enough to see through his trickery, his flaws, his monstrous character, to the extent that she had even given thought to the idea of sacrificing her pure, lovely Amalya to his perversions? Or herself? Her trust in her own ability to make intelligent, reasonable decisions was shattered.

In some ways, this breakdown made her even more dependent on God than ever. I will be more devout, more observant, she thought in gratitude, feeling doubly obligated to please Him.

Thus, instead of being wary of the wonder worker who had showed up to take Amos's place, she instead blessed God that just at this moment of darkness in her life, He had sent them a true light, a mentor, a real tzaddik, an anchor to holiness and truth who would guide them through the dangerous waters of life.

Both Shlomie's studies and activities and her own devout observance took on a new intensity. He spent almost all his time studying with Reb Shem Tov and his Hassidim in the small, run-down building near the shuk they called their *beit midrash,* and she studied late into the night every book on kabbalah she could get her hands on.

One year into their studies, out of the blue, Shlomie suggested that they move to the Old City. "The spiritual life is stronger there, better for our children. We are so fortunate that we live in an age when it is possible for Jews to live right near the Kotel."

It was easy to sell Daniella, pregnant with number six, on the idea. The secular, snobbish, moneyed people of Rechavia—most of them senior citizens—among whom they now lived treated them like pariahs, constantly complaining about the noise the children made, the candy wrappers on the staircase, the bikes and carriages in the hallway. They needed a more congenial, child-oriented neighborhood in which to raise their children, Daniella thought. The Jewish Quarter of the Old City, with its large religious families and hordes of riotous children at play, fit the bill perfectly. It was also a place where she could join other women growing in religious devotion through the plethora of women's study programs offered day and night.

They went shopping with a real estate agent. The homes ranged from tiny, cramped hovels to enormous multimillion-dollar mansions that overlooked the Western Wall from every window. They didn't want either. Finally, they came across a five-bedroom cottage with a roof garden from which, if you craned your head, it was possible to see the golden Dome of the Rock.

"This is perfect," said Shlomie, rubbing his hands as he walked through the generous living/dining room, imagining the long table with Reb Shem Tov at its head as he held classes there. He thought it best not to mention this to Daniella, the way he hadn't mentioned that Shem Tov's beit midrash was now closing down, him having been summarily evicted by the devout owner of the small building, a man who looked with horror at the group's continued efforts to master the forbidden knowledge of the mystical texts of practical kabbalah, especially the *Book of Creation.*

Throughout the ages, conventional religious leadership had always looked askance at efforts to learn the secrets of creation ex nihilo. That was not to say they refuted such knowledge was real and such power attainable. Was it not written in the Babylonian Talmud that "on the eve of every Sabbath, Judah haNasi's pupils, Reb Hanina and Reb Hoshaiah, masters of cosmology, used to create a delicious calf by means of *The Book of Creation* to eat on the Sabbath"? And had not many a great rabbi asserted that Abraham himself had used the same method to prepare a meal for his three angelic visitors who came bearing the miraculous news of aged Sarah's coming pregnancy? Some even asserted that it was none other than Abraham who had written the book, while still others contended that Adam had written it in the Garden of Eden.

Even skeptics agreed it was ancient, dating from the second century B.C.E. In a copy in the British Museum, called *The Laws of Creation*, its preface warns those who would venture to read it that its wisdom would be inaccessible to anyone but the truly pious.

Modern readers—whatever their level of piety—found it no less obscure.

It was not the kabbalah of populist preachers in Los Angeles but an older, deeper version involving techniques aimed at altering nature. It was the original abracadabra: "Twenty-two [Hebrew] letters: God drew them, hewed them, combined them, weighed them, interchanged them, and through them produced the whole creation and everything that is destined to come into being."

This sacred knowledge was only to be used for good, the book asserted. The legendary Jewish Frankenstein, called a "golem," supposedly created by the Maharal of Prague using formulas from the *Book of Creation*, was supposed to protect the Jews from their enemies. But when the golem ran amok, the Maharal removed the letters placed on his tongue, turning him back into clay.

To this day, Jewish tradition views the saga of the golem as a cautionary tale: however learned and holy the practitioner of kabbalah, rabbinic wisdom has always held that the use of such knowledge is dangerous, if not absolutely forbidden, akin to idolatry and witchcraft. Calling on angels who do not wish to be ordered about can easily turn against the conjurer at any moment, demons arriving instead, not as servants but as masters, exacting revenge by bending the conjurer to their will, body and soul.

People like Shem Tov ignored these warnings, promising their eager students that practical kabbalah was a way for man to connect more closely with God. But even he had a caveat: One's faith must be so absolute and unquestioning that hearing something must be the same as having seen it with one's own eyes. And thus Shlomie came to believe, with a perfect all-consuming faith, that he had not just heard about the great miracles Shem Tov had supposedly performed but had actually witnessed them with his own eyes.

But soon it wasn't enough just for him to believe. His wife, his children, must also believe. And so Shlomie thought longingly of the day when he could invite Shem Tov to use the Goodman home so that several times a month his family might benefit from the truths as taught only and exclusively by Rav Shem Tov, whom his devoted followers had taken to calling secretly among themselves the Messiah.

22

His mother always said, "When Menachem was born, a light filled the room."

She was a small woman who wore hats and scarves over her dark, stiff wig. The Shem Tovs were Ultra Orthodox Sephardim, the kind whose customs and beliefs from the old country had been belittled and denigrated out of them by the snobbish, elite Lithuanian school of Judaism, Ashkenazi extremists who arrogantly claimed to be the only faithful adherents to the most authentic and rigorous version of the religion of Moses. Quite the opposite, of course, was true. The Ashkenazi elites were the people radically rewriting the Torah and Jewish customs at a lightning rate, creating an ugly new religion that had more in common with Islam and the Mormons than the ancient Hebrews.

Picture her then as she remembers it: a run-down labor room in the old Bikur Cholim hospital in the 1980s on Strauss Street, where shower curtains separated mothers screaming in pain because the hospital couldn't afford to give epidurals to the fertile, devoutly religious population they served. Her final scream, and then, the walls going neon, the midwife gasping, and she, as adoring as one of those Magi in a Christmas painting she would never in her life see, holding out her arms to accept the infant. She does not remember that he was brown, small, and wiry; that he struggled, flailing, as she clasped him in her arms, as if trying to leap out of them. She remembers him shining like gold mined from the deep, dark crevices of her family's despair. A son, after so many daughters! A child who simply by virtue of his maleness had been granted the possibility of becoming a great scholar and religious leader, redeeming his own father's bitterly disappointed hopes.

They had not always been so devout. Part of the desperate flow of Jewish refugees from Arab lands fleeing the newly awakened hatred of their Muslim neighbors, their families had arrived penniless to tent camps in the desert in 1948. Slowly, the fledgling Jewish state provided them with shelter in huge, ugly housing projects. But Menachem's father, Aaron Shem Tov, joined the army and served well, making influential friends who helped him find work in the civil service. He rose through the ranks until he and his young family could afford a larger apartment near the shuk.

It was a neighborhood of outwardly charming Jerusalem stone houses built at the turn of the last century by warm-hearted Jewish philanthropists endeavoring to help the devout, visionary, and impractical immigrants who chose to leave their homes and find their way to the Holy Land. Inside, they were decrepit, damp, dark, and cramped, the alleyways between them shrinking as ugly add-ons made of tin and chicken wire grew like weeds, choking off the light and air.

But Aaron had seen the apartment's potential, taking down walls, repainting and adding modern conveniences, turning the dark spaces into spacious, light-filled rooms. Not all of his neighbors felt it was worth the effort. One by one, the descendants of the original North African immigrants for whom the housing had been built sold their picturesque homes, purchasing boxy modern apartments in dusty, outlying suburbs. Those coming in their stead were invariably stringently devout, indigent Ashkenazi Jews who looked askance at him and his Sephardic ways.

It was then his wife decided to cover her hair with a wig, to which eventually a scarf was added. He followed suit, acquiring the black velvet skullcap covered by the large Borsalino hat favored by the Ashkenazim. He began to study the sacred texts in weekly and then daily study sessions. He saw the birth of his son, Menachem, as a reward for his growing piety. In his heart, he prayed that the child would grow to be a great Talmud scholar, a light to his generation through scholarship, diligence, and good works, and that this glow would be reflected on him and his wife and the rest of his family, so that his daughters might find worthy matches when the time came.

And for a while, Aaron Shem Tov believed that this might be possible. Menachem, the elder Mr. Shem Tov would tell reporters later when they crowded around his home looking for statements, answers, insights, or simply to find someone to blame, had led the congregation in *Anim Zemirot*—the last prayer of the Sabbath morning service—when he was barely two and had to be stood up on a chair to reach the bimah; and by the age of three, he had already learned the entire first chapter of Genesis by heart. The accusations now being made against his saintly son were lies, wicked lies, he told them, spun by his son's enemies, former classmates who had always been consumed with jealousy of his brilliant, pious son's special powers. What stories they fabricated to blacken his name and raise themselves up! How could any intelligent person believe them?

How, for example, Menachem had bullied and frightened children in the neighborhood, pushing them violently off slides and swings, tripping them with wires drawn across alleyways in the dusk. How he was eager to beat up others, but unlike most of the boys didn't stop when he drew blood. How he had been suspected of tying rubber bands tightly around the necks of kittens, of being involved in the bleeding rumps of dogs whose tails had been ripped off. All of them, Mr. Shem Tov fumed, outrageous and malicious slanders with not a shred of truth.

Not that Aaron Shem Tov believed his son had been perfect. Far from it. Yes, he had gone through a hard period, his teachers often citing him for laziness and arrogance and bullying others. But what business was that of the reporters? I did everything I could to change him, his father thought, flinching from the memories.

That was true. He had punished Menachem more severely than he had ever been punished by his own father, beatings with sticks and straps that had gone on so much longer than he ever intended because of the boy's arrogant refusal to cry.

He never cried.

No matter what punishment was meted out, Menachem's dry eyes were direct and unflinching, exposing one's helplessness, daring one to try harder, until finally his father had to recognize his own impotence. Eventually, Menachem's yeshiva, too, ran into the same wall of un-abashed disdain. Running out of ways to change his character, his teachers raised their hands in defeat, informing his parents that their son would have to learn elsewhere.

To be thrown out of a yeshiva in Jerusalem was no small matter. All the rabbis talked to each other, and it was impossible to find an equally prestigious educational setting that would take him in. Having no alternative his parents, to their immense and unending shame, were forced to send him to a place that took in delinquent yeshiva boys.

The head of the yeshiva, Rabbi Kaban, was a saint, a man steeped in the wisdom of the kabbalah. It was his life's mission, he often said, to gather the errant little sparks of holiness that had not found their place in the more well regarded institutions and to bring their poten-tial to fruition.

And it had surely been so with Menachem, who had walked in that first day with a charisma that covered him like thick honey, mesmer-izing his classmates, who very soon found it impossible to do anything without his influence and approval. There followed some troubled days when even the devout Rabbi Kaban's doubts had been aroused. But he persisted, calling Menachem into his office daily for stirring private talks, attempting with concentrated love and devotion to reach the boy's soul. When nothing else worked, he threatened him: "If I throw you out, there is no place else for you to go and soon enough the Israeli army will draft you. You'll find yourself on the front lines."

Whatever the reason, a swift, almost miraculous change came over the boy. He began to earnestly apply himself to his studies. Rabbi Kaban would find him in the yeshiva at four thirty every morning, sometimes remaining until midnight, poring over texts. It was a success story, and Rabbi Kaban's gratification was immense. He quickly made Menachem his assistant, allowing him to give lessons to the other boys.

But then, something odd happened, something Rabbi Kaban could not have predicted. Instead of focusing on Talmud, Menachem began to focus solely on the *Zohar*, a medieval compilation explaining the kabbalah, which was meant only for responsible scholars over forty years of age. From there, his studies had taken him to even more esoteric texts, the *Fountain of Life*, *The Palm Tree of Devorah*, and finally, *The Book of Creation*.

When this happened, Rabbi Kaban could no longer stay silent, admonishing his star pupil, "These works of practical kabbalah are not meant for someone your age. Leave it before you bring evil into your life."

But Menachem simply looked at him with the same unblinking stare that had so unnerved his father and teachers, his eyes arrogant, his lips tightly stretched into a small, secret smile.

He refused to obey.

It was then that the stories began. How he had opened the door of a locked *mikvah* by using the names of angels. How he had used an incantation to grow money between the pages of a book. How he had driven a car with no gas all the way to the graves of the saints in Meron.

His reputation spread.

Rabbi Kaban, perturbed, decided that what his star pupil needed was greater stability in life. He resolved that it was time for Menachem to marry. And so when a rich merchant came to him for advice about a monetary matter, the rabbi asked him instead if he had any marriageable daughters. As luck would have it, he had two.

The eldest, Ruth, was a pretty, pale, docile girl of eighteen who had just graduated Beit Yaakov Seminar and hoped to teach. The father, whose heart had been set on an Ashkenazi Talmud scholar, was less than enthusiastic at first about this short, dark, Sephardi boy. He was finally won over by the rabbi's and his own daughter's endless entreaties.

Ruth had never met anyone like Menachem. She was stunned, enthralled, captivated, her mind dizzy with possibilities. He was so wise! So learned! He knew things even the greatest scholars didn't dare delve into. He was going to be a leader in the Torah world, and she would be his wife, an important rebbetzin. It was everything a devout haredi girl dreamed of.

A lavish wedding was held in a large catering hall. The entire yeshiva attended. Menachem was set up financially by his father-in-law, although not in the luxurious manner he had expected and felt he deserved: a small attached cottage in a far out suburb, an hour's drive from Jerusalem. He received a small monthly stipend from his father-in-law but not enough to cover all his expenses. Resentfully, he had no choice but to continue giving lessons, while he learned kabbalah deep into the night.

Eventually, even more outrageous stories of Menachem's miraculous use of the names of angels and the holy tongue reached Rabbi Kaban. At that point, the good-hearted old teacher finally felt compelled to act: he ordered his pupil to put aside his dangerous dabbling in the forbidden knowledge once and for all: "If you use their names to call them, they bring demons with them, and before you know it, you are at their command and not the opposite."

"What do you know, old man?" Menachem answered in contempt, turning his back and slamming the door to the study hall. Only then did a shocked Rabbi Kaban fully realize the depth of his mistake, and that it was beyond his power to correct it. He cut off all ties with Menachem Shem Tov and forbade his students any contact with him.

Menachem set up his own yeshiva nearby, in one of the poorly attended synagogues of a dying congregation that was only too happy to allow him to fill its run-down premises during the day with the sound of students learning the sacred texts. Some starstruck students from

Rabbi Kaban's yeshiva followed him, and others came from all over, drawn to his growing reputation as a kabbalist and holy man.

But he never had more than ten students at any given time. Whether this was his choice, or because people who admired him soon found their admiration outweighed by their fears, is hard to know. In any case, there was a constant flow of those who came and those who left, never to return. He always maintained that this didn't bother him. On the contrary, he claimed he wanted only those willing to submit to him completely, that the others were worthless to him and to themselves. They were weak, vacillating, undependable, and thus unworthy of learning the sacred secrets of the universe that he had to offer. Only those exhibiting the tremendous discipline he demanded would be able to reach the highest spiritual level, he said. The others were of no use to him and the sacred knowledge, being vessels too weak to hold the great light.

Soon a loyal, handpicked cadre surrounded him, willing to do his bidding mindlessly in return for sharing his powerful secrets. These men came with him to pray at the graves of saints, conducted secret rituals under the full moon in the thick forests that surround Jerusalem, daily witnessing Menachem Shem Tov's miraculous secret powers. Or so they swore.

If any one of them veered even slightly in an independent direction, ceasing to be "faithful servants," he immediately withdrew his light from them, turning his face away. Those who didn't immediately make amends were mercilessly beaten in the forests, then secretly dropped off at the emergency rooms in various Jerusalem hospitals. When they healed, they either willingly returned to a double dose of light or were no longer part of the group.

Those that left never spoke to anyone about what they had been through, terrified of Shem Tov's mystical powers to harm them. Those who remained spoke in awed whispers of the dire punishments that had befallen those who had dared to speak out against their mentor and teacher and their loved ones: how their kidneys failed, their virility vanished, and cancerous growths sprouted like summer weeds. They went on and on, feeding each other tales of destruction and retribution that filled all listeners with fear.

They swore they had seen him change all the traffic lights to green, that he had commanded the wind to pick him up and carry him, that he had thrown dice and predicted the numbers again and again and again, that people who wanted money were asked, "In which pocket, left or right?" And according to their answer, that pocket would fill with money. They swore they had seen him submerge his head underwater for forty minutes. They swore he had put his hand on the stomach of a man's father and removed his illness. They swore Aaron Shem Tov had announced to the fifteen known kabbalah masters in Jerusalem, "Here is my son, a new wonder worker." And the masters had risen to welcome him. And in the dark crowded alleyways of the place near the shuk where little yeshivot blossomed and wilted like wildflowers, everyone swore these tales were true.

People said they had witnessed these things or at least heard about them from very reliable sources. Because to those with faith, hearing about something was the exact same thing as seeing it with one's own eyes, was it not? They swore it was true and believed it was true, the way they believed the Torah was true and God existed. They made it all part of the same faith, inseparable. And it was, at least among the handpicked people with whom Menachem Shem Tov surrounded himself.

Soon after his marriage, Menachem arranged a match between his wife's sister and Shmaya Hod, one of his devoted followers. But the girl had her doubts: "He spends all his time with Menachem in the yeshiva. All day and all night. It's not the kind of life I want," she told her sister Ruth in confidence. Ruth immediately told her husband. The day before the *vort* to seal the engagement, Menachem instructed Shmaya Hod to call it off, causing his wife's family untold humiliation.

While his father-in-law cut all ties with the young kabbalist, Ruth Shem Tov was loyal to her husband to the point of obsession, refusing any contact with her parents and family for years. It is hard to know if she bitterly regretted her actions later, when Menachem lost interest in her and her love turned to abject fear. By then, there was very little left of who she had once been.

Then came a time of turmoil. A plot was uncovered and thwarted by the Israeli Secret Service among yeshiva students who planned to fire an RPG missile at the Al-Aqsa mosque to create chaos and usher in an all-out war of Gog and Magog, which the Talmud says will precede the coming of the Messiah.

At first, the students kept silent, but later, after sitting in jail for years, they would claim that Rav Menachem Shem Tov had put them up to it. But by then the statute of limitations had run out and as the crime had not taken place, and there were those who had been tried, convicted, and punished for it, police did not pursue it.

Other kabbalah masters also began to complain. "We, who truly know the magic incantations, would never dare use them." But not all agreed. They told stories of the great kabbalah master the Baba Sali, who during a *hilulah* ran out of arak. He reached under his flowing robe and pulled out a bottle from which flowed an endless supply, enough to quench the thirst of the hundreds of disciples who had come. Others argued that it was a well-accepted tradition to use practical kabbalah to heal the sick or to match the unwed with marriage partners. But even they agreed that if a person misused his power there would be a terrible price to pay.

While some would later call Menachem Shem Tov a classic psychopath, there were those who would argue that his behavior proved that the demons he had summoned to do his bidding had taken up residence within him, and now it was he who did theirs. Either theory would do concerning the events that followed his introduction into the lives of Shlomie and Daniella Goodman.

23

Just when Bina and Morris had despaired of getting Hod or Gold-schmidt to talk, a local law enforcement officer in the Galilee got assigned a call from someone who spoke Hebrew with an accent so American they thought he was speaking English. Actually, it was a mixture of the two languages. What he said was, *"Ani ausiti* citizen's arrest. *Bo* quick!"

When the officer arrived forty minutes later, he and his partner found two Hassidic types going at it, one all in white and the other all in black, each with long payot and beards, both of whom looked worse for the wear. The one in black had two black eyes and a bloody nose and was lying on the ground, as the one in white, his face scratched, shoved his shoe into his opponent's stomach after kicking him a few more times in the behind.

After separating them and handcuffing them both, police shoved them into a squad car and took them down to the station, the one in white protesting all the way. His name, he claimed, was Shlomie Goodman, and this man was responsible for injuring his children in Jerusalem and was wanted by the police. The one in black, on the other hand, claimed to be the aggrieved party and demanded to be released.

To their surprise, the one in white had actually been telling the truth.

"You're never going to believe it, Bina," Morris exulted. "They've arrested Kuni Batlan up in Karmiel."

"However did they find him?"

"Get this! Shlomie Goodman became Superman. He found him, beat the crap out of him, then called the cops."

Her eyes widened. Would wonders never cease? She was in a strange way displeased. The father's sudden attack of conscience would now force her to change her opinion of him. Perhaps he really was as unbelievably naïve as he seemed. That was the only innocent explanation for what he had allowed to happen to his children, and one she was loathe to adopt because it meant letting him off the hook.

Everything he had done, except this, went against all her ideas about a man's responsibility to protect his wife and children, to nurture and care for them. Could it possibly be that Shlomie Goodman deserved the benefit of the doubt?

"When is Batlan being brought in?"

"As soon as the traffic on Highway Six allows."

"Traffic? Tell them to put the sirens on all the way!"

To her surprise, Kuni Batlan was nothing like either Hod or Goldschmidt. Tall, slim, in an expensive tailored black suit, he was neatly shaven, his long side curls tucked up into his expensive Borsalino hat so that they were hardly visible. Also, unlike the others, he was visibly shaken, like a branch from a young tree not accustomed to storms, ready to crack from the gentlest breeze. There was no need to be harsh. All she needed was to blow on him like a birthday candle, she thought.

"So, that's quite a shiner you have there." She smiled sympathetically.

He seemed surprised at the friendliness of her tone. He studied her.

"I'm an Israeli citizen. Shlomie Goodman assaulted me. He should be arrested."

"Absolutely, Mr. Batlan. I'll see to it. Please don't worry about it. If you cooperate, I will personally see to it that you are treated the way you deserve."

"So, you'll let me go?"

"Let's not run ahead of ourselves. But as I said, if you give us something valuable we can use . . . So, let's start by my asking you a few questions, that is, if you don't mind?" She smiled once more.

"Of course. I'm happy to help."

"You know, the children of Mr. Goodman have been injured and we're investigating. If you could tell me anything useful about that, I can guarantee the police would be very grateful," she began.

He nodded. "I understand there was a fire—"

"No," she cut him off briskly. "We've established that there was never any fire. The child was held against a spiral heater until his skin peeled off, and then someone rubbed salt and alcohol on his wounds and forced his feet into his shoes."

"It wasn't me! I would never do such a thing! I would never—"

"We already have evidence that you were involved with Menchie Goodman."

He began to shake so hard, she thought he would come apart.

"Can I get you a glass of water?"

"Please," he said. He could hardly hold the glass, the water swishing in waves, spilling over the top of the glass on either side until he finally emptied some of it into his mouth. He swallowed, noticeably, as if he were trying to get down a giant pill, then put the glass down carefully on the desk, as if cognizant that one false move would herald disaster.

"Whatever they tell you, none of it was my idea. I would never do anything like that on my own!"

"Anything like what, Mr. Batlan?"

"Like what they say I did to Menchie . . . and the others."

"And what would that be?"

"You know. What they told you. Now they are going to try to pin the whole thing on me. But there is only one person responsible for all of this. And that's Menachem Shem Tov."

She took a sharp intake of breath but calmed herself. "And who might that be?" she asked indifferently.

He was suddenly silent, staring at her. "You mean, I'm the first . . . that the mother, the children . . . no one has mentioned . . . ?" His eyes showed panic along with the recognition of the seriousness of his miscalculation. But there was no going back. "We called him Messiah. He was our rebbe, our teacher. Everything we did, we did because he told us to. He forced us."

"What do you mean, 'forced'?"

"We were all afraid of him! All of us. We'd seen what he could do to those who didn't obey him. We couldn't take that chance."

"Tell me about what you did because of Shem Tov."

"He told us the children were crazy, that demons—the Evil Inclination—had taken them over and that they must be 'fixed.' It was enough for him to just nod his head at one of us to make us understand what needed to be done."

"And what exactly was that?" she asked mildly, almost sick with anticipation. It was like opening some disgusting test tube in a lab filled with deadly organisms. She realized that she didn't really want to know, to be infected with this ugly knowledge, the way that people can't stand to hear about what inventive horrors the Nazis came up with. It tainted your view of the world and mankind forever.

"He made them stand up for hours, and if they tried to sit down, they were beaten with sticks or fists. Some of them even got their teeth knocked out. He made us lock them in cellars, and sometimes he wouldn't let them sleep. He made us give them arak until they vomited up the evil. . . ." He wiped his glistening forehead.

For a few minutes, she said nothing. "So," she suddenly began, "you tortured children to save your own, worthless, cowardly hide? Is that what you're telling me?" Her voice rose.

He was shocked at her sudden transformation. It was as if someone else had taken over the investigation, someone who meant him harm. He squirmed uncomfortably. "No, no. We didn't think of it like that. He told us we were helping them, the children. The mother wanted it! She saw everything and said nothing! We only did exactly as he told us, no more, no less. We felt it was a great privilege to help him in his work. It was like following a religious commandment. We were only following orders."

She was finding it hard to breathe as he uttered the infamous phrase. Was he brought up under a rock that he didn't understand the connotations? Had he never heard of the Eichmann trial or read about the interrogation of SS officers? Was he really that ignorant and cut off from the world and his own people's history?

"Anyhow, it was Shem Tov that did the most violence. I only held the children as Shem Tov beat them. As soon as he suspected the Evil Inclination in a child, he just went crazy, beating the child the way you'd beat a devil or a wild animal. And when he used them for kabbalistic ceremonies, no one was allowed in. If you're looking to blame someone, blame Shem Tov, blame the mother, blame Shlomie Goodman!"

She felt her head splitting and an urgent desire to upchuck her lunch. She hid it, picking up a pen. "And where does this Menachem Shem Tov live?"

"In Beit Shemesh Heights, just outside of Jerusalem."

No surprise there, she thought grimly. It was a suburb with a reputation for black-coated religious extremists. How many times had the police been called to protect little girls going to school from grown men who shouted and threw things at them because they didn't think the five- and six-year-olds were dressed modestly enough? How many times had they rescued Modern Orthodox women who had been ganged up on and threatened in broad daylight because a few hairs were sticking out of their headscarves? Morris called it "little Teheran." These guys were no different than the mullahs, he often said.

It was the perfect neighborhood for a Menachem Shem Tov.

"Can you give me the exact address?" She wrote it down. Now there was no time to lose.

"So, can I go now, Detective?" He gave her a toadying smile, which she longed to smack off his face with a lawn mower. Yes, he really was that ignorant.

"I'm afraid it's not up to me."

"But, you said if I cooperated, if I gave you something valuable . . ."

"I'm sorry," she answered. "But I'm only following orders." She nodded at the two-way glass. Two burly policemen with children of their own slammed open the door. Picking Batlan bodily off his feet, they roughly handcuffed him behind his back, a little higher and more tightly than was strictly necessary. His face went white as they dragged him briskly back to his cell.

Morris was waiting for her out in the hall. "We should get backup."

They sped through the busy afternoon streets toward the Jerusalem–Tel Aviv highway, sirens blaring and lights flashing, followed by four other police cars. People walking their dogs and pushing baby carriages stopped and stared worriedly, wondering if there'd been a terrorist attack they hadn't yet heard about. In twenty-five minutes, the detectives were already riding up the wooded path to Beit Shemesh Heights. As instructed by Morris, all vehicles shut down their lights and sirens, making their approach as quietly as possible.

They found it quickly, a modest attached cottage with an oddly empty front porch bookended on either side by porches filled with red bicycles, a children's colorful playhouse, and a pink doll carriage.

A woman answered the door. She was short and heavy with a large scarf wound elaborately and intricately around her head, which dwarfed the rest of her body. Her dress was a dull brown that reached almost to her ankles, the sleeves dangling over her wrists. Oddly, she didn't seem surprised to find six policemen at her door. "What do you want?" she asked belligerently.

"Who are you?" Bina asked her, brushing past her into the house. She heard an infant's wail and glimpsed two small children playing on a living room floor cluttered with toys. Bina searched in vain for the crying baby, only then noticing there was a staircase covered with balding carpeting leading to a second floor.

"I'm Rebbetzin Ruth Shem Tov. How dare you break into my house! What do you want?"

"We're asking the questions. Where is your husband?" Bina screamed at her.

Her belligerence quickly faded under the assault. "He's . . . he isn't . . . not home right now."

"When will he be home?"

"I'm not sure."

"Can you call him?"

"I'm not sure where he is."

"Call his cell phone then, Rebbetzin."

"My husband is a saint. He doesn't have a cell phone. It's an abomination."

The baby's cries got louder, but it didn't seem to affect Ruth Shem Tov in the least, Bina noticed, a chill going up her spine. The children in the living room included a dark-haired, nervous boy about four with long payot who sat on the floor surrounded by puzzles and Legos, which he moved around listlessly, making little progress, and a tiny little girl who sat near him silently holding a doll. Neither looked up or smiled as she walked in, exhibiting none of a child's normal curiosity at the sudden appearance of strangers. They seemed unnaturally detached, indifferent. In the pit of her stomach she felt a heaviness descend as she wondered what they had experienced that had made them this way.

"Here is our search warrant. I suggest you cooperate," Morris said, offering it to Ruth, who sized him up, suddenly getting her courage back. She waved the paper away, refusing to accept it.

"You have no right to just barge in here and threaten me! I'll call my lawyer."

"Your baby's crying," Bina pointed out.

The woman walked off in a huff to fetch the child.

Police swarmed through the small house, turning everything inside out. Just off the living room was a small, dark room filled with books and a sofa. It had kabbalistic symbols on the wall: the Tree of Life, a *hamsa*, and posters of bearded scholars. It felt damp and cold, Bina thought, hugging herself.

Then she saw it. "Morris, come look at this."

He walked in and stood beside her, staring at the spiral electric heater up against the wall, the twisted coils red-orange with intense heat. He grimaced. "Come into the living room, Bina."

There, spread out on the table, were hammers, knives, ropes, plastic ties, metal handcuffs, turpentine, alcohol, guns, heaters of various sizes, and bottles of arak, just the beginning of what the police had turned up. She had a sudden vision of Lilach, her little girl, her soft skin so easily bruised and scratched. She felt sick.

Ruth Shem Tov suddenly appeared with a baby. "Don't you have a knife and a hammer in your home?" the woman screamed at them as she looked over the collected items. "Don't you have heaters? Don't you drink arak? We helped the Goodman family! We took care of them out of the goodness of our hearts, in all innocence!"

"Tell us more," Morris said mildly, indicating she should sit down on the couch.

She seated herself comfortably, taking her time. "They lived with us. We tried to save them from their insane father, who spent all of his time in cemeteries. He'd lay down on top of saints' graves and pray to them. Then he ran away and left his family without a penny! My husband gave them refuge. They stayed with us for months. Who gave food to these children? I did. Who checked them for lice while their mother was gallivanting around shopping malls? Me and my husband."

"I see. It was a kindness. But it couldn't have been easy for you, with three small children of your own. They were probably a handful, no? Did you ever have to discipline them?" Morris asked gently.

She turned to him gratefully, as if he could be made to understand. "They were. They were terrible, undisciplined, wild, nothing like my own children. But we only used personal example, that of my husband, who is a cultured and supportive man who radiates light! For twenty-four hours a day, we gave these children love, hugs, kisses, as if they were our own. We hardly got any sleep! We spent every moment cooking, cleaning up after them, doing their laundry . . . me, my husband, and friends, who all worked together, joyously, harmoniously. Here we believe in a loving way."

Her speech patterns were stilted, the words unnatural, stiff, something learned by rote. This had nothing in common with normal human conversation, Bina thought.

"And what about Daniella Goodman? How do you feel about her?" Morris asked.

The woman hesitated, her flow of words suddenly backing up in her throat. After a few moments of silence she said "She was a very good friend of mine. I still love her. But she came too far into our lives."

"And her husband, Shlomie, was he also a good friend?"

She frowned. "From the moment he came into our house, I hated him. Those silly white robes. What was he trying to prove? It was a Purim costume. Truly devout people don't have to wear silly outfits. He came as a friend and a student, and my husband, who really is a saint, tried to help him and his wife save their marriage. And now look, they've brought a holocaust down on us!"

"Can you tell us about Kuni Batlan, Shmaya Hod, Yissaschar Goldschmidt?"

The baby began to howl once more. "I . . . first, my baby. It needs to eat. I'm nursing."

"That's fine. We don't mind," Bina told her. "Look, just put a diaper over your shoulder and you can nurse with the utmost modesty."

The woman blushed scarlet. "I will do it in privacy." She went off, closing the door behind her.

Bina walked up the stairs. There were four bedrooms. Two of the bedrooms had two sets of bunk beds with a roll-out. In the third there were two twin beds and a crib, and in the fourth, a single bed. There were only two tiny bathrooms, that's all, for ten children, their mother and father, and another married couple, Bina thought. Why would Daniella Goodman agree to leave her beautiful, spacious home in the Old City and move herself and her children in here, with these people? Even if she'd divorced her husband, why not stay put? What, exactly, had happened to push her to make such a radical, irrational decision? And how could Ruth Shem Tov have accepted such an arrangement? It made no sense.

In the room with the crib, there were a number of suitcases scattered across the floor. She peered inside them. There was a dark, blackish-red stain. Blood? she wondered, taking out her evidence kit and taking a swab. Downstairs, she found a small, dark closet just under the staircase.

"Bina, come here, quick," Morris called. "Look at these."

He pointed to ten bound notebooks filled with cramped Hebrew writing. "You are not going to believe what's in them. Here, read this," he pointed to a page.

Question: In the matter of Rabbi Shem Tov's feelings towards Daniella and the matter of Shlomie passing away—is this supposed to happen the way it came to my rabbi and teacher in his thoughts, that Shlomie will give a bill of divorce and go to a distant place where he will commit suicide?

Answer: There is truth in this.

Question: Is there rejoicing in heaven about the way the matter is progressing between Rabbi Shem Tov and Daniella?

Answer: There is great rejoicing in heaven.

Question: What does the Rabbi's wife feel about the matter of Daniella?

Answer: She has her suspicions.

Question: Should the Rabbi and teacher get married to Daniella?

Answer: Yes.

Question: And what about her husband, Shlomie?

Answer: He will pass from the world.

Ruth Shem Tov walked back into the room, the baby on her shoulder. Bina snapped the notebook shut. She studied the woman. She had a sweet, young face, but frozen somehow, as if she were one of those princesses in fairy stories suffering under an evil spell.

"Rebbetzin, I'll ask you again: Where is your husband?" Morris asked, this time like the bad cop. His face had also transformed from its usual mild paternalism to something stern and almost frightening, which was not to be trifled with. Bina watched him, amazed.

"I don't know. . . . I can't be sure," Ruth answered slowly, with complacent self-confidence.

Bina exploded. "We know all about what you and your husband and your friends did to those helpless children! How they were tortured, beaten, starved, burnt. Menchie is in a coma. You are going to be held as an accessory in attempted murder! Your children will lose both their parents!"

"You know all about what happened? Who told you? Menchie? The baby told you?" she mocked, turning away from Morris and looking derisively into Bina's face. She turned back to Morris. "Yes, my husband is gone. He knew they would make up lies about him, those possessed devils! You can't believe the words of those children! They are evil! Liars! I know them much better than you! I lived with them for months! But, thank God, you're too late. You'll never find my saintly husband!" Her look was triumphant.

Morris dialed furiously. "Get Border Control at Ben-Gurion. Check to see if a Menachem Shem Tov has left the country in the past few days. Don't let him through!"

A few minutes later, his phone rang. He listened briefly then hung up. "It's too late. He's gone."

24

Their lives were good, so very good. They had a beautiful house in the Old City and no money worries. Shlomie spent all his time learning Torah, or so he said. She never questioned him on exactly what that meant, content that he had found something useful to do that kept him happy. She knew that he was learning with Menachem Shem Tov, first at his yeshiva near the shuk, and then when that mysteriously shut down, at Shem Tov's home in Beit Shemesh.

Shlomie was more than content. He was thrilled to have been admitted to his holy teacher's inner circle, feeling immensely flattered and uplifted when he was invited along to the group's raucous prayer sessions in dark forests at midnight, visits to saints' graves in Meron and Safed, and intimate sessions around Shem Tov's own table, where their holy teacher shared stories of his latest miraculous exploits, which his Hassidim confirmed, swearing they had witnessed these things with their own eyes. And when Shem Tov remarked that government bureaucrats had sinfully shut off his funding, Shlomie happily wrote him a monthly check to help further his holy teachings, never asking what he did with the money. It was tithe money, a tenth of their income, which all came from the interest that accumulated on his wife's inheritance less what they had paid for the house. They still had plenty left over, he told himself.

Daniella didn't mind that Shlomie tithed their income even though he wasn't working. Tithe money was considered the extra amount God gave you, so it never actually belonged to you anyway. You had to donate it to a worthy cause. But once she actually did say to Shlomie, "Shouldn't we spread our charity money around, not just give it all to one person?"

To which Shlomie replied, "We give it where it will do the most good. To support a tzadik increases peace in the world," he assured her.

She was pregnant again. Toward the late months of her sixth pregnancy, when she was feeling especially weary and heavy, Daniella began to begrudge the amount of time Shlomie was spending away from home. "You always used to at least help me with getting them to bed and with the shopping. Now you don't do anything! Do you know what it's like to lean over a bathtub with a pregnant belly and give children a bath one after the other? The children are forgetting they have a father."

"Reb Shem Tov says that in a truly pious household, there is a division of labor. The man learns and the woman cares for her household. A man has more important things to do than soaping down a washcloth or picking out tomatoes in the shuk," he told her loftily in his newfound voice of religious authority.

What could she answer without sounding like a woman who had lost her moral strength and betrayed her core values? Besides, this was what everyone in their new circle of friends believed, so who was she to question it? But as much as she tried to find joy in doing God's will and solace in lofty spiritual thoughts, little by little the tiny drops of bitterness and resentment against her husband seeped through all her defenses.

The baby was born around Passover. Shlomie was overjoyed with his new son, wanting to name him Menachem. But Daniella put her foot down. It was the first child born since her grandmother had passed away, and she wanted the child named for her. She was surprised that usually mild mannered Shlomie was adamant. She was even more profoundly surprised when she found herself fighting back viciously.

"Who has done more for you—and for your Reb Menachem, for that matter—than my granny? You are both leeching off her money. Off *my* money. I'm giving my son a name, and if I were you, I wouldn't fight me on this one, Shlomie! You're not as indispensable as you like to think."

He was shocked, chagrined, insulted. But he shut up about the name.

In the end, they called the baby Eliahu—the closest they could find to Elizabeth. Everyone marveled at how much the baby looked like his father. "Just like Yitzchak looked exactly like Abraham, so no one could doubt he was his son, even after Sarah had been forced to live with Abimelech," people would say, shaking their heads at the amazing likeness.

Shem Tov, on whom they bestowed the honor of acting as the baby's *sandak*, was also struck by the striking resemblance between the baby and Shlomie. And in his heart, an irrational hatred for the child was planted.

"Now he's offended," Shlomie hissed to Daniella, shrinking under Shem Tov's cold stare as they announced the baby's name.

She shrugged. "I'm sure he'll get over it in time for you to give him his next big check, Shlomie," she said dryly.

For all the lovely catering, it was a rather sad event, she thought. Joel and Esther had just had a baby, so they couldn't come. Her father had called at the last minute with regrets to say he had the flu and couldn't make it either. Daniella suspected it wasn't so much his health that was doing poorly as it was his finances. He, and especially his grasping new wife, didn't want to spend the money on airfare and a hotel room. As for Shlomie's parents, they once again begged off. The only time they'd visited their grandchildren in Israel was when Shoshana was born. She couldn't really blame them. Shlomie never called them, didn't remember birthdays or anniversaries. They bored him. As for her mother, they were still not on speaking terms.

She felt sad that she couldn't invite Essie and Yochanon and all their other good friends. All communication with people from Yahalom had ceased after their stealthy departure. As she looked around, she realized that the only people they associated with now were somehow connected to Shem Tov and his yeshiva. She didn't have a single friend of her own.

Not that she had much time for friends. Having six children did not change Shlomie's habits. Despite numerous promises, he was still never home. Daniella's bitterness turned toxic. They often had shouting matches so loud it frightened the children. But she didn't care anymore; she just couldn't cope. The venomous things that were said in these fights over ordinary, everyday disagreements turned so shockingly ugly that even Shlomie began to worry enough to seek marital advice.

Shem Tov listened carefully, his eyes narrowing as he looked over Shlomie Goodman, a man with a beautiful wife, a beautiful home, and no money worries. Impulsively and without calculation, he simply said the first thing that came into his head: "What's wrong with you? Why don't you just stay home in the evenings and help your wife with the children?"

Shlomie was taken aback. He hadn't expected such an answer. He'd expected Shem Tov to side with him, to encourage him to continue dedicating himself to study and prayer. Could such a simple solution really be the answer? he wondered. But like everything else Rav Menachem told him, he felt bound to follow it to the letter, as if it had come from God Himself.

Daniella was at first skeptical, then pleasantly surprised as Shlomie steadfastly stayed home night after night to help her with the children and the house. He bathed them, helped them with their homework, even folded laundry!

And so began a new period of calm in their marriage. The hard feelings she harbored for Shem Tov turned to gratitude when she realized it was his mentoring that had turned her husband around and saved their marriage, allowing her to recall the other wonderful things that he had done for her and her family. "We were right to make him our rebbe," she told Shlomie one night, to his delight. The reconciliation soon led to another pregnancy. Both of them reveled in their newfound happiness, considering it a reward from God at their efforts at achieving domestic harmony.

Finally, they had achieved all their goals, Daniella and Shlomie thought, rejoicing. They had found their way to the pinnacle of holiness in the holiest city on earth, the dream of every true believer in the God of Abraham. Not only that, they had also been blessed to have found a mentor who would lead them through whatever difficulties and hard decisions they would face for the rest of their days! He would make sure they never strayed off the righteous path, that they never took a wrong turn or faltered, earning punishments. They, unlike most people, would have someone holding their hands who had direct access to the glorious ways of the Divine. He would ensure that their children had the best education possible so that they, too, could live the holiest and most blessed life possible on earth.

Soon, Menachem Shem Tov and his Hassidim were spending two or three evenings a week in the Goodman home, welcome guests of their grateful and generous hosts. Shem Tov had never been in such a luxurious home. While some of his followers, like Kuni Batlan, also came from well-to-do families, no one he knew had this kind of money. Often, he would pick up crystal bowls, turning them over to see how they refracted the light, or run his fingers over engraved silver goblets and delicate silver place settings. But before long he turned his attention to the mistress of this wondrous abode, the source of all its wealth and ease.

Although she was in her thirties, three years older than him, Shem Tov found Daniella Goodman slim, pretty, and young-looking. She wore expensive, handmade blond wigs, artful makeup, and modest but expensive and fashionable dresses in jewel colors, which made her seem positively glamorous. He couldn't help comparing her to his own frumpy, overweight, prematurely matronly wife.

Once Ruth Shem Tov, too, had been a lively, pretty girl, a child of parents with considerable means. But early on in their marriage, he had forbidden her to wear makeup or to cover her hair with anything other than a simple scarf. He also saw to it that her dresses were from the proper stores in Meah Shearim and that she didn't spend too much on them.

Truthfully, they didn't have much to spend. Before he was thrown out of the building near the shuk, Menachem Shem Tov's main income had consisted solely of the amounts he got fraudulently from the Ministry of Religious Affairs for padding the enrollment lists at his more or less fictional kollel. Now, he was reduced to managing on the amounts he collected from followers like Shlomie and various other believers as payment for advice or handwritten amulets and blessings. This was sometimes supplemented by money his wife's mother secretly sent them behind her husband's back, which Menachem pretended not to know about, continuing to forbid his wife any contact with her family.

Sometimes, when Shem Tov looked at Ruth, he felt the bile rise up his throat. He felt resentful that he had married a girl from a rich family and yet had been deprived of his due, unlike other, lesser scholars who had all their needs met by their wealthy fathers-in-law. Had this not been promised him? But her father had betrayed his word. For this, it was only right that she suffer. Still, the fact that she looked like the wife of some poor pious drudge, not that of an exalted rebbe and wonder worker, embarrassed him. There were even times he admitted to himself that he had married beneath him, never considering that he might have had something to do with the fact that his pretty, stylish bride no longer dressed attractively and had ballooned from secretly eating sweets, her only respite from her husband's total control.

Fat, slovenly, and browbeaten into submission, Ruth no longer interested him. He needed a woman on his own level, a beautiful, pure, intelligent woman he could mold anew.

Thus, sometimes in the middle of a lecture on purity, holiness, and godliness, Shem Tov secretly raised his eyes, seeking out Daniella Goodman. She sat in the kitchen, her eyes lowered modestly, a rosy touch to her creamy, perfect skin. Why would a woman like that want an idiot like Shlomie for a husband? he often thought, reflecting on the unfairness of life as he looked at Shlomie, his devoted disciple, the man who stood between him and all that was out there, almost within his grasp.

The baby was born in the spring, twelve months after Eliahu, an easy birth and a healthy little boy. This time, there was no argument. They both gratefully agreed to name him Menachem.

Daniella wanted so much for Joel to be at the brit. "Please come, Joel. I want you to be sandak! I miss you so much! I want you to see my home, my children. It's been so long!"

This time, to her happiness, he agreed to come and bring his family.

The brit was held in their home. Menachem was such a dear baby, with beautiful pink skin and lovely blond curls. Everyone commented on his beauty.

"He already looks like a mensch," the *mohel* agreed.

Shlomie and Daniella smiled at each other. "Our little Menchie," Shlomie said.

"I'd like Joel to be sandak. I promised him."

Shlomie turned red. "It would be a terrible insult to Reb Shem Tov!"

"But he was already sandak to Eli!"

"As long as he is here, we can't possibly honor anyone else above him." His voice softened. "Please, Daniella, after everything the Messiah has done for our family . . . I'll talk to your brother."

She shrugged helplessly.

Shlomie approached Joel.

"Is that really you?" Joel asked him, looking over the getup, the long, untrimmed beard, the wild payot.

Shlomie smiled at him kindly, not thinking the worse of him. He understood. An eagle flying high above instills awe in everyone who beholds it. He had become that eagle. He quietly explained the situation to Joel, who had no choice but to graciously give up the honor he had not asked for but had been gratified to receive. But the slight hurt him deeply. The rebbe—if he had *any* kindness or wisdom at all— should have understood this and insisted that the child's uncle take precedence over himself, he thought, looking over Menachem Shem Tov with greater scrutiny.

Arrogantly, Shem Tov took his place at the front of the room, holding the baby in his lap with careless ease. Daniella and Shlomie were thrilled as they watched him lay his holy hands on the baby's delicate little head, using all his magical powers, his knowledge and wisdom, to call down the blessings of angels, which would ensure their child a safe and happy future.

Later, Joel approached his sister privately.

"Daniella, what is going on here?" Joel cornered her.

"What do you mean?" she countered, immediately defensive.

"Has your husband gone completely mad? He dresses like a bag lady and behaves like one of those street-corner prophets they put into insane asylums when they become annoying enough. He doesn't work. And as far as I can see, he doesn't do anything to help you either. He's never with his children. Why do you put up with it?"

"Look, Joel, if he was getting his Ph.D. and I was supporting him and he was working hard on his thesis, you wouldn't have a word to say against him! But because he is learning Torah and has elevated himself spiritually, you criticize. We have other values. You know that," Daniella argued, trying to banish her own misgivings, recognizing the truth in his words.

"People who study for a Ph.D. eventually graduate," he said dryly. "How long can you go on this way? It's insane." Esther put her hand on Joel's, restraining him.

"Look, Daniella, all Joel means is that things seem so changed now," she said gently, affectionately linking her arm through Daniella's. "The children look so different. Those long payot. And the girls, such haredi-looking dresses. Like Beit Yaakov girls." She laughed. "We're surprised, that's all. We're concerned for you and for them. Is . . . everything all right?"

Daniella abruptly removed her arm. "What are you trying to say, Esther? That we've become too God-fearing? Too religious?"

"I didn't mean to . . . All I was saying is that since the last time I was here, the children seem so, I don't know, unlike themselves."

Joel came to his wife's aid. "I noticed that, too."

Daniella ignored the larger question, focusing on the details. "They are going to schools in which all the children dress like that."

"I wanted to speak to you about that also. I was talking to Duvie about what level he was up to in English, and he said his school doesn't teach English. That they don't even teach Hebrew. They learn in Yiddish. Yiddish! What's that all about, Daniella?"

"These are the best schools for *our* children. Our rebbe picked them out personally for each of them. We are very lucky to have his guidance and blessing."

Joel shook his head. "Where are your friends, Daniella?"

She looked startled. "Since we moved, we're not in touch."

"But your new friends from *this* neighborhood?"

"I don't have much time for socializing."

"I don't see a single woman here, except for Shem Tov's wife and Esther. What is happening to you, Daniella? Why so isolated?"

Was this true? she wondered, but she answered him resentfully: "Why are you trying to make me feel bad on such a happy day?"

"I'm just worried, that's all."

"I'll tell you what you are. You are both jealous! Because I am living the better life, the holier life, and you are just going on day by day, typical Orthodox Americans who are more American than Orthodox. Worrying about your next cruise to the Bahamas," she replied cruelly, without even knowing why. It was as if after begging him to come, all she wanted now was to push him away. She couldn't stand seeing her life through his eyes.

Their words cut viciously into her newfound confidence and pleasure in her life. It was true she had no friends, but she didn't need them! She had her children, her husband, and Reb Menachem and his Hassidim. As for the children's schools, their new way of dress . . .

She was part of something special, holy, and good. Joel, with his corrupted values, would never understand that. She was sorry she ever invited him. She would have to distance herself from her family, from their discouragement and bad advice.

Joel and Esther cut their trip short, leaving a day after the brit. He left Daniella a short message on her voice mail: "I don't know what has happened to you but it scares me. I am always there for you, sister. Be careful of your new friends."

She never called him back, and didn't say good-bye.

25

They discovered to their chagrin that Menachem Shem Tov had fled the country two days after the children were brought into the hospital. He could be anywhere by now, Bina thought in despair. Through Interpol, they found out he had entered Canada but had left again two weeks later. He was now in Namibia.

"We'll extradite."

"There is no extradition treaty between Israel and Namibia. That's why he's there."

"But why would they shelter a monstrous child abuser?"

"Exactly. That's why we have to build an airtight case against him, Bina, no?" Morris pointed out.

"We have the notebooks. . . ."

He shook his head. "It's not enough. We need the testimonies of the victims, with corroborating evidence from the mother and his accomplices."

"We need the children to talk?"

He nodded, then shrugged. "There is no way around it."

"Let's talk to Johnny. He's the best child investigator in the country. If he can't get to them, no one can."

Bina, Morris, and Johnny met at Beit Ticho, a quiet, garden spot in the center of town. Once home to the artist Anna Ticho, it was now a museum with a small restaurant, where many local authors gathered to write over a cup of coffee and a Danish.

Bina looked around at the blooming garden bathed in bright spring sunshine, her mind roaming back to the windy cold day in March when two horribly abused children had been brought into Hadassah Hospital. One was healing, and the other still lay in a coma. Her heart contracted as she thought of the little boy who would never again experience his childhood, run through a garden, smell the flowers. She breathed in the jasmine and roses, trying to clear her head and exhale the poison in her heart.

This case was tearing her life apart, she thought. Any idea of having another child had to be put on hold. "I can't even think of nurturing a new life with all this ugliness inside me," she insisted to her husband. It was not only the case that was on hold, but her life.

"Johnny, we have got to get all the children to talk."

He nodded, his long fingers pressed together, roof-like, touching his lips. "It's a catch-22. As long as he's out there and they think he can still harm them, they likely won't talk. And as long as they won't talk, he'll be out there. Also, as long as they think that their mother will be hurt by their testimony, they won't talk. As long as their eldest brother has power over them, they won't talk. We need to break down these barriers one by one."

"Where do we start?"

"I think we should separate Duvie from the rest of the kids when we bring them in to talk to them. I also think we have to come to some kind of plea deal with the mother," said Johnny.

"I don't see it. She's crazy, hypnotized. She'll never agree," Morris broke in morosely.

"I didn't say it would be easy. But you've got no choice. And it's important for the kids. Talk to her lawyer. Take her out of her holding cell and put her into Neve Tirza Prison. Give her a taste of what life will be like for her there. I heard she had problems with her three cellmates in Jerusalem. Let her try dealing with a hundred drug addicts and murderers and prostitutes who all despise child molesters. Tell her if she doesn't talk she'll be there for the rest of her life."

"She deserves it!" Bina murmured.

"I'm not so sure." Johnny shook his head. "From all the evidence, it seems to me that Shem Tov is a dangerous psychopath, a person born with no conscience. Such people are often gifted with intelligence, magnetism, seductiveness. If you read the history of cults, it's the more intelligent and sensitive people who fall prey; people who are educated, idealists. Add to that Daniella Goodman's loneliness and isolation, her exhaustion in taking care of seven children with a husband who is who-knows-where most of the time. I'm sure she felt shock and terror at Shem Tov's behavior, but by the time he revealed his true self to her, like most cult members, it was too late. She was in too deep," Johnny said gently.

"So she's never going to wake up?"

"I'm not saying that. What's hopeful is that it's been shown that even cult members don't really change at their core. What they've learned, been forced into, is like a shell over their basic beliefs and personality. Eventually, it's possible for them to break out and return to themselves. To see the truth."

"We don't have time to wait for her to 'hatch'; we don't have time for 'eventually,'" Morris said firmly. "Let's start with the kids, then talk to the older boy alone. What is Duvie, thirteen? He's a scared kid. Figure out a way to ease him into telling us the truth. I think it'll be easier than with the mother, who's got a shitload of guilt to flush out of her system before she can face the truth. Some people would rather delude themselves forever than actually look into a mirror."

26

Soon after Menchie was born, Shlomie gradually slipped back into his old ways and Daniella was finally forced to admit to herself her feelings toward him had changed. She no longer felt that he was her family, part of her life. Maybe even worse, she no longer admired or respected him. Bit by bit, whatever love or connection she had once felt for him had simply vanished.

This knowledge came to her in increments: the petty disappointments that he was not there when the children needed to be cared for; the disgust at how blithely and with such self-righteousness he gave away money he had done nothing to earn, and which did not in any way belong to him. Most of all, it was the aftereffect of those brief conversations she could manage with him about what he did all day.

"The Messiah says . . ." was the way he started every conversation, a look of stupid awe on his face as he grandly expounded on his latest newfound wisdom. "The Messiah says if you want to communicate with angels, you must leave your false humaneness behind. In the *Book of Enoch*, the first perfect human ascends to God without death. . . ."

Burdened with changing dirty diapers, trying to feed, clothe, and educate seven lively children, she hardly heard him anymore.

"The Messiah says that when you light candles Friday night, you bring the Divine Feminine aspect into the home," he droned on.

"Did you remember to buy diapers? We are very low," she interrupted him wearily, his supercilious singsong reminding her of loathsome Sunday-morning television Bible-thumpers.

"Oh, diapers," he repeated, momentarily distracted.

"Amalya, sweetie," she called out. "Can you please run down and get some diapers? Also, bring me some baby cream for Menchie's rash."

She turned away from her husband, lifting a heavy laundry basket full of clothes, noting that Shlomie made no move to help her. He probably doesn't even notice, she thought bitterly. She heard her granny whisper in her ear: *Luftmensch.*

She put the basket down in the living room near the couch, using her foot to push away a pile of scattered toys. Toys, bits of cookie crumbs, used tissues, and candy wrappers were everywhere. It was sickening. But as hard as she tried, she realized she just couldn't do more on her own. She'd simply have to wait for their housecleaner, who came twice a week. She'd ignored Shlomie's frequent suggestions to have her come in more often. With their astronomical expenses and the ridiculously low interest rate the banks were now paying on deposits, she had no choice. She sat down heavily on the couch and began to fold. Shlomie followed her.

"We're learning the book *Sefer HaBahir*, the 'Book of Brightness,' by Rabbi Yitzhak Saggi Nehor, who was called Isaac the Blind. He wrote about the mystical importance of light and color."

"Right, a book about light and color, from a blind man." She shook her head, matching up tiny socks.

He ignored her. "It's about the transmigration of souls from one human life to the next. Our actions decide to which life we will return. Kabbalah is a link between God and the universe and humanity. The Sefirot are the bridge. They emanate from God, suffuse life. The Messiah says—"

"Can you go out and get a pizza for dinner?" she asked him. "I just don't have the strength to cook."

He looked up at her, as if coming out of a trance.

"A pizza?"

"Yes. Actually, you'd better bring four. Duvie can eat half a pizza all by himself."

"Duvie?" His face suddenly changed color. "Actually, I have something to tell you about Duvie."

"Yes?" she said without looking up, continuing to fold.

"His rebbe called me yesterday."

She put down the undershirt in her hands. Now he had her attention. "Again?"

He nodded uncomfortably. "He complained Duvie isn't participating in the Talmud class. He isn't doing his homework."

"Weren't you supposed to talk to Duvie about his behavior?" she accused.

"I did!" He shifted uncomfortably from foot to foot, as if on the witness stand. "I explained to him the great *zchus* of being a Talmud scholar. But he says he's bored. That the teacher is boring and mean."

She sighed, leaning back. "Maybe he needs a new school?"

"No, no. The Messiah says he's in a very good school."

"Then you have to spend more time with him, Shlomie! Learn with him. Try to inspire him. He doesn't understand yet the importance of learning. He's still a child."

"In two and a half years, he'll be Bar Mitzvah, responsible for his own sins."

"Then isn't now the time for you to try harder with him? If you were only home more, instead of—"

"Whatever I do, I do for the good of our family—you know that! I do exactly what the Messiah tells me. He says I must link myself to the spirits of saints, to bring down their holiness into my life. And so I pray at their graves all over the Galilee, hoping for grace."

"Graves? You spend your time in graveyards?"

"You can't imagine the feeling that comes over me at the foot of a saint's grave! The feeling of Divine inspiration. It's as if I'm filled with sudden holiness and understanding. It's—"

"Shlomie, I didn't have these children by myself. I can't bring them up by myself. You have to be a full-time father."

He hung his head, chastened. "I will try harder," he promised.

But when he discussed it with Menachem Shem Tov, to his surprise, this time the Messiah shook his head emphatically. "You cannot be ruled by a woman or by a child. There are ten aspects of Divinity in man, the ten Sefirot. It is a roadmap to a genuinely balanced life. But it requires discipline to learn and to practice. Before you can help your children, you must help yourself. Like on an airplane, what do they tell you to do if the cabin pressure falls?"

His eyes lit up with sudden understanding. "To put on your own oxygen mask first before helping your children."

Shem Tov nodded sagely. "Exactly. How can you help your children if you yourself are dying from lack of oxygen? To visit the graves of saints is spiritual oxygen. It allows even the most ignorant fool to absorb the greatness of spirit, the divinity of these hallowed souls. By praying to them, you are rewarded by receiving some of their greatness. Only then, when you have absorbed enough, will you be able to lead your family. You must not do less; you must do more!"

"But, my wife, Daniella, she is unhappy. She complains I am never home as it is."

"Why was Adam expelled from Eden?"

"Because he was seduced by Eve."

He nodded. "And did listening to her advice bring either of them blessing?"

A great light suddenly exploded in Shlomie Goodman's mind. He shook his head eagerly. "No. Eve was also expelled from Eden! She had to bear children in agony!"

"Yes! And the rest of her curse was?" He looked at Shlomie expectantly.

" 'Her desire is to her husband and he shall rule over her,' " Shlomie quoted, ecstatic he actually knew the answer.

"Exactly. This is your lesson, what God is trying to teach you. You must ignore your wife's pleadings and go forward to earn you both blessing and not a curse. You must rule over her and yourself. Do not be weak. Do not give in."

Shlomie bowed. "My rebbe, Messiah, how can I ever thank you?" His lips trembled and his eyes were wet with tears.

"The evil and good that befall us every day are of our own making, not that of the indifferent universe. Choose wisely," Shem Tov admonished him, allowing his fingers to be kissed. When Shlomie had gone, he went to the bathroom and washed his hands three times with soap, scrubbing them with a nail brush. As he looked into the bathroom mirror, he saw in the depths of his own brown eyes a flicker of disgust, of contempt, and of satisfaction.

In the coming year, Shlomie often didn't come home at all, sleeping overnight in Meron near the grave of Rabbi Shimon Bar Yochai, who was attributed with the authorship of the Zohar, or in the forests as dawn broke after all-night prayer sessions. More and more, he felt distanced from his wife and children. But this could not be helped, he told himself. He thought of Moses and how he had also separated from his wife Zipporah and his children. That was the life of the saint or prophet, he told himself. A man rises in holiness when he removes himself from the petty burdens and strife of everyday life. This was his destiny.

He thought of Rabbi Akiva, the ignorant shepherd, son of a convert, who had married the wealthy heiress Rachel, whose father disinherited her for her choice. With Rachel's blessing and encouragement, Akiva abandoned her to poverty and loneliness and went off to learn Torah with her admonition—"Only return to me when you are a great scholar"—ringing in his ears.

He, too, would return to his wife and his family only when he became a great scholar. With the Messiah's encouragement, he chose to dress in accordance with his new status. Every day he would put on the flowing white robes he had worn for Menchie's brit, clothes of spotless white, without a single stain or blemish, to match the yearning of his soul to be purified.

When Duvie turned twelve, he was once again kicked out of his yeshiva. Given that this was the only yeshiva that had been willing to take him in, it placed Daniella and Shlomie in a very serious bind. But they couldn't very well argue with the principal, who had kindly taken Duvie in, based on assurances that the boy would turn himself around if given another chance. If anything, Duvie's behavior had taken a severe turn for the worse. Now he skipped classes altogether, spending afternoons in the center of town, where he would smoke cigarettes and eat pizza with other yeshiva dropouts.

Daniella had done her best to talk to him, to no avail. She begged Shlomie to take him in hand. But the child had no use for his father's advice, either.

"I never wanted to go to that stupid place. I'm not learning anything there. No English. Hardly any math, no history or social studies. All they want is for me to learn about five brothers who get married and one of them dies, and no one remembers who married whom. It's stupid. They're making me stupid."

With Duvie's problems, their own seemed to grow, the fights between them erupting at closer and closer intervals, spewing poisonous fumes over everything in their wake, destroying their domestic life. Soon, their problems with Duvie spread, virus-like, to their other children.

Amalya, always so quiet and docile, came to blows with Shoshana, who was constantly in her room destroying her precious doll collection. Yossi took to clinging to Daniella even more than usual, wanting her constant attention, getting up late every morning, and stashing secret supplies of chocolate under his bed. He gained so much weight that his pediatrician told her he was prediabetic. And if that was not enough, Gabriel began wetting the bed. Even Shoshana, Daniella's bright, pretty, chatterbox, seemed quieter, sadder, burdened somehow. Only the babies, Eli and Menchie, seemed oblivious. Daniella struggled on, refusing to admit defeat, until things came to a sudden head.

It was Purim, and Duvie and Yossi had disappeared. Daniella and Shlomie were on the verge of calling the police, when the two finally showed up, long after dark, their eyes red and glassy, their words slurred.

"Where have you been!" Daniella shouted at them.

They giggled.

They were drunk, she realized, appalled. A twelve-year-old and an eleven-year-old.

"You are supposed to drink until you don't know the difference between 'Blessed is Mordechai and cursed is Haman!'" Duvie protested.

"I don't know the difference," Yossi exclaimed, before running to the bathroom to throw up.

"Did you let your brother drink alcohol? Your little brother?" Daniella screamed at Duvie.

"All the boys were drinking!"

"Now, now, Daniella, it's the custom on Purim for people to drink wine and be merry," Shlomie soothed.

"Shut up! That is not the custom for us, for our children. They're still babies, for God's sake!"

Shlomie looked as if a pet dog had jumped up and bit him.

"And what's this?" she said, shaking cigarette ashes off Yossi's costume, a scarlet king's robe, as the boy came back into the room. "Were you smoking!"

He looked down defiantly.

She turned to Shlomie. "What do you expect! He has no father to teach him. Our children are fatherless!"

The children were stunned by this, cowering. While they were already used to hearing their parents fight, previously it had always taken place behind closed doors. This was an escalation. Even Eli and Menchie looked up, startled, beginning to cry. Amalya and Shoshana picked them up, carrying them into the bedroom. Gabriel, too, seemed overcome with grief. Duvie led him off, plying him with cookies, while Yossi sat uneasily by the table, finishing off a mountain of sweets.

"Really, Daniella!" Shlomie remonstrated, shocked.

"You are a big waste of time. A do-nothing. I can't stand the sight of you. Get out!" she shouted at her husband. "Get out of my life!"

"Please, we can talk about this—"

"Aba, Ima, don't!" Yossi cried.

But Daniella was beyond reasoning, frustration bursting through the artificial dams she'd hammered together through the years composed of piety, self-sacrifice, and shame at another failure. She heard the rankling echo of Joel's words: *Why do you put up with it?*

"Get out before I throw you out!"

Shlomie took his tallis, tefillin, and siddur off the chair and left. She locked the door behind him.

Of course, he headed straight to Beit Shemesh Heights, straight to the home of the Messiah. It was almost midnight when he arrived. He was pleased to see a light still shone in the window.

Kuni Batlan opened the door. Shlomie could smell the alcohol on his breath as he shouted, *"Ah freilichen Purim,"* clapping Shlomie on the shoulder so hard it hurt. Batlan was drunk, Shlomie realized as he followed him inside. There was no sign of Ruth Shem Tov or the children, but Shmaya Hod and Yissaschar Goldschmidt were there, their heads lolling to one side or another as they lifted glasses of arak and vodka to their wet lips while Shem Tov, the Messiah, sat in his accustomed place at the table's head, watching them in amusement and contempt.

I am also drunk, Shlomie realized, sliding into a chair barely a moment before his legs gave out beneath him. And I drove all the way here that way. He found this laughable. Although he hadn't dared agree with Duvie in front of Daniella, he thought Duvie was right: Purim was the time to get roaring drunk. It was a mitzvah.

The group welcomed Shlomie loudly and enthusiastically. Soon the noise elicited a child's cries that came floating down the steps leading to the upstairs bedrooms. Following Shem Tov's lead, everyone ignored it, feeling no need to lower their voices. Batlan poured Shlomie a tall glass of arak.

He waved it away. "She's kicked me out. My wife, Daniella, has kicked me out of my own house!" he wailed.

He thought he saw a flash of contempt and amusement flit across the Messiah's face. But it was just the drink, he assured himself. He could not be seeing straight. When he looked again, the Messiah was peering into his troubled, frightened eyes with compassion. "What shall we tell our friend here, eh?" Shem Tov said, turning to Batlan, Hod, and Goldschmidt.

"As it is written: 'A man's enemies are the women in his household,'" said Batlan.

Shlomie looked at him, dumbfounded. What could that possibly mean? Yet, all the others were smiling and nodding.

"'Better to dwell on the corner of the roof than with a quarrelsome woman,'" chimed in Hod.

"'A quarrelsome woman is like a miserable drizzle on a wet day,'" agreed Goldschmidt.

"'Why is she called woman? Because she is woe!'" Batlan laughed.

Shem Tov smashed his closed fist onto the table. "Silence!" he shouted, and they cowered in fright, their laughter gone. "Is that any way to treat our brother in his sorrow?" He turned to Shlomie, taking his shaking hands into his own. "Women are the source of everything; as it is written: 'Charm is deceitful and beauty is vain, but a God-fearing woman is to be praised.' And Daniella is surely a God-fearing woman. If she is angry at you, there must be a reason."

"She says I am never home. She cannot manage the children alone. She says Duvie will become a rebellious son because of me!"

Shem Tov searched thoughtfully through his beard. He put his arm around Shlomie. "My friend, you must placate your wife. Tell her you are sorry."

"He should apologize?" Batlan shouted indignantly.

" 'When Eve was made, so was Satan!' " Goldschmidt quoted, taking Batlan's side.

" 'Give me any ill but the heart's ill, any wickedness but woman's!' " put in Hod.

Shem Tov gave them a withering look and they immediately fell into silence. "Tell your wife you will now study at home."

"What!" Hod stood up.

"We will all go to Shlomie's home every day to study, so that there may be domestic bliss between him and his wife, which is the most important thing in the world. As it is written: 'So great is peace that God's name is Shalom, and all blessings are held within it.' "

"Rebbe, Rebbe, how can I ever thank you!" Shlomie cried, kneeling before him, kissing his hand with wet, sloppy kisses, overcome with joy.

"Do not thank me," Shem Tov replied, removing his hand as quickly as possible and wiping it off with a napkin. "Go, lay down on the couch, and return to your wife in the morning."

He did as he was told.

27

Daniella took him back without much argument after a sleepless night wondering what would become of her as a divorced woman, the ultimate scarlet letter of failure and disgrace in their community; wondering how she was going to manage a household of seven children on her own, even though she was basically doing that already. Still, on the rare occasions she did see him, Shlomie was someone to talk to, someone to listen to her. And the children adored him.

She tried to widen their circle of friends by inviting neighbors and synagogue acquaintances over for festive meals on Friday night and Sabbath afternoon. But she could see people were put off by Shlomie and intimidated by their fine china and beautiful crystal. She was not surprised when they didn't reciprocate.

Determined to break the cycle of her loneliness, Daniella hired babysitters so she could get out of the house, attend exercise classes, listen to lectures, go to women-only folk dancing sessions. But often she found herself too exhausted to enjoy these outings. By the time she helped the older children with their homework, finished cooking and serving dinner, and gave baths to the youngest, all she wanted was to crash into bed along with them. By ten, she was good for nothing more than crawling into bed with a magazine or a good book. Most of the time, she never actually got to read, her eyes drooping closed from exhaustion within moments of hitting the pillow.

The isolation wore on her. She was ambivalent about Shem Tov and his students setting up shop in their home every night. On the one hand, it meant she was sure to see Shlomie. But on the other, turning her home over to strangers felt like an intrusion, a lessening of their private space.

Night after night they trooped in, somber and pious, like people paying a shiva call. With a clear sense of entitlement, they commandeered her living and dining rooms, Shem Tov seating himself unapologetically at the head of their dining table in her husband's accustomed place. Often, it felt more like a home invasion than hosting invited guests. Still, she felt powerless to stop it. What could she do? Embarrass her husband by telling them they weren't welcome? Refuse outright to open her home to a Torah learning group, thus calling down unbridled scorn and condemnation on her head as an uncharitable woman? To step forward and say anything at all would be to brand herself as wanton, arrogant, and quarrelsome, the Talmud's classic definition of a worthless woman. To be devout and respectable, the only choice open to her was silence.

And so once again, as with Amos, she brought out her china cups and plates of homemade cakes, laying them silently on the table, responding to polite murmurs of thanks with a weak smile as she quickly and silently withdrew into the kitchen. There she sat, folding laundry, straining to catch bits and pieces of the men's learned discussions, trying to discover what it was that had transformed her familiar Shlomie into a stranger.

As she listened, she began to realize this was not the usual study of kabbalah, which sought to explain the nature of God and the universe through mystical connections and meditation.

"We must look beyond our senses, otherwise our growth is stunted; we are retarded spiritually from the greater spectrum of reality," Shem Tov told them. Then he suddenly lowered his voice almost to a whisper. They all leaned in, straining to hear: "There is a sixth sense, a wondrous ability locked inside us that helps us to be aware of the non-human creatures that live beside us, unseen but not unfelt."

Daniella shifted uncomfortably.

"Those of us whose minds have been allowed to expand beyond their spiritual straitjackets feel their presence strongly." He leaned forward, raising his voice. "I am talking about spirits—angels and their counterparts, demons. They are real and they can be spoken to, just as I am speaking to you."

Now she leaned back, unconsciously distancing herself from this information, her mouth falling open, her stomach queasy. She looked around to see if anyone else was uncomfortable, but all she saw were the rapt faces of true believers, drinking in the words like Coca-Cola.

"In our unenlightened states, most of us are mentally incapable of communicating with them. But only because we don't allow ourselves to experience this. We are terrified of this reality. But if you let go of your resistance, you will quickly understand there is more in the universe than our human brains can process. There is a truth that must be felt, not understood. Our brains can't know everything, but our souls can.

"People that allow themselves to do this rise to a level in which they can command angels to do their will! They can demonstrate powers that will fill others with awe and wonderment. Such people are called Masters of the Good Name. Our prophets, our sages, the Geonim of the Talmud, were all Masters of the Good Name."

Daniella sat back, her mind in turmoil. Could she accept this? Was this the logical next step in her spiritual growth, the expansion of her mind, which she'd begun with Amos? Was it possible to speak matter-of-factly about angels and demons and magical incantations? Or was it black magic and witchcraft, activities—if she remembered correctly from her yeshiva days—strictly forbidden by the Torah and even punishable by death?

One night after they'd gone, she confronted her husband. "What are you doing with this, Shlomie?"

He seemed confused. "What do you mean?"

"Doesn't God say in the Torah, Parshat Kedoshim: 'Don't turn to sorcerers or spirits to be defiled by them'? Isn't magic forbidden and aren't sorcerers condemned to death by stoning, along with those who consult them? This can't be right!"

He was shocked at the attack. "Are you calling the Messiah a sorcerer?"

Put this way, it startled her. She thought Shem Tov was a wonderful mentor, someone who had brought good into their lives, who had actually saved Amalya from terrible harm. But why did one need to put intermediaries, however pious and devout, between oneself and God? Wasn't that the essence of idol worship, the Golden Calf? "I sit in the kitchen night after night, listening to you talk. Magic amulets and magic incantations and calling on angels? You're not talking to God; you're talking to the devil."

"You are so confused, Daniella! So very wrong! What we do is the height of holiness. You are a woman, you just don't understand, you aren't on a level to understand, not yet."

"Don't give me that 'you're a woman' baloney," she spit out venomously. "I was in medical school while you were teaching campers how to dance the hora."

In the past, he would have been devastated and furious at such an attack. Instead, he felt a strange kind of superiority over her that had previously always eluded him. Her rich family, her excellent high school grades that had earned her early admission into a prestigious college, the fact that she had been a pre-med student, had always been there between them. But now, after four years with Shem Tov, he knew that none of that mattered. She was mired in the lower worlds, hopelessly ignorant.

The first chance he got, he told Shem Tov everything she'd said. The Messiah looked at him wordlessly, then looked away.

The next night before starting class, Shem Tov walked into the kitchen.

Daniella looked up, startled. He had never sought her out before. "Can I get you something, Rebbe?" she asked, blushing.

Shem Tov smiled deeply and intimately into her eyes, as if they were alone together in the universe, as if Shlomie didn't exist. She found herself unable to breathe, unable to turn away. He spoke softly, as if every word was a great secret addressed to her and her alone: "Your husband told me you had a conversation in which you expressed your unhappiness with him and with me."

She looked down, mortified. "It was a private conversation between husband and wife. He had no right to share it with anyone."

"Perhaps you are right. Perhaps he had no right. And perhaps if he was on a higher level, he would also have no need. He could have answered your questions and doubts himself. But we both know what level Shlomie is on."

It made her sick to hear him say this. Still, it was the truth. She would have respected him less for a comforting lie.

"Do you believe in God?" he asked suddenly.

"Of course."

He nodded approvingly. "Very good. Do you pray to God?"

"Of course, every day!"

"Excellent. Then it's the same thing."

"What do you mean?"

"When you are sick, do you go to a doctor?"

"Yes."

"Good. A doctor is God's servant, His messenger. There are physical messengers, like doctors, and spiritual messengers, like tzaddikim. When you say you don't understand why your husband needs a tzaddik to intervene between him and God, what you are saying is you don't believe in God's emissaries. You don't believe in Abraham, in Moses, in King David. It is a deep lack of belief that leads you to this. It's no less than idol worship."

She inhaled deeply, devastated.

"You say that you pray. But do you really? A person who truly prays, and is not just mouthing words, talking to his own selfishness, his own ego, feels the presence of godly messengers from higher worlds all around him." He suddenly stopped, looking piercingly into her eyes. "The real reason that you object to the idea of all these things is that deep down you reject God Himself."

She felt her heart sink, horrified. "*No*, no . . ."

He persisted, more forcefully. "The real reason that a person refuses to submit himself to the words of a tzaddik, to a person who is on a higher level than himself, is that he refuses to submit himself to God."

"All I . . . all I meant is that I talk to God myself. I don't need anyone in between us! I don't understand why Shlomie thinks he does."

He shook his head sadly. "Of course, it is better to talk to God yourself. But sometimes, a person doesn't feel able. They need help. Like Shlomie."

"I talk to God all the time," she insisted truthfully.

"Do you? And does He listen to you? Are you filled with His blessings? Do you have the life you really want?"

She fell silent, filled with the misery she now recognized as living a life she didn't want at all, a husband she had no real connection with, her troubled children. She had chosen the life of a mother, but she was failing. She thought of Duvie, his failures in school, his rebelliousness. Her children would grow into people without faith, without character, who would live miserable lives. She prayed so hard, all the time, but God didn't seem to be listening.

"I need help, too," she finally whispered.

"You can only get help if you agree to submit. You're a stubborn person, and that is why it is hard for you to submit yourself to God's will. You don't believe in God, not really, and this is the way it reveals itself. If you believed that God was involved in your life every minute of every day, in everything you do, you'd understand that every moment angels and tzaddikim are being sent to you by Him as the answers to your prayers. If only you would be willing to submit yourself to God the way you are willing to submit yourself to a doctor. Let Him heal you."

She looked up at him, touched by a sudden revelation. Perhaps he had been sent to her by God. Perhaps he was the answer to her prayers! "Please forgive me, Rebbe!"

He smiled sadly. "There is nothing to forgive. If practiced by the impure, those who are not holy enough to strip away the evil that surrounds magic, *it is* black magic and absolutely forbidden. Only the very few are allowed to delve deeper, special souls who have reached the highest level of wisdom and purity required to crack open the black shell and reach the purity within.

"You say you were never taught these things by your rabbis in yeshiva," Shem Tov continued. "Either it is because they did not know, or they understood that their students were too young to understand. The Talmud itself permits the use of the mystical names of God, the invocation of angels and demons. As the sainted Rav Moshe Isserles wrote, 'Such deeds might seem strange in appearance, but the Kabbalist only brings out the true, inner nature of things as God created them, to harness the infinite energies of the universe to better serve God.'" He looked deeply into her eyes. "Do you understand now, Mrs. Goodman?"

"Yes, Rebbe." She nodded gratefully, hardly having understood a single word, simply relieved he wasn't angry. "Please forgive me. And thank you for your patience and understanding. For trying to help our family."

He nodded, satisfied. "You are a pure, God-fearing, intelligent woman with deep spiritual values. I would be surprised if you did not question what you hear us saying in the next room! Of course these ideas must seem strange, as it does to all devout Jews before they are fully initiated into the secret knowledge."

She searched his eyes. They were those of a kindly father, the eyes of the wisest, best teacher you had ever had, the eyes of a rebbe who was the exemplar of benevolence and goodness, a living example of all that could be achieved by mortal man. But then, startlingly, and to her great shock, even as she looked, they began to change.

But it could not be!

She blushed violently at the profane thoughts going through her head, which disgusted her. She felt as if he were physically caressing her. She lowered her eyes in confusion.

"Please, Mrs. Goodman, join us at the table whenever you like. You are most welcome. And feel free to ask questions. He who is ashamed to ask can never learn," he added with avuncular politeness.

"Thank you," she whispered, afraid to look at him again, her stomach churning.

She did not take him up on his offer, remaining in the kitchen whenever classes were held in her home. But even from there she could feel the waves of energy aimed in her direction, emanating from Shem Tov, enveloping her in their spell. She found herself listening carefully, suddenly eager to be convinced. Who would not be? To learn techniques for acquiring the hidden power of the universe? To learn how to affect and influence the higher spheres, to bring them down to the world? She, who was so helpless, who couldn't control her own husband or her children?

From then on, it became a habit of Shem Tov to find his way into the kitchen to be alone with her during each study session. He came to ask for a glass of water, to wash his hands, or to compliment her on her home-baked cakes. And always, his eyes sought hers. She could feel herself shiver with excitement as she anticipated him stepping into the room.

"Rebbe, I have a question."

His eyes were brilliant, mesmerizing.

She felt her lungs empty of air. "Can a woman . . . I mean, would it be possible for a woman . . . to acquire and exercise this special knowledge?"

He moved as close to her as he could without touching her. "It is not meant for man or woman, this power. It is meant only for great

souls, and only those among them who prepare themselves properly."
He looked into her eyes meaningfully. "You, Mrs. Goodman, are such
a soul. A magnificent soul."

She felt her heart miss a beat.

"You do not believe me?" He wrinkled his brow, but his lips were
smiling. "What you could accomplish, with your natural abilities, why,
it would be higher than the Prophetess Devorah, who was the judge of
all Israel! If only . . ." He shook his head and bent down, as if a great
burden had landed on his shoulders.

"If only what, Honored Rebbe?" she asked timidly.

"If only you would not be so afraid of reaching your full potential
in this world. If only you had the courage to tear away the shells that
hide your inner light."

Daniella, mired down in dirty diapers, in cleaning the pin feathers
off of endless chickens, checking heaped-up towers of rice for bugs, suddenly felt a flicker of hope in her beaten-down soul. "How can I . . . I
mean, how does a person purify themselves, if they wanted to . . . if
they were interested in . . ."

"They need only attach themselves body and soul to a tzaddik who
is already at that level. They must never question, even if they don't fully
understand. They must be like Abraham when God tells him to sacrifice his beloved, only son. They must saddle up the donkey and ride
forward unquestioningly. Only then will they rise to the level necessary." He hesitated, his flow of words stopped. He seemed to be examining her carefully. Satisfied, he pressed on. "A person must pray
devoutly. Fill their minds and souls with holiness and abstain from all
sexual intercourse. . . ."

He saw her astonishment and bewilderment, but pressed on: "You
must have complete mastery over your body before you can complete
the mastery over your soul."

She looked down, staring at the floor, her eyes a bit wild.

"Nothing in life is trivial," he went on soothingly. "Everything has
meaning. The kabbalist seeks to create acts of perfect beauty in the
physical world, to crack open the shell and reveal the light within each

tiny object in the material world. Sex, too, has its evil shells. To crack open that shell and release the light takes great mastery. Everything in our world is a dream in the mind of God."

"A dream in the mind of God," she repeated, as if hypnotized by the words. And in a real sense, she was, her rational mind receding to leave room for this new information, which seemed more real than her daily life or her past understanding of life and the universe.

Her own life with all its suffering, then, was also just a dream. Shlomie was part of that dream, a part that no longer made sense. What had he to do with her, really? She must purify herself to be ready to gain this secret knowledge, those infinite, indescribable rewards. Only then would she be fit to nurture and educate the numerous little souls entrusted to her care by God; only then would she fulfill her obligations as a true mother. She wanted so much for their lives to be a good dream.

A few days later, Shem Tov suddenly called Shlomie over. It was 2 a.m. in the inky forest that surrounds Jerusalem. They had all been shouting in an ecstasy of prayer since midnight.

"I have had a great revelation," Shem Tov told him. "It was about you."

The idea of his sainted Messiah having a vision about him before the Celestial Throne was overwhelming. "Really, about me?" He was excited, happy as a child.

"Yes. You are to spend a month at the grave of Rabbi Nachman of Breslov in Uman and read the entire Book of Psalms a hundred times by his gravesite, saying each word out loud. If you do this faithfully, you will finally break through the barriers that are preventing you from reaching the Holy Light."

Shlomie was in ecstasy. Just the idea that he had traveled so far and that the goal that had eluded him for so long was just around the corner was earth-shattering. But then his mind was suddenly troubled. "Rebbe, isn't Uman in the Ukraine? What of my wife, my children?"

"What of them? You are doing this for them, are you not? The angels assure me that your wife will fully understand your absence, and when you return, all strife in your marriage will disappear. You will be like a bride and groom on your wedding day once more, full of the grace of God, your connection stronger and more loving than ever."

Shlomie's eyes shone with unshed tears. "That is all I wish for, Rebbe."

Ignoring Daniella's vociferous protests, warnings, and exhortations, Shlomie said only, "My dear wife, when I return our lives will be set right again. You must believe me." Then he shut the door behind him, running down the steps to a waiting taxi.

The day after Shlomie left, Gabriel came down with the chicken pox. While it seemed to be a mild case, it soon spread to Eli, Menchie, and Shoshana, who had the worst cases Daniella had ever seen. All four of them had high fevers, and the little ones even had spots on their tongues and the insides of their cheeks! It was a nightmare. She kept them in the bathtub more or less constantly, covering them with calamine lotion four and five times a day. Menchie, though, was already taking antibiotics for a very painful ear infection. The poor child was hysterical, keeping her up all night. In the morning, half-dead from fatigue, she realized the refrigerator was almost empty. But with Menchie in this state, it was impossible to leave him for a minute with the cleaning girl or a baby-sitter. There was nothing left for her to do but wait for Amalya to come home from school so she could send her out shopping.

Even on the days that the cleaning girl did come, the house was a wreck within an hour, the sick children spreading out their toys and games all over the place. It wasn't a time for discipline, Daniella told herself, just glad to keep them occupied. In the evening, everyone, sick and well, were on top of her head, all wanting attention, all crying for their father, whom they missed terribly. She did her best to comfort them, to keep to a routine, but it was impossible. The laundry piled up because she was playing cards with Shoshana instead of loading the machine. And when they were finally in bed and asleep, she had no strength to fold and iron and put away the clothes that were still in the dryer from the day before.

Yossi and Gabriel, who usually played Legos nicely, were terribly out of sorts, demolishing each other's creations after hours of painstaking work and catapulting the red, white, and blue bricks everywhere. The result was all-out war, the two of them brutalizing each other. Every time Daniella got up to intervene, or to take care of Menchie or Eli, she found Shoshana clinging to her legs hysterically.

Amalya, usually so well behaved, got into a screaming fit with Duvie: "Where have you been, you stinker! Ima is collapsing from tiredness and you are smoking with your friends in Zion Square and who knows what else," she shouted at him, whereupon he slammed her roughly against the wall and told her to mind her own business.

A clamor rose from their apartment, a cacophony of misery, Daniella thought, listening to her screaming, crying children, who were also unfed and unwashed. Mortified, Daniella shut the windows, ashamed the neighbors might hear. Then she sat down, immobilized by the task ahead of her. When she thought nothing could possibly get worse, there was a knock on the door.

Oh no! she thought. Could it be that Shem Tov was still going to show up, even if Shlomie was out of the country? Duvie opened the door, and sure enough, in walked Shem Tov and his Hassidim.

He looked around at the horrible mess, heard the screaming, fighting children, and turned to Hod, Goldschmidt, and Batlan, making a small gesture with his hand. Immediately, the three spread out through the house, picking up toys, sweeping and mopping. Shem Tov made a call, and soon the pizza delivery boy appeared with five boxes. Daniella didn't hear what they said to the children, but suddenly, there was absolute silence, except for the whimper of Menchie, who quieted down as soon as Hod placed him in her arms. Like robots, the children sat down around the table and ate their pizza, and when they were done, they picked up their plates and cups and took them into the kitchen, placing them in the sink. Without being told, Amalya loaded the dishwasher while Duvie helped Menchie and Eli with their baths. With Hod, Batlan, and Goldschmidt supervising, the children got into pajamas and brushed their teeth, climbing into bed without a murmur. Soon, there was quiet.

Daniella looked around at her spotless house, sighing with relief as she put Menchie into his crib.

"How old is he?" Shem Tov asked her, smiling at the baby.

"Almost two and a half." She smiled back. "And really old enough for a bed. We've just been so busy."

"I'll bring one for you tomorrow. The boys will take apart the crib and put it into your storage shed."

"Oh, I couldn't ask you or them . . . after all you've done, Rebbe."

"Do you ask God to make the sunrise? Are you embarrassed to ask Him to keep the world spinning? To keep your children well? We are all so needy. It is arrogant to think otherwise."

She began to cry, great heaving sobs of tragic pain that filled her with the sure knowledge that she could not go on with her life as it was. Not an instant, not a split second more. She did not see Shem Tov motion to Hod, Batlan, and Goldschmidt, who hurried out of the house, leaving him alone in the living room with Daniella Goodman.

He handed her a tissue.

She accepted it gratefully, their hands suddenly brushing across each other. She moved away quickly, as if she'd been burnt. "I'm sorry!"

"You have nothing to be sorry for."

"I know that the rebbe is a tzaddik and all you do, you do in purity. But my mind, it makes me see things, things I don't want to see. When you look at me . . ."

"What, what do you see? Tell me," he demanded, almost harshly.

She was stunned out of her reticence and embarrassment. "In your eyes. I see . . ." She choked.

"Tell me!" he demanded.

She covered her face with both hands, shaking.

Suddenly, his voice softened, becoming secretive, intimate. "Please, Daniella. Please tell me what it is you see in my eyes."

He had used her first name! She looked down at the tips of her shoes, shaking with emotion. "I see desire," she finally whispered.

"And what if you are not mistaken? What if that, too, is God's will?"

She looked up at him, pierced with uncertainty, shock, and shame. "Oh, how could it be?"

"And what if I told you that was God's plan for us? To unite our souls?"

She shook her head and turned away. "I am a married woman!"

"To whom are you married?"

"Shlomie," she answered in confusion.

"No. You are married to God. Shlomie is just a messenger. If he succeeds in bringing you closer to God, he is your rightful husband on earth. But if not . . . Who do you want more, Shlomie or God?"

"God," she said without hesitation.

"What is desire?" he said, his eyes hypnotic. "Desire is a spark that rises out of flames, a spark of holiness. You know that I am the only one who can succeed in bringing these sparks out of you. What is your desire? What is my desire? We both desire God, in purity and holiness. You must give in to God, and so must I. That's it. That's everything you need to know."

"Still, I think . . . Isn't it . . . ? It must be forbidden. . . ." Her voice trailed off uncertainly. She was suddenly not sure of anything anymore.

"What's forbidden?" He raised his voice demandingly, passionately.

"For you to betray your wife."

"How do I 'betray'?" he said angrily. "Have I touched you? We are speaking here only of feelings. Do you think it is forbidden to have feelings? Yes, I have a wife, but I am also a servant of the Lord Most High, and He has given me the task of doing tikkunim in His world. It is my task to fix what is broken in the world of the spirit. And sometimes, in order to make something that is broken whole again, I must penetrate deeply, go inside the shell. You can't see the hidden flame that is dying within you, but I can. So clearly. It is my task in the world, my duty, to bring those sparks within you to life again. And you, what do you see? Desire, jealousy, a married woman, adultery," he mocked. "Have we done anything together that is impure?" he challenged her.

She suddenly felt like a stupid child. Of course, they hadn't. He was talking of something else entirely, and she, with her impure mind and her defective, lowly character, had brought this lofty discussion down into the gutter, made it all ugly. She had simply misunderstood. She hung her head, ashamed.

"Do you know what I see when I look at you?" he suddenly asked.

She shook her head.

"Batsheva as she bathed on the rooftop."

Her blood ran hot, then cold. She shivered. No, she had not misunderstood.

"You must know, Daniella, your husband no longer loves you. Otherwise, why would he leave you alone so long? And I see in your soul that you no longer love him."

"Please, don't say such things. Don't condemn me to such a fate!"

"Your fate is in your own hands, Daniella. Tell me, am I mistaken?"

She looked at him, shivering in dread.

"When King David came upon Bathsheba, was she not a married woman? And was not he a married man?"

"Yes, and it was a terrible sin, and David was punished for it."

"No, he wasn't. Because it was God's will. When David married Bathsheba, she was already a widow. And a man can take more than one wife. Our holy forefathers did: Abraham and Jacob."

She looked down, still listening intently.

"And their union, was it not blessed? From Bathsheba was born King Solomon, the wisest leader the Jewish nation has ever known. And from that union, are we not told that the Messiah himself will be born?"

A lengthy silence descended on the room.

He broke it. "This is all God's will. It's not up to me or to you. Please don't resist what I am telling you! You feel trapped, but the door is open. God has heard your prayers and opened it for you, Daniella. And for me."

"Please . . . don't . . ."

"If for once you would give up your very rational mind, and you would agree to feel deeply, I would not need to say another word. You would no longer need proofs. You would experience a truth that is stronger than any argument. You would see what I see. You would reach the highest level of purity, higher than your husband could ever reach."

"But he tries so hard."

Shem Tov shrugged. "Some are born short and some tall. As much as they try, a short man can never reach height. He will die short. Why should you let this hold you back?"

And then he did something thrilling. He reached out and touched her, holding both her hands in his, then bringing them to his lips. He kissed her knuckles, his beard tickling her arm.

The effect was electric, all her senses shocked into paralysis, her mind numbed.

28

In preparation for the meeting with the children, Bina replayed the tapes of their previous encounters, trying to gain some insight. What she saw was not encouraging. They were uniformly and hopelessly hostile. Duvie, especially, had to be physically restrained from attacking the officers. They cried, they kicked, they threw loud tantrums. It was impossible to talk to them. And yet . . . She thought of the interview with Eli. What a charming little boy: smart, articulate, polite, and basically scared out of his wits. Children like this, she thought, had been raised by good parents. Parents who cared.

Then what had happened to them to produce this kind of bedlam? Whatever it was, she sensed, it had taken place over a short time and hopefully had not obliterated their core, producing instead a thick, hard carapace under which was still hidden their true personalities. If she could only find a way beneath, Bina felt sure, she would find a bright, soft center that was still intact.

What was the way to peel back their armor?

A sudden light came into her mind. Armor. Unwieldy, iron clothing worn to protect a soldier from harm. And when did a soldier take off his armor? Only when he was sure that the *war was over.*

But Shem Tov was still out there.

She called up Morris. "I have an idea."

"I'm ready to listen," he said, deeply frustrated, angry, and a bit hopeless. The clock was ticking away and no extradition papers had yet been filed. They needed a breakthrough, and they needed it now. He listened to what she had to say with interest. "We need to discuss this with Johnny." With Morris's encouragement, Bina outlined her plan to the child psychologist.

"Brilliant." He nodded.

Once more they gathered the children together, but this time without Duvie.

"We want our mommy," Shoshana, the seven-year-old, cried.

"I know, I know, sweetheart," Bina said gently, lifting her up in her arms. To her surprise, the child cuddled against her. She felt her heart melt.

"Shoshana, Gabriel, Yossi, Amalya, we know you all miss your mom—"

"And our dad!" Gabriel cried out.

"Yes, of course, your dad, too. And they miss you. We want to bring your parents to you as soon as we can."

"You locked up our mom and won't let her see us!" Yossi, the twelve-year-old, accused. He looked miserable and on the verge of tears.

"Yes, we will. But we need your help," Johnny said gently.

Their eyes were big and round and questioning.

"Duvie told us that you just want us to help you against our mom!" Amalya declared hostilely, her sweet face distorted with hatred.

Well, this is going just great, Morris thought.

"Duvie is mistaken. I'm a mom, too. I would never do that," Bina tried.

"How many children do you have?" Gabriel, the eleven-year-old, asked.

Bina took a deep breath, encouraged by the question's neutrality. "I have two. Ronnie, who's five, and Lilach, who's two."

"Do you play with them?" Shoshana asked suddenly, her small hand clutching Bina's shoulder.

"All the time."

"What kind of games?" Gabriel wanted to know.

"All kinds."

"Taki? Three Sticks?"

"Sure. I'm very good at Taki. Not so much at Three Sticks. I usually wind up falling down."

The younger children laughed, imagining her no doubt sprawled over the floor trying to jump over sticks.

"It's lovely you're laughing. You're very good children," she told them.

All of them suddenly went quiet, drinking in her words like milk.

"And I know you all want to help your mom. But if I was ever in trouble like your mom, I'd want my children to help the police."

"Why is our mom in trouble?" Yossi asked, surprised.

Did they really not know? Bina wondered. "Because you children got hurt, and it's a mom's job to see that doesn't happen."

"But it wasn't her fault! She never hit us," Gabriel shouted.

"Yes, our mom loves us!" Amalya declared, and all the children nodded.

"Just, sometimes, she didn't see, she went away . . . ," Shoshana said hesitantly.

"Didn't see what?" Johnny pressed.

"Don't talk, don't talk!" Amalya reminded her.

"We'll get punished!" Yossi agreed.

The children froze into silence.

"I know they hurt you, Shem Tov the Messiah, and Batlan, Goldschmidt, and Hod. They punished you. But you didn't deserve it. You didn't do anything bad. They were the bad ones," Bina told them.

A thaw came over their faces.

"Who told you?" Gabriel asked, astounded.

"Eli told us. He told us everything . . ."

"He wasn't supposed to!" Gabriel shouted. "He wasn't supposed to talk. Never allowed to tell!"

"We can't. Please don't make us. We'll get into a lot of trouble. You don't know what it's like!" Yossi begged.

"He'll get really mad," Shoshana said, her eyes filling with tears.

"Who, Shoshana?"

"The Messiah. Never allowed to tell. You get stuck in the suitcase. . . ."

"Shhh!" Amalya hissed. "Remember what Duvie said!"

The children went silent.

"What did Duvie say?" Bina probed gently.

"He said we will all have to live in Shem Tov's house again, like before, and if we talk he'll do more tikkunim!" Gabriel answered.

She saw the horror in the children's eyes, the slight thawing disappearing at once and a new ice age brought on by acute terror taking its place.

"But he can't hurt you anymore, the Messiah or his Hassidim," she told them flatly.

It took them a few moments to drink that in.

"Why not?" Yossi finally asked, unconvinced.

She looked at Johnny and Morris. They nodded. "Because they are all in jail!"

Gabriel seemed aghast; then his face broke out into a radiant smile. He looked at the others: "The Messiah is in jail!"

"And Kuni Batlan, Shmaya Hod, and Yissaschar Goldschmidt? Are they also in jail?" Yossi pressed.

"Yes. Every single one of them are in jail!" Morris told them. "And you have the key to keep them there. Just tell us the truth, tell us what happened. They are saying they didn't do anything to you . . . that they should be let out."

"That's a lie!" the children chorused fiercely. Suddenly and miraculously, a cacophony of childish voices competed with each other to supply the details the police so desperately needed.

"When we moved into Shem Tov's house, everything changed," Amalya began. "He said that we had 'demons' inside us and we needed tikkunim to get rid of them so we could be tzaddikim. At the beginning, he left Menchie alone. He was only a baby. But then Menchie hid our mother's car keys so she couldn't go out and leave us. That's when Shem Tov started looking at him differently. He started beating him. Punched his face with a fist."

"He told Batlan and Hod to do it, too!" Yossi added.

"He'd tie Menchie with chains," Gabriel said eagerly. "He'd tie him to the chair and tie his hands behind him so he couldn't move."

"And then Kuni and Shmaya would punch him in the face and hit him with sticks," Amalya continued. "They'd slap one cheek, sending his head flying in one direction, and then they'd slap the other cheek, and it would fly back. They'd do it again and again and again. . . ."

"They slapped him thousands of times until his face got all swollen and square," Shoshana said, bursting into tears.

"His eyes were almost swollen shut," said Yossi. "He could hardly see. You could just see his nose sticking out of his face."

"Then they'd make fun of him," Gabriel added, his voice full of righteous indignation. "They'd call him an 'ugly mongoloid.' Say he was retarded. They'd laugh. And when it was time for Menchie's *chalakah*—"

"That's when they're three and they get their hair cut for the first time," Bina whispered to Morris. "It's a celebration. A party for the child."

"—they took all of us to Meron to do it at the saint's grave. They made Menchie run at night through the streets. And then, on the way home, we stopped near a forest. It was very dark. They took Menchie out of the car and drove off. They hid in the forest and made noises just to scare him."

Bina closed her eyes, wondering how much more she could stand to hear. Morris nudged her. "Go on; you are doing great," she told them.

"Hod and Batlan would hold him by the shoulders and shake him so hard, his head swung back and forth like a rag doll's. A lot of the time, he'd faint, and they'd pour cold water on him to wake him up," Amalya said with passion.

"All day long, the Messiah would make Menchie stand by him and jump up and down, up and down, for hours," added Shoshana hoarsely, hiccuping.

"He'd tell Hod and Batlan to shove food into his mouth until he choked or threw up," Amalya continued.

"And don't forget to tell how they hit his fingers with the wooden kitchen hammer," Yossie added urgently.

Amalya nodded. "They'd hit his fingernails until finally they just fell off." She took a deep breath. "And once they shook him so hard they broke his arm and—"

"But they didn't even take him to a doctor!" Gabriel interjected passionately.

"They'd just put on an elastic bandage," Amalya confirmed bitterly. "They tied his arms behind him in the chair. He screamed and screamed for days until suddenly, he just stopped. After that, there was nothing they could do to make him scream," Amalya said, choking up. "Nothing. The same thing happened to Eli. After a while, he just seemed not to feel anymore."

Bina felt herself going faint. If only half of it were true! But as she looked into Amalya's innocent young face, she knew deep in her heart, it was all true. Where would an innocent, good Beit Yaakov girl like Amalya, and the others, even little Shoshana, be able to imagine such cruelty if they hadn't witnessed it? It was like the stories Holocaust survivors told about what had happened to them in the camps—acts so depraved only the sickest and most wicked of minds could have conceived of them, deeds so debased no decent person could imagine them.

But it was not without logic, she thought. In a very sick way, it all made sense. Shem Tov, the psychopath, was able to seduce and terrify the others so that they feared, believed, and worshiped him. But not Menchie. He was too little to be affected by any of the magic tricks and charisma that had so mesmerized the adults and older children.

With a toddler's simple, true vision, he saw right through Shem Tov. And Shem Tov couldn't stand that. With his impulsive, violent, psychopathic personality, he viewed Menchie, the three-year-old, as a threat, an adversary to be vanquished. And Eli's only crime was looking too much like his father, the inconvenient husband Shem Tov hated for his good fortune and his gullibility.

"Are you all right? Do you want to take a break?" Morris whispered to her.

She shook her head. They mustn't. Having broken the dam, they must soak up every last drop of the evidence flooding through that they'd waited so long to gather. Besides, if the children had the courage and strength to continue, she could do no less.

"Go on, kids. You are all doing great," Johnny encouraged them.

"Yes, your mom would be so proud of all of you," Bina agreed.

Amalya took a deep breath, continuing, "With Eli, Shem Tov appointed Goldschmidt to be responsible for him. Goldschmidt would just look at Shem Tov and he'd wink or nod his head, and Goldschmidt would start torturing him."

"What, exactly, did you see him do to Eli?"

"They made Eli stand in the corner for hours and hours with his face to the wall and his hands up."

"He was like a piece of furniture in the house," Gabriel said.

"And when he was standing there, sometimes Shem Tov and Goldschmidt would kick him until he fell on the floor," Yossi added. "Then they'd put him outside on the porch in the freezing cold rain and snow in his underpants. A lot of times, they'd force arak down his throat until he gagged or threw up. Sometimes . . ." He hesitated, looking significantly at Amalya, as if asking permission. She nodded. He took a deep breath. "They wouldn't let Eli go to the bathroom so he made in his pants. Every time that happened, they'd beat him, then wash him off in ice cold water."

"Hod made him eat the piss and doody," Gabriel blurted out.

The other children went silent, nodding in horror at the memory.

Bina saw Johnny blanch.

Amalya took Shoshana into her arms, kissing the little girl's lovely, bright curls. "They never let Eli eat. If the Messiah was in a good mood, he'd throw Eli some scraps from his plate. Once, he decided to do Eli a 'favor' and got Hod to force a lot of food into his mouth and pour arak down his throat. When he threw up, he told Goldschmidt to feed him his vomit."

The children were all nodding in agreement, looking at each other. They seemed strangely relieved, as if they, too, were throwing up poison and were glad to have it out of their systems.

Morris shifted in his seat, his hands gripped in fists.

Amalya looked around questioningly.

"Go on." Bina nodded to her encouragingly. "We are upset, but not at you, at how much you've all suffered. You were victims. You are all very brave."

"Once, I heard a noise in one of the suitcases underneath the play-pen in the children's room. I opened it, and I found Eli, tied up like a chicken, a kippah shoved inside his mouth. I wanted to take him out, but they wouldn't let me. The next day, I saw Eli walking with a limp," Amalya said, almost choking on the words.

"The Messiah hated Eli even more than Menchie!" Yossie declared. "He made the rest of us keep away from him."

Gabriel nodded. "He told us we should also hate him and called him Stinky."

"He even said a few times that in the end, he'd kill him," Amalya whispered, suddenly overcome. "I wanted to help Eli! I wanted to help Menchie, too, but they wouldn't let me!" She sobbed as if her heart would break.

Bina put her arms around the girl. "You are helping them both right now, this very minute, Amalya. Remember that."

"But you haven't told us what he did to you, Amalya," Johnny said gently. "Won't you tell us about yourself?"

Her pretty face drained of color. "It was nothing like he did to

Menchie and Eli. Sometimes, though, he'd hit my back with a whip. He said he liked the sound it made against me." She closed her lips, trembling.

There was more, Bina felt. Much more. A beautiful fourteen-year-old girl in that house among those beastly men. But she didn't press. Truthfully, she had heard all she could stand for one day. And it was certainly enough to issue an arrest warrant through Interpol to have Shem Tov extradited. But was it enough to get a conviction?

29

Detective Tzedek walked in through her front door, kicking off her shoes, then reaching for the remote. She just wanted there to be some normal voices in the room, something to drown out the incessant repetition of words and phrases going through her head along with unbearable, nightmarish images. She made herself a cup of hot green tea, sitting on the couch and staring at the screen without seeing or hearing anything.

This was taking over her life, she thought helplessly, spreading evil and darkness over all the good things she believed in: marriage, motherhood, faith. She picked up the phone and called her mother.

"I came home early. I'll pick up the kids today."

Both Ronnie and Lilach's kindergarten and nursery school were in walking distance of Bina's house, but it was her mother who usually picked them up, caring for them until Daniella got home from work.

"Hard day, honey?" her mother said with sympathy.

A child survivor of Auschwitz, her mother was one of the kindest people she knew. All that horror, all that evil, had just washed over her, never touching her essential being. Daniella often thought it strange that she, a second-generation survivor, probably felt more hatred for those responsible, people she would never forgive or forget. At a very young age, she told her mother that after the Holocaust every Jew needed a gun and to know how to use it. But her mother had simply smiled and shaken her head. "Not everyone," her mother disagreed. "That is why we have Jewish soldiers and Jewish policemen," she'd say. "Why we live in a Jewish country." It was one of the reasons Bina had gone straight from the army to the police, starting out as a policewoman and working her way up to detective.

"How can you tell how hard my day was, Mom?"

"You never come home early."

Bina smiled to herself as she hung up. No one knew her better than her mother. The bond between them was so strong, so intimate, so protective and caring. She'd never imagined the word "mother" could mean anything else, until now.

As she set out to fetch her children, she breathed deeply, exhaling her stress. It was a beautiful spring day in May, the smell of blooming jasmine and honeysuckle perfuming the streets of Talbiya. Once she retrieved her children, she walked along slowly, holding Ronnie by the hand and pushing Lilach in her stroller. Their childish voices rose and fell, tinkling with innocent laughter and incessant sweet chatter. They sang songs and told her stories about the pictures they had drawn and the new tunes they were learning for Shavuot, the harvest festival. Once home, they ate their usual pre-dinner snacks of fruit and cold chocolate milk. And when she bathed them that night, she took a long time drying off their childish bodies, unable to stop herself from kissing Lilach's little chubby wrists and ankles over and over again, until the child finally wiggled out of her grasp, begging her to stop.

She had been brought up to believe in God. To believe in people. To believe that evil didn't really exist, that it was simply an absence of good, the way darkness is an absence of light.

She couldn't believe that anymore.

Evil was real, a force in the world. The Holocaust had proven that. A million and a half children tortured and murdered by mass killers who considered themselves idealists, pioneers, visionaries of a new master race. It had happened in her own century, not in the Middle Ages, at a time when people went to the movies and spoke on the telephone.

And now, terrorists claiming loyalty to Allah slaughtered and kidnapped children in schools, used them as human shields to hide rocket launchers, sanctioned the sexual abuse of little girls by old men, calling it "marriage." The Internet was flooded with thousands of images of child pornography, each one a horrific murder of some innocent child's soul. And these images were uploaded by people all over the world of every race and religion. It was a war against children, and many of the people involved called themselves religious idealists or strict fundamentalists.

Of one thing she had no doubt: if you hurt a child, you could not be a God-fearing person of any religion, certainly not of the Jewish religion. She took out a Bible, flipping through the pages. There it was, the passage she'd been looking for, Leviticus 18, verse 21: *And you may not make any of your children go through the fire as an offering to Molech, and you may not put shame on the name of your God: I am the Lord.* And those who did were to be ostracized, condemned, stoned.

She tried to imagine the Jews of biblical times, people who had seen and heard God in the desert, laying their precious babies on the outstretched arms of a cruel stone statue, watching as the fire in its belly consumed their children. It had happened around the corner from her, in the Valley of Hinnom, where people now picnicked. What irresistible force was it that could make a person go against everything decent, everything human, allowing him to hurt a child, his own child?

Perhaps it was the other side of the same yearning that urged him to connect to love, goodness, and the Divine? The devil, whoever he was, needed that yearning, needed that idealism to produce the opposite. Perhaps even a Shem Tov must have once sincerely hungered to reach God, a longing that had taken a 180-degree turn to the opposite. Certainly Daniella and Shlomie Goodman had been pursuing goodness when they had been seduced to pursue the opposite.

She went to her computer and Googled the word "devil."

In kabbalah, he was called the Sitra Achra, literally, "the other side," the side opposed to the sacred and divine, the side of impurity and darkness. In Islam, he was Shaytan, the "whisperer," who speaks into the chests of men and women, urging them to commit sin. To Catholics he was the fallen angel, Lucifer, the great seducer, who destroys man's desire to be good out of envy. The Hindus actually consecrated temples to the worship of Kali, the all-devouring, who delights in destruction, perdition, and murder in any form.

Bina thought of the years stretching ahead and the never-ending war she was involved in, the infinite stream of criminals causing havoc in the world. Did she have the strength for it? And would the little she could do actually matter in the larger picture? It was like using a teaspoon to bail water out of a sinking ship.

Noah came in at eight.

"What's up? You look wasted!" he said cheerfully, kissing her cheek and sitting down next to her on the couch.

She leaned her head against his strong shoulder.

They had met in the army. He was a young corporal and she was assigned to Intelligence. She remembered the first time she'd seen him from afar, standing on a hill in the Golan peering through binoculars at a Hezbollah terrorist outpost. He looked so tall and manly, his back straight, his arms and face chiseled with strength and youth and determination, his knitted skullcap sloping at a jaunty angle. Before she even met him, she'd fallen in love with the firmness of his stance, his calm, business-like demeanor as he faced the unknown. There had been an attempted Hezbollah terrorist kidnapping just weeks before, two soldiers killed and a third wounded. The enemy was always there, always waiting for the slightest lapse in vigilance.

"I think I'm in the wrong business," she whispered.

"What's up?" he repeated, stroking her forehead.

"I'm just . . . I don't know anymore." She shook her head.

"Don't know what, honey?"

"This Shem Tov, the things he and his Hassidim did to those helpless kids while the mother stood by hypnotized and the father was off in Wonderland . . ."

"So, you'll put him and his cronies behind bars for a long, long time so they can't do it again." He shrugged. "And you'll teach the parents a lesson they won't forget."

"And then what? This Shem Tov will just be replaced by another Shem Tov. The parents by other brainwashed, naïvely religious morons. And the children . . . the children . . ." She felt herself suddenly sobbing. She buried her head in her husband's clean, warm shirt, listening to the steady beat of his reliable heart.

He stroked her head. "You remember that passage in the Torah? The one that has your name in it?"

"My name?" She took the tissue he handed her, blowing her nose. She was embarrassed. She never cried.

"Our name," he corrected himself. " '*Tzedek, tzedek tirdof,*' " he quoted.

" 'Pursue justice'?"

"Right. Did you ever wonder why the Torah doesn't say, 'Justice, justice, do it'? Why 'pursue it'?"

She shrugged, mystified.

"I'll tell you why. Because you can never really catch justice. You can run after it, but it will always be just beyond you. But that doesn't absolve us from trying. Bina, keep running after it. That is all God asks of us."

"But how can I bring another child into such a world? I feel my whole body has been tainted. My soul feels polluted."

He pulled her closer, squeezing her shoulder. "Then we'll wait. This, too, shall pass, my love. Consider it a war wound, shell shock. Take the time you need to heal."

She gathered him in her arms and held him to her, the incarnation of all that was good in the world, she thought, of all she loved and would fight to keep safe.

She thought about the coming meeting with Daniella Goodman. How, *how* was she going to break through to that soul so long encased in permafrost? On a whim, Bina went to the computer and searched for "mothers in cults." What she read astonished her, changing completely how she viewed not only the entire case but Daniella Goodman herself.

That night, when she lit the Sabbath candles, shutting her eyes as was customary before reciting the prayer ushering in the holy day of rest, she pressed her fingers against her eyelids a little harder than usual as she peered into the thick, heavy darkness. God, she prayed silently, may it be Your will that evil be wiped from the face of the earth. And in the meantime, please make me understand how to put Menachem Shem Tov and his accomplices behind bars for a very, very long time. Please, God, show me the way!

When she was done, a sudden image lit up in her brain. The image of Daniella Goodman.

That, she understood, was God's answer.

30

He was the president and the prime minister. He was Aaron the High Priest and Elijah the Prophet. He was Mick Jagger and Paul McCartney. He was an angel on a platform so high above the earth, she could barely see his outline. It was as if Moses had climbed down off Mount Sinai, the tablets of Law in his hands, and instead of talking to the wise elders, he had inexplicably pointed to some obscure woman in the throngs, choosing her alone out of the minions.

He was the Messiah. And he had chosen her.

Daniella's head swirled with amazement and incomprehension and joy and pride. *He* had chosen her!

How was it possible? She was nothing, no one. And yet, the miracle had happened. He could see things in her soul that she herself could not even imagine. Great things! He, the all-seeing, all-wise, closer to God than the angels themselves, had chosen her!

He loved her. He wanted her.

Oh, the miracle of it!

When Shlomie returned from the Ukraine, she hardly noticed him. Nothing changed. The Messiah and his boys had, more or less, moved into her home, helping her with the children. At Shem Tov's insistence, she no longer allowed Shlomie to sleep in her bed.

It took several weeks, but even Shlomie began to understand that things had permanently altered between them. Of course, he went to his rebbe for advice.

"What can I do to bring peace to my home? To return my dear wife to me?" he asked with real agony, torn apart with sorrow.

"You must give her a divorce immediately," Shem Tov told him, looking straight into his astonished eyes.

"But Rebbe . . . I love my wife. And you said . . . you told me, if I went away—"

"You asked me for my advice, right?" he replied with annoyance, cutting him short. "Your marriage needs a tikkun. If you divorce your wife and live apart for a while, this will repair your marriage. Afterwards, you will remarry and it will be as it was when you were a young couple."

Shlomie thought about this. To be again as newlyweds! It was the deepest desire of his heart to win Daniella back to him, the bride of his youth.

"Thank you, Messiah," he replied. "Thank you."

The divorce became final almost immediately. And as Daniella stood before three rabbinical judges and caught the bill of divorcement Shlomie threw at her (as was customary) she felt her heart leap up in joy.

Finally, she thought, an end and a new beginning. She could not have dreamed what was to come next.

31

Early Sunday morning, Detective Tzedek met with Daniella Goodman. While the warrant for Shem Tov had already been issued, she knew in her heart that Daniella's testimony was vital not only to ensure a conviction but, most important, to give this woman's children some peace. They were brokenhearted not only because of the horrors they'd experienced, but because their mother, whom they dearly loved, had betrayed them. For them to heal, she, as their mother, needed to confess her wrongs and ask their forgiveness.

They sat there silently, facing each other.

Bina began slowly. "Tell me, Daniella, what did it feel like to watch Menachem Shem Tov and his 'saints' starve Eli and beat him and lock him in a suitcase, make him eat his own vomit and feces?"

Daniella turned white. "How did you . . . who told you?"

"Who told us the name of your great 'messiah'? Would you be surprised to hear it was one of his 'tzaddikim,' who also blamed you for everything that happened to your children? Who said it was you who wanted them abused?"

She covered her ears with her hands, shaking back and forth.

"What did it feel like to watch your baby, your beautiful little Menchie, treated like a punching bag, beaten black and blue with fists and hammers, until his face swelled up like a balloon? To hear his cries when they broke his arm then tied it behind his back? Menchie, your baby, your little baby, who now lies in a coma because of what your 'friends,' your 'tzaddikim,' did to him just so he wouldn't talk and tell what had happened to him?"

Daniella rocked uncontrollably.

"I have to tell you, Daniella, I'm a mother. And yesterday I found myself kissing my little girl's chubby knees, her little fat arms so much she had to tell me to stop. How, how does anyone *deliberately allow a child to be hurt? Any* child, let alone their own? I must tell you the truth: Every time I've met with you, I've felt a sense of such disgust, such outrage. I thought: What kind of worthless, despicable person lets someone do this to her babies? But you know what? Once I got to know your children, I also thought this: What kind of person raised such lovely children, children so brave and resourceful and intelligent, and so loving and loyal they refused to say a word against her?"

At these words, Daniella suddenly looked up, a new light burning in her pale face, her eyes—for the first time Bina could remember—really alive.

"And so I decided to research this. I went to my computer and typed in 'mothers in cults.' One of the first articles I came across was on a Web site called International Cultic Studies Association. There I found an article written by Attorney Susan Landa called 'Children and Cults.'"

Daniella's eyes didn't leave Bina's face.

"Did you ever hear of Jim Jones? The cult leader, the mass murderer, who fed hundreds of his followers Kool-Aid laced with cyanide?"

She saw shock in Daniella's eyes as she slowly nodded.

"His cult was called the Peoples Temple. One little girl, no older than five, was restless in class, so he ordered her to be taken from her home at night and left a quarter of a mile away. They told her that snakes and monsters were waiting for her. They made her walk home, blindfolded. On the way, they snaked a slimy rope around her shoulders and made animal noises. Sound familiar?"

She saw Daniella's eyes drop down to her fidgeting fingers.

"One fourteen-year-old girl was kept for weeks in a plywood box with only two holes for air and a can for a toilet, while adults taunted her. A boy—whose 'crime' was that he took time out to rest at work and argued about the amount of fertilizer to add to the earth—had his teeth knocked out. Another boy was stretched by four adults, who pulled on his arms and legs until he was unconscious."

Daniella gripped the edge of her chair as if keeping herself from flying away.

"The children were also punished for their parents' behavior. If a couple was discovered talking privately, the children were forced to masturbate or have sex with someone they did not like in front of the entire congregation."

"Please . . . ," Daniella moaned.

"Your 'messiah' isn't special. He is one in a long, long list of cult leaders who decided to physically hurt children in order to 'teach them a lesson' or 'break their spirit.' There was a cult called the Garbage Eaters group who wrapped a piece of wire around a two-month-old baby's thigh and screwed it tighter every time he cried. Thank God, his grandparents were able to get custody. The wire was only discovered when his grandparents took him for a medical exam after they got custody. Doctors told them there were fresh scabs around the wire, which means the torture had continued until the very moment he was handed over to them, and that the wire had cut so deeply that skin had begun growing over it—"

Daniella jumped up: "Stop, I beg you!"

"Why, Daniella? What bothers you? Stories about other people's children? Doesn't what happened to your own children bother you? Enough to punish those responsible?"

She sat down.

"You think your 'messiah' is the only Jewish cult out there? *Cult*, Daniella—you hear what I'm saying? You were not involved with a holy man but a psychopath who hurt your children, not to make them holier, but to satisfy his own sick, narcissistic lust for power and domination. He couldn't have cared less what happened to you or your children. He didn't love you."

"You're wrong!"

"Psychopaths can't love. They can only exert their charm and will and power over people they select. You, Daniella, were selected. It wasn't random. They have a nose for sniffing out vulnerability, for finding people who are troubled and depressed, who've lost confidence in themselves. You were the perfect victim, Daniella. Can't you see that?"

She shook her head violently. "We were not a cult! We were close to God, we spoke to angels—"

"In the House of Judah cult, the children were beaten with cords, switches, branches, broom handles, and ax handles. They weren't allowed to cry when they were hit or saw their brother beaten to death. In the River of Life Tabernacle in Montana they beat a five-year-old boy to death with electrical cords and a stick. When the toddlers behaved the way toddlers behave—like your Menchie hiding your car keys so you wouldn't leave—they believed their child was *possessed by the devil*. If parents couldn't make their eighteen-to-thirty-six-month-old toddler 'behave,' they were told they were guilty of not submitting to God's will. Sound familiar, Daniella? And right here in Israel, in Jerusalem, there was the cult of Elior Chen, who tortured eight children, beating and starving them, while their mother watched."

Stunned, Daniella said nothing.

"And it's not just about your babies. Think about your older children, Amalya, Duvie, Yossi, Gabriel, and even Shoshana—think how they must have felt when they were forced to watch as Eli and Menchie were hit with hammers, starved, frightened, tortured. . . ."

Daniella covered her face. "Please," she begged. "No more. I can't . . ."

Bina pulled Daniella's hands away from her face. "Don't you understand? Your children feel responsible, especially Duvie and Amalya, because they were the oldest and they saw it all but weren't able to do anything to help!"

"God!" she cried out. "Help me!"

"That's exactly what *I'm* trying to do! Listen to me, Daniella. What I'm saying to you is that what happened to you has happened to many others. Your precious 'messiah' and his 'tzaddikim' were no different than those in many other cults, and what they did to your children has been done to other children in the name of many other crazy, psychopathic gurus. It had nothing to do with God, Judaism, kabbalah. These other cults were Christian, Mormon, atheists, and yet they believed the same things, did the same things. Your 'messiah' was not a saint; he was a criminal who tricked you, like your Reb Amos tricked you. Are you getting that! You and your husband were victims, Daniella. Victims. You were taken in, fooled, manipulated—"

"You don't know what you're talking about! You're a liar!"

Bina continued calmly, "Think, Daniella, think. Use your brain, your reason! I know you haven't done that in a long time. In these cults, they don't let you think. They make you believe anything outside the cult is dangerous and satanic, that your family outside the cult hates you and your only chance for salvation is inside the cult. They tell you that if you are even thinking of your child or another human being, with any kind of softness or tenderness, that it is going to lead to your destruction and to the child's destruction."

Daniella suddenly raised her eyes in wonderment. "That is exactly what I was told. Exactly that!"

"Of course you were, because you were a *cult* member, and you had a *cult* leader, not a holy man, a rebbe. Shem Tov's whole purpose was to get his victims' unquestioning loyalty and undivided devotion. He wanted *absolute control over the minds and bodies of his followers.*"

A sudden, radical change came over Daniella. She slipped to the floor, her body twisting into a fetal position. She moaned.

Bina thought over the last thing she'd said, wondering exactly what in her words had triggered this response. A sudden insight came to her.

"Is that what happened to you? Did Shem Tov take control of your body as well as your mind?"

There was a tiny, almost imperceptible nod, Daniella's face clenched in horror. For a long time, they sat in silence.

"After the divorce, Shlomie moved out. Shem Tov wouldn't let him come anywhere near me or the children, even to visit. He was crying when he said good-bye, and the children were hysterical. 'It is only temporary,' I heard him say to them, just like my father had said to me so many years ago. This triggered something inside me. I began to regret what I'd done, not so much for myself but for my children. But soon after, the Messiah came to me. 'Shmaya will watch the children,' he said. 'Come with me.'

"I was confused. I followed him out to the car. It was very cold and already pitch-black. I remember searching for the moon, but it had vanished. For some reason, this frightened me even more. Kuni Batlan and Yissaschar Goldschmidt were sitting in the backseat. I remember my body shaking as I got into the front seat next to the Messiah. He drove too fast, too fast! I thought for sure he would kill us all. The strange thing is I wasn't frightened of that. I was even hoping something might happen. Isn't that strange? When we got to the edge of the Ramot forest, he parked. Everyone got out. Without speaking, the Messiah walked into the woods—"

"Daniella, please. Stop using the word 'messiah.' He was a man, a psychopath named Menachem Shem Tov."

Daniella hugged herself without responding. "I remember standing there, cold, frightened. I didn't want to move. But then he, Shem Tov, turned around. I couldn't see his face. It was hidden in the shadows. 'Come,' he said to me. And I did. I followed him like a little child, followed his voice. I remember feeling sick, but also that I had no choice. I put one foot in front of the other and I walked into the pitch-black woods. The branches brushed my face, and the brambles scratched my legs. I was wearing my good Sabbath shoes, and the hard rocks and small stones cut into their thin soles.

"It was only the four of us. Someone held up a flashlight. I saw Shem Tov walk toward me." She stared at the wall, unseeing, her face a blank.

" 'The trees are our wedding canopy. These men are our witnesses,' he said. Then he took a wedding ring out of his pocket. I was amazed. I couldn't think anymore. I remember looking towards the headlights of the cars on the road to Tel Aviv. I imagined myself inside one of them, speeding far away. But then I looked up at the dark branches, heard them rustling in the cold wind, whispering, as if they were alive and wanted to tell me something. But I couldn't hear, couldn't understand. . . . Then I heard him say, 'You are consecrated to me according to the laws of Moses and Israel.' He tried to slip the ring on my finger, but it was too small. I felt him struggling, pushing it down hard, bruising my knuckle. I wanted to scream, to tell him to stop, that he was hurting me. But I didn't say anything." She shook her head helplessly. "I don't know why. And then, we got back into the car. He drove to the Ramada Renaissance Hotel at the entrance to Jerusalem, then handed the car keys over to Goldschmidt. We both got out and the car drove way.

"He took me inside. No one looked at us twice. Why should they? A Hassid and his wife. He signed the register, took the keys."

She trembled, hugging her knees to her chest.

"Do you want something to drink?" Bina offered her.

But she shook her head. "I can't stop. If I stop, I don't know if I'll ever be able . . ." She trembled. "I remember that I felt a sudden numbness in all my limbs. All I kept thinking was: Is this possible? To marry the Messiah? But he already has a wife! But I didn't ask, because I didn't need an answer. Jacob married Leah before he took Rachel. Abraham was married to Sarah when he took Hagar. King David was married to Michal when he took Abigail and Batsheva.

"We rode up an elevator. We didn't speak. He put the key in the door and opened it. Inside, it smelled of air fresheners and clean sheets. He did not turn on the lights." She rested her chin on her fists, looking into the far distance. " 'Take off your clothes,' he told me. I couldn't believe my ears. He said it again, this time more crudely. I felt shocked. But then I forced myself to believe that it was the same as if he'd said, 'Keep the Sabbath holy,' or 'Love thy brother as thyself.' It *was* the same; words spoken by a saint are always holy.

"I did as he asked. I stood there, naked, humiliated, waiting." She put her hands on her head. "He yanked off my wig. 'This, too,' he said. He ran his fingers roughly through my hair.

" 'Get into bed,' he told me. 'And wait.'

"I did. The sheets were cool and starched. I thought: Why am I here? I couldn't remember an answer. That's when I panicked. I thought about jumping up and running away, but my body, it was so heavy, as if my hands and legs were tied to some thousand-pound anchor that had been thrown overboard into a black sea." She looked up. "I just couldn't think of a way out anymore. So I lay there, waiting." She exhaled slowly. "I felt the bed suddenly tremble as he climbed in. His body was so strange, so different from my husband's. And the way he touched me . . . Shlomie was always so gentle. But he was like a machine, almost inhuman. Everything he did was hard, hurtful, shameful. I felt him turning me this way and that, like a piece of wood, as if I wasn't human."

She stopped talking. The two women sat in silence.

"He did things, unthinkable, shameful things, things I never knew could be done to a woman. 'Please,' I finally begged him. 'Please, stop—it's wrong!' He looked up for a second. 'A man can do anything he wants to his wife,' he said. 'Shut up.'

"I was stunned. I had never heard him speak that way, not to me or to anyone. After that, he seemed possessed. I gagged. I ached. It felt, I felt . . . raped. My soul felt murdered."

She wept, choking on a grief that poured out of her like a river overflowing its banks.

"Maybe . . . it's enough?" Bina said gently, handing her a tissue. Daniella used it, shaking her head vociferously. "No. I want to . . . I have to . . ." She composed herself. "Just when I thought, 'I have to scream or die,' the bed suddenly lightened. I was afraid to call his name. Afraid he would come back. He didn't. He was gone.

"And I thought: Please, God, let it all have been a dream. Let none of it have happened. But in the morning when I lifted the sheets, I breathed in what had happened between them." She pounded her knees with her fists. "I was . . . so ashamed. So humiliated. But instead of wanting to escape, I thought: I must continue to believe. If I stop now, how will I be able to live with myself? That was the moment I knew I was lost. I couldn't escape, couldn't go back."

"So you gave him final authority in all things, even over your own body, and the bodies and minds of your innocent children. You moved in with him, into that tiny, miserable house, because he wanted you to, he wanted to have you whenever he felt like it."

Daniella squeezed her knees, distraught. "It's true, it's true," she suddenly sobbed.

Bina got off her chair, sliding her back down the wall; she sat down next to Daniella Goodman on the floor. "You're a victim, Daniella. Don't you see that? A victim of mind control. People like that are capable of doing things they would never, ever have dreamed of doing outside the cult. They commit the most awful crimes and they do it willingly, consciously, even enthusiastically. One way a cult leader tests his members' devotion is by seeing how far they will allow their children to be abused."

A high-pitched, almost animal sound burst out of Daniella Goodman, a scream of loss heard from lone survivors of genocides or natural disasters. Bina held her by both shoulders.

"Do you understand now? You were his prey. Once he injected his poison in you, your emotions were numbed, he made you passive. You felt you had lost control over everything. And once you felt like that, you really did lose control. You felt helpless, and so you became helpless. You surrendered to Shem Tov because he, and everyone else around you, made sure you couldn't see any other options."

Daniella's body went limp. "Giving in made everything so much easier. It was so simple, so clear," she whispered. "To resist meant to struggle. I had no strength left. I'm such an idiot! How could I have let it happen to me?"

"People who get involved in cults never know that it's a cult. Did you know that most prime candidates for cults are smart, inquisitive? They're leaders, idealists, people who want others' love and approval. But they are also people who are full of self-doubt, people who fear for the future. People who get involved in a cult never know it's a cult. What happened to you can happen to anyone at a certain vulnerable moment in their lives."

"But what I let them do . . ."

"In the Love Family cult, children were considered possessed by the devil if they cried or spoke out without being spoken to or expressed any need. You see now, Daniella? Even that wasn't Shem Tov's idea. It's classic cult manipulation. Nothing he told you had anything to do with kabbalah or Judaism. Nothing he did to you was even original. It's been done a million times to people of every religion, race, and belief system."

"But why? Why did he want to hurt me or my children? Why did he want to?" She wept.

Bina leaned back, closing her eyes. She thought of the many criminals she had met and put behind bars, and the twisted nature of the terrible ways in which they had damaged others. "I wish I had the answer to that. Some people are just born that way. They're monsters filled with rage. Some express their hostility and aggression by controlling other people, the way Shem Tov controlled you, Shlomie, his wife, his Hassidim, the children. They enjoy it. It makes them feel powerful. But I think he had another motive for wanting to control you, a sexual motive. In order to do that, he had to smash your personality, your sense of identity. You were a mother. He needed to destroy that to make you his own."

"My God!" Daniella rose up slowly from the floor.

Bina watched her. She no longer seemed like the powerful White Witch who had been such a formidable enemy, but just a weak, pathetic, destroyed victim who, like so many others, had had the misfortune of running into a very sick, damaged human predator. The only true thing Shem Tov had told her about himself was this: he *could* communicate with demons. They were living right inside his head.

"What am I going to do?" Daniella moaned.

Bina thought for a moment. "I want to tell you a story. A true story. There was a young couple with a baby daughter. Somehow, they met a man they thought was a healer. They honored and revered him as their spiritual father and leader. Over three years, they wound up giving him most of their money. They also allowed him to discipline their daughter, watching as he scalded her with hot water and beat her; and her husband watched him rape the child's mother."

"*Stop, STOP,* I beg you. . . ."

Bina ignored her. "Both parents submitted to violence and beatings. Why? Because they believed, like you, Daniella, that the purpose of these punishments was to help them grow emotionally and spiritually. They were normal people, Daniella, just like you! Both of them had college and post-graduate educations. Eventually, they escaped and went to a cult victims' clinic. When the mother was asked why she'd allowed these things to happen, she explained that she'd just moved away from her family and friends, and her husband had fallen ill and required surgery. They couldn't afford to entertain coworkers or keep in contact with old friends. They weren't on good terms with her husband's parents, who were intrusive and judgmental. She lost confidence in herself. She was depressed, anxious, fearful of what the future held. . . . Sound familiar?"

"How did they . . . break free?" Daniella asked.

"Their daughter got so ill she almost died, which forced them to take her to the emergency room of a hospital, which filed abuse and neglect charges against them. And guess what? The child had a serious untreated burn."

There was a stunned silence. "What happened to them?" Daniella asked, tears rolling down her cheeks. "To their baby?"

"The parents got into therapy, which helped the mother with her guilt, which was preventing her from making any progress. You need to make some progress, Daniella. You need to deal with your guilt."

Daniella sat, transfixed, as if she'd been given an incredible revelation. For the first time in years, a sliver of insight pierced her frozen heart. She wasn't alone. Her sins were not even unique. And she would never, could never, forgive herself.

"Please, please let me see my Menchie. *Please!* And afterwards, I promise, I will tell you everything."

Bina picked up the phone, speaking briefly to Morris. "Come, I'll take you to him. It's okay—you don't have to cuff her," she told the two policemen who accompanied them.

"Sorry, Detective, it's standard procedure."

She put her hand forcefully over the handcuffs: "Don't!" she commanded.

He blinked, then put the handcuffs back into his pocket.

Bina walked Daniella to the police car. On the ride to Hadassah Hospital, Daniella turned to her. "Please, Detective Tzedek. Can you call my brother, Joel, and my sister-in-law, Esther? Can you tell them for me that I am grateful for all they did and are doing to help me and my children?"

Bina nodded. "Of course. You can't imagine how helpful they've been. But why don't you call them yourself?"

She shook her head. "I'm too ashamed."

Bina patted her hand. There was nothing she could say.

They walked through the hospital corridors together until they reached the room where Menchie lay, a beautiful little boy lost in permanent slumber. He looked small in the large, standard hospital crib, dwarfed by beeping machines from which he had long since been detached, medical science having no further tools to help him.

"Go, be with your baby," she told Daniella Goodman, leaving her alone with her child. "I'll wait outside for you whenever you're ready to go."

Daniella nodded. There were tears in her eyes. "Thank you."

Watching from the open door, she saw Daniella approach her baby, lifting him in her arms and carrying him with her to an armchair. She sat, cradling the almost lifeless form of what from all accounts had once been a smart, charming, active toddler, a child of intelligence and insight who had seen through the façade to the heart of the beast, perceiving instinctively what none of the adults who were supposed to protect him had been able to see. It was an insight that had probably cost him his life.

Bina watched silently as Daniella Goodman rocked her baby, singing softly. The song surprised her. It was a Sabbath hymn, a song of thanks to guardian angels that accompany the faithful on their way home from synagogue Friday nights.

Shalom Aleichem malachei ha sharat, malachei elyon.
Mi melch, malachei hamelachim, ha Kadosh Baruch Hu.

[Peace to you, angels of peace, angels on high. Who is the King of Kings? The Holy One, Blessed be He.]

The mother held her unmoving, silent child in her arms, her hot tears wetting his beautiful little face, his open, unseeing eyes, his soft lips and chubby cheeks. Up and back she rocked, as if she would never stop.

Whatever human justice would mete out to this woman as punishment for her deeds, Bina thought as she closed the door, it could never equal the lifelong hell she had now entered: the harsh, unvarnished realization in the cold light of day of what she had done to her children.

32

"Please raise your seat backs and buckle your seat belts," the steward-ess said politely but firmly. It was the third time, and the plane was about to take off.

Menachem Shem Tov, with his weak command of English, looked up at her, confused and annoyed.

"Vhat?" he said.

She rolled her eyes, pushing his seat upright and reaching around him to buckle him in.

He closed his eyes, waiting for the moment of liftoff, hardly daring to breathe.

When it came, he exhaled, a small smile of victory playing around his lips.

His plan had been simple. Find a country with a haredi Jewish com-munity that he could sell some sob story to, and get their help and support in avoiding extradition back to Israel and the clutches of the stupid Israeli police.

His first stop, Canada, had almost worked. But now the story and his photo were all over the Internet, and even his newfound haredi supporters had started asking embarrassing questions. It was time to pack up and move on. Namibia was a place with no Jews, but its remoteness was a plus. But he soon got tired of the heat, the unfamiliar food, the lack of decent company. . . .

Now he was on his way to Peru. He had no doubt he would succeed eventually. But the fact that he found himself in such straits annoyed him to no end, putting a chink into his inflated sense of self-importance and invulnerability.

The only problem was time. But on that score, he felt confident. Daniella Goodman wasn't about to open her mouth. Neither was his wife. As for Batlan, Hod, and Goldschmidt, if they weren't in jail already, they soon would be. They'd have no reason to talk, and even if they did, what good would it do them? He'd made sure that their hands had as much, if not more, blood on them than his own.

He leaned back, sighing. To be a fugitive . . . it was a failure. Where had it all gone wrong? he wondered, his sense of anger and self-pity deepening. It was that woman. Daniella.

He felt a surge of lust at the memory. Her slim, pliant body in bed, so different from that of his fat wife's. But Ruth had not always been like that. She, too, as a bride . . . He licked his lips. His desire for Daniella had made him lose control, he thought. Wanting her. Wanting to get her into his house, into his bed anytime he wanted her without all that traveling up and back from Beit Shemesh to Jerusalem. But her children were a nightmare, brought up without the discipline his own children were used to. He had lost control, especially with the two youngest. Menchie, that defiant little wretch, who seemed to see right through him. Whatever he did, the child wasn't afraid. And then, in the end, it had been too late. If he talked . . . So he had to make sure the child would never be able to talk again. Batlan, that moron, as usual had screwed up, almost killing the kid and then panicking and calling an ambulance. He felt incensed all over again.

As for Eli, there had been no rational reason for how he had treated the child, except for one: he looked exactly like Shlomie.

He took out a new notebook, regretting he'd left the old ones behind. He'd fled in a panic, telling Ruth to pack them when she came to join him with their children. He wasn't sure when that would be.

He settled back in his seat. He'd already called the head of the Neshamah Amuka cult, Reb Leibel, his mentor, who had fled to Peru with his entire congregation when the Israeli Police had started investigating him. Much of what Shem Tov had done, he had learned from Leibel, who was a master.

Leibel, born to secular parents on a kibbutz in southern Israel, had become a born-again Jew sometime after his dishonorable discharge from the army, when he was caught stealing and selling weapons. In a newly grown beard, wearing the black suit and white shirt of the pious, he had roamed B'nai Brak looking for a yeshiva to take him in. He had attached himself to several, and on the way had watched with envy the way the rebbe was treated in these congregations, the way money was collected to keep him in a luxurious home with lovely furnishings. How people kowtowed to him, serving him, and hanging on to his every word. In that moment, he saw his future.

Beginning with only a few of his fellow students and their wives, Leibel created a small, proselytizing cult that told followers that his way was the purest way. He made up strange rules about what foods could and could not be eaten that went far beyond the kosher laws, outlawing rice and lettuce and many other things with the contention that they might contain tiny insects, which were forbidden to eat. He imposed a dress code for women that rivaled the Muslims in its severity, and went beyond, imposing the strictures on little girls older than twelve months, and forbidding women to ever remove their stockings, even in private. And the more stringent his laws became, the more he was astonished to see how people flocked to him, begging to be part of his congregation. He started experimenting with his power, seeing how far he could push people to go against their instincts. He married off eleven-year-old girls to thirty-year-old men in secret ceremonies. He took in runaways and had sex with them, before handing them over to other cult members. Discipline was harsh and physical, often requiring medical attention, which was not forthcoming. And the more he did, to his delight, the more his fame spread, and the more a certain type of religious seeker begged to be let in.

Unfortunately, one of his members, a nineteen-year-old drug addict, turned out to be from a prominent family of lawyers from Tel Aviv, who looked into what had happened to her and had wound up whisking her away to be deprogrammed. She had sung like a canary, and the next thing Leibel knew, he and all his cult members were on a plane bound for Peru.

A food cart rumbled by. A stewardess handed Shem Tov his meal. He stared at it, incensed. "Not kosher!" he screamed at the stewardess, who hurried to take it back.

She looked it over in confusion. "Sir, you see here," she pointed to a large stick-on label on the carefully wrapped meal, "it says clearly: 'Kosher.'"

"Not *glatt* kosher!" he screamed, slamming his fist on the tray table, which made the person in the seat in front of him jump.

"Please, sir. We'll try . . . Please calm down!"

He slammed his hands violently against the seat in front of him, pushing the chair forward. The passenger turned around, alarmed.

"Sir, if you don't calm down, I'll have to call the head of security."

He looked up and saw two burly men heading down the aisle toward him. At this, a miraculous calm came over Menachem Shem Tov. He let his hands fall limply to his sides, closing his eyes. When he opened them, he looked at the stewardess. "Sorry," he said. "Going to funeral of my father. Very sad. Take meal. Sorry."

She looked at him doubtfully, handing him back the meal and nodding to the two men, who turned around and went back to their seats. After that, he behaved himself, quietly eating his meal then closing his eyes to sleep. It was going to be a long trip.

33

In the next few days, Daniella Goodman's lawyer negotiated a plea deal for his client. She would receive a five-year prison sentence in exchange for turning state's witness. Five years behind bars, Bina thought, wondering if it was just.

"How hard did her lawyer try to get her out of serving jail time?" she asked Morris.

He shrugged. "Not very. I understand Daniella didn't want to walk scot-free. She thinks she deserves it."

Yes, Bina thought. I can understand that.

Daniella Goodman's full and complete testimony, which was immediately sealed by court order to protect her children, was shocking, putting the finishing nails into the airtight cases they were now building against Shem Tov, Hod, Batlan, and Goldschmidt. But there was still one star witness that they had not been able to interview: Duvie Goodman.

"Do you think he will talk to us now?" Bina asked doubtfully. From the beginning, of all the children, Duvie had been the most problematic, behaving like a wild horse they were trying to saddle for the first time every time they approached him, screaming curses, biting, and kicking. Not only that but, until recently, he'd intimidated the other children into silence with spoken and unspoken threats.

Bina found his behavior inexplicable. Why was he so determined to protect Shem Tov and his accomplices? Could it be that he had been recruited? That he was now as brainwashed as his mother had been? Or perhaps he hadn't experienced the horrors the others had at Shem Tov's hands?

"I think you'll find that he, of all the children, was the most abused," Johnny said to her surprise when she discussed it with him.

Her eyes opened wide, and she shook her head, thinking of Menchie and Eli. "How can you say that?"

"Because he, according to his mother, was the most rebellious, the most outspoken. Who knows what they did to him to get him to cooperate? And being the big brother, he probably feels the most guilt at not having been able to protect his younger siblings. In his own way, by threatening them to keep quiet, he's trying to do that now." He shook his head sorrowfully. "He's terrified that Shem Tov will find out and take revenge. It's no different than the Mafia. Don't be fooled by his tough-guy act. He's a child, Bina. He deserves our compassion."

"But we can't get near him."

"He isn't different than the other children. Try the same strategy. Make him feel safe. We'll not only get our evidence but help him to understand it was not his fault. I think you'll find that Duvie, of all the children, is the most eager to tell us what was done to him."

She doubted it.

"Go, Bina. Talk to the kid," said Morris. "Take Johnny with you."

Duvie was also now living with Joel, while the others were in foster homes.

They knocked on the door. Joel answered, nodding. "He's in the living room."

"Hi, Duvie," Johnny called out to him.

He was thirteen, going on fourteen, a short boy with beautiful blond hair covered by a black, velvet skullcap. His long silky side curls hung down on either side of his rosy cheeks.

At first glance, he seemed younger than his age. Only when Bina looked into his eyes could she tell that his childhood was long gone.

"Do you remember me, Bina Tzedek?"

He nodded hostilely.

"And you remember Johnny?" Joel said encouragingly. "They've come to talk to you."

"You know that Shem Tov is in jail, right?" Johnny told him.

"I know that's what you told the others to get them to talk. But how do I know you weren't lying?" he responded warily.

Luckily, this time it was actually true. Shem Tov had been picked up trying to enter Peru. He was already sitting in a Peruvian jail.

"Here, look at this." Bina said, pulling out a photo she'd downloaded from the Internet, anticipating this question. It was a clear picture of a bareheaded, shoeless Shem Tov being led away in chains by Peruvian police. CHILD MOLESTER CAPTURED BY PERUVIAN BORDER CONTROL was the headline. "Now he'll never be able to hurt any of you again."

Duvie took it. Suddenly, he sat down. Holding the paper in both hands, he stared at it for a long time, until his hands began to shake and tears ran silently down his cheeks. The transformation was unbelievable. In front of their eyes, he went from a belligerent teenager to a confused and hurting child. "*Baruch Hashem*," he whispered, closing his eyes. *God be blessed.* He sat there, without saying another word, sobbing uncontrollably.

There was nothing to do but wait patiently, unable to help, their hearts sore.

He opened his eyes, looking around the room. "Now I'll tell you everything."

So that's all it ever was, Bina thought. A child's simple terror. She'd misjudged him.

"When my parents moved from Yahalom to Jerusalem, I started a new school. It was a yeshiva in the Old City. And the rebbe there used to hit all the boys with a stick whenever he felt like it. This made me nervous, so I started biting my nails. Every time I did it, he'd smash me over my fingertips with a fat ruler. Once, it hurt so bad, I took it out of his hands and broke it in two, and told him to go to hell."

A small smile lit up the corners of Johnny's mouth.

"So, I got kicked out. They sent me to another place. It was even worse. I got kicked out of there, too. The third place was *the* worst. The kids were retarded or criminals. I was afraid of them. So I cut classes and started hanging out in the center of town by the place they call Cat's Square. Lots of kids like me hang out there. My father tried to talk to me. I said I'd try harder to be good. But I was very angry. My parents kept getting complaints about me from my teachers. They kept grounding me. But on Purim, I went out anyway with Yossie. We went to town and had a pizza and had fun.

"When I got back, my parents flipped. They called Shem Tov. He told my parents to send me to live in his rat-infested beit midrash, and that he, himself, would teach me for my Bar Mitzvah. I begged my parents not to, but they sent me away. They said I needed 'a strong hand.'" He looked down at the photo of Shem Tov in handcuffs, his hands trembling once more.

"Whenever Shem Tov showed up at his beit midrash, he would beat me with a long stick. He'd smash it into my back and my face. And when he wasn't there, he appointed Goldschmidt to be 'responsible' for me. Whenever I did the smallest thing he didn't like—if I yawned or went to the bathroom during a lesson—Goldschmidt would call Shem Tov on his cell phone, and when he hung up, Goldschmidt would smash his fists into my stomach and my face. He'd kick me and bend my fingers back until they almost broke." Tears filled the boy's eyes. "And there was someone else there, Bannerman . . ."

Johnny and Bina exchanged glances. It was the first time they'd heard the name.

"He was then put in charge. He was supposed to 'neutralize' me, to make sure I didn't lift a finger without permission. He made me—" he stopped, breathing hard "—suck his thumb. He made me drink water after everyone in the yeshiva had spit in the cup. To drink coffee they filled with paprika or salt, to drink the leftovers in everyone's coffee cups. And when I wouldn't, he . . . he beat me with a baseball bat, and . . . he squeezed my . . ." He looked down into his lap.

Bina could see that Johnny's continued silence came at a price, his gentle hands squeezed into rock-hard weapons.

"Even right before my Bar Mitzvah, the whole bunch ganged up on me and beat me. They broke a tooth." He opened his mouth and pointed inside. "They told me my parents knew all about what they were doing to me, and that they were happy about it, that they thought I deserved it, that they didn't love me anymore because I was such a disgrace to them, which is why they sent me away in the first place. I started to believe them, and that's when I decided the best thing would be to kill myself. A few times, I even tried. I almost threw myself in front of a truck. But it didn't work out. I was too slow or the truck was too fast."

"Did you ever try to tell your parents what was going on?" Johnny asked gently.

"I was never allowed to be alone with them. The only time they'd let me go home was if the whole group came with me. I tried to talk to my father, to hint to him . . . but Goldschmidt overheard and I got hit so bad. Anyhow, I couldn't make my father or my mother understand. They didn't want to believe me. That's when I started thinking that everything Shem Tov told me had been true. They really *were* in on it, my father and my mother."

Bina had a vision of this child standing up on the bimah on his Bar Mitzvah day, such a joyous occasion, his face black and blue, his teeth broken, his terrified voice trembling as he read the words of the sacred Torah, the book of kindness and love that had governed the lives of Jews from their inception as a nation. It was an obscenity.

"Then my father was suddenly gone, and Shem Tov moved us all to his house. They were all there, except Bannerman. And Shem Tov was the king. They did whatever he said and did it like it was fun for them. Like they enjoyed it. They were a bunch of Nazis! Sometimes Shem Tov watched, and sometimes he joined in. They made me sit in weird positions and stay up all night learning. And if I fell asleep, Goldschmidt would lock me in the storage room for two days, every time, with no food or water. They gave me a bowl to use as a toilet and told me I wasn't allowed to fall asleep. They never opened the door except to throw me a little food or beat me. They kept a cell phone in there, so that Shem Tov could listen to everything going on inside. And when the battery died, they'd open the door and beat me, telling me I shut it off on purpose. Once, they tried to force pills down my throat. I think it was Ritalin. They took me to the mikvah and on the way beat me with a cell phone until they broke another one of my teeth. And when I tried to talk to my mother, I got dragged away and beaten so badly I couldn't move.

"So I made a plan. To run away and take Yossi with me. But we got caught. They forced liquor down our throats. Shem Tov told Batlan and Goldschmidt to beat us up. I thought I was going to die. Then they locked us both in the storage room. After a while, I stopped counting the days."

Bina inhaled, then exhaled slowly. How much more, how much more? she silently asked. But if this is what the child lived through, I have to have the strength to at least listen.

"But that wasn't the hardest part," he said suddenly.

Johnny and Bina looked up at him and at each other, startled, afraid of what they were going to hear next.

"The hardest part was watching what they did to my kid brothers. One night, I heard Shem Tov tell Batlan to beat Menchie. I sat there watching all night long as he hit Menchie with his fists, slapped him, kicked him. And I couldn't . . ." He began to weep, in heartbreaking sobs. Bina went to him, but he shrugged off her attempt at comfort. "No, don't. I don't deserve it. I sat there and watched and I was too afraid. . . . I was a coward! I didn't do anything. I didn't say anything. I just watched, you understand? They hit him with a hammer, until he bled, while Shem Tov watched, this fucking smile on his fucking face. . . ." The boy wept. "They burned his fingertips with a lighter, they stuffed his mouth with food until he almost choked, they put him under a faucet and almost drowned him. And I saw it all, I saw it all."

"It wasn't your fault—do you understand that!"

"*No! You* don't understand anything. Once I tried to stop them and they beat me up and then . . . then . . . *they made me help them*!"

A current like a bolt of electricity went through Bina's body, a sudden sense of darkness clouding her vision. The root of Duvie's violence was self-hatred.

"I saw them taking Eli into the kabbalah room, Shem Tov, Batlan, and Hod. They closed the door. I heard Eli screaming and screaming and screaming. Hod came running out. When he opened the door for a second, I caught a look at Eli. He was pressed up against a spiral heater. Batlan was holding his skin in his hands. They'd just burnt it off! They brought my mother from upstairs. I could hear them telling her some stupid freaking lies—that Eli had stood too close, that they'd tried to move him away—and she swallowed it! Didn't complain to them! Nothing. Shem Tov didn't want him taken to a doctor. He told my mother to treat him herself. I think she tried. But then she saw it was getting worse. And Shem Tov kept beating Eli. I think she was afraid they'd kill him. So she told Shem Tov she was going to get him out of the house, give him to some lady she knew. And Shem Tov, who hated Eli most of all, said yes."

He was breathing heavily, sweat pouring off his red face. He wiped his forehead on his sleeve.

"Duvie, I know this must be very hard for you. But you are doing great!" Bina said, trying tentatively to put a hand on his shoulder. To her surprise, he let it rest there.

"Can you tell us what happened to Menchie?" Johnny asked him after a short pause.

"The last day we were in Shem Tov's house, he made me tie Menchie's arms to the back of a chair with chains. They said it was to help him, so he wouldn't scratch the blisters on his burnt foot. His head was all swollen and purple. Shem Tov stood all of us up against the wall and told us that we should tell anybody who asked that Eli was burned by a fire in our house in the Old City. I heard him whisper to Batlan that he had to turn Menchie into a cripple so he wouldn't be able to tell anyone what happened to him. And that night, when we were moved back from Shem Tov's house to our own house in the Old City, I heard Batlan talking to Shem Tov on the phone. After he hung up, I saw Batlan go into the room where Menchie was sleeping. After that, I saw Menchie lying on the floor, and Batlan had his mouth over his mouth, trying to breathe into him. And then the ambulance came."

"Would you excuse me a—" Bina ran to the bathroom and heaved over the toilet, tasting her breakfast once again. She washed her face, filled her mouth with water, and spit it out. She looked up at her face in the mirror, trying to reset her features, to remove the shock and horror so the boy wouldn't see. She needed to be calm, professional, she told herself, closing her eyes and breathing deeply.

She came back and sat down. "Sorry, please, go on, Duvie. This is very helpful."

"In the next few days, Shem Tov's wife, Ruth, kept calling me. She told me to keep my mouth shut and to make sure my brothers and sisters kept theirs shut, otherwise, there were going to be a lot more tikkunim in the future when we went back to live with them."

"That is never, ever going to happen, Duvie," Bina told him. "Because of your courage, because you told us everything, you are going to be the reason that all of them—Shem Tov, Batlan, Goldschmidt, Hod, and this piece of turd Bannerman when we find him—are going to sit in jail for a very, very long time. They are going to eat prison food and be locked up twenty-four hours a day, seven days a week."

"I wish . . . I wish . . ."

"What?" Johnny said.

"That you'd do to them what they did to us! Tie them up and let me be in a room with them for a day, with hammers and spiral heaters and shit and vomit."

Ah, if only real justice were possible, Bina thought, wishing for the same thing. But the state was so limited, its hands tied by its humanity, its adherence to civilized rules. For a moment she longed for biblical punishments, for death by stoning in which the entire city gathered, each individual invited to cast a rock at the perpetrators of horrendous deeds. How she would love to fling a few boulders on these men, watch them as they tried to protect their worthless hides with their cowardly hands, hands that had tortured innocent children. She could already see their defense attorneys crying crocodile tears: their poor clients were misled, brainwashed. They were only following orders!

And Shem Tov, the Messiah? What would his lawyer say? Already, he was trying to claim that Shem Tov should be granted asylum in Peru because authorities in Israel—fornicators, pig eaters, and idolators— had no sovereignty over the Holy Land, which was established before the Messiah against God's will. Shem Tov wasn't an Israeli because Israel didn't exist. He had been living in occupied territories, and thus so-called Israelis had no jurisdiction over him!

He would whine and cry and tell everyone what a great saint he was all the way to prison. He'd say that he was only trying to help this poor family who had asked for his help. That Daniella was the mother and she had watched it all, permitted it all. That it was her fault.

Would the court listen? Who knew? But Bina was going to make sure that those who judged Shem Tov heard everything she'd heard; that the words of the children echoed off the courtroom walls wherever these men were tried. Their judges would be fathers, mothers, grandparents. She would make sure not a single detail was left out.

As for herself, she knew she would continue chasing after evil, in spite of the full knowledge that she might never catch up. As a civilized human being in a democracy, she had no choice but to trust in the mechanisms put in place by human beings to administer retribution. It was a weak and flawed system, she knew, but the best one they had to deal with people like Shem Tov and his cronies. She promised herself to be there, every step of the way, watching and waiting, pursuing justice.

34

From the testimony of Daniella Goodman:

It is very, very hard for me to talk about my experiences with Menachem Shem Tov and his group because of the terrible pain and regret remembering brings to me. I wish there was a way I could throw it all into the depths of the ocean so that I would never have to think of these things again. Also, I find when I try to put into words what he, Shem Tov, convinced me to believe, it makes no sense. It makes me sound insane. Reading it over I get frightened and confused all over again.

Shem Tov told us not to learn the Torah because it was a very old book not meant for the modern generation, and we couldn't really understand its language anyway. He said that if we read in the Torah, "The donkey spoke," it didn't actually mean that but some abstract, Divine thing beyond our understanding, and that abstract things are the real things. You are not supposed to understand it, you are supposed to "feel" those things, he said, like you feel your hand. You needed to put faith above reason and have a lot of desire, and then wisdom would be "revealed" to you.

The prayer book was also nullified. Its words were meant for lesser beings. We, on a higher level, had our own prayers that needed no words; they were simply a strong desire in our hearts.

Shem Tov taught me that the most important thing was to have faith. "Faith above reason," Shem Tov said. Faith in what? In Shem Tov. And I did. I thought he was like Moses. That if he had to, he could split the sea. He was not a human being like others, like myself. He said he knew the secret of how to be like God. After I divorced Shlomie, Shem Tov promised me that if I followed him without question, he would teach this secret to me. But before that could happen, he said, I needed to reject God and reality, to put up a masak, a screen, between us. Only then, he explained, could I begin to receive the light of chochma, wisdom, which was supposed to open my eyes and turn me into a god.

That's when I stopped feeling like I wanted to be close to God. I wanted to be God. I wanted to have power, too. I felt shame, horror, and frustration that I wasn't yet on that level, God's level, Shem Tov's level.

There was a time, right at the beginning, that all these teachings broke my heart. I remember crying uncontrollably without even knowing why. Shem Tov called it "the Pathway of Sorrow." He took hours and hours to explain to me why this was a good thing, how it was bringing me closer to God. Hod, Batlan, and Goldschmidt and my husband also told me they had gone through this, that every person who is climbing the ladder to holiness must go through this.

Something happened to me. Deep in my soul, I began to feel the pulsing of something dark, something I had never encountered before. Images passed through my head of blood, death, killings. All the images were monstrously ugly. I would imagine ways in which people could be tortured. I enjoyed this. I enjoyed the hate. Everywhere I went, I imagined the people I saw being crushed and annihilated by evil things, as if lightning from my body could electrocute them. I couldn't understand what was happening to me. Everyone around me was an annoyance, a hindrance, slowing me down in my progress to pass to the upper levels of spirituality and godliness, in becoming the Creator. I became antisocial, unhappy, cold, distant. I despised everyone and everything. I was frustrated with my children for not being completely integrated in our group, for making trouble, for not accepting Shem Tov's ways. I was embarrassed to have such children. I felt like a failure as a mother.

I was turning into a psychopath. I think I even knew this was happening, but I was powerless to stop it.

All I wanted was the light! I wanted it more than sex, more than my children. I wanted what they call zivug copulation with the "light," so that the "seed" of the light would grow inside me. I had some euphoric moments, but they were surrounded by a despair that led to complete emptiness. Shem Tov said this was a good thing, that this is the price we pay our Creator for our progress.

I was all that mattered. I was told this was a positive thing. The "vessel," that is, my ego, was expanding in order to contain the endless "light" now flooding it. I never questioned how holy light could make you self-centered and evil or how such a light could come from a good Creator who wished us all to love each other and be good. These questions were inside me but never allowed to surface. I spent a great deal of effort to batter them down, to obliterate them.

Shem Tov taught that we lived in a false world. That everything we had ever known was like a movie, a setup, unconnected to the true reality. Like that movie The Truman Show, everyone was the puppet of the "Creator"—they were just pretending to live.

From the moment I began to believe that, nothing ever made sense again. I became detached from myself, my core beliefs, my intelligence, my humanity. I was totally without any ground under my feet. I felt I couldn't believe my own eyes, my own brain. I was told that this was a wonderful thing. It even had a name: "crossing the barrier." Shem Tov's circle considered it a fantastic breakthrough, *proof of progress. Now I understand that it was probably a psychotic breakdown. I lost track of what was real.*

I found myself fainting all the time. Shem Tov gave me "vitamins." I realize now they were probably Xanax or perhaps the antipsych medication some of his other followers were on. All I know is that hell was constantly on my mind, along with the promise of becoming like God.

At a certain point, I gave up the struggle to find myself again. I thought how much easier it would be to just stop struggling all the time against these new ideas. When I finally gave in, I did feel a sense of tranquillity. A calm came over me. I thought this was proof I had made the right decision. I didn't know that the peace I was feeling was a kind of death. I had ceased to exist.

I began to have night terrors, and depression, and anxiety, and suicidal urges, and I wanted to run away, and scream. I feared everything. I took more and more "vitamins," sometimes a half dozen a day. If I didn't, I could not get out of bed in the morning or go out of the house. My heart began beating very, very fast, and I started to lose a tremendous amount of weight. It just fell off me. Finally, when I looked skeletal, Shem Tov allowed me to go to a doctor, who took blood tests. I had Graves' disease, which is autoimmune, the body attacking itself. And that makes sense because among those I hated, I hated myself most of all.

I lost track of what was going on with my children. I would hear the blows, hear them screaming, crying, in anguish, but I told myself if I interfered, I would only make it worse, it would just take longer and they'd suffer that much more. Each day I hoped the demons inside them would be destroyed and the punishments could finally stop.

Shem Tov said I was doing the best possible thing for my children. According to him, when God created the universe, He was lonely, so He created man to put in His world. Then He used magic to seduce man, tempting him to climb the tower to God's throne, which was on top of a huge mountain. When man gets close, the palace guards show him no mercy as they battle to stop him and prevent him from reaching the throne. But finally when man somehow manages anyway, all his sufferings are explained to him: it was to make him as strong and as powerful as his Creator. That was why I and my children had to suffer.

Shem Tov hinted that he had finished his climb. He was already sitting there beside the throne, speaking to the Creator as one talks to a close friend in a coffeehouse. That was where the notebooks came in. Every day, Shem Tov would sit beside the throne and write questions in his notebook, and the Creator would answer him directly, and he would write it down. He wrote down everything, then read us the answers. But most of it, he kept secret.

Even after Shem Tov left, I was wrapped up only in myself. The little bit of humanity that was still left in me was buried so deeply I could hardly find it. That was the only way I could survive day by day. I hadn't cried for so long. Shem Tov locked up our hearts so that we couldn't be human. Human beings don't behave the way I did. I wasn't a mother, I wasn't a person; I was nothing, no one, like a wall. I didn't care about anything. Now, I can't say the names Eli or Menchie without crying. But then, nothing. I felt nothing about anyone. All I thought about was myself and how I could get out of the mess I had gotten myself into. I did everything I could to prevent the authorities from finding Eli. But when I saw how determined they were, I tried to pretend everything was normal. When they wanted to take Eli for medical attention, I resisted, insulted them, and caused my children to follow suit. I felt I was in the hands of the enemy and my only friends were Batlan, Goldschmidt, and Hod. The police, social workers, doctors, investigators were all enemies.

The first time I met with my children after I was put in jail, I suddenly noticed how terrible they looked. And suddenly, the wheels in my brain started moving again. Why do my children look like that? Why are they crying? What am I doing here? How did I let this happen? The tiny ember of humanity that Shem Tov hadn't succeeded in completely snuffing out in me started to burn again. I suddenly remembered the first time Shem Tov hurt one of my children.

It was soon after our forest "marriage," after I'd moved in with him. We had tried living separately, he with Ruth in Beit Shemesh and me in the Old City with my children. Shem Tov had forbidden Shlomie to come anywhere near me or the children, and so Shlomie found a place to live three hours away, up north, near Safed. He wanted to visit, but I wouldn't allow it.

The children missed their father. Ever since the divorce, they were on a rampage. One day Menchie opened up all the bags of flour and shook them all over the house. Yossi broke all of Shoshana's dolls. Duvie stayed out to all hours. And even Gabriel started to throw tantrums at the slightest excuse. They were destroying the house, hurting each other, defiant, miserable. I couldn't bear it. It became impossible for me to manage alone.

"You will all move in with me," Shem Tov told me decisively, not a question but a command. "I and the boys will help you to take care of your children."

I remembered how Shem Tov and his Hassidim had come to my rescue when Shlomie had disappeared in the Ukraine for a month and the children were sick and I was so alone. I remembered the order, the quiet, the discipline. Yes, I thought. That is exactly what my children needed now after all their upheavals. It was, I thought, the perfect solution.

A day before we moved, I got a phone call from my brother, Joel.

"Shlomie's parents called Mom. We heard you are divorced. Is that true?"

"Yes," I answered him.

"But why, Daniella? What happened?"

His voice sounded so far away. I knew what I was doing couldn't be explained in any way that would make sense to Joel, that he would criticize, and I would have no answers. I was in a different world now, light-years away from my brother.

"I can't explain it to you," I told my brother.

"Try!" he said. He sounded angry, impatient, upset.

All I wanted to do then was to silence him. "I can't make you understand!" I shouted at him. "You are not on a high enough level!" These were the words I had so often heard Shem Tov use to answer anyone who dared to question him.

Joel didn't say anything for a while. And then he said, "Are you all right, Daniella?" He said it so kindly, even after how I'd spoken to him and treated him the last time we were together, that for a moment I almost broke down and told him everything. But I could tell he was holding himself back, that he wanted to shout, that he was scared for me. I was afraid if I told him the truth, I'd also start being afraid. And I couldn't let that happen. I was terrified to stop believing, because if I even allowed myself a second of doubt, what would that mean about all I'd already done? What had happened in the forest, in the hotel? "You will never be as all right as I am, Joel. You are lost, your world is false. It is doomed. You are going to hell. Don't call me. Don't contact my children—you will only taint them. Stay away from us," I shouted at him.

I heard his voice speaking urgently on the line and knew at once I had no choice but to silence it. Slowly, I pulled the phone away from my ear, putting it back in its cradle. Then I pulled the phone out of the wall altogether. That same day, I changed my phone number so no one could reach me and I wouldn't have to explain myself to anyone.

That first Shabbat after we moved to Beit Shemesh, we were sitting around the table eating on Friday night. By nine o'clock, Menchie, who had dozed off in his high chair by the table, was woken by the loud singing. He was very cranky and threw his plate down on the floor, then tipped over his cup, staining the white tablecloth.

"I'll put him to bed. He's exhausted," I said.

"Sit down and be quiet!" Shem Tov shouted at me. I already knew better than to defy him. I did as he asked.

"Your children need to learn discipline," he said. It was a threat.

"But he's just a baby," I remember begging.

"Wasn't Rivka already a saint at three years old when she watered the camels of Abraham's servant Eliezer? It is never too early. We are not finished eating yet, or singing Sabbath songs, or learning Torah." He looked around the table at all the children, his dark eyes menacing. Everyone froze but Menchie, who ignored him, wriggling out of his chair, dropping pieces of bread all over the floor.

Shem Tov rose quickly, striding over to Menchie. With horror, I saw him pull back his hand and slap him so hard and with such violence that he flew across the room, landing on the hard, stone floors. I can still remember the sound Menchie made. It was high-pitched and almost inhuman, like a wounded, cornered animal.

For a moment, I sat paralyzed, frozen in silence, unable to assimilate what I had just witnessed. It was incomprehensible, like watching someone walk upside down on the ceiling. It simply wasn't possible; it didn't connect with anything I thought I knew about Shem Tov, about the world I thought I was now part of, a good world, a kind, gentle, holy world. I felt as if I must be asleep, in the middle of a nightmare. It couldn't be real.

I remember Menchie sobbing: "Ima!" He held out his hands to me. That woke me up. I jumped out of my chair and ran to him.

"Don't—don't touch him," Shem Tov commanded me. But this time, his voice was soft, almost caressing, just the kind of gentleness I desperately needed at that moment.

"But why, Menachem?" I pleaded, backing away, my heart torn, my mind stretched to the limits of sanity.

"Daniella, my dearest, do you think I would hurt your child, your beautiful little Menchie?" he said gently, his dark eyes searching mine. "Can you, after all you know of me, of my love for you and your precious children, really think me capable of such a thing?"

He was aggrieved, almost in mourning, his face filled with disappointment.

"No, no, no, no . . ." I refused to let myself remember what he had done to me in the hotel room. I told myself I had misunderstood. It was not rape. It was an act of love between husband and wife. So now, what he was saying also seemed true to me! How could I think such an evil thing after all we had been through together? He was the holiest person on the face of the earth, my savior, my friend, my beloved, my husband.

I left Menchie lying there on the floor, alone, uncomforted, screaming in agony.

"Do you hear that sound? Does that sound like your child, your baby?" Shem Tov asked me.

And I thought: No, it doesn't. I had never in my life heard Menchie make such a sound. I was confused.

Shem Tov shook his head slowly. "It is not your baby who is screaming, who is in pain. It is the demon inside him who tortures him, who makes him do terrible things. Now it screams because it knows we are aware of its presence. That we are coming to annihilate it and remove it from your baby. Do you love Menchie?"

I nodded. I was speechless. I loved Menchie more than my life.

"Then you must let me heal him, take out the demon who is inside him. If you interfere, show the demon pity, then the demon gains new strength, new ability to torture your baby. It wins, and Menchie loses. But if you are not strong enough to stand aside in order to help your baby, I can't stop you." He shrugged.

Now I understood. It was all illuminated. I must not interfere. I must go against all my motherly instincts. If I was weak, if I gave into my desire to protect and comfort him, it would only take longer, and my baby would suffer that much more. I had to be strong, to stand back and watch as Shem Tov did his holy magic, saving my baby, making him whole again.

Shem Tov nodded to Batlan and Hod, who grabbed Menchie roughly by his little arms, slamming him back into his high chair.

"*Stop howling, or we will punish you again!*" *Shem Tov told the child.* "*Sit still.*"

Menchie slowly stopped weeping, his terrified eyes yearning toward mine, but I refused to meet them, convinced it was the demon trying to trick me. I looked away.

It was the same with the others, with Eli and Duvie, who also suffered. Yossi and Gabriel were more pliant and tried not to anger him, so they were punished less, as were the girls, although I often heard Amalya sobbing into her pillow at night. I assumed it was because of what she was seeing happening to her brothers. But now, I am not so sure. Amalya never told me anything, but I always felt she was holding back.

By court order, the remainder of Daniella Goodman's testimony as it pertains to her minor children is sealed from public view.

In conclusion, I have told the entire truth as I witnessed it. Although I never raised a hand to my children, I am not innocent, but participated fully in what happened to my children, except it wasn't me. I had been canceled, destroyed, nullified, unable to act, to speak, to think.

I have come forward now to speak the truth not, as the lawyers defending the criminals who hurt my children accuse me, because I want to put the blame on them and save myself. It is impossible for me to save myself. The past cannot be erased. I believe I deserve to be punished for what happened. I was their mother. I do not expect a lesser sentence because of my testimony. I speak the truth now for one reason and one reason only: For so long, my great sin was my silence. I did not speak up. I did not try to help my children. The tikkun for that sin is simply to speak, and speak and speak, all the truth. May God and my children forgive me for what I've done.

Epilogue

Despite strenuous efforts to avoid extradition, Menachem Shem Tov was brought back to Israel a year and a half after fleeing. While his wife and children had joined him in Peru, they did not return with him and have since gone to live with relatives in Canada, where they remain. For some reason, the Israeli police never charged her or asked for her extradition, perhaps pitying her children and viewing her as more a domestic abuse victim than a criminal. Ruth has never asked for or received a divorce.

The trial of Menachem Shem Tov, like those of Elior Chen and Goel Ratzon, other gurus of child- and women-torturing cults in Israel, was widely followed by the public. Often, the courtroom was crowded by Shem Tov's enthusiastic supporters, Ultra-Orthodox Jews who held up signs outside the proceedings complaining the trial was religious persecution. Also like Chen, Menachem Shem Tov chose not to defend himself, maintaining absolute silence throughout. His lawyer also gave up the right to cross-examine prosecution witnesses, saying this was his client's wish. However, with the help of Daniella Goodman's detailed and reliable testimony, he was sentenced to the maximum term allowed by law. He will spend forty-five years behind bars. Batlan, Hod, and Goldschmidt were sentenced to thirty-five years each, while Bannerman received a ten-year sentence.

Daniella Goodman has been in Neve Tirza women's prison for the last three years. With good behavior, she will be out in the next twenty-four months. Each week, she is granted special permission to leave the prison grounds and visit with Menchie. While he is no longer in a coma, he cannot speak, walk, or swallow and seems unaware of his surroundings. He is a very handsome little boy, with large blue eyes and blond hair. The dedicated staff at the home for severely disabled children who lovingly care for him have nicknamed him Sleeping Beauty.

Although Daniella asked to formally divorce Shem Tov even before his case went to trial, only now has he agreed to grant her a religious divorce in exchange for certain prison privileges, like being allowed to join the haredi section in the penitentiary, where he is allowed three hours each day to study. He still studies kabbalah and is busy writing his own "sacred" text. But so far, he has not been able to conjure up the same magic he was known for on the outside world: no angels have opened his cell door for him, nor improved his food, nor made his bed softer.

Daniella has no interest in ever marrying again.

Shlomie, on the other hand, was introduced by a matchmaker to an eighteen-year-old girl from a newly observant family, a recent graduate of Beit Yaakov Seminary, soon after Daniella's incarceration. They were married a month later. They have two children and are expecting their third.

Shlomie went through a period of deep depression, which he said he was able to overcome through prayer and meditation. While he no longer studies kabbalah full-time, he is still deeply religious. He works in a store selling religious souvenirs: amulets, ram's horns, mezuzah holders, and prayer shawls. His young wife is an assistant in a religious kindergarten. With help from Daniella, they purchased a comfortable apartment near the sea in Ashdod. He doesn't believe in psychiatrists but does his best to lavish love and attention on Eli, Gabriel, Shoshana, and Yossi, who requested to live with their father and to visit their mother as often as possible.

While all the Goodman children suffer from nightmares, behavior disorders, and sudden fits of rage, with time these symptoms of post-traumatic stress seem to be lessening.

Soon after the trial, Joel and his family went back to America. While he was willing to accept custody of all his nieces and nephews, he did not fight the decision of Eli, Yossi, Gabriel, and Shoshana to live with their father. Duvie and Amalya, however, accompanied him back to Washington, D.C., after the court granted Joel formal custody, over the objections of both parents. They are good-looking, healthy, intelligent young people who want absolutely nothing to do with religion or their parents. After finishing the local public high school in Washington, D.C., Amalya is now studying computerized jewelry design. Duvie, however, dropped out of school when he turned seventeen. Both still struggle with feelings of guilt and depression and are under the care of skilled psychiatrists. Once a year, they spend two weeks in Israel with their family, visiting with their younger siblings, with whom they are in year-round contact through Skype and the telephone.

Amalya has never publicly spoken about what happened to her during the time she spent with Shem Tov. Both Amalya and Duvie realize that they will probably never really be whole again.

The Neshamah Amuka cult and Reb Leibel were raided by child welfare authorities in Peru, who took all the minor children into custody. After a long legal battle, in which it was alleged that large bribes were paid to Peruvian authorities, the children were released into their parents' custody. Soon after, the entire group found its way to a small village in Chile with a tiny Jewish community. Since their arrival, local villagers, who had always had good relations with their Jewish neighbors, are reportedly growing more and more anti-Semitic because of the strange ways of the newcomers, who are reportedly looking for yet another haven to which they can flee with their leader, who continues to exercise total control over them and their children.

Menachem Shem Tov recently appealed his conviction on the grounds that he had not received a fair trial since he had not testified or cross-examined witnesses. The Supreme Court denied his appeal, citing the many, many attempts made by the court during the trial to convince him and his lawyer to do both.

Two weeks after the conviction of Menachem Shem Tov, Johnny Mann had a massive heart attack. He died instantly. He continues to be deeply mourned by his friends and colleagues, who blame his death on the strain of dealing with the Shem Tov cult.

Bina Tzedek is still a detective in Jerusalem. Just recently, she had her third child, a little boy named Yonatan, whom everyone calls Johnny. To her surprise it was a very easy birth. She remembered to call Rabbanit Toledano to thank her for her blessing.

She has taken a few months' maternity leave. Sometimes, when the weather is fine, she takes Johnny out for a long walk in his carriage past the walls of the Old City. Whenever she approaches the spot where the hill dips down into the Valley of Hinnom, she shudders, hurrying past to the nearby park. There, with her baby in her lap, she sits on the grass watching happy children laughing and flying kites, which soar upward, out of the dark shadows, toward a pure and light-filled Jerusalem sky.

ACKNOWLEDGMENTS

My deepest thanks to Israeli journalist Avishai Ben-Chaim who in 2008 wrote a series of fascinating and detailed articles for *Maariv* concerning a case of horrific child abuse, arguably the worst ever reported in the State of Israel. In his reports, he described how a person presenting himself as a rabbi and a master of practical kabbalah, Elior Chen, and his followers abused the children of a cult member with their mother's passive participation. All members of this cult received long jail terms. Other journalists who explored this case and whose informative articles I found useful in my research include Uri Blau, Yair Ettinger, and Tamar Rotem, of *Haaretz*. The documentary of Doco 10 on Channel 10, "Elior Chen: Kabbalist and Sadist," was vividly informative.

Since the Chen case, numerous other such cults have come to light both in Israel and abroad. I thank Rachel Lichtenstein, CEO of the Israeli Center for Cult Victims, for providing valuable material on the hundreds of dangerous religious and secular cults that exist in Israel, and their many victims.

The experiences of the Goodman children Duvie, Amalya, Eli, Yossi, and Menchie are based on three hundred pages of actual court testimony from the Elior Chen trial. Still, I would like to make it clear that this is a work of fiction that does not in any way attempt to give a factual presentation of the Elior Chen case or any other case, but was rather inspired by a large number of such cases. As such, it wishes to explore through fiction the wider implications of how people seeking spiritual guidance can naïvely wind up in horrific cults led by psychopaths, particularly cults that abuse children.

By court order, no information is legally allowed to be published identifying child abuse victims or their families. Thus, Daniella, Shlomie, and their families and children—indeed all the characters in this book—are purely products of my imagination and bear no resemblance to any person, living or dead. Instead, these characters represent my extensive research into the psychology of cult victims, mothers in cults, and child abuse in cults, as well as books on the psychology of psychopaths, many of whom are cult leaders.

Among the sources I consulted on these topics, I found the following most helpful: "Children and Cults: A Practical Guide," by attorney Susan Landa, which I found on the excellent Web site of the International Cultic Studies Association, and on which I based the information in chapter 31 on child abuse in cults; "The Art of the Interview in Child Abuse Cases," by Captain Barbara Craig, MC USN, medical consultant for child abuse and neglect, Department of Pediatrics, National Naval Medical Center, Bethesda, Maryland; "Techniques for the Child Interview and a Method for Substantiating Sexual Abuse," published on the Child Welfare Information Gateway, a service of the Children's Bureau, Administration for Children and Families, U.S. Department of Child Welfare; "Utilization of Questioning Techniques in Forensic Child Sexual Abuse Interviews," by Monit Cheung; "Manipulation of Spiritual Experience, Unethical Hypnosis in Destructive Cults," by Dr. Linda Dubrow-Marshall and Steve K. Eichel, PhD; and the seminal book *Thought Reform and the Psychology of Totalism*, by Robert J. Lifton, MD.

Other useful books included *The Complete Illustrated History of*

Kabbalah, by Maggy Whitehouse; *Tender Mercies: Inside the World of a Child Abuse Investigator,* by Keith N. Richards; Martha Stout's popular bestseller, *The Sociopath Next Door*; and R. D. Hare's *Without Conscience: The Disturbing World of the Psychopaths Among Us.* The medieval text of Sefer Yetzirah was also enlightening. All these books were helpful in allowing me to form a more knowledgeable take on my character Menachem Shem Tov.

The description of child sacrifice in the cult of Molech is based on author Zev Vilnay's "Idolatry in the Valley of Hinnom," in his book *Legends of Jerusalem,* published by the Jewish Publication Society of America.

My special thanks to Oshrat Shoham, state prosecutor, for meeting with me and her many invaluable insights into how such a case as depicted here would be investigated, as well as how dealing with such cases affect the personal lives of all those involved in getting justice for child abuse victims.

I thank Alexandra Stein, author of *Mothers in Cults,* who kindly and generously allowed me to read unpublished chapters from her book on this topic, an expanded version of the material she has published on this subject online.

Chapter 34, Daniella's confession, is based on an e-mail by a heartbroken victim of an unscrupulous kabbalah guru published by Hannah Katsman on her Web site www.amotherinisrael.com. While the author wishes to remain anonymous, I thank her for allowing me to use her words and experiences. It is my hope that this cautionary tale of the dangers inherent in allowing oneself to be swept away by any spiritual system of beliefs will get the wide distribution it deserves and prevent others from undergoing these horrifying experiences.

I thank my editor, Jennifer Weis, for her belief in this project, as well as my agent, Mel Berger at WME, for his outstanding support throughout.

A very special thanks to my son, Akiva Ragen, who explained to me some of the true beauty and poetry of kabbalah as it is meant to be learned and practiced by normal people interested in exploring an interesting insight into spirituality. I also thank him for explaining to me just how an unethical cult leader could use kabbalah to manipulate and destroy innocent seekers of wisdom.

Last but not least, I thank my husband, Alex, for being my first reader, for his many sensitive and helpful suggestions when I took this book from first to second draft.